Hope you enjoy reading it - as much as I did
Writing it. Best Wishes

SCENARIO

Alistair Dalziel Wright

self published

Cover design by: Karen Wright
Printed in the United Kingdom

CONTENTS

For my dear wife, Karen.
Without her love and support this book might never have seen the light of day.

PREFACE

What could be more perfect than a free train trip to Cornwall just in time for a last family holiday together?

However, strange events would quickly lead William to suspect they were being manipulated by unknown forces, but not even he could imagine where their tracks would lead them.

As future Earth wrestles with it's very existence, unexpected discoveries leave William in peril and risking all for a last taxi ride home.

TO CORNWALL AND BEYOND

They hadn't been there before but a huge stroke of good luck was about to change all that. Not that all the family shared Jane's delight. She'd entered lots of competitions but this was the first time she'd actually won something. She was on the phone to their daughter Anita,

'I still don't see why you're determined we all go, why you can't take a couple of your wrinkly friends?'

'Anita, it might be the last time we all holiday together, there are four tickets and we are a family of four, it was meant to be.'

'We still have to book accommodation. Train tickets, that's all you won.'

'Steven, will you talk to your daughter, we'll have a great time.'

'Listen to your mother, and she'll tell you herself she always knows best.'

'Really, is that like our trip to Greece, when you promised us lots of summer sunshine, chucked it down for two whole weeks!'

'Your brother will be back in a minute, he's really looking forward to it, give you two some valuable bonding time before he goes to Nottingham.'

'The only things he wants to bond with are his precious computer games, what a nerd'.

Ten days later, they were on their way. The taxi deposited them in the proximity of Paddington Station, with half an hour to spare. William had managed to find them somewhere to stay, thanks to his trusty laptop. He had used the same booking company that had donated the train tickets. Anita was now looking forward to getting as far away from home in Hertford as possible, ever since the ring she expected from John failed to materialise. The fact was, he had dumped her for a six foot blonde Latvian shot putter, living in Oldham. Anita had managed to book time off from the vets where she was training to be a nurse. Somehow, she seemed to understand animals better than Humans. Steven and Jane owned a Rare Breads Farm near Oxford so they had left their manager in charge.

The platform number came up and they rushed for the gate. Jane clutched the four train tickets she had proudly won, fifty pence well spent, she thought.

'Looks like we've got seats together, can you stand over four hours with your depressed sister?'

'I'll be too busy planning our week in Cornwall, it's all here on this website and Padstow looks perfect.'

'Oh God get a life you geek, anyway, all they do is eat pasties, drink Doom Bar and fart.'

'Anita please mind your language, there are other people on this train.'

The 12.05 First Great Western pulled out of Paddington on time, bound for Bodmin. The Hawkins family united in their desire to get on together for a whole week.

'Smile please 'cried William, 'Hold up your tickets, say cheese.'

'Please don't point that thing at me.'

On leaving Reading, the conductor passed down the carriage checking tickets.

'Pass them over dear if you can bear to part with them, the man wants to have a look.' Steven was making a brief attempt at being in charge.

'Thank you sir, looks like we're off on a nice family holiday,'

'If we survive more than two days it'll be a miracle.'

'Anita, the man's just being friendly.'

'Excuse me Mrs Hawkins, where did you purchase these tickets?'

'Why, is there something wrong?'

'Shut up Steven, I won them in a newspaper competition, my son checked online, they are authentic.'

'I'm sure it's fine, I just need to look at some of these figures on our system, I'll be back in a moment.'

'Where exactly did you check Will, *Duff Tickets.com* or was it on *E Bay?*'

'This is serious Anita, they might throw us off the train.'

'Calm down Jane, don't you trust your son to do the right thing? Where did you look Will?'

'If you want to know it was.... '

'Everything's fine, just seems to be a misprint on the date but I would check all the details on any future tickets before you travel, relax and have a pleasant trip.'

The conductor moved on down the carriage leaving the Hawkins in various states of shock, relief, and in Anita's case, dismay at missing a chance to wind up her brother.

The rolling hills of Devon beckoned as they headed into the West Country. William was passing the time trying to reach the next level of *Time Warp Alien Invasion,*

'What you see in that rubbish escapes me, the time you spend trying to get to level two, it's really unhealthy,'

'At least I'm not sulking after being dumped for a steroid pumping freak from Eastern Europe.'

This friendly sibling banter continued as the train sped on, passing Dawlish heading towards Plymouth.

'This place we're staying in sunny Padstow, does it have running water and electric or do we have to fill buckets from a well by candlelight?'

'No, it looks very nice, handy for the harbour, lovely garden with great views, we were lucky to get it at such short notice, especially since there's a local festival on Monday, something to do with a horse and local virgins.'

'God, you get worse William, these computer games have a lot to answer for.'

Mid afternoon and their train pulled into Plymouth station, soon they would cross the Tamar and into Cornwall.

'Steve, do we need to get a bus from Bodmin Station?'

'Yes dear, there's a direct connection to Padstow.'

'Probably some sort of horse drawn affair, did anyone bring carrots for Dobbin?'

'Anita!'

Approaching Bodmin Parkway Station William, who had been following their journey closely on his laptop, noticed something strange, there seemed to be a tunnel ahead, which, to his knowledge did not exist.

'Steve, get the cases down, we're nearly there. What the.. !'

DARKNESS

UNINTENDED CAPTURE

'Incoming shuttle from London Central Depot 443 has departed Central at 13.40 and will arrive at Reception Centre Q at 13.47. We regret to confirm that four unidentified beings have been detected in pod No 4.'

'Professor Huntley, we cannot allow any displaced creatures to reach awareness, the shock would kill them.'

'Send full android security to pod No 4 and prepare them for simulation, the key is to transfer the displaced before awareness.'

The Hawkins family had rented one large apartment in an Eighteenth Century town house, plus a separate room for Anita. It wasn't that they thought she would spoil their holiday, however, best to be on the safe side. The family could remember some sort of accident, but the doctor assured them they would all be fine. Their luggage had been processed and transported with them to Padstow in the *ambulance*. They had all come round with vague memories of a tunnel and then darkness.

'If there was a train crash there would be something on the news, try and get a News Channel Steve,'

'I could try my laptop, that's funny, no power.'

'It's alright the television seems to be working.'

'Helga, put my trousers on, no, not on you, on me....'

'This is some old edition of Allo Allo, try News 24.'

William flicked through all available channels , there was no news anywhere just really old TV repeats.

'We're lucky to have electricity at all if you ask me.'

'Shut up Anita!'

They decided to see if anyone else was staying in the house, they might have heard something about a train crash.

'Do we have a connection yet, we know they all came through during the same transect?'

'Dr Honey had a theory that they were taking part in an ancient Human ritual called holidaymaking. The amount of spare clothing in their luggage seemed to point to this. He had also managed to extract sufficient information about the family's holiday plans from William's laptop to set up the appropriate scenario.

'We need to work quickly Professor, the individual calling himself William seems particularly inquisitive. If they break the simulation we all know what the consequences would be.'

There were no other guests in the house. The family decided that some fresh air was needed and a brisk walk around the harbour might provide some answers. Just as they were about to step onto Duke Street, they were met by a cheery gent dressed all in white except for some blue ribbons around his waist and a button hole of spring flowers.

'Morning my lovers, not from round these parts eh, thought not. Wouldn't venture too far at present, locals wouldn't take kindly to your sort snooping around, not on May Day, tis only for local Padstow folk you see. Might end up thrown in the quay for your troubles. Best watch from a window. Clear off then and be sure and have a nice day.'

Before they knew it, the door was firmly closed in their faces.

FROZEN SEAGULLS

The Fox Institute was the major local Think Tank for Padstow Federal District Six. It devised all native life scenarios for the local structured population. Their head of Internal Affairs, Hafey, had formulated an interesting theory concerning their unwelcome guests.

'Look at this Professor, some sort of transit permit, and they were all carrying them. They display primitive information, however these figures look interesting, 2514.'

'Let me see that!'

'Gloves Dr Honey, be careful of contamination.'

'Yes, but these figures could relate to a date, 2514, this Earth year, in local terms, they have information relating to this year.'

'When in history did our historians calculate these intruders arrived from, Professor Huntley?'

'The year 2014, five hundred years in the past, and three hundred years before our arrival preventing the.....'

'Exactly. '

In times of confusion, tea was always a good idea. Fortunately this had been provided, along with milk, sugar and biscuits, by the *owners*.

'That view is stunning' observed Jane, as she stared from the window, looking over the roof tops to the Camel Estuary. 'Will, don't you think so, William!'

'Yes, it is Mother, but isn't that strange,'

'What's that Einstein?' yawned Anita, staggering to the window.

'Nothing's moving, those sailing boats, clouds, seagulls, they are all frozen. Open the window.'

'It's stuck, it won't budge.'

'It's a picture painted on the window it's not real, what's going on?'

All the intruders had the same date on their tickets. The Think Tank came to the conclusion that a mistake had been made by the Local Native Life Scenario Department when they were studying native history. The transit permits must have triggered a Time Link Jump resulting in the Hawkins family skipping five hundred years and ending up in Federal District Six. The Think Tank had to find a way of stopping this happening again. The survival of the planet may depend on it. No one was taking responsibility for this slip up if that is what it was.

'We have a problem Professor Huntley' exclaimed unit XJ2P, head of all android security. 'The intruders are breaking out of the accommodation scenario, there is a high risk of contamination. Should we instigate our cleansing protocol?'

'Are we able to extend the May Day scenario, Professor Huntley?'

'Units have been trained and taken to *the streets*. Perhaps we can contain the intruders, giving us the chance to pick them up.'

'Good, there is little time to spare.'

The Hawkins family had again decided to venture forth to find out the truth about the static seagulls. The street was full of merriment. Locals singing and dancing around some strange horse type contraption... '*OSS OSS WEE OSS!*' they all chanted as they began to surround the family.

'Well this is certainly different' pointed out Anita.

'It's all quite exciting, and they seem really friendly, I think we'll be ok if we just follow them, not try and get involved,' said Jane.

They continued a short way down Duke Street, the local androids in close attendance. Suddenly, William noticed something out the corner of his eye.

'Did you see, at the window over there, It's like something out of a horror film.'

'Told you that tea tasted strange, Einstein's having hallucinations.'

'No, I saw a face staring straight at us, a bright red face.'

'It's probably a mask of some sorts, part of their festival, it won't be real' noted Steven.

'You outsiders fancy some local drink, proper strong stuff mind you. Go easy she'll blow your head off just be warned.'

DARKNESS

LEAVING SO SOON

At Think Tank Headquarters there was much cause for concern.

'We have android units for many reasons Dr Honey. For one they maintain a secure barrier between us and any irregularities. What exactly do you think you were doing on the edge of the scenario, the ancients might have seen you, possibly causing contamination again after all these years?'

'How are the outsiders are they ready for expulsion?'

'Yes professor, they will be returned very soon.'

The Hawkins family, not wanting to be party poopers, were all rendered senseless by the local brew. They were sent to recover in a local *hospital* while a suitable scenario could be constructed for their return journey.

'What I don't understand is how one little sip of that hooch managed to knock us all out, except that is for Anita, she necked it so fast even the locals looked surprised, do you remember Jane?'

'No, it's funny, the last thing I remember is Will mumbling something about red faces.'

'I saw it as plain as you are to me now and it was no mask, those eyes, I'll never forget those eyes.'

'Well, I'm just pleased we've all recovered and they say we can go home tomorrow. Maybe winning those tickets wasn't such a good thing after all' said Steven.

They thought about taking a wander outside but were persuaded to rest up and take care of Anita's enormous hangover.

The intruders were to be transported by blacked out *ambulance,* to the Terminal Building to avoid any glimpses of reality in 2514. An android reception committee would convince them they were leaving from Bodmin Parkway Station in 2014. If all went well, the new *tickets,* showing the correct date, would permit passage back to their own time without arousing suspicion.

'We can't even catch a glimpse of the beautiful Cornish countryside with these blacked out windows.' noted Jane.

'If you would follow me into the Ticket Office we have a pleasant surprise for you,' exclaimed android XP104.

'If they offer us an extra weeks holiday in Cornwall, just smile and say no thanks' said Anita.

'Now, we noticed your tickets seem to have a misprint on them, the date should read 2014 not 2514, here, we have printed new tickets for you. We would like to buy the originals back from you, by way of compensation, for say £500,' noted the stern Station Master.

'£500 for four worthless train tickets, is this some kind of joke?'

'No, I mean £500 each ticket, a total of £2000 I think, is that right?'

´Yes that's absolutely right, no wonder the railways aren't making a profit. I'm not going to ask any more questions but I hope you don't get into trouble with your bosses over this,' pondered a confused Steven.

'Actually I would quite like to hold on to mine if that's alright with you Dad?'

'Are you out of your mind William, that would help no end with your student fees which, may I remind you I am paying so no, just shake the man's hand and let's get on that train.'

The Station Master handed over a bundle of freshly minted fifty pound notes with the family shaking their heads in disbelief.

'I wouldn't get too excited they're clearly toy town money, we'll never be able to spend them' noted Anita.' '

There's something not quite right here,' pointed out William .

All was going to plan. The First Great Western mock up train arrived and the Hawkins family boarded clutching their £2000 windfall. They would soon pass back through the tunnel and back into 2014.

'Well professor, a satisfactory outcome I think,' noted Hafey.

'I hope we avoided any contamination after the incident on Duke Street, Dr Honey' noted a worried Professor Huntley.

'Yes, that would only lead to one thing.'

'You're telling me, let's get back to work.'

'That tunnel's showed up again, it shouldn't be here, I knew we should have asked more questions,'

'Shut up Einstein and count your dosh, I'll be off to the shops soon as we get home. What the ..?'

DARKNESS

KEN GOES MISSING

'We haven't seen Uncle Ken for ages is he alright?' enquired Mario.

'He's probably locked away in his shed inventing something really useless out of donated rubbish as usual.'

exclaimed Karen.

She was at the age where everything people did had to be questioned and then, dismissed as a waste of breath, sixteen, with an I.Q far too high for her own good.

'Maybe we can all go round and see him this afternoon, we're not doing anything are we Andy?' asked Dina, mother to Mario and Karen and wife to Andy, the local librarian and town oracle.

'If we must, he might have come up with yet another theory on life the universe and everything.'

'You three go ahead, I've got to file my report on farmer Smyth's prize cow, it's gone walkabout again.' Mario was twenty and had just been appointed local Crime Officer. The last owner of this distinguished title had recently retired quoting utter boredom as the main ten reasons for his decision. Crime in Padstow was almost entirely confined to animal misdemeanours of one type or another.

Padstow was blessed with an almost perfect microclimate. It rained every day, but only for half an hour or so each time. The sun shone with the same regularity, but it never got too hot and the seasons came and went with predictable regularity.

The soil was rich and produced bountiful crops which never failed, more than enough food to satisfy the almost constant population of 2,000. It was a little piece of heaven, you might think.

Uncle Ken lived in Old Dennis Road, an elevated location just a few hundred yards from the town centre and overlooking, well actually, not really overlooking anything worth talking about.

'Should we signal him we're coming?' said Andy.

'No point, we'll most likely be there before he gets the message,' pointed out Karen.

'Yes, you're probably right.'

'Don't forget to bring in your washing Mum, it's going to rain in six minutes.'

'Well done Karen, I always forget.'

'Right, come on, we'll be there before it starts.'

As usual Ken's front door was unlocked. More unusually, it was wide open.

'Hello Uncle Ken, you mad old bugger, we've come to inspect your latest insane creation.'

'Karen, show some respect.'

To say his house was a mess would be an insult to the local rubbish tip. The search for Ken in the scattered debris proved fruitless. The only place left to look was *The Shed.* In contrast to the rest of the house, this was as ordered as Andy's library. Row upon row of homemade scientific instruments, many of which were designed for observational purposes, binoculars and the like, lined the shelves. There were books entitled '*What is on the Other Side*', '*Breaking Free*' and '*Restrictive Power*'. Karen, intrigued by the potential content, was surprised to find many of the pages had been removed or rendered illegible.

'What do you make of this dad? Uncle Ken wouldn't have done such a thing, would he?'

'Who knows Karen, Ken never sticks to convention you know that.'

The only thing they could find out of place in the shed was a carefully worded note, left on a scrap of paper. It read, *At last some evidence.*

PLANS TO RETURN

'This had better be really important for me to give up my only free weekend this month, little brother. I'm supposed to be revising for my exam on the inner workings of the common hedgehog.'

Anita was on the phone to William. He had sent her six text messages this week alone, and was at his wits end.

'What's wrong, finding it hard to deal with real people in Nottingham? Life beyond the laptop's unpredictable isn't it?'

'Just meet me in the Trip to Jerusalem at 1.00pm on Saturday. If you're lucky I might even introduce you to some of my new friends.'

'O.K. but I think I'll pass on your nerdy palls. '

He had sounded stressed, could be his new life, but Anita was concerned enough to catch the train to Robin Hood country. She found her brother in a dark corner of the bar guarding what was clearly not his first pint. Some friends were nearby but he was saving space for his sister. On her arrival, he wasted no time on sibling bonding, getting straight to the point.

'I've been having nightmares, and always the same subject, that blotchy red face and those strange piercing eyes, just staring, starin.'

'Can I just remind you, it was Cornwall, all of that sounds quite normal. If you looked a little closer, he probably had potatoes sprouting in his ear holes.'

'This is serious Anita.'

'Have you reached level two yet?'

'What?'

'Your precious computer games, they're enough to drive you ga ga.'

'I've been back.'

'What?'

'There is definitely no tunnel.'

'Get a life Will.'

'Just before fresher's week I took the train back to Bodmin, exact same journey we all took in May. I was ready at the spot where it happened, but there is no tunnel between Lisguard and Bodmin Parkway. There was a viaduct at the spot and a shopping centre called Trago Mills just below, but no tunnel.'

'You spent valuable student drinking money on a trip back to pasty country, raving mad!'

'I continued on the bus to Padstow took about an hour, lovely place. I actually got a proper look round this time, even the clouds, seagulls and boats, all moved as you might expect them to. It was all there, the old house where we stayed and, yes, the window where the haunting eyes had peered from, curtains drawn this time. I only had a cheap day return but did have time to enquire at the local library and looked in back copies of The Cornish Guardian. They had no reports of a train accident when we were there, strange don't you think?'

'They've got newspapers in Cornwall, I'm impressed!'

'Please take this seriously, I can't sleep, it's doing my head in. Anyway, no tunnel on the way home either, weird, don't you think?'

'Bang on the head, Einstein, we were in an accident, does funny things to the brain, mind you, there's little evidence, in your case, that one exists.'

A brief smile passed Will's lips.

'That's better little brother. One thing did bother me though, £500 for an old railway ticket was a bit excessive, but I just thought compensation, great!'

'You see, you are interested, lots of things don't add up.'

'So what's your conclusion Sherlock, alien abduction?'

'I don't know, but there's more,'

'I'm all ears, by the way, it's your round.'

Will went to the bar and had lots of requests for him to introduce his sister, he resisted saying they were discussing important family business.

'What were those blokes talking about?' enquired Anita, with a smile in their direction.

'Oh, they all wanted your phone number. I told them to form an orderly queue at closing time.'

'Really?'

'No, I said we had important business to discuss.'

'God, how did you get to be so boring brother?'

'Years of practice, now can we get on. The travel company mum won the train tickets from, the same one I booked accommodation with, they're back.'

'I didn't know they'd gone anywhere.'

'Website and all, disappeared for six months, but it's back.'

'What's that got to do with the price of a Cream Tea?'

'Fast Trax Holidays, that's them. They've only run another competition with free travel for four to Cornwall, by train again! This time, they've included accommodation, a long weekend in Padstow over Christmas!'

'Well, thankfully none of our family is lucky enough to win two competitions in one year. Anyway, much as I would love another trip to the depths of tin mine country, I'm otherwise engaged over the festive season.'

'You're not back with geriatric John? Thought he only had eyes for Eastern European hammer throwers.'

'Shot put, she did shot put, anyway, he's only thirty two and it turns out he hates Oldham. So, I've been working out in case you hadn't noticed and we're...'

'Anita I won! I won the competition, worth over £4,000 plus all the Doom Bar you can drink!'

'Now that is seriously weird, what are the chances of that happening.'

'Exactly, it's as if someone wants us to go back, like the competition was organised just for us.'

'But you said yourself you went back and everything was normal.'

'Here, look at these!' William produced the latest winning rail tickets, in the family's names, with almost uncontrollable excitement.

'Look Anita, look at the date on the tickets, see 2514 just like before, the same, so called misprint.'

'Must have had a job lot made and need to get rid of them.'

'Come on, you must admit, takes a lot of explaining.'

'So, let me get this straight. You want us all to go back to Padstow over Christmas and stay in some shitty hotel so you can prove...what?'

'The wrinklies are both up for it.'

'You've told them already, Oh my God!'

'Mum can't believe our luck and dad just fancies a cheap holiday with free beer. It's a slack time on the farm, so they can't wait.'

'Well count me out, John wants me to visit his parents in

sunny Swansea, wherever that is. I think my visits to the gym are paying off!'

BREACH OF SECURITY

'In my capacity as leader of the Fox Institute, Federal District Six, I bring this meeting to order,' Nash stood in the cavernous, circular conference room lined with android guardians. He had ultimate control over District Six and answered only to the Higher Council.

'I have called you all here today as a matter of grave importance. I have received reliable reports that breaks in our security and that of the community of Padstow, have recently occurred. Moreover, some of these breaches are the direct result of deliberate actions by one highly regarded member.'

Collective gasps of disbelief echoed around the enormous room, who could he possibly be referring to.

'Dr Honey, I am relieving you of all duties pending an internal enquiry. High Command may well be involved at some point. I need not remind you all and any other members of our community of the core reasons for our existence here and the strict code to which we continue to adhere. Any actions which contravene this code could easily result in our shared destruction! There will be no further discussion on this matter until proper investigations have taken place. We are all under close scrutiny from above until these matters are resolved. I sincerely hope that we are not already too late.'

Dr Honey was led from the conference room accompanied by a stunned silence. He had been head of Human Monitoring for over 150 Earth years, with the complete support of all his peers, or so he thought.

SAFE HAVEN

Ken was known in Padstow as a bit of a dreamer. His hare-brained schemes conjured up in The Shed, rarely disturbed the conscious thoughts of the town's contented population. Andy was aware of some of his ideas, most of which contradicted the learned texts contained within the walls of his beloved library. So even though this latest revelation, worded on a scrap of paper, was concerning, the family were sure he would turn up happily propping up the bar in the New Ship.

'Why do you think Ken would rip pages from his own books?' asked Dina

'Probably, he's realised the stupidity of his own ideas, and in frustration, tried to destroy them,' pointed out Andy.

'It's all a bit strange though. Maybe we're in for some excitement in old Padstow town, centre of the entire universe!'

'Wash your mouth out Karen, remember how blessed we are to be here at all. Time you caught up with some truth reading. I'll bring you a couple of informative books home from the library.'

'I'm only joking dad, it's just so frustrating at times stuck here with nothing to do and nowhere to go,' exclaimed Karen.

'We should be getting home, Mario might have some news on Ken,' pointed out Dina.

Andy was very protective of his family and the Padstow community as a whole. Being librarian, he was custodian of all written texts, old and new. He was perhaps more aware of their *situation* than anyone else in the town. All he knew for certain was that Padstow had been safe and happy for many generations, and that was a true blessing.

ON THE TRAIN AGAIN

'It's like bloody déjà vu, I can't believe we're doing this, at Christmas and all, we'll all freeze our bits off, Cornwall in December, shit! Do they even have proper heating in this one eyed hotel? We're all bloody mad!'

'So nice you could join us Anita, your plans not work out then?'

'Button it Sherlock!'

'Yes, I thought you were in Swansea this week Anita?'

'Don't you start dad, it's over now alright. Those early mornings in the gym and muscles appearing in unexpected places, hideous, she's welcome to him. Just don't expect me to get enthusiastic about another trip to the end of the Earth.'

'Will, what's all this stuff, it's just a long weekend not an expedition up the Amazon,' questioned Jane.

'Mother this is more than just another free holiday it's a journey into the unknown and I've come prepared this time.'

'Holy shit! What's in this bag? You really have excelled yourself this time Einstein, watch out down there, we're coming for you!'

'It's just a few basic recording devices. If we hit that tunnel this time, I'm ready. If a fly farts, I'll capture it.'

'Now there's a sobering thought, must have cost you a bomb, all this stuff?'

'No, borrowed it all from a friend in the Photo and Media

department. She said just get it all back before term starts, sorted.'

'Did you say she, you mean you've made contact with the opposite sex at last Sherlock, well done, there's hope yet!'

'Yes, no, but, well, she's just a, you know, Oh shut up Anita.'

'I rest my case.'

'Come on you two, hurry up the train is leaving,' cried Steven.

The now familiar journey to the West Country would most likely turn out to be just a jolly Christmas family get together by the seaside, with no mishaps on the way, William was secretly hoping otherwise.

'Tickets please all unchecked tickets please.'

The dozing Hawkins brood were woken from their slumbers by the now familiar sight of a ticket inspector.

'This should be interesting,' noted Anita, 'More duff tickets with travel dates somewhere in the 26th Century!'

'It was fine last time, they'll let us go again, no problem. Anyway, I think our unexplained experiences last May Day are somehow connected to the misprinted ticket dates,' noted William, with a hint of excitement.

'I'm sorry, but you will all have to leave the train. These tickets are invalid they do not show the correct date of travel, you see this, 24th December 2514. I think you'll agree, it is still 2014.' The eagle eyed inspector was in no mood to be lenient.

'But, but, it was alright the last time we came down, in late April, the inspector realised it was a printing error.'

'Shut up Will!'

"So this has happened before, you do realise it is a very serious offence to try and forge rail tickets. We will be escorting you off the train at Exeter to discuss the matter with a member of Rail Security and possibly the police. If you would gather up your entire collection of luggage, which, as far as I can see seems to spread everywhere, and be ready for Exeter.'

'I knew it was too good to be true, winning two free holidays in one year, it's clearly a scam of some sort,' Steven was not a happy bunny.

'How totally embarrassing, you really have excelled yourself this time Einstein.'

'All we need to do is contact the travel company, Fast Trax, and get them to speak to Great Western, after all, they sent us the tickets.'

'They've probably gone walk about again, so we're totally knackered!'

'You do have their phone number William, I presume?' 'Asked Jane.

'Yes, yes here, I'll ring them now.' Will tried several times but was met with the same engaged tone. email and text messages were left unanswered.

The Hawkins family were decanted onto a packed Exeter St David's platform. William desperately shovelled up the entire collection of Nottingham University recording equipment. Anita muscled her way through the crowds, her eyes searching for the oasis of a nearby bar.

'Mr William Hawkins and family, will you please follow me!'

'Anita, over here, come on,' insisted Steven.

They were herded into the Station Managers' Office and made to wait.

BREAKING LIMBO

'Dr Honey, we have been able to maintain a stable situation here since arrival. We are all aware that fatal mistakes were made during the re-organisation process. However, because of the foresight of our scientists and the diligence of our android workers, to our knowledge, no lives have been lost since then, other than by natural demise.'

'With all due respect Nash, by accepting stability, we have not developed an exit strategy, no protocol for moving on.'

'And by risking lives you believe we can precipitate an exit strategy?'

'I for one do not wish to live out the rest of my allotted span here in this limbo.'

'Our sacred code requires us to *preserve and protect intelligent life in all its forms. Prevent conflicts where lives are in danger, for the good of all...etc.* My life's work, and I presume yours, has resulted in countless acts of preservation and prevention, wherever we have travelled and I do not intend ruining that record here on Earth.'

'With respect, I do not share your fears. We have much good work to complete in other worlds. It is a well documented fact that we could not prevent conflict on Marus Major because we were afraid of what might happen here if we left, doing nothing is no longer an option.'

'Dr Honey, as I stated during our recent meeting, you are under investigation and until the findings are out, your opinions are not welcomed. However, we do require answers to the following charges.

1. You are personally responsible for the manipulation of our Time Travel abilities in order to bring Pre Destruction Humans forward in time Five Hundred Earth years, to present day Padstow.

2. Wilfully causing a potentially fatal accident by appearing on the edge of a scenario, set up by our androids.

3. Actively encouraging Padstow residents to explore into potentially dangerous areas, risking the possibility of direct contact.

You alone are not qualified to conduct such experiments, which means, you are not working alone, is this correct, is this correct Dr Honey?'

'Yes it is correct, I am not working alone.'

'Then you admit responsibility for the charges laid before you?'

'Charge one was not my doing, but the opportunities arising as a result are immense. Charges two and three came about as a result and, yes, are my responsibility.'

'Then I demand to know who started the whole process, Dr Honey, an answer please.'

'It's not a case of who, rather what, I think you need to talk to XP100 and its team about that Nash'.

KEN DOESN'T DRINK COFFEE

'You say Ken turned up at the Ship this afternoon, thank God for that, he's been missing for a week, did he say where he had been?' enquired Dina.

'Hasn't really said much at all, which is not like him, he's usually the oracle on most things,' noted Mario.

'Is he still there now, I'd like to see if he's O.K.'

'I know he was on his fifth coffee last time I heard.'

'Coffee, he doesn't drink coffee, it has no alcohol content, would drive him crazy.'

The New Ship was Padstow's only true public house although a great deal of people brewed their own in their private kitchens. Andy's library talked of times when there were six, but it's not like there were any visitors any more, where would they come from?

Ken sat, surrounded by other locals. He looked like a rabbit caught in headlights, fending off questions from all directions

'Where you'm been hidin' for these past seven days young Ken?'

'Been wi some floozy I expect?'

'I heard Andy found some sort o' note on scraps of paper, what's it all mean mate?'

'Eh, while you was out there on walkabout, didn't happen to

bump into farmer Smyth's prize cow did you?'

'We've all been out searching for you, even young Mario's been kept busy on his police bike!'

'Must have knocked myself out, woke up in a puddle of water in the old disused Social Club, fine now!'

'Ken, old chap, you'm alright, not soundin' your usual irritating self?' asked Jan, the landlord of the New Ship, concerned that his beer sales might drop if Ken had turned to coffee on a regular basis.

'I'm fine.'

"It's O.K. Jan, I'll take it from here!' Dina shouted from the doorway.

She took the confused Ken by the arm and walked him back to his house, the long way, he seemed unsure of the route. How did he survive a week and, more importantly, why did no one find him. Padstow was not a big town and everyone was aware of their limits. Dina kept coming up with the questions, but Ken seemed reluctant to answer, he was definitely not himself.

WHERE AM I?

He woke up in complete darkness. The aroma of strong disinfectant filled his nostrils. How did he get here, and where was here anyway? He remembered jumping from his makeshift craft onto the shore, a brief feeling of achievement and then darkness, slowly drifting off into an unconscious state. He just kept thinking, how did I get here, this strange sterile room?

MORE TICKET CONFUSION

'Just try and phone Fast Trax Holidays again, they were the ones who issued the tickets, we travelled with them in May this year.'

'Our people are doing that right now Mr Hawkins. However, have you sufficient funds if we have to return you to London?'

'Yes, yes, Einstein here can pay, he seems to have money to burn these days. He has a particular attraction to one eyed Cornish towns.'

'Alright Anita, that doesn't really help,' Interrupted Steven.

The Station Manager burst into the room.

'Good news, we've got through to Fast Trax and they can confirm the validity of your tickets. They seem keen for you to complete your journey. They have been having disputes at their head office and had to close down for a while. Also, they asked us to assure you that your hotel in Padstow is still expecting you. They are arranging a special surprise for you to make up for any inconvenience caused. We will be happy to issue you with new tickets in First Class on the next available train to Bodmin Parkway, paid for by your travel company, which includes your return journey after Christmas.'

'Could we please keep our old tickets, you know, as a bit of a souvenir?' asked William.

'Oh not again Will, you and these flaming tickets, they're

no bloody use anyway. You're pushing your luck, especially since you've re located half the Media department of Nottingham University to a Great Western train carriage,' exclaimed Anita.

'Not now Anita, I'll explain later, please can we have all four of the original tickets?'

The station master was happy to hand them over, they were of no use to him, or, as he thought, anyone else. The family collected all their belongings ready to continue their journey. William carefully pocketed the original documents and let Jane look after the new ones.

'You owe us all a few drinks when we get to pasty land Sherlock.'

'It's ok Anita, all the drinks are free anyway, remember' pointed out Steven with a satisfied grin.

First class suited them all just fine, but especially William. They had the carriage to themselves, so he was able to spread his recording equipment all over the place. He was convinced that if anything happened on their approach to Bodmin, he would catch it.

'Wonder what the surprise will be at the Metropole Hotel, slap up meal I would think!' drooled Jane.

'More like a slap in the face with a wet kipper and three rousing choruses of '*I am a cider drinker.*'

'Anita!'

'William?' Steven was getting serious for once 'Why do you insist on keeping hold of those old tickets?'

'Well, if you're really interested, they are the only connecting factor with our last trip in May. When I came down on my own in September nothing out of the ordinary happened, but I had normal tickets. When I won the second competition, the first thing I noticed was the printed date 2514, just like our first trip when the people at Bodmin station gave us all that money in compensation. Coincidence? I doubt it.'

'You really are a brainless bonehead. Are you seriously suggesting a few bits of paper with dates on can cause our train to crash in an invisible tunnel? What does 2514 mean any way? Time someone talked some sense into you, maybe Miss Photo & Media could help!'

'Alright Anita, have it your way, but one thing's certain, in less than half an hour, we'll find out one way or another.'

FISH?

His eyes adjusted to the darkness. He was in a small room, sparsely furnished but in no way unpleasant. There was still that unusually strong odour of disinfectant. He could not find any clues as to where he was but he had no feeling of being in danger. He had spent so much of his life craving any evidence there might be of life outside the danger zone, could this be it?

An illuminated panel in the wall caught his eye. It emitted a strange artificial glow. He hesitantly crawled towards it, his heart rate increasing as he approached. Behind the glass panel he could make out the shape of a container of some sort. The flashing of the panels light was clearly meant to encourage him to pull the protruding handle and open the door. His inquisitive nature took over and he reached for the handle and instantly, the door sprung open. The container appeared to dissolve revealing a metal plate holding an arrangement of inviting hot food. In the centre, lay a strange object which he thought oddly familiar. He might have seen a picture of one in a library once. Yes, he remembered, it was called a fish, a fish! It really was. He was extremely hungry and without hesitation consumed the contents of the plate. He sat back to ponder the situation.

'Oh my God', the fish, was a revelation, where did it come from? He concluded it must be some sort of artificial concoction, It certainly looked like a fish, but he had never tasted one, how could it be, unless..

Perhaps there were others, out there in the darkness. After all these years, the centuries, the generations. His mind couldn't take it in. Then, a veil of white smothered his consciousness, he was, once more asleep.

ANDROID INTERVENSION

It was a sorry sight, the component parts of XP100 disassembled on the instrument table.

'Professor Huntley, you have had ample time to probe this androids memory banks, are we any nearer to finding answers?'

'Answers, yes, but the evidence points to a rather more disturbing truth.'

'Don't talk in riddles Dr Huntley we need answers, hard facts. Is XP100 responsible for manipulating our time travel abilities and, as a result, putting our entire existence at risk, and who, if not Dr Honey, made it possible?'

'Dr Honey does not enter into the equation. He was not aware of the androids plans.'

'What do you mean plans, androids, as you know, are not capable of independent thought, or decision making, outside their remit. No, someone must have instructed XP100, and we must find them.'

'There is more, and it may shock you,'

'Get on with it, what is it?'

'Take a seat please Nash, this may take some time. As you know, our androids are designed to serve, more importantly, to provide a safe buffer between ourselves and the Humans we protect. They are programmed with the knowledge that we must remain on this planet until our mission is successfully completed. They are also encrypted with our sacred code, to protect all intelligent life forms, and prevent conflicts that may threaten lives. Their memory banks contain records of the reaction caused while sedating the Humans, in order to set up safe communities. The fact was that we could not integrate with the Humans and influence future behaviour patterns. We feared, as we still do, contamination and ultimate loss of life. A catch twenty two situation which we still live with. We cannot leave and we dare not allow Humans to mix for fear of a catastrophe.

Androids are problem solving units and they are trying to find the way out of a three hundred year old impasse. Logic tells them that if we cannot interact with Humans from the present time, perhaps it may be possible with those from before our arrival. They would not have been contaminated therefore we may be able to interact freely with them. Not conscious thought but simple problem solving.'

'You are saying androids have taken three hundred years to potentially solve a problem our Saviorian scientists could not?'

'Perhaps you should say, would not. We would not contemplate using time travel other than to cover vast distances in manageable time. This is an unwritten code we abide to. As far as I am aware, this code is not stored in the workings of our androids. They have simply used it as a tool to solve a problem.'

'Send for Dr Honey, he has some explaining to do. Well done Huntley, amazing work, but where we go from here I'm not quite sure'.

THE CHOSEN FEW

'I've read all this before and believe me, I do appreciate how *lucky* we are to be here and for our predecessors to be the chosen few, for want of a better way of putting it, but it still seems a bit farfetched.'

'Karen, for generations we have had to remain content with our meagre lot, you, as an intelligent young woman should realise what the alternative is'

'Yes, and I also know from the few original records remaining, how vast our world used to be. Billions of people interacting, travelling, experiencing new things, not stuck in a little community, staring at the endless blackness on the horizon.'

'Yes, and you will also have read how that vast Human race almost completely destroyed itself through greed and stupidity.'

'Almost, yes, except for us, the chosen few. Come on Dad, why us in little old Padstow. Most of the people in this town are either too scared or too lazy to question why. Only folks like Uncle Ken dare to question if we are really alone.'

'Karen, you need to see something that might convince you, but we have to take a walk to the library.'

Meanwhile, on the other side of town, Dina was worried about Ken's behaviour. He had completely lost his appetite, and showed no interest in finding out where his lost week had taken him. He sat bolt upright at the kitchen table.

'Ken, you need to eat and drink to get your strength back. We need to talk about your missing week.'

'Ken is fine, just need to be alone, please close the portal on your way out Dora.'

'Dina, my name is Dina. I think I should take you to the Metropole Hospital to look you over. I fear you might have concussion!'

'Please, go now, Ken will see you very soon.'

Reluctantly Dina gave in and walked away. She needed to see the rest of the family and together they would visit Ken later in the day.

THE FAMILY VANISHES

This is Liskeard our next station stop will be Bodmin Parkway.... Bodmin Parkway your next station stop.

'Right you lot, get your things together, we're off soon. I can taste my first pint already.' Steven was jumping around, looking forward to another free holiday, hopefully with no further mishaps.

'Hold on dad, we should be approaching the *Tunnel* point any minute now, just looking out for the Trago Mills shopping centre. If we get past that, then I'll pack up my instruments.'

'Might as well do it now Sherlock cause nothing's going to happen this time'...

The 12.30 pm Cornishman Express from Paddington arrived at Bodmin Parkway on time. The passengers alighted from the busy carriages, except that is, from First Class. The seats were empty, the Hawkins family had vanished. The deserted carriage was littered with recording and surveillance equipment, but this remained undiscovered as the train pulled out. As the Cornishman approached its destination in Penzance the guard did his checks of the carriages. A few passengers were leaving from Second Class but as he approached, he could see First Class was empty. However, it had clearly been occupied recently and it looked like they had left in a hurry. On arrival in Penzance, all the scientific instruments were removed by local police aided by the South West Bomb Squad. In this age of terrorism, every eventuality had to be covered. Why would anyone leave such sophisticated equipment on a train? What did they want it for and more importantly, where had they gone?

A POSSIBLE HUMAN SOLUTION

'Androids have simply been searching for a source of uncontaminated Humans. They struck upon a way in which pre-ancient Human subjects could be brought here to this time and tested for purity. Then our scientists could find a way of decontaminating our present day Human population, using their forefathers for first contact experiments.'

'You realise, Dr Honey, the consequences if we harm any Humans, not to mention using time travel for any purpose other than actual travel. We jump from one potential disaster to another, pre-empting catastrophes, using our time travel capabilities. We do not use it to remove beings from their natural time frame.'

'Nash, we have not jumped for hundreds of Earth years. We have had to pass on tens of problems to others in our fleet to solve, because we are stuck here. Perhaps it is time to bend the rules in order to move on.'

'Can our androids return these Humans to their own time, unharmed and unaware?'

Dr. Honey was not sure how to reply. He knew he had acted without permission from above but the androids were convinced it would work and it had. Professor Huntley and Internal Security head Hafey, would also be implicated. They had covered up the first visit from the Hawkins family. If he was to press forward with his plans to escape this slow death on

Earth, he had to come clean.

'I apologise in advance for what I am about to admit, but it may help make your mind up about the validity of the androids theories.'

'Spit it out Honey, you cannot sink any deeper into the mire than you already have.'

'Alright then, it will work.....because it already has!'

The silence was deafening, Nash was trying to comprehend the enormity of Honey's admission.

'We recently captured four Humans from the year 2014 in a time displacement. They arrived unharmed and remained unaware throughout their *visit*. At no point was there any danger of possible contamination.' He was stretching the truth.

'The androids set up convincing scenarios to fool them. Huntley and Main were led to believe it was all an accident and I went along with them. They thought the travel documents they were carrying caused some sort of time jump. They are still working on a solution to how this would be possible. I have not told them the truth for fear of implicating them even further.'

'And at no time were these Humans aware of any time difference?'

'They thought they were spending a holiday in 2014 Padstow, our androids and scenario set ups took care of that.'

'Can you prove they returned to their own time unharmed, you surely didn't follow them back!'

'No, no, that would have been fraught with unimaginable dangers.'

'Then you don't know, they could have carried some contamination back with them. They may have died, spread disease, changed the course of history, Honey what have you done!'

IMAGES OF DESTRUCTION

However nice the fish might have been, he woke up frustrated and wanting answers. Once accustomed to the light, he realised he was not in the same room. His everyday clothes had been replaced. He was now wearing a rather fetching white one piece with blue slippers and matching plastic cap. His skin had been scrubbed to the end of its useful life and he stank like a disinfected toilet. The walls of his new room were decorated with rather disturbing images of nuclear destruction which altered every few moments with pictures of Padstow in all its idyllic glory. A running audio loop explained how the war of all wars destroyed every vestige of Human existence, except Padstow. It was the only surviving pocket of humanity out of the billions that went before. He found himself resisting the urge to accept this scenario. He had always questioned the accepted truth about their privileged position in the world. He had built crude instruments from the meagre supplies available to him, in order to penetrate the darkness that surrounded his town.

At last he had the evidence he needed, the fish!

Whoever his captors were, they were not fishermen from Padstow, who were sadly victims of the war and the contamination of the seas. For generations, the residents of Padstow had longed to venture forth into the waters, but the eerie green glow that emanated beyond the shores at dusk, along with the endless warnings from books and posters, had prevented this. Stories of lost lives documented in Andy's library, and the threat to this unique community's existence, had tempered the most adventurous of spirits.

The repetitive sights and sounds invading his conscious mind were beginning to have the desired effect. Perhaps he was just a dreamer, longing to venture beyond the darkness to a better world outside. He should be happy with his lot. The confusing thoughts of fish and strangers soon faded away as he drifted again into the welcome arms of slumber.

KAREN NEEDS CONVINCING

'O.K. Dad, convince me.'

They stood in Andy's small library, in part of what used to be the trauma centre for disaster survivors and before that, the largest hotel in Padstow, the Metropole. Most of the literature contained within its shelves was post destruction texts. These documents strived to explain the horrors of Earth's self inflicted destruction, and, by some freak of nature, how Padstow was saved. How a little bubble of humanity lay safely cocooned behind a dark veil, masking the horrors that lay beyond.

There were also texts on how to be self sufficient, living off the land and using Human resourcefulness to its maximum potential, always cherishing their unique gift of life. Other books explained that, unless another miracle occurred, the population would eventually die out from the lack of new stock from outside and the Human race would cease to exist. Mostly, texts were written to reinforce the theory that attempts to enter the dark zone would result in contamination and death to those exposed to it. These books and pamphlets were supposedly written not long after the nuclear war by those who first experienced its results.

'I've read most of these before Dad,' noted Karen. 'Have you never wondered why there are no first hand accounts of the destruction. No details of how we survived, only that we did and should be eternally grateful that fate dealt us such an amazing hand. There are lots of gaps, that's all I'm saying.'

'I said there was something I needed to show you. I've only shown it to the most inquisitive townsfolk, like you.'

'Andy, Karen, I've contacted Mario, we're all meeting at Ken's house, he's really not himself. We need to persuade him to get checked over.' Dina had just rushed in at the wrong time, the opportunity was lost.

RETURN OF THE HUMANS

'Why was I not informed of this at the time? This will no doubt be referred to the Fleet High Command, we could all be banished to Correction Colony Three. Earth would be left to perish before they discover the truth.'

'We did not inform you because the process worked. The four Humans were returned to their own time, unhurt and unaware. The opportunity is there to free the Human race and move on. The mission has not failed, but stagnated. Fear has gripped us so tightly that we have lost the will to try for a solution. Our androids have presented us with an opportunity to free humanity and our own beleaguered people.'

Nash was clearly impressed with Honey's enthusiasm and belief. If Humans had been returned safely, the status quo had been protected.

'You still haven't explained how you know these Humans are alive and well.'

There was a long silence before Honey replied.

'I know because, they are on their way back here on another *holiday*!'

Nash collapsed into his chair in disbelief.

'The androids saw the logic. If the first capture succeeded then why not again? They simply used the same technique, tempting them with another free *holiday*. There was also evidence that one of the party was very keen to return.'

'What do you mean, one of the Humans suspected foul play?'

'Perhaps, but it meant he persuaded the rest to follow.'

'Dr Honey, you are using a lot of assumptions here. You must prove to me, and High Command, that your scheme will work. I need full details of how you intend using them to solve our dilemma, that, not one more Saviorian will be harmed in the process. Also the methods needed to expand you're so called solution to cover the entire Human population, allowing direct contact, rapid integration and the release of both our races.'

'I can produce our outline plans within one Earth day, Nash.'

'Then do it, but, with all due care.'

'You will not regret this Nash and thank you for your support.'

'The jury is still out on you and your team Dr. Honey, you are still in very deep water.'

A FIRST CLASS SHUNT

'Does anyone remember getting off the train, or is it just me?' Jane was confused. She sat in the waiting room at Bodmin Parkway station, luggage and family members loosely arranged around her.

'I remember feeling like this after a particularly heavy night out with Suzie from the vets,' mumbled Anita.

Steven was watching William rummaging through their luggage.

'It's gone completely, disappeared.'

'If you are referring to the contents of your brain, they wandered off years ago!'

'No, really Anita, all my monitoring and surveillance equipment has vanished!'

'Oh God no!, bang go your chances with Miss Photo and Media. How much do you reckon that little lot is worth?'

'Just rein your mouth in for once Anita, can't you see he's worried.' Steven did wonder at times where his nerdish tendencies came from, but that could wait.

'You must have left it all on the train, we can get someone to phone ahead and keep it safe, we can pick your stuff up before we go home.'

'But all my evidence could be recorded on that equipment.'

‘We’ll get it back, don’t you worry. ’ Jane continued ‘So anyway, no one answered my question, who remembers getting off the train?’

A long discussion ensued but the conclusion was…

‘Ah! You must be the Hawkins family. We were about to call an ambulance but you appear to have recovered, do you think you’re ok to catch the next bus to Padstow?’

‘Sorry, did I miss something. We’ve been racking our brains trying to figure out how we ended up in this waiting room, none of us can remember getting off the train.’ Steven was voicing the concerns and confusion all the family shared.

‘Oh yes, let me explain. Just passing Trago Mills, you were shunted from behind.’

’Anita, not a word, don’t even go there.’

’Yes, a runaway goods train struggled to brake and collided with the rear First Class carriage you were travelling in, the impact must have knocked you all out, fortunately, no derailment took place and we were able to retrieve you from the carriage. Yours was the only carriage affected. We do most sincerely apologise, thankfully, no harm done.’

‘No harm done! We could all be suffering concussion or worse, at least call an ambulance and have us all checked out at A & E,’ demanded Steven.

‘We will arrange it straight away. In the meantime, I will rustle up some food, you must be hungry.’

‘Yes ok, but please no pasties, they tend to make me vomit!’

‘Anita!’

‘Well, that would seem to explain things, does everyone feel alright?’

‘Explain things! It doesn’t even begin to explain things.’

‘Watch out, Sherlock’s on the case!’

'For starters, we were put on a later train at Exeter. First Class was at the front of the train. They haven't explained where my equipment has gone but they managed to get the rest of our luggage. Also, if the so called shunt knocked us out, what state was the carriage in? The train just carried on regardless? I don't think so.'

'He does make some good points, I must say' noted Steven.

Even Anita seemed to be pondering something, or was she just thinking up her next wise crack?

'When they come back with the food we'll demand some answers,' cried Steven in his most forceful tone.

'Oh! And in case the coincidence passed your minds, the so called shunt happened just after Trago Mills, if you catch my drift.'

The station porter arrived with the food. This consisted of sandwiches and some sort of fruit drink. The appearance of said sandwiches was more convincing than the taste, but they put it down to typical railway fare. The vaguely orange drinks were strangely addictive and they gulped them down without question. An ambulance appeared soon after. Following some tests they were passed fit and well to board the bus bound for Padstow. The spiked drinks they had just consumed were beginning to have the desired effect. The list of questions they had prepared in their heads vanished as they all burst into a chorus of '*oh! I do like to be beside the seaside.* ' Even Anita was in jovial mood, expressing her love of everything Cornish and how she couldn't wait to eat her first cream tea.

Not surprisingly, they were the only passengers on the bus, save for their very attentive *minders*. The powers that be had asked for their *journey* to Padstow to be as long as reasonably possible. Things were brewing at the Think Tank.

NEW CLOTHES!

'Uncle Ken, we've brought you some of your favourite biscuits to cheer you up.' Mario and Karen were leading the family up to Ken's front door.

He lived in a lovely street of ancient houses overlooking the Camel Estuary. Directly overhead, the sky was blue, but with 2.30pm fast approaching they knew it would soon be time for rain. Locals had long since resisted the temptation to lower their eyes to the horizon, they knew what awaited them if they did. A constant line could be drawn where welcoming blue sky met the impenetrable black of the contaminated world beyond. The lime green stagnant waters slopped against the deadened shores of the estuary. They learnt to keep their eyes firmly fixed on the immediate surroundings and, of course, remembered just how lucky they were.

There was no reply at Ken's house, so they walked right up to the front door and pushed. Usually entry could be gained easily, as he, like most Padstonians, never locked their doors. It was firmly locked.

'Ken, are you in there!' shouted Dina anxiously.

She was sure she could hear muffled voices coming from inside. 'There's someone in there with him.'

'It's probably Mrs Young from top of town, you know, they had a bit of a thing going until she discovered he was more interested in his latest invention than her cream buns!'

'Mario, I am surprised at you, knock again.'

'We should leave him alone, he's clearly feeling better if Mrs Young's come to call,' noted Karen.

Just as they turned to leave, Ken opened the front door, hesitantly.

'Oh Ken, I was getting worried, and when the door was locked, but if you have company we'll talk later.'

Ken had changed clothes from his last encounter with Dina, and his latest attire concerned the family somewhat. His green wellies gave way to an expanse of bare leg topped with blue and yellow checked boxer shorts. On his upper half, he modelled a pale pink blouse and matching accessories. The whole ensemble was topped off with a red balaclava and ear muffs!

'That's it, down to the hospital with you. That bang on the head was worse than I thought, what on Earth are you wearing?'

'Ken just wanted a change, does it not please you Dora?'

'I'm Dina, Dina, and since when did you start wearing Aunt Lisa's things. I thought you got rid of them years ago?'

Mario, forever the attentive police officer, had his notepad out and was scribbling furiously. He could not take all this in, so was recording the evidence for a later date.

'This is the most exciting thing to happen for years' exclaimed Karen.

'What does Mrs Young think of your new taste in clothes, she is in there, isn't she?'

Karen pushed past Ken in fits of laughter.. 'Mrs Young, are you responsible for Ken's fashion revolution...........Oh my God, what the hell!'

NEW PLANS

As he came once again to consciousness, he was sure he could hear voices. All he wanted to do was to get back to his lovely home in Padstow. His mind was strangely clear and uncluttered. They were alone in the world, but had survived, fortunate beyond belief. Whoever was out there, just open the door and let him go home, that's all he wanted.

'The Human subject has responded to treatment and is ready to return, once we have retrieved his android double.'

'Plans have changed, he is going nowhere, he is now needed for important experimentation,' Hafey had brought instructions from the local Think Tank, things were moving fast.

'Shall we sedate him again, ready for transfer?'

'No, his body needs to be free of any administered chemicals. You may feed him and perhaps encourage a little light exercise, but that is all.'

Hafey left in a hurry, she had been summoned back to headquarters for an urgent meeting.

He stalked the room, demanding to be released, but there was no reply. The feeding station in the wall sprang into life. It had been a mistake to offer fish last time, having clearly aroused suspicion in the Human mind. A succulent steak briefly took his mind off the situation. They had to get him in good condition for the tests ahead. As he tucked into his food, the ceiling opened up to reveal a selection of exercise equipment lowering into place.

'I just want to go home, let me go home!'

ALVIS PRINCE HAUNTS US

A meeting involving Fleet High Command was a rare occurrence. It involved bringing together representatives from all Saviorian districts on Earth including Federal District Six and the Padstow Think Tank. Fleet High Command was in charge of hundreds of Saviorian operations throughout the galaxy and beyond. They were busy creatures whose time was precious. The Earth Scenario had long been a thorn in their sides. The lack of a solution, or the willingness to find one, was a severe drain on recourses and needed to be resolved.

In the light of the new developments in the remote commune in Federal District Six, Commander Aragon had swooped in from his current deployment on Dorogon Three. The stakes were high as no further loss of life would be tolerated. Since the accident after the sedation of the Human race, in order to prevent a nuclear holocaust, the Saviorians were gripped with fear. More loss of life would certainly result in transportation to a Penal Colony for all involved.

Dr Honey had convinced the rest of his team that his plans would work. Professor Huntley had drawn up some preliminary strategies for implementation after initial contact. Both Main and Hafey were clear on their roles going forward. One step at a time, that's how it had to be. Failure was not an option, they all knew that. The decision to go ahead or not was one for the whole Saviorian community on Earth to make, not

Fleet High Command, they could only advise.

The proceedings were being beamed live to all parts of Earth, except, of course, the Human race. They continued to live out their lives in thousands of Micro Community Pods, still convinced they were alone in the world, the lucky chosen few. Whether or not they could cope with a new reality was a question for the future. Could they comprehend, that for the last 300 years, the Earth had been patrolled by alien's, suppressing Human nature for, so called, good reasons. Would they accept their explanation, or resent centuries of quarantine put in place by an alien race. With an overwhelming mixture of dread and excitement, Main called the meeting to order.

'Dr Honey, are you and your team ready to present your plan to Fleet High Command and our fellow Saviorians here on Earth?'

'Thank you Main, Commander Aragon, honoured guests from High Command and fellow Saviorians here on Earth. We were all a lot younger when we arrived here, all eager to save this race from ultimate self destruction. The breakdown of a collective Human desire to keep the planet safe led to a proliferation of nuclear weapons in the hands of rogue states. Earth had turned its back on fossil related energy and invested greatly in nuclear fuels. From North Korea to Iran, Israel to the new Islamic State and beyond, fingers poised over buttons. We have seen it time and again on other worlds, a point of no return had been reached, and we had to intervene, the W.M.Ds had just been launched. Instant sedation was the only solution. Freeze the Earth at one point in time and create a post destruction scenario, the same one we all now live through.

Isolation communities were set up all over the globe. We vacuumed the entire planet of all nuclear weapons and were ready to introduce ourselves to the human race. Commune Sector Twelve in California was chosen as the first contact point and Human disguises would be used to avoid shocking our Human subjects with our appearance. Instead of contact on a massive scale, we sent in one of our most experienced negotiators, Alvis Prince, a name now revered throughout Saviorian culture.

He walked into a saloon bar in Commune Twelve, posing as a Public Health Officer. His intention was to gauge public reaction to the post destruction scenario, set up in this small sector of San Francisco. The native population had recently awoken from their imposed slumber and were trying to digest the vast number of information leaflets that had mysteriously appeared in most public places explaining their new situation. The sleeping gas administered, contained an element that allowed them to be more accepting of their new world, but they still had countless questions. The Human disguise, known to Saviorians as a Simu-Suit, seemed to work, why not, it had been used on many other planets in various forms.

As the area chosen was an urban one, strangers were not uncommon, so Alvis Prince did not attract suspicion. Conversation began to flow between the two species and then... a sneeze from an innocent Human bystander entered one of Alvis's four lungs, he collapsed on the bar room floor. Androids were dispatched immediately to remove him from the scene but he died soon after. Our sacred code of conduct had been broken, a life had been lost. Fortunately, no one else died and the Humans seemed unaffected, but our project of integration was dead in the water.

We could not put any more lives at risk, and this holding pattern has continued to this day. Something has to be done, and we now feel we have the solution, a calculated risk worth taking. If you will permit me, I will put forward our proposals.'

PADSTOW FOR CHRISTMAS

It had been more than three hours since they left Bodmin station, they now arrived at the Metropole Hotel in Padstow. The effects of their doctored orange drink were beginning to wear off as they stepped off the bus, directly into the hotel foyer.

'I'm surprised a service bus brings you right up to the front door,' pointed out William.

'Because of your ordeal on the train we arranged with the bus company to make an extra stop here, welcome to the Metropole Hotel.'

The android Hotel Manager showed the family to their rooms, a double and two singles overlooking the estuary to Rock, however, it was already dark.

'This really is a special prize you have won. The drinks package allows all four of you to have any drink, even champagne and three meals a day with our very special Christmas lunch. Really, there's no need to leave the hotel!'

'Sounds great, but I'm sure we'll want to stretch our legs at some point,' replied Jane

'Oh, I forgot to mention, you also have your own personal driver and car, twenty four seven, just call for Paul when you want to go out.'

'That sounds like fun' perked up Anita, 'Is he a bit of a Cornish hunk, rugby player type, huge biceps and all that?'

'We'll see what we can do to arrange that (*was there time to construct a suitable prototype?*), dinner will be ready in the dining room at 8.00pm, it is now 7.30pm, have a pleasant stay, I know we'll enjoy having you.'

'Oh, before you go, some of my belongings from the train are missing, some pieces of scientific equipment. could you ask if they have recovered them in Penzance, they are very important to me?'

'Not to mention what Miss Photo and Media might think, wouldn't want to ruin your chances there Will.'

'I will get our people to look into it sir, we should have them back by the morning.'

'I must say son, you have excelled yourself this time, we don't even have to worry about drink driving, it sounds like Paul will look after us.'

'He can take care of me anytime.'

'Anita!'

The transportation delay had allowed those at the Think Tank some breathing space, however, the meeting at the Fox Institute went on. Dr Honey and his team knew that, no matter what decision the Saviorian people made, the unfolding situation was now beyond their control.

THREE HEADS ARE BETTER THAN ONE

'Karen, what's wrong?' Dina rushed into Ken's house as soon as she heard the shout.

On the sofa in front of her sat two more *versions* of Ken, each with parts of their anatomy missing. One of the Kens was talking to himself while the other had his head missing. Karen sat on the floor, mouth wide open, just pointing. In rushed Andy and Mario closely followed by Ken, version one, wellies clomping on the floor.

'I think I'm going to need a spare notebook!' cried Mario, standing in the doorway.

The spray knocked them out instantly.

Ken had to work quickly, there wasn't room in the town for identical triplets.

ESCAPE

The combination of more food and a little exercise had cleared his head. This had somewhat counteracted the effect of his therapy sessions. Once again he was ready to take on the world. He was determined to get to the bottom of where he was and who his captors were.

He searched the room for a way out without success. It suddenly dawned on him, what if he could open the flap in the ceiling where the exercise equipment appeared from. It was a long shot but worth a try.

He used the equipment to climb up to a point where he could reach the flap. With surprising ease he managed to prise the flap open. With determination he pushed his body up and clambered out of the room. A chill breeze wafted over his face. He was in some sort of service tunnel which stretched out to his left. The darkness was almost impenetrable so he crawled along using the side walls as a guide. He followed the direction of the breeze, thinking that at any moment he would discover a route to freedom.

Either his eyes were adjusting to the darkness or there was a faint light ahead. His crawling picked up pace, he was feeling his old self again. Then, his passage was halted by a glow coming up from the floor ahead of him. He crawled up to it and peered down. The room beneath was identical to the one he had just escaped from. The woman sitting at the desk was not distracted by his banging and waving from above, she could not hear him. The video screen in front of her took all her attention. He squinted to see its display. The woman was not familiar to him. This was strange because everyone in Padstow knew everyone else, she was a stranger. Dressed in her white one piece, she had clearly been through the same process as he had. She continued to stare at the screen, scenes of nuclear destruction alternating with those of idyllic rural community life. He looked closer, that wasn't Padstow. He did not recognise the streets or people. He had been concentrating so hard on the content of the video he had not heard the alarm. He instinctively sprang into action. The woman could not be helped, he had to find his own way out of this maze. He flew along the tunnel, bruising his arms and knees in the process. Voices were calling out but using a language he could not understand. Suddenly, he tumbled out of the tunnel, falling several feet onto soft sand.

A QUESTION OF RADIATION

'We have to go back five hundred Earth years for our plan to make sense. Radiation levels, although increasing, were under some control. Fast forward nearly two hundred years, control was lost. Humans were constantly exposing themselves to higher levels due to widespread nuclear activity. There was an almost total reliance on nuclear energy combined with the indiscriminate testing of weapons. Our scientists are now convinced that the combination of our sleeping gas and increased levels of radiation in Humans, made them lethal in our company. We miscalculated the content of our sleeping gas. Once that human sneeze entered Alvin Prince's Saviorian lungs, it poisoned him. Our android scientists, unknown to us, have been working on the problem for years. While fear of failure gripped the Saviorian people, they worked on a solution. They have found a way to replicate that Human sneeze with a much reduced radiation level. Our plans could be put in place, and at last, we could move on.'

'Just how do you plan to test this theory, Dr Honey?'

'As you are aware Nash, our androids found a way to bring Humans from five hundred Earth years ago, forward, to the present day. During their Time Jump visit, unknown to them, tests were carried out which revealed low levels of radiation in their bodies. These Humans were persuaded, by means of our scenarios, that they were visiting Padstow in the year

2014.

We are now convinced that we can utilise these ancient Humans in tests resulting in safe contact with Saviorians. The next step would be to compare the physical makeup of ancients with that of present day Humans, especially related to radiation levels. Our scientists believe that with three hundred years of zero radiation exposure, present day Humans will have similar, if not lower, levels in their bodies. Then, ultimately, we would be ready for direct contact with the Human race. There would be safe contact, integration and an end to our time on Earth. The ancients would be returned to their own time, unaware that they had spent their *holiday* in the 26th Century, and their involvement in saving the Human race. The details of how to implement integration would be worked out with Saviorian Command here on Earth. We will back up our plans with the extensive scientific evidence contained in these documents,' Honey pointed to the evidence saved on electronic devices, then sank, exhausted, into his chair.

'We thank you Dr Honey for all the hard work put in by your Think Tank, and the androids at your disposal. While we do not approve of the methods you involved in reaching your conclusions, we applaud your intentions and will retire now to examine your evidence and finalize any agreed proposals to put before the Saviorian community here on Earth. We are aware that time is of the essence. Your proposals will be studied with speed and absolute accuracy.'

The room emptied in complete silence, each delegate consumed with their own private thoughts. For many, half a lifetime had been spent on this distant planet, could the end finally be in sight?

A VERY CONVENIENT FOG

After a round of drinks at the bar, swiftly followed by another, the Hawkins family strolled into the dining room and headed for a table by the window. Not that there was anything to see. Not only was it dark, but there seemed to be a thick fog outside, clinging to the window panes.

The waiter came over. 'Are we ready to order, we have a large party due soon, so the kitchen would like to get your food prepared first.'

'Yes, fine, we thought it was a bit quiet for Christmas Eve' noted Steven.

'Don't you have Christmas decorations in darkest Cornwall, can't help noticing, no tree, no tinsel, crackers on the table, is it a Cornish custom or something?' 'Anita, don't forget, this is a free trip, good idea not to upset the locals'

The waiter looked confused, could this scenario be incomplete, what else had they missed?

'Oh yes miss, eh.....' A message came through on his kitchen order tablet as a means of explanation. 'Renovations Miss, we are closing soon for redecoration, and the manager didn't think it was worth it. We will put it right straight away, more drinks anyone?'

The family were poking around in their rather bland starters searching for any recognisable ingredients while consuming the next round of drinks, when the confused waiter returned.

'Looks like you have our undivided attention tonight, our other guests have cancelled, fog is too thick for them to get here from Truro.'

'Oh great! Christmas Eve getting legless with Mum, Dad, and the nerd from Nottingham, my idea of heaven!'

Will staggered off in search of the toilets.

'Let's just enjoy our meal Anita, then we can go for a walk around town, find some life,' suggested Jane.

'Good idea, and here comes our main course, this is the life, cheers!" at least Steven was relaxed with the situation.

Will came back from the toilets. 'You have to come and see this, it's incredible, come on you lot.'

The family left their food and ran to the foyer. The hotel had been decorated with not one, but three Christmas trees and a vast array of coloured lights and paper decorations.

'Wow! Where did this lot come from, in less than half an hour, it's impossible!'

'You're right dad, it is impossible, I smell a rat. I bet this hotel's empty, no other guests. Someone's covering up their mistakes, no decorations and then, boom, this!'

'Who gives a s..., I think it looks great. You haven't had enough to drink Sherlock, come back and you can try and guess what you're eating, I'm still working out why my pasta is blue, they certainly do things differently down here. How's your shoe leather steak Dad?'

'It's fine if you wash it down with a few glasses of red.'

'Don't you go complaining now.'

'Yes I know, it's all free.'

The sound of clanking cutlery echoed in the sparsely occupied dining room. The Hawkins clan were well oiled by now and decided to get into the Christmas spirit with a few carols. The hotel staff stood back bemused, they were clearly not familiar with the lyrics.

'I've got an idea, let's stagger down town and sing to a few locals, someone in Cornwall must speak English.'

'Good idea Anita, I could do with the fresh air.'

'That's the spirit Mum, you two coming?'

'Just let me finish my barely sticky toffee pudding,' spluttered Steven.

'We'll all meet in ten minutes in the foyer' shouted Jane, already on her way to the door.

The girls went back to their rooms to fetch their coats, Will had other ideas. He hadn't come here to sing carols, he wanted answers and what had happened on this visit, so far, only added to his suspicions.

The androids were experiencing a serious circuit overload. No further instructions were coming from the Think Tank. They were led to believe that this would be a brief holding situation and that the Humans would be removed from the hotel scenario quickly. They had dealt with the Christmas decorations, now there was talk of walks into town. The hunky chauffeur had been hastily constructed, but was showing signs of malfunction, his Cornish accent frequently lapsing into pseudo German.

Now plied with drink, the Hawkins family were acting in a very random manner and carol singing in Padstow could easily spiral out of control.

'Excuse me, sorry for disturbing your staff meeting, or whatever it is.'

Will was standing at the hotel desk staring into, what could have been, the office. Several hotel staff were there clearly having a heated conversation.

'Ah yes, Mr Hawkins, we hope you enjoyed your meal.'

'Yes, thanks, I did, except for the fish bones in my chicken.'

'Yes, sorry about that, our kitchen staff got a little confused with the order.'

'Have you managed to track down my missing equipment yet, it is really important to me.'

'Oh yes, we are still looking into that.'

'Well, just give me the phone number of Penzance Station, and I'll do it. Oh, no my phone is missing too, can I use the hotel phone?'

'Oh yes, sorry, not possible now, think the connection down due to err, fog, yes, the fog.'

Will was sure he could actually see smoke coming out of the receptionists ears, no, not possible, was it?

'Fog doesn't cause phone problems. Come on, lend me your mobile.'

'What's up Will, come on, we're going for a walk,' Steven and the girls were approaching reception.

'Just trying to locate my equipment.'

'Anita! Don't even go there.'

'Forget that, they said it will be here in the morning, come on!'

They headed for the front door but their path was suddenly blocked by a huge muscle bound figure dressed in Cornish rugby shirt and tight jeans. Anita keeled over on the spot, her every prayer answered in an instant. Suddenly everything about Cornwall was first class and she would be moving here next week.

'Can me lift you up, bitte, my lover?' proffered the linguistically confused android. 'Let me fetch der autobus. She won't be ein minute, be back dreckly, my handsome.'

The Hotel Manager jumped in to the save the situation

'Not a night to be going out on your own, fog this thick, you could easily get lost. If you want some air, Paul will drive you around for a while, point out a few things you won't be seeing on the way.'

'Oh, that would be great' drooled Anita. 'The rest of you can stay here, as he says, too foggy to go out, you'll only get lost.'

'Oh no you don't young lady, you've had far too much to drink, I'm not letting you lose on that poor young lad, he seems confused enough as it is without you getting your claws into him!'Jane had spoken.

The hotel manager made them wait in the foyer for the car to materialise from the fog. They had to be kept under control a little longer.

Will had no intention of having a guided tour of foggy Padstow. He was heading out on his own. Just as he reached the hotel door, Paul pushed in.

'Der auto wagon is outside, please commen zi 'ere and park yer bums in yonder chariot, she's a beauty, is her not, zi auto bus?'

Will saw his chance, he got in one side of the car and straight out the other, he was away into the fog, and into the future. The Saviorians worst nightmare was unfolding, loss of control.

MYSTERY OF THE THREE HEADED KEN

When they came around, all of the Ken's were gone. The house was tidy, and there were fresh flowers on the table, along with a hand written note.

Sorry, had to rush off, will explain all very soon. Just some experiments I was doing, gets lonely on your own, needed to create some company, nothing to worry about, will soon be over.

'What just happened there, were we all knocked out, did Ken do it to us, answer me Andy?'Dina was understandably in a state.

'When I came round you were all still out, but Ken was gone,' pointed out Mario.

'Which Ken, you saw them, didn't you, there were three if him, well, two and a half if you count the decapitated one.' Karen was close to hysteria but Mario was searching for a logical answer to this strange situation.

'He said in his note that he was lonely, needed company. We know he experimented a lot, perhaps he had managed to build some spare Kens.' Dina was desperate to find a logical explanation of her own, but nothing made sense.

'He did have access to some knowledge from before the nuclear war, I let him borrow some texts that had survived. He is a very clever man, but how could he build a functioning copy of himself from the junk in his garden, let alone two?' pondered Andy.

Karen had recovered enough to realise there may be some excitement around the corner after all, the fact there was no logical explanation only heightened that feeling.

'Let me see that note, what does this bit mean, *will soon be over*, sounds a bit final don't you think?'

Android Xb430 had returned to the monitoring facility in the buffer zone. It had been recalled after its slip ups in Ken's house. It was meant to solve the ongoing Ken substitute problems without being detected, now it had aroused suspicion in the local community. To compound the situation, the real Ken had just escaped from the same installation and was presumably trying to find his way home. Hafey was called in to give guidance.

'I suggest we monitor Ken's activities carefully, but don't intervene. Things are moving fast at the Think Tank, but we have had no instructions to pick him up yet. Android Xb430 needs to be decommissioned, and lessons learned.'

BEYOND THE GREEN WATERS

It took time to find his bearings, he must have fallen further than he first thought, thankfully, no broken bones, the soft sand must have cushioned his landing.

There was a faint glow coming from the facility he had just escaped from, otherwise, he was engulfed in thick black smog. The undulating terrain beneath his feet resembled some kind of sand dune, where was he?

His immediate thought was to get as far away from the installation as possible. He was surprised he hadn't already been followed. The thick smog didn't hamper his breathing and did not seem to be toxic in any way. One thing was certain, he was not in Padstow.

He decided his safest course of action was to crawl across the sand dunes in a straight line, away from the glow, his marks in the sand a reference point for his progress.

After a good ten minutes crawl, he could detect a thinning out of the black smog. He thought he could make out another strange glow spreading ahead of him. He knew he had not circled back on himself, the eerie green glow grew brighter. The sand beneath him began to drop away and he began to slide. To avoid tumbling forward, he stood up, the mist was melting away. In front of him lay a shoreline and the green polluted waters of the Camel Estuary.

His eyes were dazzled by the bright sunlight and he took a moment to focus. He visually traced a line across the menacing green waters. He could clearly make out the outline of his home town, all be it from an angle he had never thought possible. All his life he had sat in his shed looking out to the shore opposite, and the blackness beyond. How did he get here and what did it all mean. He slumped to his knees, exhausted and confused as a crowd gathered on the crumbling harbour walls of Padstow.

CONTACT WITH THE GLASS WALL

It had all happened at speed, William had gone. His family assumed he was on his way for a couple of pints in town, little did they know.

'He could have waited, follow that geek, handsome!'

They sat for a few moments in the car before realising they had not moved.

'Das auto is broken, she be going nowhere, please to wait in der hotel while I try to find der problem my hansoms.'

News soon spread to Think Tank headquarters. A Human from five hundred years in the past was loose in the 26th Century.

He was moving quickly, too quick for them to extend the scenario in front of him. If he was not apprehended, the future would soon hit him smack in the face. William sprinted through the thick mist, he could see nothing ahead but believed he was heading in the direction of the harbour. He wanted answers because he wasn't here for a holiday.

The glass wall of the Think Tank laboratory halted his progress with a smack. The impact knocked him backwards and out cold. He lay on the sterile floor surrounded by concerned androids. Scenarios take time to construct and Will had outrun the technology of the Saviorians, ending up in their world, what was to be done now?

After checking his vital signs, William was immediately quarantined for his own good and that of the Saviorians on Earth. The team at the Fox Institute had not experienced this level of anxiety since Alvin Prince's tragic death.

They were waiting on the decision regarding contact with Humans but this latest incident would hardly inspire confidence amongst their superiors.

A BIT OF A COCK UP

'Major Main, you are asked to report to Nash's office immediately, Commander Aragon of Fleet High Command has some serious questions he wishes to ask.'

The telepathic message could not have been clearer. The incidents with the two Humans could not have happened at a worse time. While Saviorians on Earth were making up their minds on the integration question, two major security breaches had taken place in Federal District Six.

'Come in Main, I have asked Dr. Honey to join us. What is the latest situation?' Nash was clearly disturbed and under pressure from his superiors.

'The Human, known as Ken, from present day Padstow, removed himself from the Buffer Zone Installation ten Earth hours ago. Under your instructions, we have not intercepted him, but are monitoring his activities. He is currently on the Northern shore of the Camel Estuary, in a somewhat confused state. There is a real danger of widespread panic if his fellow villagers recognise, and try to reach him.

The Human known as William, an ancient from five hundred years in the Earth's past, escaped a scenario set up in the Fox Institute. William and three other ancients had been brought forward in time to assist in our integration experiments. We are sure he rendered himself unconscious while impacting with the laboratory wall. He is unharmed and detained in a hospital scenario.'

Commander Aragon rose, 'As they used to say on Earth, a bit

of a cock up all round Major Main, would you not agree? Your people have brought us here to judge on your planned experiments with Human integration and find you unable to maintain security in one of your smallest Human pods. Clearly, you and your team have taken your eyes off the ball in your pursuit of the ultimate prize, leaving Earth. While we await the verdict of our people on Human integration, I suggest you sort out these *problems* before the Human race discovers our grand subterfuge, you are dismissed.'

They had to hope William had no recollection of leaving the scenario and Ken could be picked up without arousing suspicion, the clock was ticking.

THEY CALL IT SNOW

It wasn't yet time for the 2.30pm rain shower, or in fact, the one before that. The stuff falling from the sky over Padstow was white and very cold. The crowd assembled on the harbour walls frozen, literally, in fear. They had never experienced anything like it before. They ran for shelter in the New Ship public house, shouting and screaming. Children stopped to gather up the strange frozen white material in small balls. The distraction had momentarily made them forget the image of a man on the contaminated shore opposite.

The sky was grey, the sun had gone. Was their world about to end, their charmed existence at last submitting to the poisoned world beyond their little Eden.

'Fetch Andy, he'll know what this be, he got the knowledge. Little uns, get inside, this 'ere white stuff might be contaminated.'

Pushing to get a view from the pub window, all they could see was a mass of grey and white. The ground had even turned white now and they shivered in the hostile environment.

'Snow, it's snow!' Andy and the family had arrived at the New Ship.

Having left Ken's house, heading for the library, they too got caught in the storm. They had followed the crowd leading to the pub.

'In pre war days, our climate was much different. People could not rely on regular rain showers and warm sunny skies. There were frequent storms and floods, people lost their homes, and quite often their lives.'

'How dreadful! Can't imagine living wi such uncertainty.'

'Why yea, picture going to fetch washin' in and not being sure she'll be dry.'

'Or coming down pub and gettin drenched, weird, or what.'

'There were also times when thousands of people died because their crops wouldn't grow because of something called drought, no rain for years.'

'Stop can't stand to hear no more, best just be grateful for what us ave now.'

'Yes, but what do it all mean Andy, is things to go back to them bad old days?'

'Tis the end ain't it young Andy?'

'It does seem strange, but all we can do is wait and watch, see if this is a one off situation or, a sign of things to come.'

'What is strange' piped up Karen, 'Is, for three hundred years nothing has changed, just as if something or someone was controlling the weather and such like, while we play out our mundane lives, watching for the 2.30pm shower!'

'How dare you, have you not been payin heed to your father's teachings? We be the lucky ones and us parents and grandparents afore us. I've been to Andy's library, as many of us 'ave. We've all seen them pictures of that terrible day when world destroyed herself. Why we was spared is a proper mystery. But I tell ye, young lady, I wakes up every morning, and give thanks that we was.'

'Well,' said Mrs Bishop,' I'm surprised at you, Karen, a clever young girl, talking such rubbish. We've kept us little world going by stickin together and making the best of our little garden in a sea of darkness. I suggest you hush up and start pulling your weight.'

'Sun's back!' Little Molly Brown ran from the window, 'The funny white stuff's gone, can we go out to play?'

While the people were arguing, everything outside had returned to, what they called, normal. The diversion had worked. Ken had gone from the shore and from their minds, for the time being.

The snow storm had been just that, a storm, gone forever. A reminder of how lucky they were now. Keep your heads down and be thankful.

OFF HIS TREE

'Will's been gone an hour now, I knew we should have followed him into town. It's not another planet, Cornwall it just seems like it. What can harm us out there, a bit of fog?'

Anita was heading for the hotel door when she found herself face to face with Paul, the linguistically impaired android. He seemed a little flustered, waving his muscle bound arms in all directions.

'Ya, yes, please to listen to Paul now, bitte. Your brooder, Wilhelmina, Villiam, is kaput, how you say, legless, my handsome, off his tree! Hit his head on ein glass door of yonder bar, beer keller pub, fine now, in bed now sleepzing in der hospital.'

'What's he saying, is William ok, where is he?'Jane sobered up immediately.

The Hotel Manager rushed over, they all huddled round to listen.

'As Paul was trying to say, William has had a slight argument with a glass door in the Customs House Pub. Seems the fresh air and alcohol didn't mix well. He lost his balance and, unfortunately, knocked himself out. A local fisherman came to his rescue and called an ambulance. He is on his way to Truro Hospital, we can follow if you wish?'

'Yes, yes! Let's go now, thank you,' called out Steven.

'I'll kill that little nerd when I see him, bang go my chances with Paul the Penzance Pirate, mind you, I could stay here and hold the fort while you go to the hospital.'

‘Anita, this is your brother, how can you be so selfish!’

‘I’m sorry Miss Hawkins, but William has been asking to see you in person, I think you should go.’

’God, must have taken a bad knock if he wants me there, ok, we’ll all go.’

It had been decided that the entire Hawkins family had to be re-united at the Think Tank laboratories. Events had dictated that the subjects to be involved in the direct contact experiments, had to be more closely guarded until a decision on whether to go ahead or not was made.

The car that was ‘kaput,’ had miraculously been repaired. They climbed back in and the scenario was running. A mock up within a confined space, such as a car, was easy to control. The fog story meant there was no need for the illusion of passing scenery. The sensation of movement had been developed by the android scientists over centuries of using such scenarios. The Hawkins thought they were on the half hour journey to the hospital, in fact, they were crossing the Think Tank compound to join William at his hospital bed.

The Fox Institute lay in the buffer zone between Padstow and Wadebridge. A vast interconnecting honeycomb of underground walkways and ground level express transportation tubes, kept the Saviorians in contact with neighbouring districts. These buffer zones maintained the thousands of small Human population pods, covering the world’s native population. The Fox institute and Think Tank was but a tiny speck in this worldwide network. Like Padstow, each and every small collection of humanity, thought itself unique and alone. They were almost completely unaware of the alien presence cocooning their planet. Strays, like Ken, were few and far between and, until now, easily contained. Change was on its way, but how would the world’s population react?

THE LIE OF THE GREEN SLIME

Ken needed no reintroduction to his surroundings, the white one piece and sterile aroma said it all, but memories were fresh in his mind. He had stood on that shore and seen the familiar outlines of fellow Padstonians. He had witnessed the descending grey and cold of a snow storm, the confusion in the people's ranks. He also remembered stumbling into the green slimy waters, so long a barrier to the inquisitive minds like his own. The shock of realising that it was harmless green dye placed into harmless blue water, a lie perpetrated by who, and why? His mind was awash with confusion and mixed emotions. Invisible strangers had invaded his world and created so many questions, too many even for Ken's inquisitive mind.

He had to be treated like a new born, Ken's mind and body had to be cleansed and made able to work to his full potential. They must not let him leave the bunker again. Androids would have to make direct contact with him to prepare Ken for possible integration. It had been agreed that he would be one of the Humans used in the Ultimate Experiment. They believed his mind would be more accepting of the incredible situation he would find himself in.

A CASE OF FISHERMAN'S FLU

William's determination had brought him to this point. He had been the one to persuade the rest of the family to come *back to Padstow* for Christmas. He had always been the inquisitive one, reluctant to accept all was normal when, unknown to them, they Time Jumped, via the *tunnel*. It was this questioning mind that drove him to escape the latest scenario, and cause panic in Saviorian ranks. As he lay in Think Tank quarantine, he still had to believe all four of his family remained in 21st Century England. The logical part of his brain convinced him of that, aided by the excellent work undertaken by the androids. The rest of the Hawkins family were on their way. Surely they would know what really happened after he left the Metropole Hotel?

Unknown to William, he had been chosen, out of the four ancients, to be tested and undergo first contact with the aliens from his future. However, unlike Ken from 26th Century Padstow, the plan was to keep him unaware of his part in the scheme to release the Human race from its three hundred year isolation. Somehow, the family had to be returned to their home, five hundred years in the past, unharmed, unchanged and unaware, thus, keeping the course of history intact, what could possibly go wrong?

'What do you mean he's in an isolation ward? We were told he banged his head, but was fine,' Jane was clearly concerned.

They had been expecting to take William back to Padstow with no more than a hangover and a bump on the head.

'Is this some sort of joke, I mean, we all know Cornwall is in the back of beyond, but If I thought we needed immunising against local bugs before I came, I would have ducked out.'

'Anita, you're not being helpful here, let the doctor explain.'

'We think your son may have contracted a very rare virus called Fisherman's Flu. He was found on the floor of the Customs House public house by two local fishermen who, we believe, are carriers of the virus. People who have contracted this virus in the past, have always made a complete recovery within a few days. We are giving William a course of Cod Liver Oil tablets. He will be safe to go home once the symptoms of gasping for air and blowing bubbles subside.'

'It sounds rather strange, I've certainly never heard of Fisherman's Flu' commented Steven.

I must admit, it certainly had us scratching our heads. The last known case was reported on the Caribbean island of Aruba in 1994. Fortunately, our doctor Ling spotted it, William should be fine.'

'Can we see him now?' asked Jane, impatiently.

'Yes, of course, but I'm afraid you will have to talk to him from behind his isolation screen, just until he's been given the all clear.'

The speed by which William's hospital scenario had been set up, and the news that he had to be placed in isolation, put extreme pressure on the androids to come up with a plausible explanation, they would struggle to explain Fisherman's Flu if seriously questioned.

THE RESULTS ARE IN

The logistics involved in organising a worldwide vote amongst the Saviorian community was not a problem. However, the painstaking process to provide detailed information on the plans put forward by Dr. Honey and his team was time consuming. Now, all was in place at the Fox Institute, with the chosen Human subjects, no longer at large. If the vote was yes the practised procedure could be activated.

The Central Co-ordinating Office for Saviorian activities on Earth was in New Zealand, close to one of the Human population pods in the former city of Auckland. Results of the pole were pouring in from all parts of the world. The assembled scientist at the Fox Institute waited what seemed an eternity. Saviorians were by nature a calm logic driven race. Today, however, the air was heavy with nervous tension. The enormity of the situation brought back distant memories of three hundred years ago, when they were all young explorers saving a distant planet from self destruction. How did a relatively short deployment turn into a sentence of half a lifetime? Could it really be coming to an end?

The holographic video screens sprang to life. The Auckland Co-ordinating Centre had collected all the votes, this was it.

'Fellow Saviorians, the choice you have made today will, potentially, release us from our mission here on Earth. You have made a bold and brave decision to allow direct contact, once again, with the Human race. You have voted by a ratio of five to one in favour of attempting integration once again.'

You might have expected an outpouring of spontaneous emotion from those assembled at the Fox Institute. Instead, there was stunned silence, this was actually about to happen. Commander Aragon rose to address the shocked delegates.

'Well, members of the institute, the Think Tank and all associated with Federal District Six, there you have it, the approval you asked for from your peers. We will now begin the implementation of your contact and integration plan. As I understand it, you have a time frame of ten Earth years to bring about stability amongst the native population and facilitate our exit from this planet. Let there be no doubts, each stage of this plan is fraught with danger. If the contamination problem has been solved, there is still the unanswered question of how the Human race will react to our presence. How we imposed segregation on them for generations. The lie that made them believe almost all of the entire world's population had been destroyed in a nuclear war, never mind the fact that an alien race has roamed their planet for three hundred years, without their knowledge or approval. Be prepared for these and many more eventualities as you attempt to bring about an outcome, long overdue.'

Emotions were now released in the room. Professor Huntley and his team allowed themselves a brief moment of congratulations before the hard work began.

A TRICK OF THE LIGHT

Mysteries were rare in Padstow 2514. Mario Rollins was in the middle of an interview with Tom Bradby, a carpenter from Boyd Avenue.

'So Tom, you say this man was standing on the beach over on the other side of the estuary.'

'Yes, other folks with me must have seen he too, but they deny it now.'

'Could you see a face or the build of the man?'

'Well, he be a fair way off and that, but 'e sure reminded me o' young Ken, you know, that bloke who went missing and turned up at Ship wi' a few marbles short.'

'Do you think this person could see you watching?'

'I'm not sure twas all over mighty quick see, that snow stuff came and we all ran!'

'If it was Ken, or anyone else for that matter, how do you think he got there?'

'Well, tis impossible, we all know that water's poisoned, has been for centuries.'

'So, would you agree, you imagined it, a trick of the light? That would be why the crowd with you now deny it.'

'You're probably right, but that there image is still in my mind.'

'Thanks for your time Tom, I have your statement on record, and will keep you informed if there are any developments.'

Mario was always keen not to prolong any investigation, so he was happy to wrap this one up.

'And that's it, mystery over is it?' quizzed Karen.

The Rollins family were meeting at Ken's house trying to make sense of the past few days events, he still hadn't turned up.

'You must admit, the last few days have been seriously strange. Ken walks off into the sunset, only to turn up with a bump on his head and a fondness for women's clothing. Suddenly, he produces two fellow Kens, supposedly created because he was lonely. We all wake up, he's gone again but says, don't worry, it will soon be over. Then, apparently, swims the green river of doom, and is seen waving from the opposite shore. We nearly freeze to death in a freak snow storm, the like of which has not been seen in living memory, and all you can tell poor old Tom is, we'll let you know of any developments. If I wasn't so confused, I'd really be enjoying this, it's the most excitement we've had since we discovered a new type of potato on farmer Smyth's farm.'

Andy took some time to comment. He too was dumfounded by recent events. He had prided himself on keeping the community contented and on an even keel. His family were the first place that people came to in time of need and confusion, but this was different. However you looked at it, there appeared to be some outside forces at work, and inside he knew it wouldn't just be Karen demanding answers.

'Don't you think we should call a Public Meeting, before anyone does something foolish, like trying to cross the deadly green river, or enter into the *darkness*?' questioned Mario.

'He could be right Andy' added Dina. 'For the sake of calmness and sanity, please let's do it.'

'I can put some posters up and walk around with my loud

hailer,' Mario was showing some uncharacteristic enthusiasm.

'Ok, but give me some time to formulate a reasonable explanation, to avoid unnecessary actions.'

'Good luck with that Dad!' said Karen, as she went to answer the door.

THE NEW SCI-FI HERO

'Just when you thought you'd heard it all, along comes Fisherman's Flu. Only in the depths of creepy Cornwall could you come across a virus where you blew bubbles, and my brother had to be the one to catch it! I can't wait to quiz him about that.'

'Come on Anita, take it easy on him, it could have been serious.'

They were ushered into a small waiting room area and asked to shower and change into white Sterile Suits, blue cap and slippers. They were certainly taking this harmless virus seriously.

'William has been sedated to regulate his breathing so please keep questions to a minimum, simple yes or no answers would be good, we can only allow a few minutes.'

'This sounds a lot more serious than a mild viral infection' insisted Jane.

'Just taking precautions to facilitate a rapid recovery Mrs Hawkins please come this way.'

The screen around William's bed was translucent and there was no way to recognise who lay in the bed.

'Will, can you hear us, we came straight away, are you ok?' enquired Steve.

'Yes.'

'Can you remember banging your head in the pub?' asked Jane.

'No.'

'Is there anything we can get you, son?'

'No' came the abrupt reply.

'Oh I've had enough of this, Will, which university are you at?' asked Anita.

No reply.

'O.K. what age am I Will?' No reply.

'Will, are you feeling alright, just answer.'

'Yes' came the reply from behind the curtain.

A sudden impulse made Anita reach for the screen surrounding the bed. The framework gave way and toppled to the floor. On the bed, there was no sign of William. There had not been time to construct a convincing android substitute with William's voice print.

'What the hell's going on, where's my son!' implored Jane.

Androids rushed to the improvised hospital room. Steven and Jane were stopped in their tracks, but Anita escaped, she was loose within the corridors of the Fox Institute 2514, this was no hospital, this was not her time.

Android security was for once, a little light on the ground. Major resources had been deployed to sector three, where the two chosen Humans were being prepared. Anita's blue slippers lost grip on the polished floor as she bounced from one wall to the next. She didn't take much notice of the various rooms she rushed past on either side, until she collided with an open door, a family trait you might say. In her dazed state she struggled to focus on the form facing her. Stumbling to her feet, Anita realised she was looking at a Holographic Image projected in remarkable detail. It first reminded her of a Sci Fi film she'd seen on DVD. She was drawn to the green and red eyes with their strange hypnotic properties. The figure was clothed in black, but its proportions seemed all wrong, stumpy short legs supported a stout frame, and she was sure there was a hint of a tail beneath the black cloak. Short sleeves covered the even shorter arms, and a huge hood covered the head. Only the eyes could be seen, penetrating the darkness.

Professor Huntley was addressing an unseen audience,

'Fellow Saviorians of Federal District Six, you will now be aware of the monumental decision you have all made. Our entire population here on Earth will be watching every step we take towards integration and ultimate exit from this planet. As is our way, we aim to keep you fully informed before each step is taken. Our brave colleague here at Fox, Dr Arthurian Honey, has put himself forward to be the first of our kind, since our illustrious hero, Alvis Prince, to come into direct contact with Humans. As you all know, step one will involve an ancient Human from the year 2014. We feel it important for us all to share this encounter as closely as possible, and you will no doubt be hearing a lot about the Human subject, Mr William Hawkins, and his unique role in this endeavour. When we have further news, we will inform you straight away.'

Up until the mention of William's name, Anita was trying to remember if this was the film she had seen recently. Now, her jaw hit the shiny metallic floor of the information room. 'Holy shit is this some kind of a joke. I knew Will was short of money, but I didn't realise he was into acting in low budget Sci Fi flicks!'

She could hear her voice talking outside her head as footsteps approached.

'Miss Hawkins, please come with us.'

CONTACT

All was going to plan. William Hawkins had gone through rigorous testing and was proving the model subject. Calculations made about the makeup of standard humans, circa 2014, were proving 98% accurate, well within acceptable levels.

William was feeling great. Most testing had taken place while he recovered from his argument with *the pub door.* He had been told a Dr. Honey would visit in an hour to pronounce him fit to leave. His family were, apparently, on their way to collect him. Will still had loads of questions about their latest trip to Padstow, but they could wait 'til he got out of the hospital.

He was alone in the small hospital room, but beyond its walls, things were different. Teams of scientists had been brought in to cover every breathing moment of this first encounter. Highly sophisticated monitoring equipment would cover each of the three heart beats, Human and Alien. At any moment, the process could be halted. Both Dr. Honey and William were the worst kept secrets in Saviorian medical history, everything was being watched.

'It is very important that you keep him calm. The adapted Human version of our Simu-Suit should convince him you're a *regular guy*, just don't stare at him, remember the May Day scenario, he spotted your eyes then, there may be a memory link.' Huntley continued 'Once you feel he is relaxed, and does not suspect anything, you can start the procedure, good luck Dr. Honey, all Saviorians will be watching, feel the support.'

'Hello William, this is Dr Honey, he's here to check you're fit enough to go back to Padstow.'

The android doctor left the room. It is safe to say Dr.Honey was by far, the more nervous of the two species in the room. He was in possession of all the facts. William spoke first.

'Hi Doc, can we get this over with, I feel really great and I need to get out of here to sort a few things out.'

Dr. Honey remembered William well from their first encounter during the May Day scenario, he prayed this time that the time travelling Human, did not. Dr.Honey circled the room, still very wary, but he knew he had to do this and he did have faith in his scientists.

'Have patience Will, I can call you Will, can't I?' William nodded. 'Firstly, let me re-check your blood pressure.'

Will thought the doctor was a little strange. His movements were slow and very cautious, and he avoided eye contact.

'Your left arm please Mr Hawkins,' Dr.Honey suddenly became very formal. The doctor reached out and made direct contact with the Human, the first direct contact in three hundred Earth years, he pretended to check the pressures.

'Good, thank you, blood pressure normal.' Both the doctor's hearts were beating fast and he fought hard to control his emotions.

'You seem a little shaky Doc, rough night last night, a bit like me, eh, not enough lemonade with it!'

Dr. Honey ignored William's remark, he had to focus.

'Now, I just want to check your breathing, you are aware there was a knock to your chest when you hit the door?'

'No, but nothing surprises me after last night.'

Dr. Honey was now very close, the two species sharing the same air.

'God Doc, your breath stinks, smells like you've eaten a crate load of rotten fish!'

The scientists had missed the point that Saviorian dental hygiene was not the best. In fact, they had no teeth as we know it, just two long rows of digesting suckers. Food was half digested in the mouth, before swallowing, hence the pungent smell.

This Simu-Suit had better keep working, thought Honey, if not, my cover's blown.

'Excellent, your breathing seems normal.'

A slight smile spread across the doctor's fake face, so far so good. Dr. Honey had shared William's breath with no ill effects, hopefully the same could be said for Mr Hawkins as he had turned a little green.

'Is everything alright, William?'

'Yes, but could you wear a mask next time, you really do need to see a dentist Doc.'

The next test was the most critical. The sneeze that ultimately cost the life of Alvis Prince must be replicated here and now. The scientists had prepared a special facial wipe which would produce a sneeze upon contact.

'Sorry about that oversight Mr Hawkins, here, please wipe your face with this, it will guard against any potential germs.'

Will gratefully scrubbed at his face which caused an immediate reaction.

Dr. Honey had to position his face so as to receive the full force of William's sneeze. The explosion from the ancient Human's nose and mouth covered the alien in a shower of mucus and exhaled breath.

'Oh God I'm really sorry doctor, I don't know where that came from, wipe your face with this.' He offered the same wipe without thinking.

The doctor's immediate reflex reaction was to dab his eyes

with the cloth. He quickly withdrew, realising his mistake.

'Thank you, thank you, I think I'm fine.'

For the first time today, William found himself eye to eye with the alien and suddenly had a strange feeling of déjà vu, but it was gone, the doctor realising, distracted him.

'Well, judging by that sneeze, there is clearly nothing wrong with your breathing. I'm pretty sure you will soon be free to leave, probably just coming down with a Cornish cold.'

Dr. Honey had been covered from head to tail in sensors and monitors of all kinds. The scientists in the next room feverishly devoured the data received from the alien's body, so far, so good, no adverse reactions.

'I'll be back very shortly, and give an update on your family's whereabouts. It's been a real pleasure treating you Will.'

'No sweat Doc, thanks for looking after me.'

Dr. Honey left the room with a thrill in both his hearts, he was alive and apparently well, and so was his patient.

POWERFUL DRUG

The development of Saviorian science in the field of altered memory had enabled them to cope with complex situations with a certain amount of ease. This was such a situation. The unpredictable and inquisitive nature of Humans was to the fore in the makeup of the Hawkins brood, especially the younger generation. In order to send this family back to their own time in a state of splendid ignorance, some of these techniques now had to be employed. Humans were far removed from the inhabitants of Slugbot Five in the gullibility stakes. A memory similar to that of a goldfish, combined with a determined desire to believe black is white, or any other colour suggested to them, made their species easy to control. Humans were an entirely different kettle of fish.

Three quarters of the Hawkins family had been picked up, kicking and screaming. They were clearly worried about the whereabouts of William, and why he was suddenly appearing in Sci-Fi films.

Not unlike the reboot of a computer, their memories had to be reset to the point where they entered the hospital to pick up William. If their drugs worked properly, there would be no residual memory of intervening events. William, however, because of the tests carried out, could not be rebooted.

'Where have you lot been, sightseeing tour of Cornwall? I've been waiting ages.'

William, having been discharged, was ready in a waiting room. He wanted to thank Dr. Honey personally, but he was nowhere to be seen.

'We came straight here, they were very helpful in the hotel, brought us here in a nice car,' noted Jane.

'So, knocked some sense into you did they?' asked Anita

'Can't believe the number of tests they did, felt like some kind of guinea pig.'

'Probably had trouble finding any brain activity.' Anita, compassionate to the end.

'Come on, we've got a car waiting for us, it's Christmas Day, time to celebrate.' Yes, Steven was his old self, clearly the drugs had worked.

DEADLY GREEN SLIME

'Hi Jan, come in and join the party.' Karen was clearly enjoying events, 'It's Jan from the pub.'

'Hello Jan, what drags you away from the bar?'

'Sorry to bother you Andy, but I'm a bit worried. Some local boys are talking about building a boat! You know, to try and cross the estuary and find Ken. I think it might just be drink talking, but thought that Mario should hear about it.'

'But they know, one toe in that green slime would mean certain death,' cried Andy.

'Are they still in the pub?' asked Mario.

'Yes, I think so.'

'Then I'll come and stop them. Dad, I think it's time for that public meeting.'

Andy quickly drew up some posters and fliers warning again of the dangers out there and reinforcing the positives in their lives. He also called for a public meeting for two days time in the Metropole Hospital. This would give him the opportunity to scour the library for more images of the war and some showing the idyllic lives they enjoyed now.

Mario co-ordinated search parties for Ken, to keep the locals occupied, stressing all the time to keep within safe areas and not to go near the water. The Rollins family knew that nothing would be gained from panicking. They were all still safe if no one did anything stupid. Karen went along with the plan for now.

REVELATIONS

Dr. Honey was hooked up to a sophisticated monitoring system, checking all aspects of his physical and mental wellbeing. There was real excitement within the institute and the wider alien community. The Human subject, William, had been sent back to the hotel scenario with a clean bill of health, so plans were being made for the next stage. Everyone knew that this would be much trickier. The tests carried out on Ken and William showed similar levels of radiation on their bodies, much lower than those in the Human that contaminated Alvis Prince. In order to provide a degree of continuity, Dr. Honey would again be the Saviorian subject exposed to the present day Human, Ken. There would, however, be one major difference with this encounter, no scenario. Because Ken was from the present time, he would be the first to meet a Saviorian face to face, with limited use of a Simu-Suit. Not only would they be testing for physical compatibility, but also for signs that Humans could accept the appearance of the aliens and the implications of their presence here on Earth. Because of Ken's inquisitive mind, he was thought a suitable subject, who might even embrace the situation.

It had been decided that, in order to gain Ken's trust and obtain the same degree of contact achieved with William, a Simu-Suit would be used initially. Only when Dr. Honey felt the first stage had been a success would he be revealed as his true self.

Ken was fully alert, and free from any mind altering drugs. An android appeared at the door of Ken's room, dressed as a doctor. Shock and disbelief were the reactions etched on Ken's face.

'Please do not be afraid, you are perfectly safe. We know your mind is full of questions, and they will all be answered in time. There is no need to try and escape us, we are all on the same side, believe me.'

'I....I don't recognise your face, you're not from Padstow, how is this possible? I remember now, the water is safe... I could see my friends in the distance... but who are you? ...I knew it, we're not alone, are we? All my life I've been trying to prove it, they wouldn't listen. You survived, your ancestors, they too came through the war.'

All Human emotions were visiting themselves on Ken now, but the strangest was undoubtedly, excitement, he wanted this to be happening. 'So...so, you're from where, let me see, across the estuary that would have been Rock. Wadebridge your families survived in Wadebridge, is that it?'

'All in good time, I am here to explain what will happen next. You're inquisitive nature brought you away from the safety of your own village to where you are now. We need to carry out some tests before you are allowed to go home. Yes there were, what you call survivors......'

In the Think Tank there were concerns the android doctor was not handling the conversation with Ken very well, but they allowed it to continue.

'Firstly, we need to confirm your body is free from any contamination, will you please co-operate.'

'Oh! You mean from the dark zone, radiation belt, from the war. Yes, please do your tests. You promise then to give me answers?'

'We certainly will, all the answers you need, and many more. I would like you to meet one of our most renowned scientists, Dr. Honey. He will guide you through the testing procedure.'

'Yes, thank you. I didn't catch your name.' 'Me, oh I'm ZX120 answered the android on his way out.'

'Strange sort of name for a doctor, must do things differently in Wadebridge, I suppose it's been a long time' pondered Ken.

Dr. Honey had just got over his contact session with William, but was keen to complete the process. He entered the room with the same caution as before, but this encounter was going to be very different. He was happy the way the Simu-Suit had worked with William, so he had confidence this part would go well.

'Good day, err...'

'Ken, my name is Ken, from Old Dennis Road.'

'Yes, thank you, my name is Dr. Honey, please let me explain what is going to happen...'

'Sorry for interrupting, but I only know of one doctor in Padstow, my niece Dina Rollins, and you're clearly not her.'

'Yes I know this is confusing, but please let me continue. You were picked up in the buffer zone, probably after getting lost, and we need to check you are safe to go home.'

Ken thought the best course of action was to go along with this Dr. Honey, even though his mind was racing in a strange way, he felt, for some reason, the doctor could be trusted.

Ken's room was in the same vicinity as William's *hospital* scenario and the scientists were ready again to analyse Ken and Dr. Honey's results. The doctor had acquired some strange Human mouth cleanser after his breath nearly knocked William out. The close contact and breathing tests went well as did the sneeze, although Ken could not apologise enough for covering the alien in projectile mucus. Both species appeared to be feeling well and the scientists in the lab were quietly confident.

'I am just going to go over the results with my colleagues and then I will attempt to answer the questions I know you have.'

Dr. Honey left the room. Ken sat on the bed with a fixed expression of bewilderment on his face. If these people were survivors, how many more were there. Andy's books and records all referred to total destruction but for Padstow. If they were wrong, who provided the false information?

A good hour later, Honey returned with a slight smile emanating from his Simu-Suit.

'Good news all round Ken, you have a clean bill of health, and so it would appear, do I.'

'Why do you say that doc, it was me having the tests, not you?'

'No Ken, you had already been tested, it was me in the spotlight.'

'You've lost me doc.'

'It is true, isn't it, that you have an open and inquisitive mind, Ken?'

'Yes...but why?'

'You see, we've been watching you for a long time now. At first you were thought of as a danger to the stability we created. This is why pages from the books you were reading were removed, in case you stumbled upon evidence. But now, now you are going to be so important to us and your kind in the integration process, sorry, I'm getting ahead of myself.'

'O.K, I've listened to enough, just who exactly are you?'

'I think you'd better brace yourself for a shock.'

The Saviorian pressed a point on his forehead and the Simu-Suit vanished.

MISSING EQUIPMENT AND LOST FAMILIES

'So you say your daughter and her family won this short break holiday to Padstow over Christmas?'

'Yes, that's right officer, Steven, her husband, was particularly excited because it included free drinks!'

'But, in fact it was William, your Grandson, who arranged it all, is that correct?'

'Oh yes I think so, last May they won some rail tickets to Padstow, and had a bit of an adventure by all accounts.'

'What is the great attraction in Padstow then?'

'Oh, I think William likes it there, he had a day trip to Padstow from university not long back.'

'Yes that would be Nottingham University, is that correct?'

'Yes, that's right. Can you tell me what this is all about officer, only they're due back in a couple of days, you can speak to them then. Has something happened, you see Jane doesn't phone or anything when they're away she never has. They've always been fine so I don't worry.'

'If you could try to ring her please, there are some questions I need answered.'

'Oh, ok, now where's her number, yes, here we are, can't be doing with mobile phones and such like... Oh, no reply, phone seems to be dead, oh! Now I'm worried, you'd better tell me what's going on.'

'It appears your Grandson was carrying some recording equipment he borrowed from Nottingham University over Christmas. We know this because it was picked up from a train in Penzance.'

'But, they would be getting off at Bodmin, if I remember it right.'

'That is correct only they were not seen at Bodmin and did not arrive at any hotel in Padstow, they were not even booked in anywhere in that town. I really need to know if there was anywhere else down there they might have stayed instead?'

'Well no, I don't think so. They haven't been to that part of the world much until recently.'

'I don't want you to worry, they probably changed their plans, but please, would you get in touch with me as soon as you hear from them?'

'Yes, yes, I will, but tell me officer, why are you so interested in their whereabouts?'

'Probably nothing, but we need some answers about the images we found on your Grandson's recording equipment, we do need to talk to him right away. Please try not to worry, If we find them, you will be the first to know.'

He handed his card to Mrs Shaw, and was gone. Vera was confused and very worried, she tried Jane's phone again without success, what on Earth was going on?

LEAVING SO SOON?

Here they were, back at the hotel after what seemed like an eternity but in fact was little more than twenty four hours. Their recollections of the previous day were, at best sketchy. They put this down to the worry over William, but he seemed well now. Little did he realise the service he had given to his future world. The priority for the Saviorians was to get William and his family safely back to their own time without endangering the course of history in any way.

'Hey look! Sherlock, I think you've got a special Christmas present.'

There, in the middle of the Metropole Hotel reception was a collection of scientific recording equipment.

'You found it, oh thank you so much.'

'It had been left on your train from London, they sent it over from Penzance,' informed the Hotel Manager.

'Looks like the romance of the nerds might be back on track,' cried Anita.

'Now I can look to see what it recorded when we had that so called shunt outside Bodmin.'

'Oh no Will!' cried his mother, 'Can we just have a normal few hours before you start all that again.'

'But I need to check it out.'

'Here look at this,' said Steven. 'What hope is there when so called centres of excellence can't even spell properly.'

'What do you mean?

'How would you spell Nottingham?'

'Ask Anita, even she could answer that.'

'Less of the wise cracks, geek boy, that's my domain.'

On the side of one of the boxes was a label which read *PROPERTY OF NOTINGHAME UNIVERSITY*.

'Probably just a misprint, come on, time for Christmas dinner, I'm starving.' shouted Jane.

While Dr. Honey was in the middle of testing Colonel Hafey was put in charge of bringing about a smooth return to the 21st Century for the Hawkins family. There was a continued concern that William had suspicions.

'We cannot afford to be casual. The error on the mock up recording equipment is slack, we need to more vigilant.'

A breakthrough seemed so close and everyone was rather edgy.

The Hawkins family were just relaxing over coffee when the hotel manager came over.

'We do hope you have enjoyed your Christmas dinner.'

'The giblets left in the turkey was a bit of a surprise, is that a local tradition?' enquired Jane.

'You would have to ask chef about that madam.'

'They're probably left overs from some sacrificial rite they perform in these 'ere parts.'

'Nice to see you back to your old self Anita,' remarked Steven.

'Anyway, I have some news that may interest you. We are well aware that your stay has not been without mishap.'

'You can say that again!' cried the family as one.

'As you are aware, our hotel is about to close for re-decoration.

The owners would like to offer you a small cash amount, if you would agree to leave one day earlier, that being tomorrow. Trains are limited on Boxing Day, but we have checked and one is available at 11.20 am tomorrow.'

'May I ask, what this small amount would be?' enquired Steven with interest.

'I have been allowed to offer you £500 each,' Saviorians had very little idea of the value of 21st Century money but they were, however, excellent forgers.

The last mouthful of Steven's coffee plastered the tablecloth. Anita jumped in 'Right, I'm off to pack, make it £1000 and I'll go now!'

She jumped up and kissed the hotel manager, a move she soon regretted. His skin had a metallic cold feel 'Oh my God, sorry!'

'No need Miss, an old war wound, metal plate in the cheek, long story.' he had been well programmed.

Will was pondering, 'Our holiday was free, along with the train tickets, right. Now you are paying us the grand total of £2,000 to go home early? I smell a rat.'

'I assure you sir, out hotel is spotless, we exterminate vermin at the first sign.'

'No, no, I am very suspicious, why do you want rid of us so badly?'

'Shut the f .... up Will, if the tin man wants to give us money, I say thanks, where's the door, sorry, no offence meant.'

'That's fine Miss. We simply want you to go home quickly, I mean happily, with a small Christmas gift. I will leave you to discuss it over another round of drinks, waiter!'

'Do you remember our May Day trip, how much did we get to leave those *special* tickets behind?'

'You know very well Sherlock, it was £500 each, so what?'

'Rather a coincidence, £500 each time.'

'So what? Very generous people the Cornish, I've always had a lot of time for them.' Anita crossed her fingers.

'Son, you may not be aware how much it is costing us to put you through university, this might not cover it, but it will help, don't you think?'

'Your dad's got a point Will. Let's just take the money and go home early. It's not like we're seeing much on this trip.'

'I was the one who won you this free holiday in the first place. Something just isn't right I need to look at that imaging equipment now.'

William was up and gone before they could react, he needed answers, whoever was behind this wasn't going to buy him off this easily. In his room, he assembled the universities, state of the art equipment. He just needed to check on any sound and visual recordings collected around the time of the *shunt*. All was prepared and he sat back to watch the playback screen. To begin with there was just snow and zigzag lines with no sound then the picture cleared. He sat forward in anticipation.

'Stupid boy Pike, how do you expect Captain Mainwaring to believe that, and where's your scarf, you know what your mother will say.'

'Sorry Uncle Arthur.'

'What the hell is this?'

He found himself watching an old episode of Dad's Army. He only recognised it because Steven had the box set. William frantically searched for something meaningful but all he got was three more episodes of the dated comedy. He rushed from his room only to be met by Anita on her way to pack.

'What's the rush Sherlock, found something?'

'Four episode of flaming Dads Army, that's it.'

'Looks like your girlfriend has a fondness for old men in uniform, got a bit of competition there Will.'

'It's impossible, all the memory was clean when I packed the equipment, where's the manager?'

William showed the android the recordings.

'This is not what you expected to see, I take it Mr Hawkins.'

'What do you think, does it look like they're on a train? And why are they wearing 1940's army uniforms?'

This clearly did not compute to a 26th Century android from Saviorian.

'Sorry if you feel let down in any way, we simply passed the equipment on to you as it was found.'

'Come on Sherlock, come and have a drink in the bar , unless that is, you want to watch episode four where Jones utters the immortal words '*They don't like it up 'em.'*

Back at the bar, Will was a broken man. The family decided they would leave the next day pocketing the cash.

'Well done everyone' exclaimed Hafey, 'Get the leaving scenario ready for tomorrow, there are to be no more mistakes.'

KAREN AND DINA HAVE DOUBTS

Andy, Dina and Karen were formulating a strategy for the forthcoming Public Meeting. Dina rarely ventured into Padstow public library even though it too was housed in the old Metropole building, she saw it as Andy's domain. However, like many of the town's residents, she did like a good read. Almost all the works of fiction had been created by residents of the town over the past three hundred years. The visitors thought it best for mankind to start afresh, leaving mostly references to the war and survival of the few as reinforcement in the minds of the *lucky ones*. Factual books mostly referred to the likes of animal husbandry, getting the most out of your crops and home crafts. Only the likes of Ken felt the need to delve into the unknown.

Dina saw Andy as the custodian of any residual pre-war texts, as his father was before him. He was trusted to be the oracle in this field and few others bothered regressing into the past. Karen would like to be one of the few.

'I feel we need to get back to some sort of normality after the events of the past few days. We can use this public meeting to reassure people to be thankful for what we have here.' stated Andy.

'Yes, and bury our heads in the sand yet again.'

'Karen, I thought you agreed to go along with this strategy and not confuse the people further?'

'People are going to ask questions, I have questions. Where is Uncle Ken? What caused the snow storm? Are we really alone in the World?'

'Now is not the time for flights of fancy, people need stability. We need to point them in the right direction, so no more arguments!'

Karen stormed out of the building; this was not good enough for her.

'Let her go Dina, she'll come around in time.'

Andy proceeded to show Dina images of nuclear destruction he had not shared with her before. Then she saw some pictures taken by post war residents on the few cameras to survive. Happy smiling faces, families playing in the fields, people working hard on the land and sharing the fruits of their labours.

'How can they not see how fortunate we are? I have a few images here of snow storms from the old world. I don't know how I have missed them all these years, strange. Look, children playing safely, throwing balls of snow, nothing to fear, it's lucky they turned up now.'

'What about Ken, how do you explain the sightings, his letters and his strange behaviour?'

'It was clearly a trick of the light. We have learnt not to raise our heads to the distance, we all know what lies there. The people who thought they saw Ken, their eyes were straining to see that far away, they were mistaken, it simply could not have been him. Mario's search parties will find him then he can answer your questions.'

'You're probably right Andy, but I just have one more problem.'

'Oh no, you're beginning to sound like Karen.'

'Those horrific images of nuclear destruction, have you ever thought who took those photo's, how did they get into your library?'

Andy looked bemused. Few people had asked to see them. He had always used them as a positive reinforcement for the odd doubting mind. As far as he knew, they had always been there, his father had shown them to him, without explaining their origin.

'Dina, now is not the time, we do not need more mysteries, especially now.'

'Then you admit, it is a mystery you don't have an answer to?'

'Yes you're right,' was all Andy could say.

This public meeting might prove more difficult than he had anticipated.

A HUMAN'S FIRST FACE FULL

Simu-suits had been developed by Saviorian scientists for a variety of reasons. It is safe to say that this species was not the most attractive in the galaxy. They had been on the receiving end of so many adverse reactions from other aliens they encountered so it was considered research money well spent. As William had recently experienced, their digestive processes had a particularly vile bi-product which, if this had been a violent race, could have been developed into a useful weapon. Finally, the Simu-Suit translated the Saviorian language into any other found in space. A useful tool as theirs consisted of a long series of gurgles and slurps.

It had been decided at the Think Tank that Ken's initial exposure would be a brief one. If he was, in fact, an open minded person, this exposure time could be increased, but was not thought essential.

'Holy shit! What the hell, that can't be real!'

Ken covered his face and eyes, partly to mask the stench but mostly the shock. He had lasted longer than many other species on first contact. Dr. Honey risked a brief Saviorian greeting.

'Goo shoach missau sleemph ushii, ' inadvertently spraying the unsuspecting Human with yellow bile.

Quickly, he reinstated his Simu-Suit and Ken gratefully accepted half a box full of anti-bacterial wipes.

'I'm sorry if my appearance upsets you Ken but in fact, your initial reaction is encouraging.'

'What the f... are you?'

'Your continued use of Human expletives seems to suggest my un- veiled appearance is a source of concern to you.'

'You can say that again, are you for real?'

'To answer you factually, yes I am real, as are the other fifty thousand of us here on Earth.'

'So, I take it you are the by- product of the nuclear war, some sort of extreme mutation?'

'I could feel deeply insulted by that assumption. I have, in fact, not lacked female admirers amongst our kind.'

'Sorry Doc but these admirers need a serious eye test!'

'By your jovial demeanour I suspect you are ready to hear some hard facts.'

'Sorry, yes, please continue.' Ken's nervous laughs only masked his heightened state of shock.

'I will continue to employ my Simu-Suit to control your anxiety and to translate our beautiful language into yours. As I stated earlier, there are fifty thousand of us here on Earth. We have been present here for just over three hundred of your years. We come from the planet Savioria in the Andromeda Galaxy 2.5 million light years from Earth. We were guided here in order to prevent mankind's self destruction and to leave only when we were sure you would not make the same mistakes again. We are Saviorians, our sole purpose is to preserve what we recognise as intelligent life in all its forms, wherever possible.'

'Wow, that's quite a story, but there's only one rather large problem Dr. Honey, you failed, we did destroy the Human race, except for the few fortunate souls in Padstow.'

'It is with continued thanks to our scientists and androids that that myth perpetuates to this very day.'

'You're talking rubbish again doctor, we and our families have lived in the shadow of our nuclear history for over three hundred years. I have often wondered if we were left entirely alone but, until today, have seen no evidence to prove otherwise.'

'I can see this is a lot for you to take in. You are a very important part of our plans, so let's take it slowly. I should leave you to rest for a while and check on my own progress. This is just the beginning Ken, so please be patient.'

Dr. Honey left Ken to rest and hopefully absorb some of what he had just been told. He was also anxious to confirm that he was fit and well and of no danger to his fellow Saviorians. As he left Ken's room he was met by Professor Huntley.

'We are all so grateful to you, doctor for your bravery in taking part in these history changing tests. While you were consulting with the Human subject we have collected a great deal of data on your physical well being and that of the two Humans. If you are up to it there is a meeting scheduled with Major Main and Commander Aragon in one Earth hours time. Plans are already in place to expand exposure and ultimate integration, as soon as possible.'

'Thank you Professor, I can understand your desire to speed the process along. However, having just experienced the Human Ken's initial reaction to the limited amount of information I imparted, we need to proceed carefully. I will report to your office in one hour Professor.'

Ken lay down and tried to come to terms with everything he had just seen and heard. In a way, he had spent a lot of his adult life searching for something like this. In reality it had probably been a source of escapism from the mundane existence in idyllic Padstow. Could all this really be true, he secretly hoped it was. He couldn't wait to talk to the slobbering alien again.

A knock on the door and XY304 brought Ken's evening meal, fish.

'I suppose you're going to tell me this is real fish from the waters around here, something we've been deprived of all these years?'

'Well, yes sir, it was harvested only yesterday off the Cornish coast.'

'So the waters have not been polluted for centuries, it was all a lie?'

'I am not at liberty to talk on this subject sir, enjoy your meal.'

Ken had many questions and he was ready for the answers.

HOW CAN THEY JUST VANISH?

The recording equipment and video images removed from the train in Penzance had been sent to Police Headquarters in Exeter. Their contents were being played back over and over again at various speeds down to freeze frame. Were they dealing with a simple hoax or was there more to it? Why did William Hawkins set up this gear in the first place, what was he hoping to capture?

'Let's play it back once more at normal speed' requested the Chief Investigating Officer Jim Hammond.

The first few moments showed the interior of the First Class carriage with the Hawkins family relaxed and in good voice, getting their luggage ready to disembark at Bodmin Parkway. They were the only passengers travelling in First Class. The daughter, Anita could be heard '*Might as well do that now Sherlock cause nothing is going to happen this time.*'

The picture then flickers and changes to negative instantly. The family have vanished with their luggage. There are a few unrecognisable sounds on the recording before the screen goes blank.

'Play those sounds back again at half speed' asked Hammond.

Shoorish coshee ampoo...

'They are not part of any language known to us, but our analysts confirm they have a definite structure not just random sounds, we are still working on them sir.'

'Have we had any luck tracking down the family?'

'No I'm afraid not sir.'

'They can't have just vanished, and they certainly have not left the country.'

'No sir, we have checked the borders, no sighting so far.'

'Are you sure the recording is continuous, no breaks?'

'Yes, as we concluded before. Split down into individual frames, family talking in carriage, recording in colour, next frame family gone, recording in negative. Nothing and then the unrecognisable speech sounds.'

'The girl Anita, her last words suggest something had happened on a previous occasion, what might that mean?'

'The only thing we have to go on is the statement from Mrs Jane Hawkins mother, Vera Shaw. She stated they had '*a bit of an adventure by all accounts on their first visit to Padstow.*'

'Why did William go to all that trouble, borrowing this equipment from his university, what was he trying to record?'

The room fell silent, they had drawn a blank.

'Ok, we can't afford many more man hours on this. Get back to Mrs Shaw and see if there is anything else she can remember about the previous trip to Cornwall. One way or another, they will turn up eventually. Keep someone working on the recordings, good luck.'

As yet, no actual crime had been committed and the police had more pressing matters.

YOU DON'T REALLY WANT TO GO OUT

'So let me get this straight, it's our last night in Padstow, the free drink is great but, let's face it, the food's rubbish, what's wrong with eating out?'

Anita was trying, without much success, to get the family to go out for the evening, walk down town, maybe see something.

'That fog hasn't lifted the whole time we've been here and as you say, the drinks are still free, so I vote to stay put, we're off in the morning. Just relax.' Steven was on his third pint and very happy.

'Your Dad's right,' added Jane, ordering another bottle of white. 'Just relax, we can order a take away if you want.'

'Have they developed that concept in Cornwall yet? They probably think take away is when the white van comes to remove your dear old Granddad.'

'Anita!'

'I'll come with you sis', I could do with the fresh air.'

'What did you call me Einstein, sis', you've never called me that.'

'Haven't I, come on get your things.'

'Ok you're on, but yours is the first round. Give me ten to get my face on, verbally impaired Paul might be around, he can show us the sights of downtown Padstow.'

Little did she know that Paul was minus his android brain and a couple of limbs, he may well be for the spare part depot.

'Did I overhear you say you two were going out?' The hotel manager was on the prowl.

'We told them it was a horrible night but you know what young people are like' noted Jane, aware that her lips were becoming numb on Saviorian Sauvignon Blanc.

'Christmas night in town is not all that great, not many places open, best you stay here, more drinks anyone!' The android was trying hard, but it wasn't working.

'Miss out on my brother buying a drink, no we're off to the bright lights, he might even stretch to some local fish and chips if I'm really lucky.'

Anita and William went off to get ready.

'Be quite nice a few hours on our own, I'll be back in a minute good time to empty the tanks.' Steven stumbled off to locate the loo.

The manager came back with more drinks. 'Mrs Hawkins, it really would be a waste of time them going out. The kitchen can prepare any dish they might want, will they not stay?'

'Oh, it's alright, they'll soon be back, neither of them likes to put their hands in their pockets but thanks anyway.'

'Two of the ancients intend breaking out of the hotel scenario Colonel Hafey, they will not be dissuaded.'

'We do not need this distraction at such a delicate time. Very well, round up all available androids and set up a party scenario alongside the hotel, one that should satisfy their curiosity.'

'The only androids available might have some slight defects, for example XP120 Paul, can we use them in a convincing way Colonel?'

'We have no alternative but if the ancients are under the influence of alcohol with some luck they won't notice, see to it now.'

'Yes Colonel, our androids usually come through for us in the end.'

PADSTOW FIRST

'Come in Dr. Honey and please take a seat.'

The doctor took his place at the circular table along with his colleagues from the Think Tank, Commander Aragon of Fleet High Command and Earth's Logistics Officer, Jackie Green.

'Thank you for joining us at such short notice Dr. Honey,' noted Professor Huntley

'While you have been performing heroics under testing, we have been making plans. May I introduce Chief Logistics Officer Jackie Green. Both of our teams have formulated a scheme to bring about progressive contact and integration with the Human population, Jackie would you explain.'

Dr. Honey remembered Jackie Green from an incident over one hundred Earth years ago. It was connected with a crop failure in a Human commune in Eastern Canada. A team of androids had been sent into the Human population to sort the problem out and the doctor had helped Jackie with the mission by providing historical background to programme the androids. She had come across as very capable then and, he was not surprised to see her at the top table.

'Dr. Honey, good to see you again, if I can get straight to the point. We have concluded that we could aim to commence Human integration using the inhabitants of Padstow. It would seem the logical starting point as it was your Think Tank that discovered the potential solution to our enduring dilemma here on Earth. In addition, it is a relatively small commune and therefore easier to monitor. We see this happening over a very short time frame and commencing soon.'

'Dr. Honey, your comments please.'

'Firstly, it is a great pleasure working with you again Jackie. It is an honour to be chosen as the first contact commune since the ill fated incident involving our tragic hero, Alvis Prince. My recent experiences with Human subject Ken has made me realise the enormity and complexity of the task ahead. His reaction to my physical appearance was dramatic, and he is an open minded Human. We have to be prepared for possible hostility and aggression when the population discover what we have done. Humans do not like to be controlled or manipulated.'

'Yes, we are aware of this possibility and may need to employ emotion suppressing agents in our initial work,' pointed out Major Main.

'We can use subject Ken as a test model and so I now need to answer all his questions and gauge his reactions. This I can do without delay. What were the results of my physical reaction to Ken?'

'As far as our extensive analysis can tell, direct contact is perfectly safe. You have not shown any adverse side effects to Human contact, but this will be constantly monitored.'

'So, we have agreed a course of action.

One, Dr. Honey talks in detail to Ken about our mission and its effects on the Human race.

Two, through Dr. Honey and Ken we enlighten the population of Padstow.

Three, the buffer zone around the town is removed.

Four, the plan is taken forward into the wider world.

Five, the Human race take their planet back.

Six, Saviorian withdrawal from Earth.'

All present in the room agreed, the entire meeting had been watched by all Saviorians on Earth, the plan would begin.

Ken was becoming restless, he needed answers. Dr. Honey entered the room and his wait was over. The Simu-suit was in place, progress would be quicker that way.

'Ken, it's good to see you again. Are you ready to hear our version of Human history for the past three hundred years?'

'I'm more than ready to hear your side of the story, but I may take some convincing and you might not like some of my reactions.'

'Can I just say, our intention all along was to protect the population of Earth from its determined desire to destroy itself. We arrived just in time to do this. Nuclear weapons had just been released from numerous locations, no one was talking anymore. They wanted to obliterate their enemies from the face of the Earth.'

'Yes, I know all this, mostly from reading the books in Andy's library in Padstow. I have also seen the accounts and pictures of destruction, the war did happen!'

'No Ken, the fact is we stopped it. We planted those pictures in your library and thousands like them all over the world. Who do you think removed the pages from your books at home, our androids did. You were getting too close to finding out the truth. Yes, it was all a fabrication but we did it for the right reasons, to protect humankind from itself.'

'You have to do better than that, show me the evidence, show me there are others out there, your so called survivors.'

'You already did see proof of survivors, when you removed yourself from your room earlier in the week. You saw a woman in another room didn't you? She is from a town known as Wadebridge, you might have heard of it. Do you remember the woman?'

'Yes, I do now, it's all a bit of a blur, I think I tried to get her attention but her eyes were fixed on that screen, the one showing ...no, I can't remember that part. I had to run, thought I was in danger.'

'Ken, we need to make progress here, your memory will focus itself soon enough. I want you to watch this recording and please try to accept that everything on it is genuine, it is a condensed record of our time on your planet.'

The video showed the arrival of the Saviorian Fleet as they circled the Earth.

'All the Weapons of mass destruction on Earth were vacuumed clear of the atmosphere and temporally stored in a collection of vast weapons disposal ships. The entire population was simultaneously put to sleep while the segregation process was set up. Human communes were established in manageable units depending on the topography of each area. Buffer zones were set up where possible, between communes. This is where the Saviorian people and their androids exist, parallel to their Human neighbours.

Fake news items and evidence was placed in every commune portraying the end of the world, showing the one local 'Garden of Eden' which was spared. The sleeping gas contained a memory depressant which left survivors with vague recollections of the time leading up to destruction day.

Micro climates were set up around each mini community providing the ideal environment for the few lucky ones to thrive and be content. Once stability had been restored, the artificially induced slumber slowly wore off.

Gradual integration was supposed to take place with the human population in a controlled manner. However, a fatal accident involving our great Saviorian hero Alvis Prince halted the plans, and the delay has continued for three hundred years, which brings history up to date, nearly.'

'We now believe we are ready to introduce ourselves to the world and unite Humans in safety.'

Ken was gobsmacked. He slumped back in his chair rubbing his eyes in an attempt to clear his thoughts.

'You did all this for us, to save us from ourselves?'

'It's what we do, all over the vastness of space. As you put it, saving life forms from themselves.'

'But why, because if it is true, we probably deserved to perish through our ignorance and stupidity.'

'It is our sole reason to exist. Written in our sacred code –

'To *preserve and protect recognised intelligent life in all its forms and to prevent conflict where lives are in danger, for the good of all.'*

We need no other reason to exist, it's what drives us on.'

Ken felt humble in the presence of this intriguing alien.

'If we were so close to self destruction what makes you so sure it won't happen again?'

'Saviorians do not judge Ken, there is no guarantee. You are by no means the most hopeless species out there. That dubious honour so far belongs to the moronic people on Odious Peev Minor. They are a totally dysfunctional race of cannibals with little short term memory retention. We converted them to vegetarianism five times, but they forget every time and continued munching their way through their own population. No, Humans have a conscience and this gives us hope.'

'So, when the accident happened with this Elvis what's his name?'

'Alvis Prince.'

'Yes Alvis. Surely you could have left your androids in charge of uniting the Human race again and gone onto your next mission. They were clearly unaffected by shared breathing problems.'

Dr. Honey laughed, 'Our androids are indeed very capable. However, they are not designed to think for themselves, let alone deal with complex interactions between intelligent life forms. You Humans would soon have worked them out. No meaningful progress would have been made. We need to interact with you face to face in order to maximise your survival potential, we never return to problems we have already dealt with so this is a one and only chance to get it right. There are too many desperate scenarios out there for us to come back again.'

'Face to face interaction might be a problem, don't you think doctor?'

Both of them laughed.

'Yes, Simu-Suits are a great invention!' joked Dr. Honey.

'Ken, do you accept what I am telling you? We need your help to convince the people of Padstow that what we are telling you is the true version of your recent history, and that we are really here to help.'

'I know there will be many different reactions to your invasion, because that's how many will see your presence here. Life as we now know it is very simple and many will not welcome change, even resent interaction with other communities. I certainly can't predict what any outside people might think, two minutes ago they didn't exist to me, and still don't. As for the people of Padstow there is no wider world. People may indeed see you as saviours and accept what you have done, others, I'm not so sure. Violence and hate have not been part of our lives for generations, you may have a chance.

To answer your original question, yes, I am an open minded person and accept, with reservations, your version of events. It is not Human nature to live in isolation, so let's get out there and mix!'

'Thank you Ken, you are truly a credit to your kind. Tell me, are there any others in your community that share your open mindedness and sense of adventure?'

'Well, let me think, most of them are either too scared to venture far or are so content with their lot, their only concern is the size of their prize winning cucumber! Saying that, yes, there is someone, my Great Niece Karen, Karen Rollins, she has an enquiring mind. She gives her father Andy a hard time with her questions about the past and whether we could possibly be alone.'

'Andy Rollins, he runs the library doesn't he?'

'Yes, how do you know him?'

'Well, with his knowledge he has been very useful to us. He believes our one village survival story and is only too willing to share the false evidence we planted in the library with anyone who wants to listen. It was the same with his father before him. Now we have to tell him the truth, which may not be easy.

For now, do you think Karen might help back up our version of events?'

'I would say that is a distinct possibility, however, she is still young and I am reluctant to give permission.'

'Very well, but we may need to look for her support when we reveal our presence in Padstow.'

'She will be the first to show interest, I'm sure of that.'

'Do you feel you are ready to meet some of my colleagues, true Saviorians, not androids? They will, I assure you, be as reluctant as you, but we need to make progress.'

'On condition you wear, what do you call them, Simu-Suits? I have no desire to drown in a sea of snot and bile, no offense meant.'

'Well, if it makes you feel more comfortable. I will now go and prepare a meeting.'

AN ANDROID CHRISTMAS PARTY

'See you later oldies, sure you won't come with us?'

'No fear Anita, besides, your dad might not make it past the front door, have you seen the state of him? You go and have a good time and Will, look after your big sister.'

'Him! You must have a short memory, we all know what happened the last time he went out, lost an argument with a glass door. I'll hold his hand Mum, see you both later.'

'When will you be returning?' enquired the over anxious hotel manager.

'Why, is there a curfew, do the living dead rise up after midnight?'

'I'm sorry, I do not understand, how can the dead be living?'

'Get a life Lurch, you need to get out more. You're always hanging around here, do you ever get a day off, re-charge your batteries, let your hair down?'

'No miss, battery re-charging is done overnight.'

'I suppose employment rules don't apply down here in pasty land, oh never mind. Will we're losing valuable drinking time.'

'Doors will be locked at midnight miss, please be back in time.'

'Now you're seriously pissing me off, just give us a key. We promise to be quiet and not disturb all your other guests, oh yes I forgot, there aren't any others are there.'

'Yes, can we please have a late key, we may not need it but just in case.'

'Listen to you goody two shoes it will probably take us 'til midnight to get out of Strangeways at this rate.'

William was sure he could detect smoke escaping from the Hotel Manager's ears and nose and the Metropole had a no smoking policy.

'Very well, we will leave the front door unlocked a little longer, if you insist.'

'We do, come on Sherlock!'

The android hotel manager had delayed their departure long enough for a makeshift party scenario to be constructed. Several malfunctioning androids had been draped in what was thought as 21st Century party gear. The only remaining ill prepared androids had been pressed into service because of the imminent World Integration process. The ones left could best be described as the dregs of the stock.

Anita and William were allowed only a few steps from the front of the Metropole into the thick fog. Immediately they were confronted by a couple of the slightly better prepared androids.

'Where you hip guys be off to going, into town?' enquired a pushy android barring their way.

'Err, yes, just for a couple of drinks, maybe a bite to eat, just a bit of local life really,' answered William.

'Oh you won't be a findin' anything much open on Easter, I mean Christmas Night in these parts, oh arrr me 'ansome. Us be on us way to his sister's party just by 'ere. You'm more than welcome te join us, oh arrr, if you've a mind to my lover.'

'Sorry, I didn't catch most of that,' replied Anita, puzzled.

'They're inviting us to a party, says there's not much on in town.'

'Oh great, yes we'd love to. Got no costumes mind you, it looks like you're in fancy dress!'

In their haste to assemble contemporary attire, the androids had been dressed in 1960's hippy, laced with a touch of punk and heavy metal. They were ushered to a front door almost before they realised. The unmistakable sound of Village People's Y.M.C.A. drifted through the fog filled air.

'Are you sure this is a good idea Anita, we don't know these people.'

'You're the one who wanted to get out and mix Sherlock, just chill.'

'I'm sorry, if I'd known we were going to a party I would have brought a bottle.'

William was giving their apologies as they reached the living room only to realise they were being stared at from every corner. Their hosts didn't seem to be in the party mood, looking vacantly at one another for someone to take the lead. The two characters who let them in, Will thought they were called Bono and Gaga, were clearly acting as hosts.

'Your bottles Mr Hawkins, as requested, please make yourself at home, come and meet my friends,' ushered Gaga with a sickly smile.

As Y.M.C.A. played again for the third time, a speeded up version this time by means of variety, William and Anita decided to try and mingle. They deposited their bottles on a nearby table, they were empty anyway.

'So, are you all locals, this is your house is it, sorry, didn't catch your name? I'm Anita.'

She held out her hand then realised the guest had only the one arm.

'Oh! I'm really sorry, fishing accident was it?'

'Suggs.'

'I'm sorry, didn't quite catch that.'

The android, dressed like Johnny Rotten, appeared to be getting prompts from an invisible source.

'Suggs me am, not lost it fishing, old war wound, blown off, yes, we be local types, Federal District Six.'

'No you say Padstow!'

'Padstow me lives in Padstow!'

Anita either needed a drink, or better still needed to get out of there. William was also in a state of confusion.

'So Gaga tell me, how do you know my name, Hawkins, I've never met you before?'

'Oh, err ... this be a small commune, town, pod my lover, me know them folks in yonder hotel, they say you be ancient William Hawkins, Ha Ha!'

Bono approached, 'ready for more bottles, you and Anita, we've prepared red ones this time?'

'Yes, could we have something in them this time, I seem to have sobered up since coming in here, can't imagine why.'

'Will, come here a minute I need a word.'

'I know what you're about to say sis, this is a seriously weird place, these people can't be for real surely?'

'I know, look at those two in the corner, they haven't moved a muscle since we arrived, could be a couple of shop dummies.'

'They seem to know a lot about us seeing we've just met them, I get the feeling we've been set up somehow.'

'Shall we leave now or try and find out what's going on?'

'Hey Anita, I brought us all to Padstow again because I thought something strange was going on, I think we've just found the evidence.'

'Ok Sherlock, let's have some fun!'

Anita headed straight for the two shop dummies while William followed Gaga to find out the hotel connection.

'So you two seem to be having trouble mixing, not want to mingle a bit, perhaps we could change the music? Got anything more up to date at the right speed?'

Anita's approach sparked the androids into life, they tried to escape but Anita followed them.

'Tell me, whose party is this?'

'Party, fun, music keep Humans happy, hello you warm blooded creature,' replied the easily confused android.

'Of course we're Humans, is that another local word for tourists like emmets?'

'Er ....bottles get you bottles now, I go bye!'

'Does your friend have a name,' turning to the other dummy.

'Name? Oh yes I comprendez, numero, si senor XP724, that be it number...nombre, name..'

'You're all on some local brew, off your heads, do you know that. What's it made from? Turnips I bet.'

All the tin folk, except Gaga, began to gather in the centre of the room.

'So tell me about your friend in the hotel who knows us, what's his name?,' enquired William.

Gaga seemed confused, trying to join the android slow waltz.

'It wasn't Paul the hunky rugby player with the German accent?' asked Anita on her way over.

'Need input from Think Tank, got bottles, here got to have fun, drink now please.'

Gaga rushed away to join the others smoke clearly emanating

from her ears.

'I'm going to try something, back me up Anita. There's a door over there, look. I want to see more of this house. I don't think any of this is real, these people certainly aren't, try and distract them somehow.'

Anita made for the centre of the confused huddle, there was no need for distraction, they were all out of it, motionless unplugged.

'Wait for me Will!'

In the next room Colonel Hafey was more than a little concerned. She had been left alone to *entertain* the ancient Humans with a rag tag collection of defective androids. Now there was a potential breach of the scenario and all the androids had just shut down!

UNINVITED GUESTS

Dr. Honey led Ken from his room on the way to meet Professor Huntley, Nash, Jackie Green and Commander Aragon. Security was tight and androids lined the corridors to the reception room. The doors to Nash's management suite hissed open.

'Please come in,' Nash welcomed the first Human to his office and a three hundred year wait was over. His Simu-Suit allowed him to proffer a hesitant hand in welcome. He introduced Ken to all the Saviorian dignitaries.

'It is a great honour for us all to meet you face to face. I know that Doctor Honey has explained the situation we all find ourselves in. It is now my responsibility to explain our plan. Your help is vital in this initial process in order to ultimately hand your planet back and let us move on. Please before we proceed, give us your thoughts Ken.'

'Well you will excuse me if words don't come that easily. I am still trying to absorb, never mind accept all I've been told. I have always prided myself on having an open mind. Indeed, I have never really accepted that we were alone in this vast world of ours. Aliens from another world did not, however, enter my thoughts. Your good doctor here has done a very good job explaining where we find ourselves. You think you can count on me to help you implement your plans. I cannot however predict how my fellow Human beings will react. I wish you luck with the task ahead.'

'We are all in your debt Ken, as we are to Dr. Honey for his bravery. Now we must explain our plans for your community in Padstow, Major Main will say more.'

'Thank you Nash, please let us all be seated. Our androids on the ground have made the following observations. The residents of Padstow, under the guidance of Andy Rollins, have planned a Public Meeting. Many are concerned about your whereabouts Ken since you disappeared a few days ago. Some residents reported spotting Ken on the opposite side of the estuary before our timely snow storm. Andy plans to reassure the townsfolk that all is well and Ken will soon return. You will indeed return alongside Dr. Honey, to explain our current situation. Using reaction from your fellow villagers we will plan the expansion of awareness. As the meeting progresses we will gradually dissolve the Dark Zone and remove the stain from the sea. At some point Dr. Honey will switch off his Simu-Suit to reveal his identity. This is essential to prove the validity of our situation. Androids will be in attendance at a discreet distance in case events take an unplanned route.'

'We can talk about plans all day but progress needs to be made. I am convinced now that Saviorians and Humans can breathe the same air safely, so can I suggest we make a start now!' Commander Aragon was becoming impatient as he had other fish to fry in the great out there.

The meeting was about to break up when the door hissed open, in rushed Anita and William running headlong into Nash and Jackie Green. Seconds later they were joined by a desperate looking Colonel Hafey and a bunch of malfunctioning androids. The scene that developed might have appeared amusing to the outside observer, in fact it was deadly serious, potentially devastating.

'What the..!'

QUESTIONS PLEASE, NOT YOU KAREN

It was clear that the Public Meeting was attracting unprecedented interest. The generally apathetic attitude to anything thought provoking had been replaced with questioning fear. Ken had not been found despite Mario organising countless searches. The people wanted answers. Almost every able bodied person in Padstow was heading for the meeting. Hostility and anger were not emotions normally exhibited in 26th Century life. They may however emerge again if Andy couldn't come up with some acceptable answers. There was one large public room in the Metropole Hospital that was rarely used. Its huge picture windows overlooked the Camel Estuary and the blackness beyond, a dramatic backdrop for a potentially dramatic meeting. The residents were still behaving in an orderly way, queues stretched up and down the hill. Elderly and infirm were seated first and it was clear there would be standing room only. Those residents who had reached well over one hundred years of age could not remember a situation like this ever before.

'I don't know what these young boys are thinking of, wanting to build boats again, I just need to get back to me jam making.' This was all too much excitement for Mrs Salvage from Drake Road.

'I just hope Andy can settle them down quick, my pigs get restless if they be left alone for a spell,' pointed out Jake from Stile

Pasture.

'I tell you, I saw him clear as day, it were Ken alright, wavin' like a mad thing he was, then that dam white stuff came down, could see bugger all. Where is he now? Answers, that's what we be wantin' and before six and all, there's a darts match in the pub.' John Evans spoke for many younger men, standing restlessly at the back of the room.

The meeting was planned to coincide with the 2.30pm rain shower. The last few stragglers were late but so was the rain. Locals at the door checked their watches, looked to the skies, no cloud, no rain. When it started it was a good ten minutes late, residents were confused, the rain was never late.

'What is happening, this place is fallin' apart, Andy had better have answers, a good ten minutes late it were!' cried Mrs Bishop a local hairdresser.

Happy that everyone who wanted to be there had arrived Andy rose to hush the chattering crowds. He was flanked by Dina and Mario on a hastily erected platform. Karen was also there but in the front row of the crowd. Would she defy her father and question his beliefs or keep her thoughts inside?

The room fell silent in expectation.

'Fellow residents of Padstow, thank you all for coming to this Public Meeting. I am astonished, as many of you are, by the turnout here today. The last time we had so many people in one place was, I think, a good forty years ago. I remember a couple of hundred of us congregated in the old church to celebrate the first twins born in living memory. Nothing much really happens here to disturb our idyllic lives.'

'Boring, you mean,' Karen wasn't quiet for long.

'Quiet, let him speak!'

'So it is not surprising, when something out of the ordinary does happen, for us to be concerned and anxious. I hope we can reassure you that all is well and you have nothing to fear. With the help of some of the more historically minded amongst us, I have managed sort out some images to share with you from the library archives.'

A few moans and groans filtered across the room, but they were soon silenced.

'Please pass these images around, I hope they will calm your fears and put your minds in a better place.'

Stacks of photographs were passed around the assembled townsfolk. Andy had put together his best selection of photos. He had even discovered a few he didn't know he owned. Quite how he had missed them was a mystery. He aimed to reinforce the message of good fortune and continued prosperity enjoyed by the residents. They enthusiastically examined the images, some had never seen any of them before, others not for many years.

Karen was the first to speak. 'We're all aware of how we got where we are or your version of it anyway, if it is true, we are indeed lucky to be here. It is the things that have been happening recently that concern me, and I suggest it is the reason why so many people are here today.'

No reaction, and Karen suddenly had the feeling she had overstepped the mark.

'My daughter has always had strong views, I want to hear what you all think, so please indicate if you wish to ask a question and we'll do our best to get to you.'

In usual orderly fashion numbers were given to those who wished to speak and then randomly drawn. Many of the early questions were more like statements, all in praise of Andy, thanking him for reinforcing their belief, consoling Dina and Andy for having such an awkward child.

Then it became more tricky.

'Yea, I know you've shown us that the snow stuff is harmless and even fun, but why, after generations, did it fall on us and, might it happen again?'

'As we've just seen today, with the rain coming late, things might be changing. In pre destruction times climate and weather patterns changed all the time. We've been lucky up until now, I'm confident we can cope even if the washing gets wet when it shouldn't.'

'Andy, some local boys want to build a boat and go looking for Ken. All the searches Mario has organised have failed to find him, is it worth the risk?'

'I haven't seen any evidence to suggest the glowing green slime in the estuary is any less dangerous than it was three hundred years ago, in my view it's a suicidal plan. Ken is one of my family, we are equally if not more, concerned for his safety but there is good reason not to put one foot in that polluted water, if I didn't warn you I could never live with the consequences.'

Mario stood up. 'There are only a few places yet to search but we will find him. We need to extend our search to the toxic shoreline, but no further. Perhaps the boat building boys could join in this search instead?'

'We're with you there Mario,' was the cry from the crowd.

'Soon as we're done here we'll get to it!' shouted Carl Brown the blacksmith.

'This is the town spirit, we need to banish negative thoughts.'

'We will be fine if we all stick together.'

Andy was relieved how the meeting was progressing so all they had to do now was find Ken

'I don't think there are any more questions, so with your approval I declare this meeting closed.'

'There is one more question Andy, No 24,' pointed out Dina.

'Who has No24?'

'Yes, Dad, that's me I have another question.'

'We can talk about this at home Karen.'

'No, others might want to hear it.'

'Yes, let the girl speak,' shouted a portion of the crowd.

'Ok, but make it quick, we've important business to deal with.' Andy was clearly not amused.

'Just answer me this, who was around to photograph the nuclear destruction of the rest of the world? All those graphic images you've got stored in the library. Yes of course! It was one of the chosen few from Padstow that survived to record the event before being fried alive! I tell you what happened, nothing, it's all a lie, we've been living under a lie for three hundred years and I bet Ken has found out the truth if we can only find him.'

'Rubbish, you're talking rubbish girl, look out the window, what do you see? Raise your eyes, blackness in yonder distance, death in the water,where did that come from if not that retched war?'

'Take the maid home Andy, we've heard enough.' Molly Dan was a down to Earth Padstonian who had the ear of most residents over the age of one hundred so when she spoke, most listened. 'Well done Andy, you're doing a good job, your old dad would be proud of you. Now come on you lot, haven't you got homes to go to, let the men folk search for Ken.'

Mary had spoken and the room began to clear. Andy breathed a sigh of relief, normality had resumed, for now.

.

THE UNRAVELLING SCENARIO

'You lot aren't part of the party down the hall are you, Wow! Fancy dress or what!'

Anita was referring to the Simu- Suits worn by the Saviorian dignitaries she had just made contact with.

'Colonel Hafey, just who are these creatures? They appear Human but we can account for all the residents in the local commune and these two don't seem to fit.' Main was clearly embarrassed in front of Commander Aragon.

'They are clearly not android stock, can you explain Colonel Hafey?'

'I think I'd better leave that to Dr. Honey, his contact with these creatures goes back a long way. I think when you hear the full explanation, the picture will become plain.'

'Oh no!, you don't mean they are the ancients? How did they escape our scenario, this could be catastrophic?!'

'Well yes, I'm afraid they are,' admitted Colonel Hafey. 'We tried to sedate them again when they broke out but they appear to have become immune to our drugs.'

A sudden hush fell over the room. Ken looked at William who was staring at Dr. Honey. Anita was catching flies by the bucket load while the androids shuffled around in circles, clearly lacking direction.

'Eyes, your eyes, they seem familiar, from some nightmare I can't quite remember.'

William was wrestling with the memory of the Hawkins first visit to Padstow, the eyes in the window.

'Never mind his soddin' eyes, who the f... are you lot, some sort of freaking religious sect of midgets? I've heard about the likes of you down here in the wilds of Cornwall. You must be on some crazy trip, local whacky backy or what? Trying to mess with our minds, Will let's get out of here, now!'

'Wait a minute Anita, I remember now. It was you at that window in Padstow last May Day, watching us.'

Will was pointing at Dr. Honey who appeared very uncomfortable.

'Don't start Will, what are you on about?'

'When those locals were dancing round us on May Day, he was watching from a window. You remember, I said something was going on. You'd better explain, just what's this all about?'

While events unfolded in Nash's office, a security cordon was erected around the room allowing no one to enter or leave without Main's permission. A decision had to be made quickly. Could the ancients still be sent back as planned tomorrow, or had events overtaken them. Ken was about to make that decision for them.

'So, I don't recognise you from Padstow, just where do you come from?'

'Hi! Pleased to meet you, I'm Anita and this here is my nerd of a brother William. I'm from Hartford and he's at university in Nottingham.'

'Then what these creatures say is true, there was no nuclear war, there really are others out there in the world like us?'

'Oh Christ, not you as well! What are you on man, is this whole town high as kites?'

'Unless we missed something on the train down here, the world is still out there' noted William.

'No, we thought we'd been saved from the nuclear war that destroyed the rest of the world but it was all a lie, there was no war and you're the proof. These aliens stopped it.'

'Will can't you see, they're all freekin loco, out of it, coke heads from Cornwall, let's go now!'

'No Anita, this could be the reason we came back to Padstow, you remember the business with the tickets, the date 2514. What's your name?'

William was pointing at Ken.

'Me I'm Ken, Ken Rollins, why?'

'Right Ken, can you tell me what year it is?'

'What year, well you must know, it's 2514, three hundred years after the Great War, well if there was a war that is.'

'Did you hear that Anita, we passed through that tunnel and jumped five hundred years, creepy right?'

'Listen to yourself Captain Kirk, you've been brainwashed by those computer games, get real and get out of here now!'

Anita made a break for the door but her progress had been blocked by an android arm. Dr. Honey stepped forward.

'Please Anita, calm down. My colleagues and I will try to explain the situation but we need to meet in private for a few moments, Ken please come with us.'

Androids guarded William and Anita while the others left the room. They made their way to a small anti-chamber where they could observe the ancients in private. The atmosphere was tense, Commander Aragon spoke first.

'It is now clear to me why your team has been detained on Earth for so long. In my long life I have never come across such incompetence. We have a potential catastrophe on our hands. You all assured me that there would be no danger of the ancients breaking your scenario, now not only are they in the 26th Century, they are also fully aware of the fact.'

Main spoke up 'To be fair Commander, our resources were sorely stretched in preparation for initial integration. The ancients are very inquisitive, far more so than Humans of this age. We have had to sedate them several times so our drugs no longer work too well on them.'

'Fine, but what is your plan now?'

Professor Huntley spoke next. 'We have two problems to solve. Our priority must be to advance the integration process using Ken. Nash, I want you and Dr. Honey to take charge of an initial meeting with local residents and Ken will make the introductions.

At the same time, Colonel Hafey and Major Main need to sort out the ancients. Decide whether we can send them all back safely to their own time or replace William and Anita with two convincing androids to return to 2014 with the parents and persuade the young ones to stay here in 2514. I fear we must make haste, Anita still looks in a volatile mood, she may try to break out again and the androids are not programmed to use force to restrain.'

Nash, Ken and Dr. Honey went off to prepare for contact with 26th Century Humans while Colonel Hafey and Major Main decided what to do with Anita and William from the 21st Century. It really was a dreadful mess.

'So you really buy this garbage about time travel, aliens and the war that never was?'

'Put it this way, I'd sure like to find out one way or another. These guard guys don't seem forthcoming so let's wait 'til the bosses return.'

They didn't have to wait long as Colonel Hafey and Major Main returned.

'We realise how difficult it must be for you to accept anything we are telling you. It may be easier for you to believe this is all some sort of role play game you've got caught up in. We could send you home on your train tomorrow as long as you promise to forget all about this and not tell a single person back in2014, I mean anyone at home.'

'Oh no! You don't get out of it that easily, I've suspected all along there was something strange going on. Anyway, I need to convince my sister here that I'm not completely round the bend.'

'Mr. Hawkins this is a very serious situation where your actions could cause the course of history to change, if you see proof that we are telling the truth, you cannot go back.'

'Come on Will are you really taken in by all this bullshit? Oh, I've heard enough of this, show us your Earth shattering proof then,' Anita was calling their bluff, thinking how it may shut William up for good.

'If you are sure Miss Hawkins, there is no going back.'

'If Anita says she's sure that's it.'

William was surprised but more than willing to find out. Neither of them really believed they would not be able to go home. The Major proceeded to switch off his Simu-Suit, followed by Colonel Hafey. The stench that filled the room almost choked William, Anita fainted on the spot.

ALIENS FROM BODMIN

Ken was to make his return to the Rollins family first and only introduce Dr. Honey and Nash after he'd explained his life changing experiences with the Saviorians. His Alien friends would not enter Padstow until Ken deemed it safe to do so. It was their hope that Andy, once convinced of the validity of their story, could persuade the rest of the town to slowly take events on board. A tall order but it was what they had waited for all these years. The feeling was that if Andy could be convinced of the truth the town would follow. The Saviorians had calculated the Human reaction would be more of stunned amazement than aggressive revolt. Earth had been in a state of tranquil resignation for over three hundred years, it was hoped the fight had been drained from Human nature. If the opposite applied their only hope was further sedation but would that still be effective, it no longer worked on the ancients.

It had been whispered in quiet corners that they should simply lift the barriers and leave, 'the Humans would be fine', but that was not the Saviorian way, the job had to be finished properly, they must never make return visits.

Luckily for Ken, all the family were at home, even Karen. She had made peace with her father agreeing to disagree and not rock the boat.

'Was that someone at the door, I thought I heard a knock?'

questioned Dina.

'We're not expecting anyone I'll go and see,' Mario went to the front door. 'Oh you're joking! I don't believe it. Hey you lot, look what the cat's dragged in, don't just stand there come in!'

Everyone rushed to greet Ken with several rounds of hugs and kisses.

'Is it really you Ken, we've searched every corner of our habited world, no stone unturned. You look remarkably good, where on Earth have you been?' Andy was in a state of delirium, all was now well with the world.

'Dina, get round town with your loud hailer, tell the whole world Ken is back!'

'No, no, please wait, I really need to talk to you all first if you don't mind, the rest of Padstow can wait a while, please!'

'Yes sorry, how insensitive of me, you must be starving, Karen get some food and drink for Ken.'

'Why me, I want to hear what he has to say, I've a feeling it could be very interesting.'

'It's ok Karen I'm fine, I've been well looked after while I've been away, so don't fret.'

'But we searched all the houses in town, was someone hiding you?' Mario was confused.

'No, nothing like that, I was with others you don't know.'

'You're talking in riddles Ken, you know very well, I am acquainted with everyone in Padstow, in fact, in the whole world.' Andy's new found self assurance was slowly diminishing.

'These others, they come from a far off place, in fact, they are not of this world.'

'I knew it!' Karen was suddenly enthused. 'Come on, tell us everything Ken. All those notes and messages you kept leaving us, I knew you were on to something, come on where have you really been?'

'Karen, Ken's clearly not well, Dina needs to check him over. You remember the day we found him wearing women's clothing, thats not normal is it?'

'Womens clothing?! That wasn't me Andy they sent a copy, what they call an android. It pretended to be me while I was at the Think Tank.'

'This is fantastic, tell us more, these others, where are they now?'

'That's enough Karen, Ken clearly needs help.'

'Actually' Mario pushed in. 'I think we need to hear Ken's story from the start. Can we all sit down calmly. If nobody minds I will treat this like a police interview, I think I need the practice anyway!'

'I'm not going to stay and listen to this nonsense, I am sorry Ken, you are clearly ill.'

'Sit down Andy, you need to hear what I have to say and I have proof that this is not the ramblings of a sick man, so please, let Mario ask his questions.'

'Yes, come on Dad, you might find out you're not right about everything after all.' Karen was on the edge of her seat in anticipation.

Ken proceeded to tell them the whole story, right from when he thought he spotted something through the nuclear darkness, risking all to cross the estuary in a makeshift boat carefully avoiding contact with the poisoned sea. When he got to the point where the Saviorians informed him there had been no war, Andy jumped up.

'You talk of the proof you will supply us with, I have all the proof you need that the war really did happen, you have seen it all Ken.'

'Yes I have, and for many years I was happy to accept it. Then I began to wonder how did we alone survive, why us, it didn't make sense. I began studying the dark edges of our community. I built telescopes, probed into the darkness, saw something through the gloom, a light, movement, then took the plunge. All your books and photos, they were planted here from the generations before you were born. You were perfect, you perpetuated the myth, convinced others, except young Karen, she knew there was something more out there. Now she too will witness the verification of her suspicions.'

'What does this mean Ken, how many more like us are out there. Is it safe beyond the darkness? Who are these others, where are they from, Bodmin I bet?'

Karen was so full of questions she didn't know where to go next.

'Stop this now Ken. How dare you try and fill my daughter's mind with even more garbage, enough!'

The room fell silent for a moment then Dina spoke. 'Do you remember before the Public Meeting, showing me all your collections in the library? I asked you who took the photos of nuclear Armageddon you are so proud of, you couldn't answer?'

'Oh! We've been through all that.'

'Just listen, you couldn't answer, you, for a moment, were puzzled. What if there is some truth in what Ken is saying?'

'Dad, can't you see, Ken might be right, he says he can prove it, please let him finish, at least listen.

Mario spoke 'I think they are right, we should see his evidence and then judge.'

Another silence this time longer, everyone was staring at Andy.

'Oh very well, let's see his evidence. I still maintain he needs help, perhaps you all do.'

Andy slumped in his chair, he felt his own family were turning against him.

There was another knock at the door, Ken jumped up, I'll get that, I've a feeling I know who it will be.'

A few moments later Ken came back into the sitting room.

'Andy, Dina, Karen, Mario, may I introduce my new friends.'

From behind Ken the diminutive Simu-Suited figures of Dr. Honey and Nash emerged.

'These two gentlemen are Saviorians and have lived on this planet for just over three hundred years along with fifty thousand of their kind. We owe our lives to them as does the whole of Humankind. You will not find what they have to say easy to accept, but please hear them out. We are a vital part of their plan to re-unite the planet and move on.'

MAY DAY REVELATION

After making sure Anita was in recovery, Colonel Hafey and Major Main moved to the next room where both parties could still see and hear each other without the threat of vomit and sensory overload. A translation device allowed continued conversation while the Simu-Suits were still switched off.

'I hope you are both sufficiently recovered for us to continue. We did not intend any distress, but you did ask for proof. I think you will agree our appearance is down to a lot more than fancy dress Anita. She slowly shuffled nearer the two way screen, her jaw scraping on the floor as she stared into the next room. William too got as near to the glass as he could, he spoke first.

'Your Dr. Honey is that his name? I know him, we've met before, at least our eyes have. I knew it was him there on May Day watching. Now I realise why his eyes appeared so strange, they are actually the most attractive part of your anatomy. Yes, and he was the doctor when I was in hospital after my meeting with the glass door, it's all making sense now.'

'Well would you mind explaining it to me? I mean don't take this the wrong way, but those two look like the result of some botched Frankenstein experiment, you are both seriously ugly. How you don't drown in your own dribble, God only knows. I will give you one thing though, Human you certainly are not.'

'Then you can believe our story, you understand who we are?'

'Hell yes why not? I mean, it's not our problem anyway, we've been dead a long time if your story's true, it's the future but not ours.'

'I think you'll find you're wrong there sis, you see by meeting and interacting with these, what do you call yourselves, Saviorians, we may have changed the course of history. So I think we're stuck, going back would risk the whole future of the world, is that right?'

'This is what we were afraid of, it is our fault for bringing you here, but we needed to find out if we could safely interact with Humans again. Will, you were a valuable component in that process. When you and Dr. Honey met in our *hospital*, it was the first Saviorian contact with Humans for three hundred years. You are in fact the catalyst for full integration along with the contemporary Human Ken who underwent the same tests. We were hoping to send you back to your time unaware but sadly that is now impossible.

'Hang on just a minute, I've got to go back, I've got a date with Mr Wright, he just doesn't know it yet. All my friends are back in 2014, they'll know I'm missing. Probably half the sick animals at the vets have died as I seem to be the only one who feeds the poor little buggers. Even Will here has a couple of vague pals, and of course Miss Media of Nottingham, his first love. That's not to mention the parents, they won't go back without us, have you thought about that?'

'I'm glad you mentioned Steven and Jane, we need to organise your replacements. Please excuse us a moment, I have to talk in private to my colleagues.'

The Saviorians switched off their translators leaving William and Anita guessing as to the content of the alien's conversation.

'Shhmush frooth eesh slootch blarthrooph sposhee,' Sprayed

Colonel Hafey.

'Oofosh slimoomph eesh blooshpoo arphump,' replied Major Main.

Rivulets of yellow green slime slowly trickled down the glass partition. An android left the room with instructions and a bucket full of gunk and a mop.

'It is all arranged, your parents will return to 2014 tomorrow with William and Anita to continue their lives as normal, no-one will suspect anything, the link will be broken, present and history intact.'

'Well thank you for that, we are going home after all, do you hear that Will. Its ok your secret's safe with us. You can cover the world with phlegm and pus to your heart's content, we won't tell a soul, isn't that right Will?'

'I've a feeling that's not what she meant.'

'Yes, I thought we made it clear, you will have to stay here.'

'Then who's going back with the old folks?'

'If you mean your parents they will be returning with android children, the latest and best models yet. They will be encrypted with all your characteristics and life history, a perfect copy of you. Our revolutionary Simu-Skin will give an authentic feel and super battery packs should last the normal lifespan of a Human. It will be the first time they have been tested outside the lab but we understand they are making good progress.'

'Bloody Hell!' Anita fainted again.

LISTEN TO THE HOTEL MANAGER

Jane couldn't sleep, she looked at the bedside clock through bleary eyes, 04.20am. They had finally gone to bed at one in the morning having enjoyed just a little too much hospitality at the bar. Steven had assured her that Anita and William would be fine, they were often in a lot later at home. She had not heard them return, however, and just felt there was something wrong.

'Steven wake up, Steven did you hear the kids come in, Steven!'

'What, oh go back to sleep, we'll see them at breakfast.'

'I haven't slept all night, something's wrong. Go and check, will you?'

'Oh for heaven's sake, they're not six anymore, go back to sleep!'

'Right I'll go then!'

Their rooms were just down the corridor. Jane first listened at Anita's door, no sound, she gently tapped and the door gave way, strange. Once inside she peered into the gloom and could clearly see the bed had not been slept in. On closer inspection she noticed the wardrobe door was open and she was sure some of Anita's favourite clothes were missing, not just what she had been wearing when they went out. Jane rushed from the room and down the corridor calling out for William. She found a similar scenario in his room, no sign of either of them. Steven was at her side wondering what all the fuss was about.

'They haven't come back Steve, look, their beds are made up and some of their clothes are missing, I knew something was wrong.'

As if by magic the Hotel Manager appeared on the stairs, he carried a poster in his hand. It was an open invitation to an all night party at the Social Club.

'I saw William and Anita return at 2.00am to get changed. They told me of the party but didn't want to disturb you. They asked me to give you a message saying they would meet you at breakfast said they had made friends earlier who told them of this party but needed to change first.'

Androids are normally programmed to be truthful but an exception had been made in these desperate times.

'There you are I told you they'd be alright, now come back to bed.'

'I suppose that explains the missing clothes and open doors, they must have been in a hurry, strange I never heard anything though.'

The manager listened at the door until he was convinced Jane had accepted his explanation, then returned to an emergency planning meeting. Time was short if William and Anita mark two were to be ready for breakfast. If all went well it was hoped the android Brother and Sister could meet their real selves to test out whether William and Anita thought they would be convincing in front of their parents, a tall order indeed.

DINA, FETCH THE BUCKET!

Nash realised that the clock was ticking but he knew that to rush integration and fail would consign his race to many more years on Earth.

'I'll give you one thing,' Andy was determined to uncover this deceit.

'I don't recognise you as Padstow folk. There are some people who rarely venture outside their homes, but Mario, you will back me up, these two are not familiar faces.'

'You're right Dad, I certainly don't recognise them.'

'Mr Rollins, we know you very well. We are responsible for nearly eighty percent of your impressive library's contents. While a state of impasse persisted you did us a great service, keeping the population happy and content, but it is now time for the truth.'

'Oh wow! This is great, I knew there was more out there than just our little town. I want to know everything.' Karen could hardly contain herself. 'I am surprised people from another world look just like us, if a bit short, something of a letdown really but it's all still fantastic, come on tell us more.'

Dr. Honey proceeded to outline their story on Earth in as much detail as the Rollins could absorb. Ken backed up their version of events but Andy was still not convinced.

'You say you saved this planet and many others from destroying themselves? Who's to say we deserved it, we may well go straight down that route again, then what?'

'Lessons certainly need to be learnt and we can help. Firstly though we need to tell the people of Padstow the real truth and gauge their reaction and you as a family can play a vital role in that process.'

'Fantastic what can we do?' Karen was all fired up now.

'Hang on a minute, that proof you were going to give us, just what is it?' Andy was still in charge at least in his mind.

'Karen, you said you were a little disappointed that the Saviorians resembled Humans, nothing could be further from the truth. I think this is the ultimate example of looks being deceptive. You are in for a shock, but Andy, this may be the proof you require. Dina, I have to ask you how house proud are you?' Ken had decided the time was right.

'Well quite reasonably I suppose, but that's a strange question, you've been in our house loads of times.'

'Yes I know, let me put it this way, do you have a good supply of cleaning implements, mops buckets that sort of thing?'

'Yes of course. I hope you're not suggesting my house is anything other than spotless!'

'No certainly not Dina you know me better than that but best be prepared. Dr.Honey, Nash would you kindly switch off your Simu-Suits.'

In an instant Andy's world and his steadfast beliefs collapsed in a sea of slime. What stood before him was most certainly not Human. The diminutive figures of no more than four feet in height were supported on two sturdy webbed feet. Their fluorescent yellow bodies were covered in green scales. Two stumpy arms flapped without control beside their huge distended stomachs. A reptilian tale counterbalanced this bulk and the whole thing was crowned by a bright red bulbous head. Yellowish red piercing eyes, two large flapping nostrils, trumpet ears and a huge mouth, lined with rows of slimy suckers completed the look.

The stench in the room caused Dina to vomit uncontrollably. Karen, awe struck, got a little too close and suffered a drenching of goo and yellow bile. Mario was sure he had an old camera somewhere but couldn't keep his footing on the sludge covered floor. Andy was completely dumbfounded. How could he possibly introduce these physically repulsive creatures to the simple folks of Padstow, if they didn't die of shock on the spot they may well expire from the stench?

Dr. Honey and Nash could recognise the concern in the family's eyes and immediately switched their Simu-Suits back on.

'How do you manage to function with such physical impairments?' Asked Mario, who had managed to keep a safe distance.

'Believe me, there are far more extreme physical models out there than ours. Humans seem to be more preoccupied with physical form than most which is why we are deploying the Simu-Suit.'

While a recovering Dina made a start on cleaning up the mess, conversation moved to developing an action plan. Andy could no longer believe in Padstow's unique position in the world. He wondered if the residents would think he had misled them all these years and turn on him.

'When do we get to meet the new people, I can't wait? I thought I knew everyone in the whole world, this is great, I'll do anything to help, anything.' Karen was clearly the sort of Human the Saviorians needed to use to champion the cause.

'May I suggest you call another Public Meeting Mr. Rollins, you could use the excuse that important developments have transpired in the search for Ken which would affect everyone in the town. They will still listen to you Andy, if you would please help us.'

Major Main knew that if they could get Andy on board the process would advance more smoothly. Andy wouldn't admit it but he was rather pleased to be asked.

'Alright, leave it to me. Come on Mario, we'll get onto it straight away.'

Saviorians watching worldwide were beginning to believe that the end might at last be in sight while the majority of humanity still believed they were alone.

WILL THE REAL ANITA HAWKINS PLEASE STAND UP

Having recovered, Anita was now on the offensive. 'So, if I get you right, I will never go home, never see my friends, and never grow old with some shitty bloke and five screaming brats. I'll be stuck here in the future with no future except a lifetime with my geek of a brother, watching the world destroy itself again while you slime balls clear off back into space?'

'That's one way to look at it Miss Hawkins. The truth is it's too late to send you back but you could have very fulfilling lives helping to shape a new world for the better. Your world in 2014 already had many of the problems that led them the point of self destruction. You and your brother could guide this re-born Human race along a safer path after we have left.'

'That sounds more like a job for young William. I would have us all at each other's throats within five minutes!'

'Sounds like a chance to be taken seriously for once,' countered William. 'But surely this is all pie in the sky? You must have your own people trained for the so called integration. A few hours ago we were an unfortunate accident landed on your doorstep, now we're going to save the world?'

'All we are saying, Mr Hawkins, it's not necessarily the disaster your sister thinks it is. You can both play your part now in 2514.' Major Main was not just trying to smooth the waters he could truly see an opportunity here.

'And another thing,' Anita wouldn't let go, 'If you think some tin headed replacement knows everything about me you really are in La La Land. Five minutes alone with my friend Lucy would be enough. She knows things about me that I don't even know, what happens then? Oh yes and by the way Lucy I've had a bit of work done on my face, nothing serious just a few rivets and a metal plate in my chin, looks great in the right light!'

'You will soon get the chance to meet your replacements and I think you'll be surprised and impressed.' 'On a more personal note' William was clearly emotional, 'Are you telling me we'll never see Mum and Dad ever again and no chance to say good-bye, to try to explain, just gone forever?'

Even Anita hadn't contemplated this scenario.

'God Will you're right, that's it, I'm not doing it. Take us back to the hotel before anyone notices, we promise to keep our mouths shut, our little secret. I mean, no one would believe us anyway. All this business wouldn't even have happened then.'

'I think you're wrong there Anita, I've read quite a lot about time travel and if you were to go forward or back in time and interact with people and events of that time, there is a chance that when you return, things will have changed. It's probably different for Mum and Dad, they've not interacted with any-one except the androids which are only glorified machines.'

'It is true what William says, we cannot risk sending you back, your future is here and now. Your parents will be unaware. They will believe the family is going home from a Christmas break in 2014, life will not change for them,' Colonel Hafey was keen to move on. By her actions Anita had forced their hand and would have to live with the consequences. The fu-ture of the world was at stake and it shouldn't be affected by the actions of a one highly strung Human.

'We must go now and check on the progress of your duplicates. I ask you to take some time to study in more detail the record of our time on Earth and concentrate on the roll you both must take up.'

Colonel Hafey and Major Main left the room.

'She's one stuck up slimy bitch, I'm dammed if I'm going to help her, all this just can't be real, I just want to go home.' Tears began to roll down her cheeks and William found himself comforting his sister, a rare event in his life so far.

He did understand her frustration and fear but secretly relished the thought of being at the beginning of a new phase of Human history. He had suspicions right from the tunnel experience that something strange had happened to them. What would have happened if he hadn't persuaded the family to come back at Christmas? He was probably responsible for their present predicament. However, he was fairly confident the Saviorians would have found a way to get them back anyway.

'Listen Will, you can stay if you want, but I'm going home. If these duplicates are as good as they say they are they won't know it when I switch with them. Miss tin head will stay here and I get my life back in 2014. Help me please, I can't stay here.'

'What about changing history, you would be risking that, can you shoulder the responsibility?'

'You don't know for sure there's anything in that mumbo jumbo, it's all science fiction nonsense. If they catch me attempting a switch fair enough I'll have to stay but I must give it a go. Please Will don't get in my way. You owe me for dragging us here in the first place.'

'When you say it like that, I can't argue. Just remember if you make it back to 2014 and find the place is run by goldfish don't say I didn't warn you!'

They avoided suspicion by pretending to study the entire history of Saviorians on Earth and were pretty impressed by their commitment to saving lives at all costs and with no little sacrifice to themselves. They couldn't help wondering if the Human race was worth all their efforts but applauded their endeavour.

Colonel Hafey and Major Main returned soon after with two companions.

'William and Anita I would like you to meet William and Anita.'

Right on cue Anita fainted again.

ANDY ACCEPTS THE TRUTH

Posters were being placed all over town with catchy headlines such as

> *Ken found alive and well- don't miss his amazing story which will affect us all, forever!*
>
> *Public meeting in the Metropole Hospital 2.45pm (after rain shower)*
>
> *Bring the whole family - refreshments provided.*
>
> *A roll call will be taken for this life changing meeting - BE THERE!*

'You don't think it's a bit too strongly worded, you know how people get spooked easily?' Dina was hanging a poster up outside the pub.

'Perhaps it should read, *Aliens re-unite the Earth after centuries of isolation.*' joked Mario.

'Seriously though, I'm really worried about all this. I mean I haven't got my head around it yet. It could all be too much for some of our residents. As a doctor it concerns me that we may have serious heart problems if not deaths through the related shock.'

'I know, from my perspective there are a few characters who might go off the rails. I don't think they would get violent. I've never really witnessed violence, but this is an extreme situation.'

'Do you totally believe these creatures? It seems they have sacrificed a lot to safeguard our future, spending three hundred years on Earth with no benefit to themselves? Still what choice do we have we are simple folk at their mercy?'

'Ken seems convinced and he has experienced much more with them than we have. The proof for me will be when other people walk into Padstow with their stories to tell.'

'Their physical appearance is quite convincing in itself, don't you think, it's a bit more than a fancy dress costume, I mean who could dream up that look, they are pretty repulsive.'

Mother and son walked on to their next poster location in silence, lost in thought, their minds filled with questions, fear and a tinge of excitement.

Andy and Karen were at the library along with the two Saviorians and Ken. They were going through Andy's collection trying to work out the right approach to take at the public meeting. Dr. Honey and Nash were keeping a low profile in case someone from the town spotted them.

'I can't believe that most of this material was planted by your people. I believed it all with a passion, in a way still do. It's been a lifetime's work to keep people safe and warn of the dangers out there. All this time we've been safe anyway. We could have moved around freely, met others from different places. Karen you were right, why was I so blind, never questioning any of it?'

A tearful Karen hugged her father for the first time in many months. 'You mustn't blame yourself Dad, you were doing all this for the best of reasons. All this evidence would be pretty convincing to most people. Just be glad you are here to witness the truth, your Father and his before him didn't get that chance. We must be positive.'

He kissed his daughter's head and looked into her eyes with

pride.

'Well said,' noted Ken. 'It must be a positive message we get across at the meeting, not dwell on what might have been.'

'Mr Rollins, you have done us an enormous service over all these years, as have countless thousands of others in your position all over the world. You have made our task a lot easier, buying us time while we came up with a solution. Our real concern is one of acceptance. Will the Human race trust us to finish the job? Three hundred years is a long time, resentment may turn to anger and delay our programme even longer. We need community leaders like yourself on our side and to guide the population when we depart.'

'Please don't take offence at this question' Andy hesitated. 'You must have some sort of weapons available in case the Human reaction is not what you hoped for?' He was really testing out how forceful these aliens might be in securing their plans success.

Nash replied in a controlled resigned manner.

'We have never, nor will ever in the future, resort to violence. Our nature and sacred code has no place for it. Weapons are what brought your kind to the brink of destruction. We do use a harmless sleeping agent to prevent any potentially confrontational situations, no more so than during the prevention of nuclear destruction on this planet. This agent acts swiftly and with no harmful side effects to Humans. It can be adapted to contain a memory suppressing component but this is only used in a few occasions as its effectiveness diminishes with repeated use. We have never deliberately caused death to any intelligent species we have come into contact with, it is simply not allowed or desired.'

Dr. Honey added. 'While the Human race slept after our arrival, we destroyed all the weapons on the planet including the potential to develop new ones in the future. The desire for confrontation was suppressed by drugs in our sleeping agents.

A lot of time has passed, we will have to see if their long term effects bridged the Human generations, or if old traits re-establish themselves. We can only do so much, the rest, as it has been said before, is up to you.'

'My son Mario, as you no doubt know, is the Padstow police officer. The vast majority of his work involves rounding up stray animals and walking drunks home after a heavy night, I think that goes some way to answer your question.'

'I hope you're right but we cannot underestimate the upheaval our life changing revelations will cause, this is one of our greatest challenges yet, mainly because of the delays in implementing our initial plans.'

Karen then asked 'Do you never re-visit planets if your plans fail, try again?'

'We have an eighty five percent success rate but saying that, there are occasions when a species is bent on self destruction. No, we do not re-visit. There are simply too many problems out there to allow that. We will use all our energies to solve conflicts but ultimately it is down to you the native population to make it work.'

This conversation could have gone on for hours but plans had to be made and quickly. Suddenly the Library doors burst open taking them all by surprise.

'Ken it's true you're back, we tore the place apart you old sod, where you bin hidin' damn it? Hold on a sec, who be you two little folk, I don't know you do I, what's goin' on Andy?'

The burly figure of Simon Wells filled the doorway. He was the local odd job man and had his fingers in most pies. Before anyone could react Mr Wells shot out the door. He prided himself on being the chief spreader of rumour in the town and he was determined not to wait for an explanation when he could provide his own to anyone who would listen, this integration process was not going to be the calm orderly process the Saviorians wished for.

SWITCH OR NO SWITCH?

Although the latest high tech androids were not living beings the Saviorian knack of finding solutions to ongoing problems had produced, on the face of it, something remarkable. The artificial awareness and intelligence encrypted in their complex brains, combined with memories and characteristics extracted remotely from William and Anita, added up to two convincing copies. So much so that the copies were convinced they were the genuine article. If there were gaps in their hastily assembled personalities, only time would tell. They had been clothed identically to the genuine articles, ready to take their place at the breakfast table with Steven and Jane.

'What do you think?' asked Colonel Hafey, feeling quite proud.

'On the face of it very impressive I must say' noted William.

'Let's hear them speak, I bet they don't sound much like us,' asked a sceptical Anita.

'Let's hear *you* speak bitch, you're the f...... copy, now can we get on with this? I just want to go home.'

'Wow!' exclaimed William, 'It's you down to your acid tongue, Anita.'

'Excuse me that's my sister, tin man, have a little respect.'

'She hasn't quite got my looks but not bad, hold up your chin a minute, wow! Even got the birth mark, impressive.'

'Get your grubby hands off me you freak!' shouted Anita.

The banter went on for quite a while until Major Main cut in.

'We really need to make progress here. I think you will all agree our scientists have done a brilliant job. Now our androids must be introduced to their new parents and you, Will and Anita, get ready for your new life in 2514.'

During the previous conversation both sets of siblings had mixed, changing places while examining each other. William had made his mind up to start a new life here. He held back as the others left the room. Aware of his sister's determination to go home, he closed his eyes as she left the room, not noticing the wink she gave him and the small tear in her eye.

Soon after, Anita and William were rushed back, to meet their parents for breakfast. The Saviorians had done all they could to salvage the situation. Valuable time and a great deal of energy had been wasted on this unwanted distraction. They were fairly certain no damage had been done to the time continuum and that the genuine siblings would settle into their new lives before long.

Anita and William were escorted to a briefing room because their next important meeting would be with fellow Humans five hundred years their junior. William couldn't help studying Anita, was this his genuine sister or a collection of metal, Simu-Skin and stolen identity? 'Stop freekin' staring at me you geek, you're really beginning to bug me. Can't you tell it's me Sherlock, I did credit you with more brains than you clearly possess.'

'You do sound like you I must admit. So you didn't manage the switch? I couldn't watch when it came to you leaving I might have blown it for you.'

'You're off on one again, Will look, we have to make the most of this now that's all that matters.'

He was having doubts now, these android copies would not

know about Anita's plans to switch they would have been programmed before she revealed her plan. If this was the fake beside him he mustn't let on, he had to give Anita a chance to escape.

DORIS HENSHAW'S LOVE CHILD

Mario got the message about Simon Wells and was tracking him down. It didn't prove that difficult as he had left a trail of confusion in his wake. However, his progress was hampered by desperate residents craving the truth. Stories soon emerged that the two strangers were the love children of Doris Henshaw, a lady in her seventies who still commanded a rather dubious reputation in the town. These two had clearly been hidden from view for forty years to avoid scandal. Another theory was that the two individuals were in fact shop dummies that Simon mistook for real people. The odd job man was frequently injuring himself as a result of short sightedness. Also, Simon had a well earned reputation for draining the whisky bottle, some thought he might well be seeing double.

Mario eventually caught up with Simon sharing his knowledge with twin brothers Pete and Paul Jervis. They were well respected in the town for talking common sense, usually both at the same time, and they were very close to Andy and his family.

'Ah!, young Mario you'll tell us the truth' exclaimed the twins. 'Spill the beans Mario and shut this drunken idiot up will you?'

Simon looked devastated that his fun was about to end.

'Have you all seen the posters about the meeting tomorrow?'

'Yes, we were going to ask you about that, what's going on? There's been too much excitement around here recently it's not good for one and all.'

'It's best for everyone if we let Andy explain tomorrow, it's not long to wait. I guarantee that by the end of that meeting everyone in town will be fully in the picture. In the meantime it would help greatly if you would use your energies in making sure everyone is able to attend tomorrow at 2.45pm.'

Mario was addressing his remarks to Simon in particular, he knew the twins would take the request seriously.

'No scoop story then young lad?' questioned Simon.

'You'll just have to wait until tomorrow with the rest of the town, in the meantime, no more rumours Simon ok?'

'Yes boss,' smiled the odd job man as he ran off to his next victim, a fresh explanation forming in his overactive brain.

The meeting could not come quickly enough. At least the ill timed contact with Doctor Honey and Nash had guaranteed a full house after the rain shower tomorrow. One thing was for certain, it would not be the meeting any of the townsfolk were expecting.

MEET YOUR NEW PARENTS

Jane knocked at Anita's door and was relieved when she got a response. 'I'll meet you in ten minutes in the breakfast room Mum.'

A similar answer came from William's room. Jane was happy to be going home. It had certainly been an unusual Christmas. She just wanted to get back to some sort of normality and see her animals again. Steve was already at the breakfast table talking to the ever present Hotel Manager.

'You are booked on the 3.30pm First Great Western train from Bodmin Parkway. We have arranged a private transfer to the station and as Paul is *feeling* much better he will drive you there. Please be ready by 2.30pm at reception with your luggage, including your son's scientific equipment. Again we apologise if your stay has not been as pleasant as you might have wished.'

'Yes it certainly would have been better if we could have seen more than the inside of taxis, hospitals and hotel rooms but I'm sure none of this is your fault, and the free booze and compensation has certainly numbed the pain. Oh you're there dear, the kids awake then?'

'I think we'll have to stop referring to them as kids, their nocturnal habits are certainly not those of children!'

'Let's not be hard on them Jane, we were all young and carefree once. This kind man has arranged our travel, even down to a taxi to the station.'

'The least we could do Mr Hawkins.'

The ever attentive Hotel Manager vanished as he was ready for a battery re-charge. William emerged first, both Anita and he were being monitored at the Think Tank next door. Colonel Hafey wanted to make sure they would function properly and pass the Human validity test.

'You're a sight for sore eyes, good night was it?'

William seemed confused, was it one question too many for his circuits to cope with? The colonel took one step nearer the observation screen, surly all the preparation had not been in vain?

'Leave the boy alone, he can't have had more than three hours sleep, you'd be confused in his shoes.' Steven had come to the rescue.

Anita soon took her place at the table. 'And before you start Mum, we had a great time, so can we postpone the third degree, I've got a rollicking great hangover and this room's still moving.'

'Your mother's just pleased to see you both, can't you tell?'

The Saviorian version of a full English breakfast was consumed by all, well mainly Steven who ate most of William and Anita's as well as his own. He would have preferred if the shell had been removed from his fried egg but for once the manager was nowhere to be seen. Jane couldn't wait any longer for some details on the night before.

'So come on what made this party so great that you had to come back and get changed?'

Again it was Anita who replied. 'We fell lucky there, got talking to these guys at this party, they gave us some written invites to this celebrity chef's do, Paul something, booze, food more booze. We had to get dressed up a bit so came back to change. Bit of a laugh wasn't it Will?'

'What was that, oh yes probably?'

'It's usually Anita who's the worse for wear after a session. You're looking a bit grey Will, are you going to be alright to travel?'

Colonel Hafey was really concerned now, there was no plan B, then.....

'I'll be fine, just give me an hour or so. Need to get all my equipment together for university, make sure it's all in one piece, it has to be back on Wednesday for another project. Waste of time, all that effort, I was sure I was onto something.'

'Never mind Einstein I'm sure Miss Audio Visual will provide something suitably comforting to cry on.'

Relief in the Think Tank, all sounded well now, especially with Anita, they were really impressed with her performance.

The Hawkins family went off to pack. The weather was terrible again, couldn't see anything outside. They'd all be glad to get home to hopefully some decent sunshine. William caught Anita's arm on the stairs.

'I don't remember a party, seems to be a blank in my memory.'

'Don't worry Will I'll cover for you, didn't know you could dance like that though.'

'What, oh really, search me.'

He had to perform better than this or they would soon arouse suspicion from the parents. She knew they were being watched and wondered if she would be able to contact Colonel Hafey. No, that might only make things worse. Hold tight and watch his back, this whole thing had to work for everyone.

HUMAN INPUT

'As you know, you two were not in our original plans but we could use your help in the integration process. We're pretty sure that generations of stagnation in Human behaviour have resulted in a high degree of apathy amongst the native population. We will need to energise the Human race at the same time choosing credible leaders and role models for the people to follow. We do not profess to understand Human behaviour completely and would value your input greatly.

You have been lifted from a time of high octane Human activity to one of virtual comatose stagnation, mostly caused by our interference. We made the only decision available to Saviorians to prevent the destruction of your planet. However, we owe it to the Human race to give it the best chance for a functioning normality. Advice is what we seek from you, will you help?' asked Major Main.

'Sounds like quite a challenge, it gives us a good reason to be here, so we would be honoured, wouldn't we Anita?'

'Back off brain box, I really don't want to be here. The thought that I won't be joining the wrinklies does my head in. I had some sort of control over my life, all be it a bit sketchy at times, before you dragged us into Santa's grotto 26th Century style, and all the madness that comes with it. If aliens invade in 2014 fine, I can deal with it. I would be in familiar surroundings with my friends and family. Here and now, everything is alien even dear old Ken, five hundred years our junior. As for our intergalactic saviours, a bit too good to be true don't you think. Do you know anyone who would sacrifice everything to save a bunch of losers like us? So excuse me if I'm not overwhelmed with excitement at the prospect of being stuck here in the complete unknown, but stuck here I am.'

William was rather taken aback by Anita's reaction. He thought she was meant to be the android that Anita switched with earlier in the day. Either the Saviorians had done an amazing job with the new androids or this was the real article and her plot had failed. Those in the Think Tank were not impressed with Anita's attitude towards them yet were secretly delighted as it confirmed to them that this was the genuine ancient Human article. Even they could not produce an android more foul mouthed than the real thing. William wanted to take Anita aside, ask her directly, but he had to wait until he knew his parents had gone through the time jump. It would clearly take much longer to persuade Anita that their mission was a selfless one. Major Main and Colonel Hafey felt it even more important that she witness the public meeting in Padstow today, in order to give the whole process validity. William would have to be charged with controlling his sister's outbursts.

'Would you at least agree to witness the first mass contact with 26th Century Humans later today? It may help you accept our position here on Earth?'

Major Main was trying to reach out but realised it might be too early.

'Whatever, I mean it's not like I've got anything else planned for the rest of my life it. Might be a laugh but go easy on the gunk and bile show, it turns my stomach.'

If she was typical of 21st Century women what hope was there? Anyway, there were far more important issues to attend to. They were on their way to a remote observation post on the edge of Padstow, to witness the first stage if integration.

THE WORLD IS WATCHING

Commander Aragon and Jackie Green had based themselves in a Command Centre located in part of Old London. They were there along with other Saviorian dignitaries from around the world to monitor activities in Padstow. If all went to plan they would trigger similar operations all over the globe. It had been agreed to start with rural areas, leaving large urban communities until later in the integration process. It was felt that any problems arising from their exposure in wider spread Human groups would be easier to control. Once they were confident the plan was advancing safely they would concentrate resources in urban communes where sheer numbers alone might create their own complications. Observations and measurements taken over the past three centuries seemed to point to the following,

Verbal disputes were on the decline and compromise was usually the outcome of any disagreement between Humans.

Physical violence was rare and short lived.

Contentment levels were high but ambition was rarely shown.

Stagnation had become a reality in many communities.

People still worked to produce food, sustaining life, but that was about it. Acceptance and resignation had become dominant traits of Human nature. In short, it was looking more likely that Humans would accept the alien's and their version of events. The worry was that they had gone so far down the stagnation route they would not be up to the challenges ahead. Humans were a complex species making prediction almost impossible.

All eyes were on that tiny rural community in South West England because, if the process failed there, what hope was there for the rest of the world?

A GRAND DAY OUT FOR PADSTOW FOLK

Midday in Padstow, the sun shone brightly out of a clear blue sky. The lurking menace of the dark zone encircled the town as it had done for three centuries. Light reflected back from the polluted waters of the old Camel Estuary. The derelict harbour was a constant reminder of how a world conflict had almost destroyed this haven of tranquillity. No logic could explain why they were spared. The whole town had collectively held its breath for all this time praying for things not to change, for the darkness not to devastate them as it had the rest of the planet.

If tickets had been sold for this public get together someone would have made a killing. It was a little after twelve and queues were starting to form. Many of the senior residents had brought chairs and stools to sit on while they waited. Mrs Cope, one of the local bakers, had produced baskets of filled rolls, hot soup and pasties for the hungry hoards. As the crowds grew there was a great deal of idle banter, the sort that usually accompanied any gathering, but this time the people sensed something out of the ordinary was about to happen.

Stories about Ken were ten a penny but none of them came within a million miles of the truth. One thing was for certain, after this Metropole meeting, their lives would never be the same again.

'Dr Honey, Dr Honey' Nash was at his side.

'I have just had a conversation with Major Main. He reports that all is well with the ultra advanced androids William and Anita, they were accompanying Mr and Mrs Hawkins to the Bodmin Parkway scenario building ready for the time slip back to 2014. The ancient Human siblings have been installed in Observation Pod 5 overlooking the town ready for initial contact. They have been briefed to observe proceedings, input where necessary and anticipate any future problems. At present we have no plans to introduce them to present day Humans, this should be done once the veil is lifted from the town.'

Several hundred androids waited just beyond the dark zone. They would not be deployed unless serious civil unrest broke out. They had been supplied with powerful sleeping gas spray guns but the Saviorians were very reluctant to use them. This would amount to a serious setback to any integration plans.

Andy, Mario and Karen were to initiate the meeting but would quickly introduce the long lost Ken. Dr. Honey and Nash would be the only two aliens there and Dina would monitor the crowd carefully on their introduction. They could only guess how the meeting would go, after all, it had only been tried once before, three hundred years ago, and that ended in disaster.

Reaching what used to be New Street round the corner from the Metropole, the Rollins family were still taken aback by the size of the crowd. Old and young, healthy and infirm waited patiently in line for the doors to open. There were very few faces missing. Some folk that were never seen out from one year to the next were there, hiding behind other friends and family. There was suddenly an eerie silence, a sense of impending doom. People watched as the librarian and his family walked briskly on, no questions just fixed staring eyes. The sisters Jones who were always at the head of any queue gave way with a vague smile as Mario opened the door to the hospital.

The meeting hall overlooked the town and the black void beyond, perfect for the upcoming proceedings. Although vast, the room was soon packed with expectant residents, no one was to be left outside on this special day. At 2.30 pm very few people seemed to miss the absent rain shower. Once everyone was settled inside, Nash and Dr. Honey took their places outside in the garden, awaiting their cue. The crowd seemed to take a collective intake of breath as Andy rose to address the good people of Padstow.

ON THE TRAIN AGAIN

Paul, the beleaguered taxi driving android, had been pressed back into action, resources were stretched for obvious reasons. His vocal confusion had not been resolved but that was not a priority right now.

'Der taxi he is well and waiting for you my lovers, nice to be seeing you again young maid.'

'Sorry, do I know you?' Anita was carrying the cases for the others while William fussed about with his scientific equipment.

'You no remember me, I is der Paul my lover, I been das chauffeur, driver type persona for you peoples before yes, no?'

'No sorry, a lot has happened lately, nice to meet you Paul,' she shook his hand in a strangely formal way.

'Come on Jane, William it's time to go home, we've got a train to catch.'

Steven thanked the Hotel Manager for a holiday with a difference and gratefully pocketed the compensation money while William dumped his bags in the boot. The taxi had been fitted with the latest visual technology. The changing Cornish scenery would pass before them. The implanted videos in the windows gave the impression of moving countryside outside while the mock up taxi found its way to the Bodmin Parkway scenario. The air con was on and the windows did not open.

'William are you ok, you've hardly said two words since breakfast?'

'Me, yes I'm fine, just a bit, you know.'

'I think what he means is he's still a bit hung over after last night, am I right Sherlock?'

'Could be, have you got the tickets Dad?'

'Oh yes, I thought I'd lost them at one point but the Hotel Manager said I had left them on the breakfast table.'

'Let me have a look please Dad. Well what do you know, they are dated 26th Dec 2014, four tickets for First Class to Paddington, we're going home!'

'What did you expect William, more of that Back to the Future stuff? These are the tickets we were given at Reading on the way down.'

'It's ok Anita just my little joke. I give in, there's nothing strange going on I'm just an attention seeking nerd with an overactive imagination.'

'Ve are at zi station in fumph minuten my handsomes, been a vuderba time having you all, safe back to your own time journey, I mean your own homes, bitte.'

Luckily no one was really listening to the ramblings of the confused tin man. They jumped from the taxi just in time to see the *train* arrive.

'I'd like to say some day it would be nice to come back to Cornwall, but I would be lying!'

'Anita, at least wait 'til we get on the train!'

Jane led the way onto the *platform* and found First Class. No one noticed the lack of passengers as they settled into their seats. Steven and Jane were too preoccupied with going home to notice anything out of the ordinary about their children's behaviour, why would they? The last possible thought would be that they were bringing two androids from the 26th Century back to suburban London 2014.

ALL IS REVEALED

'Thank you all for your attendance here this afternoon. It doesn't seem five minutes since our last meeting but these are monumental times for our little community.'

A tear came to Andy's eye as he struggled to find the words, where to go next, how to drop the bombshell. Dina held his hand, an action not lost on the crowd.

'You ok Andy, tell us what this is all about,' came a lone cry from the crowd.

'Yes please just get on with it I couldn't sleep last night with worry, and where is Ken, we were told he would be here?'

Andy didn't want this growing unease to spread in the crowd.

'Please everyone just listen.'

'Yes let the boy speak.'

'Thank you, Ken arrived back yesterday but he was not alone. He brought with him two strangers.'

'Then it were true about Doris Henshaw, they be her children out of wedlock, hidden away for all these years, shame on her.'

A movement in the middle of the crowd and a frail old woman got to her feet.

'It's her it's Doris!'

'They can't be mine I had no children, it was all a lie then as it is now, so leave me be!'

A general murmur of disbelief spread across the room.

'Quiet please, Doris is telling the truth, these strangers are not her boys.' Andy hesitated to clear his throat, 'You won't find any relation of theirs in this town, they come from....outside.'

'Outside, did he say outside, there is no outside he knows that better than all of us.'

'Dina I think your old man's been on the bottle, sort him out will you.'

The huge door at the corner of the room creaked open, the crowd turned as one.

'He's right! Please, everyone, I promise you will know everything before you leave today.' Ken wandered over to join Andy.

Ken was determined to keep things moving, there was a lot more to come out yet. He had deliberately never spoken about the woman held in the Think Tank with him but knew he had to cut to the chase.

'After you saw me on the beach I was again picked up by my unseen captors. Waking up in a strange room I knew I had to get to the bottom of this mystery. It was clear that I had been right all along, others had survived and were trying to contact the good people of Padstow.'

'That's impossible, Andy tell them, we've been alone for ever, I can't take it in, you must be wrong Ken, we all know you've not been well lately,' June Lyons expressed the thoughts of many in the crowd who really didn't want to hear this.

'Please listen to Ken, he has convinced me that all he is saying is true and believe me, it goes against all I've been telling you over the years, I am truly sorry.'

'Andy please, this really isn't about you, you know that. Please be patient all of you, I must move on. Eventually my suspicions were confirmed, we are not alone!'

More disturbances in the crowd, suddenly everybody wanted to speak.

'So Ken, what you sayin' is some other folk from another town got spared as well, where are they let's meet them?'

'Yes, my family before the, you know, they came from Wadebridge, a few miles away then, are these folks from there Ken?'

'Bring them in, we need some proof of your tale Ken.'

Ken held his hands up gesturing for the questions to stop. He was aware Doctor Honey and Nash were outside, waiting patiently for the cue to join the meeting.

'The *people* I spent the last few days with are from much further away.'

'Bodmin, they from Bodmin, my great, great aunt, her family came from there, that was a long way off mind, weren't it Andy?'

The general feeling in the crowd seemed to be one of confused excitement, not fear. They didn't know how it was possible but the thought of meeting new neighbours filled them with anticipation.

'I'm sorry to say there is no chance these strangers are long lost relations of yours, any of you.'

Ken braced himself 'They come from Savioria, another planet, not from here, they have been on Earth just over three hundred years, they say they saved our planet from destruction and are now preparing to leave.'

The crowd stirred again 'Come on Ken you're talking rubbish. You well know our town's seen no one from outside, not a soul we don't know, never mind little green men from outer space.'

'That's right we didn't come here to listen to the ravings of a mad man. You been in that green river and swallowed some of that poisoned rubbish, young Ken, you'm makin' no sense boy.'

Andy stood up and tried to settle the crowd. 'It pains me to say that Ken's story is indeed based on fact. I didn't want to believe him either but I've seen the proof.'

'Let's see it then, show us all the proof.'

'Yea stop messin' about, my tea's getting cold.'

'You can't tell lies to us any longer Andy we deserve the truth, or let us all go home.'

The townsfolk were really restless now.

'Andy, will you go and bring our guests in,' demanded Ken.

The librarian made his way to the door his footsteps disturbing the stunned silence.

'I have to warn you, many will be shocked with what you are about to see. So if you wish to leave please go now, especially those of a nervous disposition. If you chose to leave please make your way to the garden and wait there, I'm sure it will be worth it.'

Everybody looked at one another in bewilderment, not knowing what to do. A few started to make their way out but really wanted to stay to find out what the fuss was about. Some parents took their children out as a precaution, but not all. Most of the townsfolk stayed rooted to their chairs whispering to their neighbours.

A few minutes later Andy returned with two strangers in tow. Dr. Honey and Nash looked far more nervous than anyone else in the room. This was the first time they had been exposed to so many Humans at one time. They still secretly feared contamination even though their scientists had shown there was no danger. Standing next to Andy they waited to be introduced.

'Wait a minute.' A voice came from the floor 'I recognise these two jokers.' It was Simon Wells the odd job man. 'Doris, these is your boys isn't they, what's to be shocked about Ken. Maybe was a fright to Doris when they come along! Look at they, couple o' frightened little rabbits caught in a light. Should be ashamed Ken, worrying the poor folk for no good reason.'

A ripple of laughter crossed the room, this was rapidly turning into farce. Ken hammered on the table, he was clearly frustrated.

'These two *gentlemen* are not what they seem. They have disguised their appearance to protect you. Good people of Padstow it gives me great pleasure to introduce Dr. Honey and Nash from the planet Savioria. They have waited a long time for this moment, please listen to what they have to say.'

Again there was much hilarity in the room.

'Dina you really need to take a good look at young Ken 'ere, he's clearly not all there.'

'Sandwich short of a picnic if you ask me.'

'Tis funnier than that comedy bloke from St Edmunds Lane, you know 'e does a turn in the Ship on occasion.'

'You talking' about me? You'm right though, lots of new material 'ere boy!'

Dr. Honey spoke 'You good people clearly need convincing of our validity. Please turn your eyes to the window and the darkness beyond.'

The laughter died away as everyone craned their necks for a view. Nash sent a telepathic message to the Think Tank to dissolve the barrier. At first they could see no change, then slowly the impenetrable shroud that had stifled their very existence for generations began to thin. They could begin to see the outline of hills and fields through the gloom.

Within minutes the horizon was clear and they could make out the shiny silver outline of the huge Think Tank Headquarters and tiny figures moving about outside. Covered roadways stretched into the distance, a whole different world existing right on their doorsteps. Quite a few people fainted and needed Dina and Anita's help. Many just pointed, others stood, mouths wide in stunned silence. The few who had left for the garden rushed back in shouting.

'Have you seen this?'

'Look, I can't believe my eyes!'

'What's happening?'

As if by habit, many turned to Andy for an explanation, he just stood, arms around Dina and Karen his daughter, who had a broad smile on her face and tears of joy streaming down her face. With help, many who fainted began to come round after the initial shock.

'We do not intend to distress you in any way but we need to show you the reality of your situation. We, the Saviorians, are responsible for the last three hundred years of your planets history. There was no nuclear destruction of the World, we stopped it just in time. The rockets had taken off but we stopped and removed them, all of them. The process of normalisation was supposed to take only tens of your years. We wanted to give your planet back sooner but a contamination disaster stopped the process. Only now can we give you back what is truly yours. Our two species need to work together to achieve this goal now that the contamination is no longer a threat.'

Nash stopped to catch his breath in reality the Simu-Suit was not comfortable for long periods of language translation. He looked at the sea of Human faces, the expressions of incomprehension and total disbelief etched on every one. Years of stagnated existence in a tiny community had taken its toll, they seemed incapable of fathoming what was happening. A lone voice came from the crowd.

'Andy, you told us we were alone and we lived our lives accordingly and never questioned. Now this stranger says it was all a lie, what do we do, can we even trust you anymore?'

Ken spoke 'Please, this is not Andy's fault he did what he

thought was best, what he believed was right.'

'Yes and it was our people, the Saviorians, who filled your library with propaganda, false images and phony war stories long before you or he was born. We needed to buy time to help the Human race heal its wounds. So please do not blame Andy, he did a superb job on our behalf without any knowledge of our existence. He kept you safe and calm and brought you to this moment.'

Nash wanted to move on but were these people, these lost sheep, ready for more?

'So what you be sayin' is no one died, all them folks are still out there thinkin' they'm alone too, how sad is that?'

'Well, just like you the families of those people lived on, yes. It's not just that you are not alone, there's a whole world of people out there. However, the people of the commune of Padstow are special. You are the first in the whole world to become aware, all others remain in isolation. We need to see how you cope before moving on to other parts of the world.'

A loud gasp could be heard from those locals sitting by the window.

'Look at this 'ere look! That nasty green slime, she's gone,'

'ere maid look at that beautiful blue water, wow, did you do that an 'all?'

People ran from the room to get a better view from the garden. The clear water of the estuary shimmered in the dazzling sunlight. Children jumped up and down in joy wanting to run down the hill and dive in. Their world was changing and evolving before their very eyes

'Please come back in the room, we have much more to tell you!'

People slowly filed back in chattering and smiling, full of hope and expectation.

'So that water's now safe is it, just like that?' It was Carl from the New Ship.

'Yes, it was only a coloured dye, we have just flushed it away,' noted Dr.Honey, not calculating the man's mood.

'So we have all wasted a huge chunk of our lives and whole generations before us watching the boats in our harbour rot away, for nothing? Many of our forefathers before the war, that we now find out never happened, were fishermen. Hands up anyone who has tasted fish?'

No one responded.

'Of course not, we thought they'd all died out in your *polluted* waters. How many other things have we been denied all these years, for nothing? Why didn't you just lift the black veil from our lives and clear off years ago?'

Ken intervened 'None of us would be here if the bombs had been allowed to fall. This race of selfless aliens came to our rescue and we should be eternally grateful.'

Dr. Honey continued 'We understand your frustrations and will now work towards a speedy withdrawal. We too are anxious to leave, there are countless other planets and peoples out there who need our help.'

Carl was not finished 'Where is the proof that you are who you say you are. Most of these folks are finding it hard to believe there's someone else just over that hill never mind little green eyed monsters from outer space. I mean, no disrespect but you look more like dodgy salesmen, in fact come to mention it, you're the image of Pete Adcock's boy Harry. He keeps trying to sell me dodgy spuds and carrots.'

'That's a lie wash your mouth out Carl.' Came a call from the floor.

'You raise a very good point' continued Dr. Honey. 'Saviorians are very different to you in physical appearance. We think of ourselves as quite attractive in fact. However our limited contact with Humans has told us that you do not share our opinion, quite the opposite. Our clever scientists, many years ago now, developed what we call Simu-Suits. To the native species of a planet we appear just like them, a type of disguise I think you call it. These suits even translate our beautiful language into what you are hearing now. We find it allows us to cut through many barriers and prejudices, allowing progress to be made without distraction. I think the proof you require can be easily provided by switching off our Simu-Suits. However, our real appearance seems to cause distress amongst Humans as was the case with Andy and his family, but it seems to me a risk we have to take. You need to expose yourself to the real Saviorian in order to accept our explanation.'

'There is no apparent danger involved, they are peaceable creatures whose whole ethos is to preserve intelligent life, however, their appearance can cause revulsion. We must try and accept their physical differences and trust these creatures.' explained Ken.

Dr. Honey continued, 'For those who do not wish to watch live, we will record the event and you can watch it back later, we will provide Andy with the wherewithal to do that.'

'If they're not dangerous what's to fear. I for one need to see the evidence myself so bring it on, I'm not budging.' Carl was adamant and pushed himself forward for a better view.

'Those of you who wish to leave please make your way to the garden again and we will tell you when to return.'

Mario opened the doors and many with young children and some of the elderly followed him to the sanctuary of the fresh air. Once the remainder had settled Ken spoke 'I will invite our guests to remove their Simu-Suits, we ask you not to panic and to stay in your seats.'

ANYONE FOR A SQUIRREL BAR?

Only one member of the Hawkins family was feeling nervous as they reached the point in the scenario where they would be reunited with their own time. Jane and Steven were chatting about whether they could afford that new car along with concerns about their animals while they'd been away.

William had switched off, literally, something he had been programmed to do in order to conserve the life of his batteries. Anita was counting down the seconds to the moment she thought the Time Jump would take place. She estimated only another fifty seconds left. In the time it took to wink back at William in the Think Tank she had decided. Anita was sure he hadn't seen her parting sign. Was he still wondering who the android was, surely he could tell that the sibling who remained with him in the 26th Century was a collection of nuts and bolts and clever scientific stuff? It just seemed the right thing to do, she hadn't asked to be Dr Who's assistant. He was the one convinced of strange goings on, and he had been right. William had got what he wanted, a life outside the norm. No need now for computer games, he was living in one. She already missed him. Did she regret constantly taking the mick of him, certainly not, the little nerd deserved it! A tear formed in the corner of her eye and trickled down her cheek. She was unaware, lost in thoughts of guilt and foreboding.

Anita had never believed in unproven theories of time travel.

She couldn't see how her returning home to her own time would affect the future or the past. They had interacted with others in 2514 yes, but most of them were aliens! She pushed the thought from her mind....ten seconds to go, oh well this is it.

A bright white light swept through the carriage. Anita looked back from the window to see an old brick tunnel recede into the distance.

Jane and Steven were still deep in conversation seemingly unaware, but where was William?

A few additional passengers now sat in First Class relaxed in their seats. Anita read the date on a young woman's newspaper, 26th December 2014, they were back! But where on Earth was Will?

'Have either of you seen Will, he seems to have vanished?'

'Probably gone to the loo, why the sudden interest in your brother, are you feeling alright? You usually can't wait to see the back of him.' Steven and Jane laughed, they hadn't noticed anything out of the ordinary.

'Yes sorry, just wanted to ask him something that's all, it can wait.'

An eternity seemed to pass and still no sign of William the android. Could it be he had just vanished, maybe tin men can't travel in time, lost in the celestial junk yard for eternity?

'Sorry, wanted to check out the Buffet Car, I'm peckish,' William appeared behind them.

Liar thought Anita but she was very relieved to see him.

'Your sister was worried you'd vanished from the face of the Earth, quite sweet don't you think? Buffet's a good idea though, you two go and get some drinks and sandwiches for us all, here's some money, didn't seem to spend any this Christmas,' laughed Jane handing the money to Will who eyed it suspiciously.

'It's ok, you can buy dinner when we get back to London if you want.'

Anita pushed her android brother through the carriages to the buffet car.

'We all know you don't need real food, just a regular supply of scrap metal, so where did you vanish to?'

'You're not android are you? You're the Human Anita, that wasn't meant to happen, was it?'

'Well done Sherlock and for your information there only ever was one Anita, that's me. Your silicone sister will be taking care of my real brother five hundred years from now. God, I'd get locked up for saying that if anyone was listening. Anyway, your job is to keep mum and dad convinced you're the real deal for the next sixty odd years, so come on where were you?'

'I'm afraid sixty years might be impossible. You see when we passed through the Time Switch some of my batteries were damaged. I went to check them out, it's not good news.'

'So how long do you think they'll last, we could drop into a local hardware store and buy some more, what do you take, double A's?'

'It's serious, I calculate more like sixty days.'

'Bloody hell, can you fix them?'

'Its Saviorian technology, too advanced for your primitive science. Without getting back to 2514 I will burn out in three months time. However, I'm afraid that's not the worst of your problems.'

'I know, you don't have to tell me, you've got limited scrap value, substandard materials. Don't worry I've got a couple of mates that'll get a good price for you!'

'How can you possibly tell jokes at a time like this?'

'Sorry it's just a defence mechanism I have when things go belly up, the really bad news is, what?'

'While checking my circuits I detected something abnormal, I have a built in location detector.'

'Bit like a SatNav in the car you mean?'

'Perhaps, anyway, the fact is, when we switched time we also moved location. My sensors show us to have jumped to a Parallel Universe.'

'A what...?'

'To you and your family it appears normal and for much of the time, events, places and people will be very similar, but this isn't Earth 2014.'

'I think you damaged more than your batteries Einstein, you're talking rubbish just like the real Will.'

'I've checked several times, we're not where you think we are.'

'So where are we?'

'On parallel Earth, one hundred and fifty light years from where you want to be.'

'God, that's a bit of a cock up! Is this my fault, trying to come home when I should have stayed with Will? They were right I should have kept myself in 2514.'

'It is true, it would have caused fewer problems had you remained but, there might have been another cause, me. The drain on my batteries came when we attempted the Time Jump. Power was somehow diverted and caused us to jump to where we are now, Earth but not as you know it.'

'That really makes me feel better, I don't think, so Einstein how do we put it right?'

'We don't, unless the Saviorians trace us, we're stuck and they are too busy putting Earth right in 2514. They will have noticed a Time Jump and probably been satisfied with that and not check further.'

'This parallel Earth we've landed in, is it identical to my world, in which case what's the problem? I mean we might as well be home, I wouldn't have known if you hadn't opened your big metal jaw.'

'My implanted knowledge banks only allow me to surmise. From what I can extract Parallel Universes are rarely identical. Some are minutely different others deviate in huge and obvious ways, let's hope for the former and your parents remain unaware and you can lead as normal a life as possible.'

'You could be wrong though after all you're just a tin can with a confused brain.'

'However, when did trains in England start selling *'Squirrel Bars- The Genuine Taste of Rodent in a Milk Chocolate Bar'* there on the shelf, look!'

'Oh my God, it's true!'

THEY'RE CERTAINLY NOT CORNISH

The moment of truth had arrived as the Simu- Suits were switched off revealing the true Saviorian to a mass Human audience for the first time. As Dr. Honey opened his huge sucker filled mouth to speak a fountain of eruptive, stench filled regurgitated gunk, spewed forth and drenched the first five rows of the unsuspecting crowd. Women and children screamed while covering their heads in an attempt to shield each other from the deluge. Those further back pinched their noses and tried to breathe through the pungent aroma of half digested vegetation and rotting flesh. They stared in utter horror and amazement at the two tiny forms in front of them, they were certainly not Cornish! Their story instantly took on an air of validity. As the initial postulant outpouring subsided noises could be heard emanating from the chasm of Dr. Honey's mouth.

'Shoosh oomph e googarshh arashoo ugshee Padstow intphoo'

His bright red bulbous head seemed to throb with a certain degree of excitement. Then, to the misfortune of the crowd who had just managed to mop the worst of the spew from their faces, he started to speak again. It was more than they could bare, hoards of people rushed for the door slipping and sliding on the sea of yellow and green puss. They careered into walls and chairs, knocking one another over like dominoes.

Witnessing the mass exodus Dr. Honey switched his Simu-

Suit back on. Even the hardiest of souls, with cast iron stomachs and stain resist clothing, had fled the building. Within minutes the streets of Padstow were deserted. People had forgotten their new liberty and were locking themselves away from this new unknown.

'Well, that went well,' declared Karen as she helped to rediscover the floor with a huge mop and bucket. 'Clearly our fellow residents are not too keen on our friends from beyond the stars, especially their oral habits, what's the next move?'

There was a moments silence then Dr. Honey spoke.

'Simu-Suits require a great deal of power to maintain their integrity, they need to be recharged. I still can't quite comprehend. If we are to complete out task here on Earth, our suits need to last longer than a few Earth hours. Humans appear to have serious problems with our spectacular appearance.'

'We should wait and see what happens when the dust settles and the town's folk have had time to digest the situation, sorry bad choice of words. It's a major shock to everyone, including me,' noted Andy.

'At this moment we have all our resources ready and waiting for the all clear to start the integration process. We cannot wait for, as you say, the dust to settle. Our plans are to release the next village to Padstow tomorrow and so reintroduce the communities to one another. This process has already taken too long. We need you to visit people, reassure them and report back by midnight.'

Nash spoke with some frustration, he knew this part of the process would be difficult but not because of the mere physical differences.

'So where will you be when we try to persuade Mrs. Trevithick of 47 High Street that this nightmare is preferable to being safe and sound in a predictable little world?' asked Dina.

'We must return to the Think Tank and arrange for vast

amounts of Simu-Suits to be produced with more efficient power packs, by yesterday. Contact with Humans will have to be controlled in a much better way, only revealing out true identity briefly to prove our validity. Please help us, the future of the entire world may depend upon it.'

'Before your arrival on our doorstep this was the entire world!' pointed out Mario.

ANITA INDUCES THE TWITCHES

'Where have you two been for the past half hour, we're starving to death, did you get the food?'

Anita and William had been very careful with their choice of sandwiches and drinks. Thankfully, most of the menu was free of rodent, although Anita was disturbed to find *Succulent Rat Smoothies* available at only £2.75.

They had to be very careful not to arouse any suspicion in the parents and be one step ahead at all times.

'You didn't say what kept you all this time' continued Jane.

'A woman had taken ill in the buffet car, too many smoothies or something. We just comforted her until a doctor was found.'

Anita thought the truth might be a bit too much for her parents to take. *Actually Mum, I was having a long conversation with my android brother about how we ended up in a Parallel Universe after spending Christmas in the 26th Century.*

'That was very kind of you two, I'm very impressed.'

Anita suddenly felt twelve years old, she expected a pat on the head and a sticky sweet shoved in her mouth. William looked like he was asleep, in fact he had shut down again to preserve battery power.

'I'm sorry we dragged you down to Cornwall for Christmas,

not much fun was it? Still you'll soon be back amongst your friends. There's a lot to be said for familiar surroundings and a normal routine don't you think?

'Anita your Dad's talking to you.'

'Oh yes I couldn't agree more, the more familiar the better I say.'

'You alright dear, you seem miles away?'

'More like a hundred million light years,' Anita muttered under her breath.

'Your next station stop will be Plymouth, passengers travelling on to London Paddington please have your tickets ready for inspection.'

That all sounds pretty normal thought Anita, this might not be so difficult after all.

'Yes I'm fine Mum, just a bit tired after last night's party, they know how to have a good time those Cornish folk!'

'Perhaps you should get some shut eye like Will, never seen him so zonked out.'

'No I'm fine, need to look after you wrinklies don't I.'

Never had she spoken a truer word. Everything at Plymouth station looked normal, maybe William was wrong, and they could be back in their own world. Perhaps the railway company were experimenting with a new range of snacks and drinks with unusual names. She should try a Squirrel Bar, it might be some kind of joke.

'I'm just going to the toilet, won't be a minute.'

Anita headed for the buffet car. She picked up a Squirrel Bar from the shelf, it felt like a normal chocolate bar, no fur hanging out.

'Will that be all, Miss?'

'Oh yes thanks.' *He's a bit of a hunk*, she smiled he smiled back.

However, she couldn't help noticing how his nose twitched in a sort of uncontrollable way. She removed the wrapper from her Squirrel Bar and broke it in two.

'Holy shit!' she yelled out loud 'That's bloody raw meat for f... sake!'

'Only the best ingredients,' the hunk said proudly with another twitch, 'A very popular product, flying off the shelves it is, get it flying, Squirrel oh never mind.'

Anita ran, throwing her Squirrel down as she fled.

'Strange girl, oh well no accounting for taste, next please.'

She stumbled all the way back to First Class where Jane and Steven were in heated conversation with the ticket inspector, again.

'What do you mean it's not the right company name, you are Great Western Railways, have been for years. Oh Anita, tell this nice man, he insists they are a Railroad not a Railway company, he thinks the tickets are forged. Seems like we can't travel by train anymore without being accused of something or other.'

Anita looked at the tickets and quickly tried to cover it up with some charm. 'I'm sorry sir, what's your name?'

'Tom.'

'I'm sorry Tom but you must see it's just a printing error. We were given these tickets in good faith, it really isn't our fault one word has been spelt wrongly.' She gave him a long lingering smile and couldn't help noticing his nose starting to twitch. 'My parents have had a very traumatic few days in Padstow, so please, can't you see it's a genuine mistake?'

Tom was still staring at Anita, the twitch having spread to his left arm, he slowly pulled himself together.

'Yes, very well, but in future please check your tickets when you purchase them to make sure all the details are correct, have a pleasant trip to the Capital.'

Tom handed the tickets back to Steven and twitched off down the carriage.

'Am I right, it's in America they're called railroads, isn't it?'

'He's probably new to the job anyway, all sorted no need to fuss thanks to our Anita.'

At that moment William rebooted himself.

'All circuits are functioning at full capacity, voice activated, ready to interact with Humans. Hello!'

'What did he say, you alright Son?'

'Sorry, just talking in my sleep, one of my computer games getting to me.'

'You need to give them a rest nerd brain, I think you're turning into a bloody computer.'

EUCHRE BEFORE INTEGRATION

At Observation Pod 5 things were getting tense. They saw people running from the Metropole Hospital in all directions, back to the safety of their own homes. It had been three hours since the meeting had begun and all was not well. William and Anita were being consulted on Human behaviour, but only William had any ideas how to help.

'Humans don't like to be pushed into corners and they need time to absorb what they've seen and been told. If you go banging on doors you might make things worse, they may get defensive and lash out.'

'Do you agree Anita?' asked Major Main.

'How the hell would I know, it's your mess? I think I'd be freaked out after seeing you in the flesh though.'

These observations were sent back to Dr. Honey and Nash. It was decided to wait a couple of hours and only approach locals as they emerged from their homes. It wasn't long before a group of young men were spotted on the old slipway by the harbour. They were armed with hammers, nails and planks of wood. It appeared that they were trying to repair one of the rusting wrecks by the water's edge. Mario was sent to investigate.

'Hello boys, what's happening then?'

'If what those slimy space things say is true we're off up the old estuary to tell any folks out there what's been happening. Can't trust no one no more especially your dad, he fed us all that rubbish, all us lives. We could have been out and about to all parts, maybe met some different girls and drank some decent beer instead o' that muck they serve in the Ship!'

'Dad was just trying to do his best to look after you and the townsfolk.'

'That's as maybe but we're aimin' to make up for lost time Mario, if that be ok with thee?'

'So you're happy with all this alien stuff, not afraid of the future?'

'Them ugly little midgets don't bother us, maybe they did save the world and all that all them years ago, but I reckon it be our world now, so bring it on!'

'I'm glad to hear you say that but can I ask you one small favour, just wait until tomorrow morning to sail away. We need to be sure the whole town is happy with things then the Saviorians will be out of our hair.'

'My hair's still full of their yellow spew, the sooner they gone the better. Ok, a few more hours won't make much difference, it'll give us more time to get her proper sea worthy. First light mind, we'm off!'

'Thanks boys' shouted Mario as he ticked them off his list of approvers.

Karen was very keen to help, her positivity about the future might help sway doubters and answer their fears. On her way down Duke Street she noticed a group of middle aged women talking on doorsteps and looking around anxiously.

'Evening ladies, quite a day we're having.'

'Oh girl, we're just so confused, are they slippery little creatures for real, I mean, can we trust 'em with all that drool and dribble?'

'Our Fred, he's got a powerful stomach but he's been retchin' and heavIn' past hour, what's to be made of it all?'

'Well all I can say is if you can look past their appearance they are really very friendly. They mean no harm and have actually been looking after us for three hundred years, without us knowing. In fact without them there would be no us. If we can just persuade others then everything will be fine. They'll soon go and we can get out there and meet new friends, hear stories, live a proper life.'

'Easy for you girl, you be young and adventurous like, some of us is scared of what's out there, been happy in our little world, looked after by your Dad.'

'But isn't it good that the whole world was saved after all, I know I felt pretty guilty when Dad told me we were the chosen few. We have to be positive and embrace this new challenge.'

'Happen you're right girl, got no choice have we?'

'That's the spirit, can you lot spread the word, these aliens need to move on, open up the rest of the world and leave us to make our own way. I'm sure if you want you can carry on as normal, you don't have to leave town, just welcome strangers if they come to call.'

'My Fred'll be happy with anything so long as e don't ave to meet that there mini vomit machine again, keep them away and you've got a deal girl. Come on Doris, Vera, Eileen and you Bet lets spread the word, we be inviting the world fur tea!'

After an hour or so, lots of groups were venturing out into the strange cold and dark early evening. Pointing to the horizon they could spot stars they'd never seen before. A glow from across the estuary confirmed the presence of the alien headquarters. A hive of feverish activity, accompanied by an unfamiliar hum of generators made the locals feel uneasy. Had they really been on their doorstep for centuries watching over them, keeping them safe, or trapped, depending on which way you looked at it. A bank of cloud rolled in from the west producing a light rain.

'What time's it Ralph?' enquired Stan.

'I make it half past six, what's going on, that feels like rain to me.'

'Me too mate, world's goin' crazy, rain at half past six at night, I might get wet going to my Euchre match, never got wet at this time afore.'

'No never at half past six, can't be doing with this, taint right.'

'I'm off to dig out my Dad's old umbrella, sod it!'

'Here, what you make o they slippery little rascals at Metropole today, is they for real or what?'

'Damn well felt real, got proper drenched in spew, leave it to Rollins family, they'll sort it, I'm off, bloody rain!'

Dr. Honey had called a meeting at Andy's house for ten pm to assess the public mood. Time was running out, the entire Savorian population was watching and waiting.

'We have managed to speak to a surprising number of people and although most find your physical appearance abhorrent, they grudgingly accept your presence here, for now. Some are even vaguely grateful for what you've done. For most of the residents it was a long time in the past and generations have grown used to their simple life. Many just want to be left alone and don't care about the outside world. My name is mud in a few households but I can live with that. There is no general uprising or protest, just a feeling of *go away and leave us alone.* The younger generation are more enthusiastic and keen to mix with anyone who might be out there, which is probably to be expected. I think we can safely put Karen in that category.'

Karen smiled broadly at her father, something he hadn't seen from her in a long time.

'With all due respect, integration with Saviorians is not what they want.'

Andy was keen to re-establish his roll of guardian in Padstow, although he wouldn't admit it. His pride had taken some hard knocks recently and the burning of many of the library texts and photos hadn't helped ease the pain. Androids had been hard at work in the background re-stocking his shelves with the up to date version of recent Human history. They were also providing useful information on possible methods of re-discovering lost practical technologies from three hundred years past. The planet had regressed in many ways under Saviorian control and there was much to catch up on.

Nash and Dr. Honey had listened carefully to what Andy had to say. Padstow was the testing ground and was perhaps proving to be more of a straightforward transition than anticipated. However, this was a small rural community and always had been. More complex problems were expected in some of the urban areas across the globe.

'We have decided Andy, to take your advice and open up the next community and some others further afield. A telepathic message has already gone out, as you Humans say, the ball is rolling. Integration is not needed here and would clearly only cause unwanted distress. We will speak to you again once neighbouring communities have been released and perhaps started communicating again. We sense real hope for the Human race, but we've only just...'

Dr. Honey was interrupted mid sentence, Jean Masters from Grenville Road rushed in screaming.

'Please Dina come quick, something awful has happened. It's young Mary Brady from down our road, she's real poorly, come out in a terrible rash and just collapsed, we can't revive her, please come now!'

Dina grabbed her medical bag and ran.

WHITE NAPKINS AND RATS IN ROLLS

'No more trips to the depths of Cornwall anytime soon please William. You must be satisfied there were no strange goings on down there?'

Anita nearly choked on her coffee.

'A free holiday to Italy would be greatly appreciated though, if you could arrange it!'

Steven's attempt at humour was lost on the android.

'I expect he's looking forward to hooking up with Miss Media Studies again. I bet he'll have a few surprises for her when they compare notes in the editing room, eh Will!'

'She's just a friend that's all,' noted Will with a confused grin.

'Hey, did you see that!' cried Jane.

'What?'

'Oh, we've passed it now, a field full of red squirrels, hundreds of them, I thought they were rare. We tried to get hold of a pair for our place but no such luck, never seen so many of them together. I'm going to try and get the address, find more out.'

Anita wondered whether there was a theme developing here. In this parallel world, did they farm squirrels to produce chocolate bars?

'Must be some sort of breeding programme, trying to boost numbers, I'll enquire when we get home,' noted Steven.

'Good, I'll watch to see if there are any more.'

If the only difference between this world and ours is a fixation with furry rodents we might get by, thought Anita.

The train advanced to Exeter where it made its regular stop. First Class was now filling up as two very well dressed elderly ladies took seats near the Hawkins. They exchanged a polite hello and proceeded to open a very fancy picnic hamper holding a wide selection of rolls, cakes and hot drinks.

'You folks going all the way to the Capital today?' enquired the smaller lady.

'Yes, we're on our way home from a short break in Cornwall,' replied Anita.

Steven and Jane were nodding off trying to count red squirrels and William had gone off line again.

'Oh I do love Cornwall, especially the wild life there. Were you staying anywhere near Groundhog Game Reserve, I've heard their freezing techniques are second to none. You can pick out a hog, shoot the dear thing yourself and have it delivered freeze packed to your home address ready for when you arrive back. They fatten the little blighters up a treat, easier to shoot and there's plenty of meat to go around.'

'Fascinating,' replied Anita as she checked that the parents had dozed off properly.

The larger more rotund lady joined the conversation, 'You feeling peckish young girl, we've more food here than we can eat?'

'No, really I'm fine, just eaten actually.'

'Ok dear but if you change your mind just give us a shout.'

Anita was about to look away when she caught sight of the ladies biting ravenously into a couple of rolls. The fresh blood trickled down their double chins as they carefully extracted some fur from what was left of their yellowing teeth.

'I don't know how the supermarket manages to keep these house mice so fresh, they are delicious, are you sure you won't have one dear?'

It took all Anita's will power not to throw up all over them but she held firm, managing to wave away the offer politely. The ladies delicately dabbed away the crimson dribble with lacy white napkins before starting on their desert of chipmunk chip cookies.

'You look a bit green dear I think it's a trifle hot in this carriage. Perhaps you should take some air before we reach Reading. I'll tell your folks where you are if they wake up.'

'Thanks, I might just do that.'

The fur filled feast was nearly over so she could risk five minutes in the toilet with the window down. She threw her head into the fresh air, gulping in the blast of a cold winter's day. This parallel problem had just reached a potentially serious level. If the population were openly devouring rodents from their snack boxes, it wouldn't be long before the oldies noticed. Anita took in one last gulp and made her way back to her seat. The train was about to reach Reading and to her relief the ladies were leaving. The movement of passengers woke Jane and Steven.

'Is this your daughter, lovely girl, we were just telling her of a place to visit next time you're in Cornwall, safe journey home,' and they were gone.

'Sorry Anita we must have dozed off. What were those nice ladies talking about?' asked Jane.

'Oh I don't know something about a wildlife park where you can shoot your own dinner I think.'

'Really you get worse, if that's possible. Be careful, someone will take you seriously one day!'

'Is Will still asleep? I think he's coming down with something. Hope he didn't catch something in Padstow, he's back at university next week.'

'I'm sure he's fine. If there is a bug in his system I'm sure it'll get booted out.'

'What? I swear you youngsters talk a different language,' cried Steven.

William's eyes snapped open, his batteries temporarily replenished.

'William Hawkins - male, nineteen years of age, parents - Steven and Jane, Sister - Anita, residing in Nottingham, attending university first year... refreshing memory banks, intact, proceed. Sorry, must have dozed off again, are we there yet?

The parents just stared at him, Will clearly wasn't himself today.

'I need to go to the toilet Will, come with me and guard the door please, I think the lock's broken.' Anita marched the android down to the end of the carriage. 'Do you really have to give a flamin progress report out loud every time you wake up? You're soon going to blow your cover.'

'Sorry Anita, I'll adjust my settings straight away.'

'Right but that's not our only problem. The people here seem to have some sort of rodent fixation. Not satisfied with farming the little critters, they chase them, shoot them and eat their little furry bodies in a sandwich. We simply don't do this where I come from it's not cricket you know. We're lucky the wrinklies are a bit slow on the uptake but sooner or later they're bound to notice.'

'Should we tell them then, you know, about the...?'

'Oh yes the parallel universe, the visit to 2514 and the fact that their son is actually an android. Oh yes I nearly forgot their real son is living in 2514 Padstow helping some aliens return our world to its former state following a near fatal nuclear war. Let me think, are they going to fall for any of that, I don't really think so! We have to protect them as best we can and hope for the best. Come on, we need to get back before the next rodent revelation!'

MARY BRADY FALLS ILL

A few selected pockets of humanity were being released from their three hundred year slumber. They included communities on five continents and across a variety of rural and urban groups. News of the illness in Padstow had come too late to stop the process.

'Please let me through, where is she, where's Mary?' Dina was having problems pushing past the crowd outside the Brady house. 'Can everyone please leave the house and the immediate area until I can assess Mary's condition?'

Mrs Brady was trying to comfort her daughter who was struggling to breathe. She was flitting in and out of consciousness and the rash on her face and neck was horrific. Circular mounds of green and red throbbing sores were continually breaking out and then receding to be replaced by others. It was as if her body was trying to repel this invasion but struggling to contain it.

'I'm so worried, what is it? I've never seen anything like it, can you help her please?'

Mario and Andy had hastily cleared the house and much of the street in case the child was contagious. Dina had asked Mr. and Mrs. Brady to wait in the kitchen while she tried to make an evaluation. Suddenly Nash and Dr. Honey burst into the room.

'Please Mrs. Rollins, we will take it from here. We have the equipment to run tests and make a diagnosis much quicker than you can.'

'So much for keeping out of Padstow and avoiding distress amongst the community.'

Dina was trying to protect her patient, something she'd done all her life. 'I've tended to everyone in this town for as long as I can remember, please let me do my job, we're wasting time.'

'Please Mrs Rollins, if we found out we were in any way responsible for this infection it might put the whole integration process at risk. We must move Mary to our secure, sterile facility and treat her.'

'What part of piss off don't you understand?' Mr. Brady had heard the argument and had barged in. 'You'm been told by Dr. Rollins here. Now take yer puss spewin gobs with you and piss off back to the hellhole you came from fore I send you there me self!'

Mario tried to restrain George Brady.

'Poor Mary, she wanted to get right up close when they poxy vermin exposed themselves at that there meetin, took a full face load o that green vomit, nearly drowned the poor little mite. Took my missus a good couple hours to clean that crap off the young maid, can still smell the rotten spew now. It's not right young Mario, you get rid o' these little devils or I'll get the boys to rip their heads off!'

Though understandable, Mario had never heard language so threatening in his life before. Human emotions buried deep for so long were coming to the surface now. He needed to be strong and positive. The closest he had come to confrontation was when farmer Smyth's prize bullock had trapped Morwenna Fisher in the cow shed for three hours and had to be tempted away with a bag of turnips.

'Dr. Honey, Nash, please leave the house and let my mother

tend to this child, George go back to your wife, you are not helping, nothing will be gained by argument!'

To his surprise everyone did as they were told and left Dina alone with the stricken Mary.

Medicines on 26th Century Earth were mainly of a herbal nature. They were fine for everyday colds and headaches, but this was different. None of Padstow's residents realised that it was the aliens who had prevented any serious illnesses in the community by the careful control of the environment, keeping a watch for any potentially harmful bugs and bacteria. Pumping the water system full of life enhancing agents had increased the life expectancy to well over one hundred and fifty years. These people were as fit and healthy as they could be until now and had trusted the herbal remedies Dina had provided to keep them that way.

Mary was fighting hard but the repulsive rash was spreading to her arms and legs, devouring every inch of her skin. Dina was lost, she coaxed the poor girl to have sips of water and tried to apply a soothing herbal paste to the throbbing sores but she knew that alone would not cure her.

Something close to panic had taken over the Think Tank. No sooner had the order been given to enlighten other Human communities then this outbreak occurs. Was the rash that was taking over the young girl's body of Saviorian origin or merely a Human strain of a child's viral disease? Risks could not be taken, the girl had to be quarantined in the secure environment of the Fox Institute.

'Colonel Hatey why haven't we sent a division of androids to retrieve the child?'

'There is a very delicate situation with the child's parents who will not allow our people access to the young one. Also, the local self professed doctor of medicine, Dina Rollins, insists on caring for the child herself. There is a danger the situation could escalate, remember, we are the outsiders, still not trusted. It is a close knit community, one we ourselves have nurtured for all these years.'

'Can we persuade Mrs. Rollins to give up the child and convince the parents to let us treat her?'

Major Main knew time was against them. If this outbreak was to replicate itself in other Human communities recently released who knows where it might lead. William and Anita had been brought back from their observation pod in the hope of them bringing a Human perspective to the impending crisis. Only William could give any real practical advice, Anita, not surprisingly, struggled with a problem outside her android remit.

'All I can say is you need to let these people believe it is their decision to permit your treatment of Mary. This will avoid any more resentment down the line.'

'Have you got anything to add Anita?' asked the Major. '

Me no, just grab the kid and get her treated, why are you waiting. She could spread the infection all over the shop if you keep messing about!'

'Well yes, thank you both for your input, Will, we shall take your suggestions on board.'

Back in Padstow, Dina was at her wits end so when Andy was charged with persuading her to give Mary over to the alien doctors his task was easier than anticipated. Dina was asked to convince Mary's parents that their daughter's best hopes lay in the hands of the alien Saviorians.

'Please Mr. and Mrs. Brady, come in and close the door.'

Mary's situation had clearly deteriorated, her face a mass of ever changing angry green and red blotches, only her tearful eyes escaped the ravages of the advancing infection. Her breathing was shallow, she moaned, clearly in distress. Mrs. Brady could not control her anguish, bursting into floods of tears.

'I know this is very difficult for you both but I can do no more for Mary other than try and comfort her. We need to trust the aliens, they have the skills and better medicines to treat her. If we don't let them help I fear for her life.'

'Please George we've no choice, we have to let them outsiders help.'

'I still don't trust 'em, we're goin' with our Mary, watch 'em like hawks, you tell them Dina, we'll not be leavin' our young maid's side.'

The Saviorians had no choice, they had to allow the parents to accompany their daughter.

The crowds outside the Brady house were treated to a sight beyond their comprehension, a shiny metallic flying machine glided silently over their heads, landing in a nearby field. Four androids emerged carrying sterile suits for the Humans to wear. They vanished into the house, the crowd waited with nervous anticipation. A few moments later they emerged with Mary in an individual life support capsule, sealed from the outside world. Her anxious parents looked scared and confused as they were ushered into the craft accompanied by Dina and Dr. Honey.

Mouths wide, the ever expanding crowd watched in wonder as the vessel sped up and over the Camel Estuary, lights blinking in the darkness fell. They followed its path as it landed at the nearby Fox Institute facility. Stunned silence turned to stampede as the crowd rushed to confront Andy and Mario. Two androids had stayed behind to fumigate the house and neighbouring dwellings.

'Can we trust them little creatures Andy?'

'What they planning on doing with young Mary, she be proper poorly by all accounts?'

'We have to trust them because their technology leaves us in the dark. I believe they are good, after all we owe our very existence to them.'

'So you says Andy, let's hope you're right.'

The crowd slowly dispersed, eyes still straining to see over the water to where the other world people occupied a sprawling piece of *their* land, they could not wait to see the back of them. Meanwhile, children excitedly discussed the sight of that flying metal tube over their little town. Parents were fearful that their young ones might already be infected with poor Mary's disease and just dearly wanted their little piece of paradise back.

Mary's parents were in total shock after leaving the ground, all this couldn't be happening, a living nightmare. All they could think of was what was happening to their daughter, so the hot tea like drink designed to sooth their nerves had no effect. All the fight had gone out of George as he sat head bowed staring at the metal floor.

Dina was allowed to witness the examination and treatment process. Their contact since arriving at the Institute had been solely with androids. Dr. Honey and Nash had rushed off to attend emergency meetings with fellow Saviorians.

'Ah come in, let me try and bring you up to speed on events,' Professor Huntley was chairing a meeting with senior local Saviorian officials that included Nash, Dr. Honey, Colonel Hafey, Jackie Green from Earth logistics and Commander Aragon. There was a video link running to other Earth centres including communities in the process of enlightenment.

'First of all Dr. Honey, we would like to congratulate you on retrieving the infected Human girl to our secure facility here in District Six.'

'Her name is Mary, she has a name, do not forget that.'

'Indeed, we are awaiting the outcome of tests on the unfortunate Mary and I cannot stress enough how vital it is to have a foolproof diagnosis and plan of action to control the situation, in order to advance our ultimate goal.'

'If I may put a global perspective on this potential crisis,' Jackie Green stood up to be heard.

'I appreciate the unfortunate timing of events in Padstow but where does this leave the communities worldwide who are, as we speak, emerging from the darkness? Do we tell them, well actually we made a mistake, and it's not safe out there so please forget what we just said, trust me I'm an alien?!

'Clearly we need to buy some time to allow the conclusion of tests on...Mary. We have asked our androids to run some mandatory courses on how to cope with the outside world. Residents will not be allowed to leave their community until the course is completed. So far it seems to be holding although we clearly cannot force residents to stay put. Humans are inquisitive by nature and may tire of waiting.'

'May I ask a question?' Commander Aragon stood up to speak.

'You seemed so sure that Saviorians and Humans were safe to breathe the same air without fear of another Alvis Prince episode. Were your studies on the Humans William and Ken not extensive enough, flawed in some way, or did you rush to reach the conclusion you so clearly desired?'

An angry Dr. Honey spoke. 'Our tests were as painstakingly thorough as any we have carried out on all of our missions throughout the galaxy. I personally risked everything in the firm belief of the positive outcome we achieved. Since the initial tests we have spent hours with Humans all over the Padstow community with no ill effects on either of our species. I strongly object to your suggestion Commander. Please wait until the results are in before apportioning blame for a crisis that, as yet, does not exist.'

Nash now spoke up 'I believe Dr. Honey is correct, we must wait for the results. However, I do have this thought, the infected Human is a child as we know.'

'Why yes!'

'Human children do contract infections such as Chicken Pox at an early age, and we could simply be dealing with that here. We do monitor illnesses in our Human populations and apply remote treatments, but, we have missed the odd one in the past which usually ran their course without disastrous outcomes, we must wait and see.'

Nash's possible explanation seemed to settle the meeting and the room fell silent in contemplation.

The peace was soon shattered when android XV017 rushed into the meeting room. He handed an info block containing the test results on Mary to Professor Huntley who studied them impassively for a few moments. Clearing his cavernous throat he spoke in hushed tones.

'It is the definitive conclusion of our esteemed group of scientists that the child is suffering from a variation of the Human disease Cow Pox, a rare viral infection found in rural agricultural communities.'

'You say a variation, how has this variation come about?' asked Commander Aragon.

Professor Huntley took a deep breath.

'The report says it was altered through contact with fluids projected from the mouth of a Saviorian.'

A collective gasp circled the room.

BASE CAMP ON THE MOUNTAIN OF SURPRISES

'Isn't that your phone ringing mum?' Anita was pointing at Jane's bag from where the muffled sounds of the Birdie Song could be detected.

'Is that you Mother? I was going to call when we got to London.'

'Jane, thank God, we thought you'd been abducted by aliens or something.'

'No, just Cornish folk Mum!'

'I've been trying to reach you lot, especially William, seems he left some recording equipment from Nottingham University on the train.'

'That's odd, he's got that here with him, the people in the hotel fetched it back from Penzance for him.'

'Has he got it all because the police collected recording gear from the train when it reached Penzance?'

'Hang on I'll ask him, it's your gran on the phone, something about the equipment you borrowed, have you got it all with you?'

Will checked his bags and as far as he knew it was all there.

'Mum, he says it's all there, a bit strange though, we'll call you again when we get to London.'

'Alright but I have to call Jim Hammond, the policeman looking into this, don't be surprised if they are waiting for you on the platform. Oh and Jane, can you pick up a couple of those Squirrel Sensation Bars, our local shop can't stock enough, flying off the shelves they are, speak to you soon.'

'Was that gran you were talking to?'

'Yes of course it was, you heard her voice didn't you?'

This got Anita thinking, *if this is a parallel universe it's going to be difficult to predict when the anomalies might pop up. Clearly gran was the gran they all knew, wasn't she?*

'She said something strange though, I'm sure she asked me to get her Squirrel Sensation bars in London. I hope she's not going senile on us, mum's usually so bright.'

Anita just gave a sympathetic smile but her concerns had just been confirmed.

'I'm more worried about the police meeting us from the train. What's this all about William?' Steven had one of his frequent, I'm worried and not in charge looks.

'Well Mr Hawkins....I mean Dad, there must be some mistake on their part, I've got all my, I mean the universities, equipment here, fat lot of good it did me.'

'Never the less, what are the chances of two sets of identical gear turning up in Penzance?'

'It might not be the same sort of gear, gran could easily be confused.'

'However, it is you the police want to talk to, what's on those tapes, did you see?'

'You know very well Dad, a complete box set of Dad's Army plus ten minutes of snow and squiggly lines!'

'What if the police did retrieve your stuff from the train? And the hotel, embarrassed that they had lost the original gear, quickly organised a replacement set with the misspelling of Nottingham on the box. Dad's Army was just something left on by mistake?'

William looked pensive, his memory banks struggling to keep ahead of the game.

'So there might be some genuine evidence from the train and that's why the police are interested, that's exciting isn't it!'

'Oh William, I don't think I can take much more of this, I don't need any more surprises.'

You're in for a bit of a shock then Mum, thought Anita. *We're only at base camp on the mountain of surprises and we're running out of safety ropes.*

'Just think Will, you'll be able to take two sets of spyware back to Miss Techno 2014, she might not be able to contain her delight, you lucky boy!'

That's if she hasn't turned into a gerbil, thought Anita.

Their train pulled into Paddington and as they clambered onto the platform the Hawkins family noticed three uniformed officers of the law rushing in their direction. In the main station concourse a demonstration was taking place. Through the general shouting and babble Anita could clearly hear the chant

PROTECT OUR FREEDOM TO SHOOT HAMSTERS

HUNTING RODENTS IS A HUMAN RIGHT

From what Anita could make out this well attended protest was aimed against government plans to license the shooting of rodents in public places. Luckily Jane and Steven were only concerned with the presence of the law.

'Mr William Hawkins?'

'Yes that's me.'

'If you don't mind we would like you to answer a few questions. We have a vehicle waiting, please bring your family with you and any additional surveillance equipment you have in your possession, this way please.'

Stunned by the speed and intensity of the police action the family followed meekly to the waiting mini bus. Will was trying to hold himself together. He was desperate to configure his memory banks in order not to slip up but he knew he would soon need a rest to recharge his batteries. Anita could see the anxiety on his face, afraid that their subterfuge would be uncovered even at this early hour. She had all her fingers and toes crossed.

The blacked out mini bus soon arrived at its secret location and the family were led at speed through a maze of corridors into a room filled with sophisticated monitoring and analytical equipment. William noticed Nottingham University gear on a nearby table. He knew that the version he carried was a fake, given to the Human William to keep him quiet, but what was recorded on the genuine article? They had gone to a lot of effort to bring the family here in secret so the police must have something. However, this was a parallel universe so who was to know?

COW POX

'So, let me get this clear' asked Aragon. 'Are you saying the child already had the symptoms of Cow Pox and because she was in close proximity when Simu-Suits were removed, somehow fluids from one of your colleagues reacted with the infection and mutated?'

'That seems to be our reading of the situation.'

'You'll have to do better than that Professor Huntley. You could find yourself spending the second half of your life span trapped here on Earth.'

'I hoped, Commander Aragon, that you were about to ask how the child is doing.'

'Well?'

'Our drugs have all but eradicated the Human strain of the infection from her body. However, she is struggling to contain the effects of the Saviorian element which continues to spread and she remains highly contagious but in no immediate danger.'

Jackie Green then spoke. 'I can confirm that the process of Human integration has been paused and that we are quarantining and screening all Padstow residents for signs of the Cow Pox variation. This process must be carried out with due speed and diligence and with the assistance of Humans already involved with the process. May I suggest we also utilize the two ancients from the 21st Century?'

'Thank you Jackie, in the meantime we are working hard to

clear up the Saviorian side of Mary's infection. The last thing we want is a Human death on our hands,' noted the Professor.

ROWING UP TO WADEBRIDGE

Dawn broke over Padstow to a light rain and a cold Easterly breeze. Many locals were up and about early, marvelling at the sight. They stood gazing at the horizon wondering what lay out there, some gaining a new confidence and a desire to explore.

On the derelict harbour a group of four young men launched their makeshift craft into the cold clear waters of the Camel Estuary. Their homemade oars splashing randomly into the unfamiliar waves of the incoming tide. They were heading upstream, the tide in their favour, towards what, they did not know. No one witnessed their departure except the androids in their silver craft circling the town.

The quarantine process had started, new found freedoms cut short because of the poor stricken Mary Brady. Andy, Mario and Karen were ready to help with the planning process while keeping up with Mary's progress. Dina was on her way back in one of the alien transport craft, along with William and Anita. They had been asked not to reveal their background to any of the locals. They agreed this might be too much for them to take in. Instead, they would blend in with the androids,this would not be difficult for Anita.

Their role was to calm any concerns the residents may have about this latest *new* situation. Locals had been asked to stay indoors and wait to be screened and for quarantine to be lifted. William was finding the experience on the ground difficult to comprehend. Here he was in the 26th Century but it was like stepping back to The Middle Ages. These people lived such simple lives with none of the trappings of a 21st Century technology driven existence. No cars, mobile phones, in fact phones of any kind, no TV and no internet or computers. In William's eyes these people were living primitive lives but appeared strangely content. *Were the aliens doing them any favours? Reintroducing them to the outside world?* He certainly sensed a growing feeling of *leave us alone just go away* from many families in the town.

Back at the local Think Tank Professor Huntley was snowed under with concerned messages from around the Saviorian community. For the first time there were even calls to simply open up the entire world and withdraw immediately, leaving the Humans to cope for themselves. This prompted a hastily convened video and telepathic discussion amongst over 1,000 delegates from all over the world and beyond. This continued while the Padstow screening process gathered pace.

The boys in the boat were proving a minor headache having been headed off by an android patrol boat. They had reached the halfway point towards the old town of Wadebridge and were debating whether to enter the dark zone ahead of them when the alien craft approached, its silent engines taking the boys by surprise.

'Please you must return to Padstow straight away, quarantine is in place for all residents.'

'Yes? I reckon you full of bullshit, no intention of givin' us freedom to roam.'

'That's right John, we'm nothin' better than prisoners. You say you been looking after us all these years? Tis rubbish man. Leave us be, for we're off into that grimy blackness to see what's beyond, you have a good day now.'

The boys started to row off at a pace only to find their path blocked. There was no way they could outrun the sophisticated alien craft in their cobbled together hulk.

'You need to return, young Mary Brady has a serious illness and she may have passed it on to you. We need to check you all, back in Padstow. We cannot risk anyone spreading the infection. Once everything is cleared up you are only too welcome to set sail, please climb aboard. Leave your collection of nails and wood, we will help you build something much better when this scare is over.'

'You reckon these boys are tellin' the truth?'

'I think so Billy. If young Mary is proper sick best be on the safe side.'

'You gonna help us build a magic ship like this 'ere beauty, that right?'

'It might not be quite like this but we think you'll approve.'

'Sounds fair to me, come on lads!'

Within seconds they were back in Padstow. The androids had already built a safe landing jetty for incoming craft. The young lads were escorted back to their families with the promise of a seaworthy craft the subject on their lips.

While conducting their house to house examination of Padstow's residents, William had a question for Main, who was now accompanying him.

'All the communities you created three hundred years ago have been receiving the same level of care and attention as this one, is that correct?'

'That is correct, we maintain them all to the same degree.'

'And they have all been taken back to the same primitive balance of existence, living without the trappings of advanced societies?'

'Correct, we needed to give them a chance to grow from the same starting point once isolation ended.'

'Then I believe your plan has a good chance of success. The physical plight of the poorest areas of the Old World must have improved under your care. Those wishing to dominate others by the use of force and advanced weaponry would have found their supply cut off overnight. Now they have to concentrate their efforts on survival and co-operation.'

'You do not realise how wonderful it is to hear a Human support our strategy.'

'When the dark veils are lifted from around the world, everyone will start on a level playing field, with the chance to do things right this time, brilliant!'

'With one major drawback,' noted Andy who had been listening from a distance.

'When you lift all the protective curtains from around the world those people will again be living in the environment that existed before you arrived.'

'You are correct there Andy, we cannot, unfortunately cocoon the Human race indefinitely. We were hoping to integrate and aid with the rebuilding process, however, Mary's infection may yet change everything.'

Despite the best efforts of the Saviorian scientists, Mary's condition was not improving. The blotches on her skin had changed in nature to dark blue and angry looking. At irregular intervals the blotches exploded spreading potentially contagious infection over anything within a two metre radius. In the absence of Dina, who had gone to help in Padstow, Colonel Hafey took it upon herself to bring the parents up to date.

'Mr. and Mrs. Brady, your daughter's condition appears to be changing. We have cured one part of the infection but as yet we are unable to control the remainder.'

'Can we see her yet? We're proper worried and this place gives us the creeps, it's all too much to take in, we're just simple folk happy in our little cottage.'

'Do you trust us Mrs Brady?'

'Well I reckon I does, got no choice in the matter have us?'

'Then please try to relax and we will get you home as soon as possible. We are doing all we can for Mary, hopefully you will be able to see her soon.'

'This ere infection, sorry what's your name?'

'Hafey, Colonel Hafey.'

'Right then Colonel, you say it be half cured, so which bit be cured then, do it have a name?'

'Oh yes, I believe you call it Cow Pox.'

'Oh I heard o that. I remember our Prudence, her youngest caught that years back, cleared up proper well, and quick' noted Mrs Brady.

'So the other half, the bit you'm havin' trouble with, do he have a name?'

'Well not as such, you see it's a new strain.'

'What you mean new where'd he come from then?' Mr Brady was clearly suspicious.

'Well it appears that when you attended the public meeting and our fellow Saviorians introduced themselves, your daughter intercepted some stray saliva.'

'You be right there, she got well soaked poor maid!'

'We believe that was the point at which the infection mutated, a reaction to elements in the saliva.'

'So if I be readin your fancy words right, your man at that there meetin gave our Mary the sickness you can't cure, is I right?'

'Unfortunately Mr Brady, all the evidence points in that direction, we are making every effort to find the antidote, it's only a matter of time.'

'Our little maid would ave been fine now if it wasn't for you meddling slime balls. We're takin' Mary home now, where is she?'

'No George, wait!'

It was too late because Brady had pushed passed the colonel and his wife and was headed to where he thought Mary was being treated. Instead, he forced his way straight into the meeting room where the Saviorian dignitaries were planning their next move. Not expecting any Human interference there wasn't a Simu-Suit in sight. In his haste George stumbled and slid across the phlegm covered floor, coming to rest at the webbed feet of Commander Aragon.

'Sloogosh ash pishock!' exclaimed the amazed highly ranked officer. 'Umph tash floog pishock eephog.'

On his command Simu-Suits were rapidly deployed before the floundering Human could react. Colonel Hafey rushed in from behind.

'My sincere apologies Commander, this is Mr Brady the father of the young Human girl we are treating, he is very anxious to see his daughter and clearly took a wrong turn.'

Picking himself up, George wiped the curdled decomposing sludge from his trouser leg. 'I can't fathom which part o' hell you from, but I'm damn sure it's time you cleared off back there.'

He ran for the door but was stopped in his tracks by his wife. 'George, they say we can see our Mary now, come on it's this way.'

As they followed Colonel Hafey down the corridor a very determined android passed them in the opposite direction. It entered the meeting room unannounced.

'What now?' exclaimed a frustrated Professor Huntley.

'Another sick Human has been discovered in Padstow, same symptoms but a male child this time.'

'No!' was the collective call from the room.

NEXT QUESTION

'We have been trying to contact you for the past few days Mr Hawkins but it appears your phone, and those of your family were all out of action.'

'We were in Cornwall' interrupted Anita. 'You should have tried smoke signals or carrier pigeon.'

'This is a serious matter Miss Hawkins so please don't waste any more of our time and anyway, what is a carrier pigeon?'

'So why exactly have you got us here, we've done nothing wrong.' interrupted Steven.

'All in good time Mr Hawkins. Firstly, you say that your short break holiday was based at the Metropole Hotel. We checked with them and they have no record of you staying there. We phoned them several times, I think they were a little annoyed with us towards the end, but they are clear, you never stayed there!'

'That is ridiculous the weather was so foggy we spent a lot of time in the hotel and it was certainly called the Metropole.'

'That is very interesting in itself Steven, I can call you Steven, can I?'

'Yes yes, what do you mean interesting?'

'What I mean is, Steven, the weather over the past four days in Padstow has been clear and cold, no fog!'

Anita was strangely quiet because she knew the truth. The question was, how much did the police know?

'So the first question must be, if you were not at the Metropole Hotel in Padstow, where were you? However, where you did or did not stay is not our major concern. It is what we found on your recording equipment that really puzzles us.'

'I don't know where you got that spare set of equipment from,' exclaimed William, lying through his gleaming android teeth. 'This is my gear and I brought it back with me on the train today,' he pointed at the bags on the floor.

'Yes, and I was there when he played the tapes back, all that was recorded were old episodes of Dad's Army, so I think we'll be off now and not waste any more of your time.'

'Not so fast Miss Hawkins, I think we need to show you all something.'

What now, thought Anita, she was trying so hard to keep the deception intact. She couldn't second guess what this parallel universe might throw up. Now it would appear there may be more revelations in the hands of the police.

The family were led to a huge screen hooked up to their version of William's recording gear, which as he knew was the genuine article. His imprinted memory from the Human William told him all about his desire to capture something interesting on the tapes, was this the material the police had stumbled across?

'Before we show you what we found William, could you explain why you went to all the effort of setting up this gear in the First Class carriage of a Western Railroad train to Penzance?'

'Excuse me' interrupted Jane. 'We never travelled on Western Railroads, never even heard of it.'

'Please, let William answer the question.'

'Well, it was in connection with my university course in Media Studies. I wanted to observe passenger habits over a long journey.'

The rest of the family gave him a long questioning stare, especially Anita, she didn't realise just how sophisticated android programming had become.

'However,' William continued 'I must have forgotten to select the record function and ended up with these old recordings of Dad's Army.'

Well done William, thought Anita.

'So perhaps you can explain this?'

The huge screen burst into life showing the interior of the First Class railway carriage. The Hawkins family could clearly be seen getting their belongings ready to leave at Bodmin Parkway station. There was no sign of anyone else in the carriage.

'Is this some sort of stitch up!' cried Anita 'We all know modern trains have cameras on board for security, looks like that to me.'

'Yes, haven't you better things to do with you time?' added Jane.

'Please watch the rest of the recording,' insisted Jim Hammond, head of the investigation.

Anita's voice was clearly heard over the images *Might as well do that Sherlock cause nothing is going to happen this time.*

'Can you confirm that the voice on this recording is yours?' asked Hammond

'Well you can't see who's saying those words, it's just a voice on a tape, so no, I cannot confirm it and I suspect neither can you.'

'We can compare your voice patterns with that on the tape, so please do not be obstructive.'

'Ok, it could be me, but so what?'

'If indeed it is your voice, what exactly did you mean by the statement we just heard?'

'Well, the Sherlock bit is a family joke I assume you do understand jokes don't you? The rest, well you heard William say he was studying passenger behaviour. As we were the only ones left in the carriage, he might as well pack his gear up, it isn't rocket science is it?'

'The part about *nothing is going to happen this time,* what does that mean?'

'How much do you get paid for doing this job? Ok simple, there had been other passengers in the carriage at another time, so *this time* there weren't!'

Hammond stared at Anita and she was sure she could detect that now familiar twitch in the face men of this universe exhibited in times of stress or excitement. He knew she could be right on that point, so he moved on.

'Let's see the rest of the recording.'

They watched as the scene instantly changed from colour to negative, the Hawkins family were gone. Then sounds could be heard,

shoorish coshee *ampoo*

William translated under his breath, *We've got them*

Anita heard him but luckily no one else in the room did.

Steven then jumped in 'It must have been a result of the shunting we were involved with as the train entered Bodmin Station. We were all knocked out by the impact, it clearly affected the recording and same goes for the sound quality, distorted.'

'This is the first I've heard of a collision on that date. Samuels, go and check it out with the railroad company.'

His assistant rushed off to find out.

'How much longer are you going to keep us here? I'm starving and I just want to get home,' pleaded Jane.

'Just need to check on this so called shunting. We can rustle up some sandwiches if you like.'

'Oh no it's fine, my treat, I'll get us a meal when we're through here.' Anita had visions of rats heads squashed between two thick slices of wholemeal.

'That's very nice of you but can we get on.'

Samuels soon returned with an answer. 'I've spoken to the Station Master at Bodmin and he assures me there was no incident on that date and has the camera footage to prove it if we want.'

'How interesting, yes get him to send it over. Looks like you'll be with us for lunch after all Mrs Hawkins.'

HEADING FOR THE BLACK MIST

Young John Stevenson was discovered just as the screening of Padstow residents was nearing completion. His parents had tried to hide him for fear he would be taken away like Mary Brady in that strange flying machine. Luckily by hiding him his parents had kept him away from other children, however, he was very poorly. A transport ship had been sent to pick him up. Karen was a close friend of the family having been to school with John's sister Jenna.

'You must let them treat John, they are well meaning creatures.'

'We hear what you sayin Karen, but there's been no word on poor Mary.'

'I'll find out from Mum what the latest is on Mary.'

'That's kind of you maid, if she be alright we'll send our John to the strangers.'

The androids waited patiently outside the Stevenson's house but time was short. Using force was not in their remit but they had to move soon. Karen had spoken to Dina but the news was not ideal, there was no answer yet to the alien pox mutation. She had to be careful with her response to the Stevenson's. A degree of poetic license was called for.

'Mum has spoken to the doctors treating Mary and she has had a partial recovery but still needs some further tests before she can come home. John's best hope is to join her in their hospital over the other side of the estuary, time is something we haven't got Mrs Stevenson.'

'Alright Karen let's do it, but if our John doesn't come home fit and well them slimy little creatures will surely pay,' stated a very concerned father.

The waiting transport craft whisked the family off to join the Brady's. Screening of Padstow was now complete and the town was given a tentative clean bill of health.

Androids reported back to the Think Tank who confirmed the arrival of the Stevenson's. No one was allowed to leave Padstow until the Saviorians had a clear plan going forward.

Andy, Dina, Mario, Karen and Ken had been invited to a special conference along with William and Anita. Frustration was mounting in the wider Saviorian community.

'No, you listen to me, if they strangers from wherever says we not contaminated then to hell with 'em, let's go have a nose around, what you say boys?'

'Right on, they might or might not ave saved us great, great, grandparents but we need to see for oursels what the real truth be. Let's go meet some other folks if there be any out there.'

A group of some twenty young men and women stood in Market Place planning to break the quarantine order. They included the boys who had attempted to sail up the Camel Estuary. They were beginning to exhibit signs of the Human lust for adventure, forgotten over generations. Some were to use the boat again, others to set foot across the fields in random directions. There had never been a need for maps or compasses until now, but they had neither and they could not get access to the library during curfew. It was a cold winter's day and they were ill prepared, their artificial environment having been removed by their guardians. These intrepid explorers, the first for over three hundred years, had no practical knowledge or experience, just an inbuilt desire to reach out.

The old artificial limits of Padstow were being protected by a ring of androids. All Human and Saviorians working on the enlightenment process had removed themselves to the Think Tank for a crucial meeting, not believing that the residents would try to break the cordon. Android lines were far stretched but mobile units riding on all terrain Hyper Bikes bridged the gaps.

Four groups of five set off from Market Place in different directions. They agreed to walk towards any black mist clouds marking the edge of the next commune of Human life. Billy and four other young men managed to reclaim their floating hulk in the harbour. They were not prepared to wait for the aliens help to build a new craft, they had waited long enough! Once they set off the four groups had no way of communicating with one another besides primitive smoke signals and reflective flashes from mirrors. Portable batteries had not been re-discovered and, of course, there were no mobile communication devices. They had no idea what the terrain would be like, possibly overgrown and harbouring dangerous wildlife. In fact, the aliens appeared to be the least of their worries. However, they were determined to spread the word to whoever they met that they were not alone. If the Saviorians were to be believed there were millions of people out there ready to be reunited.

SHE'S NOT MY SISTER

The grand meeting room at the Padstow Think Tank, which had been the venue when Dr Honey had revealed his plans for the integration of Humans and Saviorians, was now the location for the latest emergency conference. For the first time Humans were invited to be involved in decisions regarding the alien withdrawal from Planet Earth, this in itself was a major step forward. One unforeseen element was the presence of two ancient Humans from half a millennium in the past. Talking of which, one such ancient was about to drop a bombshell even before proceedings got underway. William stood up to speak, addressing the dignitaries arranged around the oval table.

'If I may speak before this meeting begins?'

'Yes William, but please make it brief, we have pressing matters to resolve,' noted the chairman, Professor Huntley.

'Thank you, it is my firm belief that the *person* sitting next to me is not my sister Anita. In fact it is not a person at all but a very sophisticated android built to accompany the William creation back to the 21st Century. I believe at the last moment my sister switched with this duplicate and returned home along with my parents. It would be remiss of me not to speak up and air my suspicions. I am deeply shocked that I no longer have the companionship of my dear sister, I ask you to confirm my fears or prove me wrong.'

'You've really lost it this time Sherlock you know it's me you daft plonker. Ask me anything about this geek, I know it all, not that there's much to tell, he's a boring little shit at the best of times.'

'Please, we can delay no longer. This is easily resolved, Colonel Hafey please confirm if we have an android around the table or not.'

'You stay away from me slime ball or I'll gouge your ugly eyes out.'

Anita tried to leave the room but was apprehended by two fellow androids. The Colonel soon discovered the service hatch at the back of Anita's head and immobilised her.

'I am sorry to say it would appear you are right William, you have our deepest sympathy. It is beyond me how this was not detected before now Hafey, answers!'

'We produced a very good replica Professor Huntley, it would appear we are victims of our own success.'

'I only hope your real sister is alive and well back in your time. Your input to our present problem is greatly valued if you feel you can continue.'

'Yes thank you, it is why I stayed behind and ultimately, I fear, why Anita did not,' He wiped away a tear and urged them to continue.

Professor Huntley cleared his cavernous throat and addressed the meeting.

'Fellow Saviorians, in this room and around this planet, Human friends from past and present, we have reached a crossroads. Our plans for integration with the Human race are in grave peril. It would appear that we are a physical danger to Humans, the infection of young Mary and now John evidence of that. Other potential dangers may await us all if we continue along the integration path. Human communes already enlightened are waiting to be allowed freedom of movement, where do we go from here?'

Commander Aragon now spoke, 'It seems to me, and has done for some time, that a great deal of dithering has taken place, not just recently but throughout this mission. The time has come to exit this project, leave the Humans to survive alone. We cannot guarantee that they will not eventually blow this planet up, just like they attempted before, but our work here is done and by delaying any longer we may actually be the cause of their ultimate demise by passing on mutated viruses.'

Professor Huntley again spoke, 'For me, and I believe my other colleagues around this table, it has always been more than a clearing up operation. We have given up half our lives trying to find a way to share the same air as Humans, to guide them to a better future, leave them in a good place. I admit this new viral outbreak is a major blow to our mission here, but how can we abandon them, they have so much to learn? Yes, we saved them from self destruction, but we also returned them to a primitive existence, you might call it their Dark Ages.'

'Can I say something?' William stood up. 'As a 21st Century Human I have a different perspective on your dilemma. The situation Humans find themselves in now is purely artificial, controlled and suppressed for their own protection. We are by nature an adventurous and competitive breed, fiercely independent, always striving for more and better. Would it not be possible to leave these Humans the tools needed to develop again and trust in their better nature? If in another five hundred years they get to the point of self annihilation again then perhaps it was meant to be, a self fulfilling prophesy. At least you gave them a second chance. Perhaps it is time to take a risk, trust in Human nature, pull down your barriers and let them be.'

The room was left in stunned silence, William was proud of his input and secretly thought his sister would have approved.

'Wise words indeed' pointed out Professor Huntley, lost in

thought.

'If I may speak?' Karen rose rather hesitantly, 'From the point of view of someone who has been directly affected by your timely intervention, my father will confirm what I am about to say. I could never accept that our small community was the only one existing on our huge planet. We had many arguments on the subject, but my point is this.. . If I am typical of young people who have spent their lives in a tiny protected community, then we can't wait to get out there and meet others. If this new human race can't make a better job of living in some sort of peace and harmony, then I am a fool. It is our right to have the opportunity to build something good and the sooner the better. We appreciate all you have done for us but it is time for you to leave with our blessing. As William has rightly said, give us the knowledge and let us grow, on our own. Fill our libraries with the truth and practical advice to build a new world, but please let us do it for ourselves. Thank you for listening and by the way, we are not as primitive as you may think.'

Major Main now addressed the meeting 'These are all fine words and very encouraging from my perspective. Perhaps after all these years on your planet we have got so used to taking care of your every need we have lost sight of the real purpose, to return your planet into your safe keeping.'

The meeting was interrupted by a message from androids guarding Padstow while quarantine was still in force. They reported groups of local youngsters attempting to explore beyond their restrictive cordon. They were believed to have expressed a desire to *meet other Humans if they exist out there.* The androids wanted permission to use sleeping gas to prevent their advance.

'What should I tell them?' enquired Colonel Hafey, 'I'm sure they could have the situation under control in seconds.'

There was a spontaneous cry of *NO* coming from every Human

in the room.

'Please just let them go!' cried Karen 'This is our world now, they need to do this, I need to do this, we all do!'

'Karen's right' called out Andy. 'I understand why you used me to perpetuate the nuclear war scenario but that time is over. However headstrong these youngsters are, let them go and join the rest of the world. I believe your task here is nearly over.'

Jackie Green was about to speak but Professor Huntley intervened, 'Sorry Jackie, we need to give our androids on the ground in Padstow an answer. If we let them go and they manage to encounter other centres of population we lose control of the situation. We cannot predict what they might tell them or how they will interact.'

'We could instruct our androids to track them at a safe distance and inform us of any potential problems.' suggested Hafey.

'Good idea Colonel, let's take a vote. Our Human friends please join in, all in favour of allowing the Humans to adventure out beyond Padstow,'

Hands were raised,

'And those against?'

It would appear we have taken the first major step in Human integration even if we are not part of it, the vote is carried unanimously. Colonel Hafey, inform our androids of our decision.'

'Yes Professor.'

'Now Jackie you wanted to speak?'

'Well yes, although your vote rather makes a mockery of what I am about to say. I would like to put on record that I voted against your decision as I would on any further plans towards uncontrolled Human re- integration. The scale of our planet wide operation is mind boggling. A simple rural population is nothing compared to the vast urban conglomerations we have segregated for generations. The potential for chaos is truly immense. We have successfully kept control for centuries, we need to take our time over the next stage or all hell might break out.'

Ken, who had been very quiet up to this point, indicated he wished to speak.

'Please Ken, what would you wish to add?'

'Thank you, yes, as my family well knows I have spent most of my adult life searching for the truth. Things just didn't add up for me. As it happens, I think I qualify as one of the first Human explorers for three centuries. My point is this, the Human race are adventurers by nature, always wanting to push the boundaries. Hold them back now with the knowledge they are about to receive and you will create problems, resentment and possible anger. This is our planet to make of it what we will. You need to take to the skies again with our blessing and thanks, it's time for us to grow, thank you.'

There was a spontaneous round of applause from all the Humans in the room and the hint of a tear in Dina's eyes.

After what seemed an eternity Professor Huntley spoke. 'This meeting has been broadcast to all our bases on Earth. They have all heard our deliberations, I think it is time to make a proposal for us all to vote upon and act accordingly. My proposal is this...'

He had no time to get the words out because, bursting into the room came an android nurse, with the devastating news.

'The Human child Mary Brady has died.'

GREAT JUMPING GERBILS

They played back the video footage from Bodmin Station over and over again at various speeds, with the same conclusion. There was no incident outside the station and even more interestingly, the Hawkins did not get off the train.

'I think I've seen enough' noted an exasperated Jim Hammond. 'Time for an explanation, you are clearly hiding something.'

'I'm sorry,' answered Steven, raising his voice. 'We did get off that train, all be it in a sorry state. The people in the station were very kind and once we had recovered, they took us directly to the Metropole Hotel in Padstow.'

'Again lies Mr Hawkins, the people at the Metropole Hotel have no record of you staying over Christmas, so where have you been?'

'Did the hotel manager give you any receipts to prove you had stayed there?' asked Hammond.

'No I don't think so. You see, we won a competition, everything was paid for, even the drinks.'

'Very unfortunate that Mr. Hawkins, so you have no proof, again I ask you, where were you?'

Anita thought long and hard and then replied. 'Alright, I'll come clean.'

Everyone was all ears. 'I'll remind you, we are recording this conversation, and it can be used in evidence.'

'That's fine. We were abducted by aliens who took us to the 26th Century. William is in fact not my brother but an android replica of himself. The real one is assisting the Saviorians, repulsive little alien creatures, to help the Human race after they nearly destroyed themselves in a nuclear war three hundred years earlier. We were sent back on a train from Bodmin to our own time only to discover we've ended up in a parallel universe where old ladies eat hamster sandwiches, dripping fresh blood everywhere, satisfied now!'

'Anita, I don't know how you think this is helping. Even you can see this is an unnerving situation, yet you still can't take things seriously.'

'Thank you Mrs. Hawkins, you do realise charges can be made for perverting the course of justice,' pointed out Hammond.

'You wanted the truth I've given you the truth. Order a sandwich Mum and see what they offer you.'

'*Shoorish coshee ampoo,*' piped up William who had been enjoying a period of battery revival. 'It means, *we've got them*, it is what the Saviorians said when they retrieved the Humans from the train. You've been wondering what it meant, now I've told you.'

'Don't you start William, this really isn't getting us anywhere.'

'Mr. Hawkins, I am sorry to tell you this but I am not your son. Anita is right I am an android, a very advanced one I will admit. If you wish to confirm this you simply have to pull out my battery holder, it is located at the back of my head. Please be careful, it took ages to get my hair straight after the last time!'

Hammond, not thinking for a moment there was a grain of truth in William's story, instructed a colleague to part William's hair in order to dismiss this ridiculous claim. 'There's nothing there Jim just skin.'

'As I suspected, now my patience has run out I demand...'

'Just press on the back of my neck, a flap should spring open.'

'Well?' Oh just do it man.'

'Great jumping gerbils, what the f...?'

A friendly officer strode into the room. 'Anyone order a rat sandwich on brown bread?'

IN THE NAME OF POOR MARY BRADY

'How could this have happened? Our scientists and doctors were on top of the situation, we had rid the poor girl of half of the infection, what went wrong?'

'It would appear,' reported the nurse 'that the Saviorian portion of the virus, once free from its Human host, mutated and spread to the girl's lungs, she literally drowned in her own mucus and bile. We did all we could Professor.'

'How is the boy doing, dare I ask?'

'John's condition seems to be different. Having learnt from Mary's treatment we left the Human virus in place. It would appear it has started to battle the Saviorian strain, perhaps even to destroy it. We will keep you informed of his situation.'

The android left the room to ear shattering silence.

Eventually Professor Huntley spoke. 'It would appear our mission is failing. We vow to preserve lives at all costs and now this, I am ashamed on behalf of all our kind.'

'If I may say something?' It was William getting to his feet.

'From where I am standing you have nothing to be ashamed of. You saved the Human race from extinction, sacrificed half your allotted lifespan caring for the native population while searching for a safe way to live alongside them, helping them towards a secure future. Where is the shame in all that? The one and only error of judgement was this, you did not feel ready to believe in Human nature, to allow it to reinvent itself alone. I think now you have no choice but to do just that. This mission of yours has been a success and it's up to us now.'

'Thank you for your kind words, however, I doubt whether Mary's parents would agree with you.'

Dina spoke 'It was their choice to let poor Mary stay at the public meeting, to allow her to come to the front for a better view. We did warn people and give them the chance to leave the room and wait in the garden. You had tested thoroughly using Ken and William this could not have been foreseen. Remember, Mary was already carrying the Cow Pox infection.'

'We should not have removed our Simu-Suits it was a step too far.'

'The people would not have believed your story if you hadn't, they needed proof,' added Andy. 'It was a very unfortunate accident and there is no need for blame or guilt.'

'You are indeed a remarkable species,' cried Commander Aragon.' The Atruphix people of Numbus Seven would have vaporised us on the spot, it is time to move on!'

The android nurse returned to the room swiftly followed by Mr and Mrs Brady, clearly distressed. 'We got just one thing to say to thee,' whispered George Brady hardly able to speak. 'It won't bring our beautiful girl back but it as to be said. I never want to see thy ugly rotten faces again. Might be there's good blood in there, if ye have any blood that is, but just shuffle off back te where yer from for all us sakes, I've no fight left in me, go back to hell, now!'

They both burst into floods of tears and couldn't get out of the room quick enough. Dina followed them shortly afterwards to offer any help she could.

'I think it might be time for that proposal Professor Huntley.'

'Yes, well said Commander. I propose a swift but orderly withdrawal of Saviorians and their androids from planet Earth, without any further attempts at integration. I propose a time scale of no more than one Earth year in order to remove all artificial barriers and disseminate practical advice on growth and regeneration.'

'Can I add a further suggestion?' asked Colonel Hafey.

'By all means.'

'That we agree to remove all traces of Saviorian life here on Earth and return areas we have built on to their natural state.'

'Yes, we can ask for that too,' stated Professor Huntley. 'I'm sure more details will get approval when we appoint a Human Liaison Council. I now invite every Saviorian worldwide to vote on this, the most important of all matters.'

Huntley cast his vote and asked for a quick meeting with all Humans in the room.

'As you were all part of our first contact for three hundred years, it would be an honour to have you on our Liaison Council. Hopefully others from the worldwide Human family will join us soon.'

They all replied in the affirmative with enthusiasm.

'Can I have a private word?' asked William.

'What is it my friend?'

'I may be asking the impossible but here goes. As you know my sister Anita switched places with her Android copy and returned to the 21st Century. I miss her and my parents greatly. It is my wish to stay here and help with the Liaison Council's work. Is there any way you could find them and bring them back safely here?'

'As you know William we do employ time travel in our work, however, it is not intended for general use. There are certain dangers attached and with them come responsibility not to abuse this ability. What is more important though, it was your sister's choice to leave. Your parents could still be blissfully unaware of anything out of the ordinary and I imagine, are just happy to be home as well.'

'Yes I see your point, rather selfish of me I know, I just need to know they are alright.'

'I can't promise anything but there may still be a trace on them from the leap. This erodes with time but we could try, at least you would know they were safe. As a favour to a valued friend I will ask our scientists to look into it but I make no promises.'

'Thank you, it would put my mind at rest so I can concentrate on the work here.'

Professor Huntley asked Colonel Hafey to put a couple of the team of android scientists who had worked on the Hawkins scenario to find the answers William wanted.

VOICES THROUGH THE DARK

'You can't seriously be thinking of hanging this boy, it's barbaric, stop at once!' shouted Sue at the top of her voice, her companions by her side.

At first little notice was taken of her, then the crowd fell silent, staring, and dumbstruck.

'Good God, who the hell are you, where did you come from, does anyone know these people?'

'Never mind all that, you can't be doin this sort o thing it's just wrong, you mad the lot o you!' cried Simon.

A man wielding a clip board and some sort of makeshift loud hailer appeared from the midst of the crowd.

'Of course it's not real, just like you can't be. Where have you been hiding all your lives? We do this every week, this was a particularly good one, especially with Seth's late intervention.'

'Do what every week?' asked Gwen.

'Live entertainment, good isn't it, convinced you! We're getting quite good at it, should be after all these years. We take turns at directing, but you know all that don't you?'

'So it's all some kind of joke, a bit of a laugh is it?'

'Well yes, certainly relieves the boredom, anyway what's your story, where you been hiding, does anyone know these young folk?'

'NO!!' came the resounding reply.

'Never seen em before.'

'Tis a real mystery, who on God's Earth are you?'

'Why don't you ask Seth Trevarion, he knows where we came from, he heard us no more than an hour ago,' answered Sue.

Seth, now free from his stage prop shackles, looked nervous.

'You know these strangers Seth, surely you made up the bit about hearing voices in the darkness, thought it was a brilliant last minute addition to the play,' said Don Rogers who had been playing the judge.

Seth stepped forward to speak. 'Well actually, I were tendin to old Daisy in top field, she been havin terrible pain in her fore leg. Any road, it were right close to a spot near world's end. Suddenly I hears these voices, they be comin from the darkness, quiet first then proper clear. *Let's go spread the word,* I hears. Well, I reckoned play was startin dreckly so I legs it down off field straight ere, but I did hear them voices.'

'Would you recognise any of the voices if you heard them again?'

'Might do, not sure.'

'But you didn't see anyone?'

'No sir, like I says, I ran straight ere, didn't want to miss me part, never bin in one o they plays afore.'

Simon spoke up 'Is there anyone out there can you hear me!'

'Well I'll be......tis e, the voice, tis yours right?'

'You right there Seth twas me callin out.'

The crowd gasped in unison, did these strangers really come out of the darkness? Impossible, the poisoned mist would have killed them on the spot, they'd been told that in all the books they read from the library.

A voice from the crowd spoke up. 'You're in disguise aren't you, farmer Jones's brood, they ain't ere, reckon that's who you be. It be part of the play, well I'll be dammed, had us worried there for a spell.'

'Yes, that's it!' shouted the crowd.

'Come on, wem off home, haven't had such a laugh in donkeys!'

'Stop, this is silly, we're wasting time, we can prove who we are. We'll go back into the darkness, it's harmless, just a kind of smoke. We're from Padstow, some of you might have heard of it. It's a miracle and we just want to share it with you, come on, take five minutes, follow us,' cried Sue.

Before anyone had a chance to reply the five strangers had left the hall. Like the Pied Piper, the townsfolk of St Merryn were following in a chain along the street, down the hill, out of town towards the edge of darkness. The trail of villagers stopped well short, not wanting to risk possible death but the *Padstow Five* walked on, right up to the edge.

'Are you watching?' they cried

'No tricks, in we go.'

'No don't, you'll kill yourselves!' Shouted the crowd.

Then they were gone.

The crowd stood in silence, waiting for who knows what, shocked that these people could commit certain suicide. Then, as the good people of St. Merryn stood shaking their collective heads, the outlines of five figures slowly emerged from the mist.

'Now do you believe us?' cried the strangers.

Many fainted on the spot, some stood open mouthed, others ran for the safety of their homes. A few brave souls crept forward, hand in hand with their new neighbours. Trying not to breathe, they entered the mist. A few seconds later shouts from the darkness,

'It's true.'

'It'safe!'

'I'm still alive.'

'How can it be?'

'It's a miracle!'

They ran from the gloom, joy on all their faces.

'You people have a lot of explaining to do,' a local dignitary spoke up. 'However, this tale is for the whole village to hear. Call the people back straight away and let's hope it's not a work of fiction you are offering us.'

HAND THEM OVER TO THE U.I.D.

'So Mr. Hawkins, when did you receive the medical implant in your neck? I thought I was up to date with scientific advances, but I've not seen this before?'

'How thick are you? This is an android so do you want him to screw his head off to prove it?'

'Did you say rat sandwich, I'm sure that's what you said?' questioned Jane, beginning to doubt her own sanity, and certainly that of her daughter. 'I do know one thing, that is not my son William, so what is going on?'

The police officers were having a private conversation.

Jim Hammond came back with developments. 'We are handing this case over to the Unaccountable Investigations Department. They specialise in abnormal cases, this clearly being one. We will be finding you somewhere to stay in London while the investigation proceeds. We ask you not to talk to anyone about what we've discussed in this room. I do not confess to know what's been going on here but it's out of my hands now. Someone will come and escort you to your accommodation. In the meantime please have some lunch, I take it you do not care for our exquisite rat, so we will find something bland like cheese. I take it you must be vegetarians or some other strange foodies?'

'He did say rat. Anita, what is going on? I'm so tired, I just want to go home.'

'Let's just have something safe to eat and I'll try to explain, but God knows where to start!'

Tea, sandwiches and cake were brought to them in the police canteen. The family plus one android sat huddled round a table while Anita did her best to explain the scenario as it had unfolded. At first Steven and Jane thought their daughter was plain bonkers. William, the android, helped a little by giving further evidence of his mechanical composition. This included detailed examination of his synthetic skin and a neat trick involving interchangeable limbs. Tears were shed at the thought of never seeing their real son again but the parallel universe was the icing on the cake.

Steven was fighting hard not to descend into complete insanity while Jane just kept saying 'Rats, why rats?'

Anita was beginning to doubt her own mind hoping, she would wake up and find it had all been a long disturbing nightmare. However, there was Will, proof if ever they needed it, that a dream it certainly was not.'

'If you are all ready we need to take you to your secure accommodation. You will need to have a good night's sleep in order to be ready to face our colleagues at U.I.D. you can be sure, one way or another, they will get to the bottom of this. Please follow me.'

Hammond led them to a waiting blacked out car. Jane's request to contact her mother was refused as was Anita's to contact her friend Molly who would be desperate for a girl's night out. They were asked to make a short list of people who might be concerned and they would be contacted by the police. Anita very much hoped these contacts all existed in this parallel of worlds.

A NEW START FOR ALL

Jackie Green, who had now come round to the idea of a swift withdrawal from Earth, would take charge of overseeing this immense task, she did not have long to wait on the outcome of Professor Huntley's vote. Commander Aragon explained the results.

'Having asked the opinion of the entire Saviorian population here on Earth, the decision has been made. With a three quarters majority, we choose to leave this planet within the next twelve months.

'Steps will be taken with immediate effect to remove any restrictions on the native population. They will be made aware of our roll in their recent history and the second chance we have afforded them. Remote help through the androids and the written word will promote a relatively speedy development from the highly primitive state they find themselves in now. Ultimately it is the responsibility of humankind to build a safe and secure future, we will not be returning here again.

'Plans are already in place for your next assignment which, I personally hope, will not prove as protracted as this one has turned out to be. Saviorians and Humans will convene a working council to share ideas and plot a future path for all those living on this planet.'

Applause broke out in the chamber and smiles all round from

the Humans present. Even William, who was not from this time, was delighted for the new Human race, interested to see which direction they would take.

There still needed to be a controlled awareness programme. The main instruction to androids was to watch and advise, not to intervene. It was judged important that all communities in all areas of the world had the chance of the same start to their new existence.

The dismantling of Saviorian hardware was to begin straight away and Humans would not have access to any of it, when they leave their technology would go with them. Every small section of Human society would be given the same helping start. This would prove as interesting in formerly deprived areas of the globe as it would in previously advanced and powerful states. Large urban areas, which had experienced the greatest change when the aliens arrived, had reverted to self sufficiency amongst the decaying remains of skyscrapers, motorways and railways, useless to them when the aliens imposed their quarantine on the old world.

Probably the greatest influence on future development initially would be the climate, which had been controlled under the Saviorians.

All this was speculation for the time being, the priority had to be supporting Humans through the latest traumatic period of their history.

'William, can I have a word?' It was Dr. Honey approaching. 'You requested a trace on your family's return to your own time and our scientists have given me some news. To the best of their knowledge, and time travel is not an exact science, they believe they have found a footprint. We are rather puzzled however, it would appear your family and our android, have jumped into a parallel universe.'

'So are you saying they didn't get home? Are they in any danger, where exactly are they?'

'No, I'm sorry to say they didn't get back to your version of home. These places take many forms, they may believe they are home but then notice certain differences in the way this world or its society functions. On the other hand things could be quite unstable and therefore potentially hostile.'

'Oh no, can you bring them out of there. What could have caused this, we returned alright the first time?'

'It is likely to be one of two things. Anita might be a factor because she interacted in the 26th Century, potentially altering history, or William the android may have had an effect because he was taking the place of a Human who had previously travelled to our time.

'The only way we can possibly retrieve your family is to use the same time portal as before. The android need not return as it is disposable.'

'If I understand you correctly, they would have to catch a train with tickets for the year 2514 or 2515 as the year is about to change, and travel to Bodmin as before?'

'That is correct William, however, we are assuming conditions in this parallel universe are compatible. Bodmin might not exist there or even railways for that matter. There is also the small problem of getting the tickets to them across time and space.

'I checked that we still have our contact link, established when you were captured on the previous two occasions. We can attempt an android cyber corridor if his locator signal is still working. Through this we can send tickets for him to print off and distribute to the family. If the parallel is very similar to your 21st Century version we may be in luck, I won't depress you with the odds on success.'

'How long will the process take?'

'If the cyber corridor is still in action it should be instantaneous, I will instruct our scientists at once.'

'And If it fails?'

'If it fails, your family will be spending the rest of their lives in a confused state, not knowing what unknown turns their new world might take.'

REINTRODUCING HUMANS TO THEMSELVES

Sue had addressed the community of St Merryn and had drawn the admiration of her fellow explorers by the way she carefully explained the situation, to the best of her knowledge. Clearly not entirely convinced by her version of events, the good people required concrete proof. The meeting elected ten representatives to accompany the Padstow folk back to their own little town. They hoped to obtain enough evidence to persuade their residents that they were not alone in the world after all.

Just as they emerged from the Meeting Hall and the chosen ones started their walk to the dark zone, the horizon began to change. The dense black curtain started thinning and very soon evaporated completely. The people could see for miles over the hills and the sea beyond their village was a shimmering azure blue. They could smell the sea air as an unusually cold breeze began to blow. Clouds began to fill the sky at the wrong time of day and the world was awakening to the annoying squawk of seagulls.

'You said this would happen but I confess I thought you were barmy' cried a village elder.

Many sank to their knees and, as had happened in Padstow, others just stood and stared.

'We would still very much like to take the walk to Padstow with you, if you don't mind.'

A great deal more than ten started the walk over the fields, witnessing for the first time the alien structures crossing the landscape. Androids could clearly be seen as they began the dismantling process and great transport craft filled the skies. The evacuation process was underway, this was it and there would be no turning back.

The peoples of two villages chatted like old friends, united again after three centuries. The talk was of disbelief, boundless excitement and planning for a new future. An hour or so later this happy band crossed over from the barren wasteland of three hundred years neglect onto farmer Smyth's immaculately cultivated land, on and down the lanes into Padstow. The place was swarming with people, packing the streets and pathways, laughing and joking. Many turned to witness their arrival. Peter noticed one of the boys who had set sail for Wadebridge.

'John, youm back then, how'd you fair upstream?'

'Them folks up there thought us bonkers. One old boy reckoned we was ghosts back to haunt he for pinchin his brother's pigs, silly old duffer. Twas only when thon dark mist started liftin did they listen. Here, they got some fancy ploughin gear so I reckon we be havin to get a few ideas from em. Any roads, some o they boys ave old boat wrecks likes us, makin their way ere soon, thinks they can thrash us at darts! What they like? Others they comin on foot, tis like one big family gatherin. Who you got ere then?'

'Oh these folks is from St Merryn, I got a yarn to tell you about they, but it'll keep.'

'How do, welcome to Padstow, fantastic ain't it, come and have a warm in the pub.'

The third group of explorers had made swift contact with the people from St Issey who had also made it to Padstow. Humanity was reintroducing itself to its neighbours and the Ship was running out of ale. Soon they hardly noticed the activities in the skies overhead as transport craft zoomed out of sight on their way to the Mother Ship.

Padstow, although a tiny town, was to have three representatives on the World Council. Andy and Dina chose to stay at home and work at grass roots level to help the residents of Padstow reinvent themselves, if they wanted his help that was. Dina had learned much from the Saviorians about medicine and wished to remain in town with Andy. Mario also felt his place was at home and he knew his job would become a little more complicated in an open world. As for William, Karen and Ken, they would soon be flying off to join the fledgling Council which would convene in the suburbs of old Pyongyang where three centuries ago the decision was made by its Leader to initiate the insane destruction of the rest of the world.

MESSAGE FROM THE FUTURE

In their remarkably comfortable hotel suite somewhere on the banks of the Thames, the Hawkins and William the android, having rested, were trying to come to terms with their situation. They had been told to be ready at 8.30am the next day when they would be driven to U.I.D. headquarters for interrogation, but they didn't like the sound of that.

'So Will do I call you Will or do you have another title?'

'Will is fine Mr. Hawkins, because that is who I was programmed to be.'

'Good, well, Anita has painstakingly explained our situation, however, if it wasn't for your presence here I would be convinced that our daughter had finally lost all contact with the real world. I still cannot believe Jane and I spent two entire holidays blissfully unaware that we were actually visiting a future world, overseen by aliens, there I've said it. As for this parallel thing, well that's just crazy. So a policeman has a weakness for the odd rat sandwich, it hardly justifies your explanation, Anita.'

'We want to believe you dear, but you must admit it's a lot for us to take in,' added Jane.

'Well, if it's any consolation, I thought our William was off his tree with this magic tunnel business and his fixation with Padstow but I know now where it all led.'

'Switch on the TV, let's try and catch the news,' sighed Steven.

The riots in central London have now spread to other major cities in the country. Police have the situation under control for now but warn protestors they will shoot to kill if any rodent retailers are targeted. The latest disturbances are a response to Government proposals to restrict the sport of shooting rodents in public places. They want to charge a fee to license the activity.

In other news, the recently elected far right Ruthlessness and Fear party in Australia has brought forward legislation to impose the death penalty on anyone found surfing at a public beach. A spokesman for Donald Wiseman the new President stated that this obscene behaviour has no place in modern society and will be stamped out forthwith.

Sports news now and Global Cricket has approved the use of deep frozen warthog testicles for forthcoming limited overs matches. The authorities believe the improved bounce achieved will lead to skill levels improving throughout the sport.

'Alright Anita, please turn it off I've seen enough!' shouted Steven. 'We need to prepare ourselves for what might happen tomorrow. After watching that, who knows what rules apply here?'

William, who had just rebooted himself, made a suggestion, 'I am sure the best course of action is to stick to the facts as we know them. You are the innocent parties in my makers plan to kidnap you into the 26th Century, their motives were honourable so let's hope these people see it that way. I suggest you spend some time formulating a tight story they cannot pick holes in.'

'The tin man is right,' commented Anita. 'Let's get through tomorrow and worry about warthogs later.'

Suddenly William's head began rotating on his shoulders, like in some old horror film. When this gyration began to slow, he tried to speak. At first the others could only catch a few letters of words as his mouth passed by.

'Inc..ing .es..ge ..om ..ber l..k W. m.y .e a.e .o.esc.. h..ans .ro. p. r.ll.l uni..rse.'

'What's he trying to say because I'm afraid his head might spin off and kill one of us,' noted Anita.

'Much better now, here's the message,

Incoming message from cyber link. We may be able to rescue Humans from parallel universe, activate your printer for important documents.'

'What does all that mean Will, where's this message coming from? Tell us.' pleaded Jane.

'I must keep cyber link channels open and conserve battery power. William is downloading documents shortly, tell you all then.' His head slumped to his lap and he began to hum like some meditating priest.

I'll put the kettle on,' announced Jane, not knowing what to say or do. 'Expect we could all do with a brew, well maybe not err, him' pointing at the android.

'What do you think it means Anita, is the message coming from your friends in the future, is our William somehow behind it? Listen to me! None of this makes any sense.' Steven was starting to lose it again.

'It's beyond me but if Sherlock has a hand in it, God knows what might happen next. I'm just intrigued to know which orifice the paper comes out of!'

'Tea's up any news?'

The android's hum had turned into a series of clicks as his mouth shot open.

'Well, that answers my question, that's a relief.' joked Anita.

Three small rectangles of card shot out of the slot below William's nose, Steven caught them before they reached the floor.

This was followed by several sheets of what looked like instructions on A4 this time retrieved by Anita. The exertions were clearly too much for the android and he shut down again.

'What have you got there then Dad?' enquired Anita while trying to read the other downloads.

'I don't believe this, I'm holding train tickets dated 27th December 2514 from London Paddington to Bodmin Parkway.'

'Holy shit, not again!'

'What do your papers say Anita?'

'Oh! Let me see, it's addressed to us, the Hawkins family.'

If you receive this cyber link message through android XL100, or William as you know him, the scientists at the Think Tank Federation District Six in Padstow have managed to maintain a trace to your location.

THERE ARE CONCERNS ABOUT YOUR SAFETY LOCATED AS YOU ARE IN A PARALLEL UNIVERSE.

At the request of your family member William Hawkins, we have endeavoured to locate you and bring you here to Earth 2514. Time travel is not an exact science, as you will now be aware, however we are confident in our ability to complete this task successfully.

We are now sure that the presence of XL100 during your time slip caused your unfortunate arrival in your present location. In order for us to execute your retrieval we ask that you follow the instructions below, to the letter. Any deviation from this process will result in failure and you will be trapped in your other world for ever. There are no second chances for this delicate operation.

Here are your instructions, assuming you have access to a Paddington Station and a Bodmin Parkway, we are, as you say in business.

Board any train scheduled to stop at Bodmin, this must be completed on 28th December 2514.

Do not arouse suspicion, if asked, you are taking a holiday in Cornwall, you will be familiar with this scenario by now.

If asked by a ticket inspector, use the ticket misprint excuse again, as well as Anita's charm!

Prepare to leave the train at Bodmin Parkway as before, this is when the Time Jump will occur. The location for your arrival will be our laboratory in the Fox Institute, as there is no need to create a cover scenario this time.

Please do not deviate from these instructions, this is your one and only opportunity. Your brother sends his love, he is well.

'This is incredible, how is it possible to send messages back from five hundred years in the future let alone use good old fashioned train tickets to send ourselves forward to the 26th Century? I must hand it to you Anita, I'm beginning to believe there's some truth in all of this.'

'You'd better believe it Dad. But how the hell are we going to get to Paddington Station when our rodent loving friends are planning some sort of interrogation in the morning?'

'We must convince them that we are the innocent party in this whole unbelievable adventure, hoping they release us in time to catch a train to Bodmin.'

'Yes, as simple as that Mum. They clearly believe we are part of some sort of conspiracy. If they shoot people for breaking into pet shops what have they planned for us?'

At this point William returned from his self imposed shut down. 'Our scientists are amazing aren't they, what a fantastic plan. You must all be thrilled, no, what's the problem?'

Anita explained the small matter of next morning's grilling.

'Oh that, don't worry if things are going badly I have a few tricks up my sleeve. Remember, I can't come with you but I can aid in your escape if needs be. So, take a leaf from my book, recharge your batteries and think positively, for tomorrow you're going on another holiday!'

ARRIVAL IN PYONGYANG

William, Karen and Ken took a few unsteady steps from their Hyper Speed Transport ship to Pyongyang. For Karen and Ken the unusual stresses on the body travelling at such a speed were something, thankfully, they would not have to get used to for long. Even William had only flown in a conventional 21st Century jet a couple of times on holiday, but nothing like this.

The half hour journey had afforded them very few views of the world under the Saviorians but they did get glimpses at take-off and landing. The honeycomb of small Human communities below each had their own individual boundaries of black still intact. Hi tech alien installations between primitive indigenous settlements highlighted how much work would need to be done.

The former capital of the most evil dictatorship the world had ever witnessed was an interesting location for this New World Council to convene. Even during William's time, North Korea, as it was known then, was a rogue state with destabilising intentions. Two hundred years later the despot Ty Jung Co had brought mankind to the brink of extinction by aiming the largest nuclear weapon ever constructed at the heart of Europe, believing world domination would be his final prize. Only the Saviorian intervention prevented total annihilation.

A massive cleansing operation stripped away all evidence of

the evil tyrant's armoury and that of all warmongering nations of 2214. Some crumbling ruins, reminders of that terrible time, remained amongst the pristine rice fields of 26th Century Korea. Protected enclaves were living the same clean simple lives as their fellow Humans in Padstow, Prague and Pennsylvania.

The New World Council building had already been constructed. However, technology used in the final months of protective occupation would soon vanish, leaving the world to grow again at its own pace. This vast complex, quite eerily empty when the three of them arrived, would gradually fill up with delegates from around the emerging Human world. Signs were still encouraging, every passing hour more and more communities were being reunited, with little sign of animosity towards the custodians of their fledgling world.

Jackie Green was there to greet Ken, Karen and William, introducing them to other wide eyed newcomers from far flung places. One concession to the use of alien technology had already been agreed. Their Instant Language Translator, a simple implant in the ear, was offered to all delegates on arrival, reducing the chance of dialogue being lost in translation. The Council, when complete, would represent the whole world's population in miniature. Plans formulated and agreed here would be taken back to indigenous populations for implementation. Saviorian transport ships would be used to place delegates back in their local areas armed with practical guides to sustainable growth and social interaction. It would be years before the delegates met again, they may even have been replaced by then. Only when transport methods had developed and communications technology good enough would more regular meetings become viable. However, there would be some structure in place, in the twelve months left, for unified growth to have a chance.

Hour by hour more delegates arrived. As the first location on the planet to be made aware, the three representatives from Padstow had the privileged task of encouraging social bonding amongst other delegates, although little effort was needed, everyone wanted to share in this miracle.

For Karen, this was a dream come true. All her short life she had dreamt of meeting others, for she never accepted Andy's version of history. Now, here she was talking to a delegate from North Africa about the impact unregulated climate would have on their development once the aliens had removed their artificial weather settings. Inequalities would soon appear.

It was proving difficult for many just to accept the world had been widely populated while all the time being in isolation, it was as if they had been punished for their forefather's mistakes. Mostly however, there were tears, hugs and liberal back slapping, excitement for the future and a desire to be allowed to manage their own planet again. Now integration was off the table only the delegates would have firsthand knowledge of the visitors and their way of life. There was no point giving Humans access to Saviorian secrets, instead they would provide stimulus for creative thought through the written word and one to one sessions with the delegates, who would pass on their knowledge when they returned home.

William, like Ken and Karen, could not get enough of inter-Human contact but he was also anxious for news of his own family back in the 21st Century. He took some time out to see if there was any news, and was grateful when Jackie Green linked him up with Professor Huntley back in Padstow.

'Hello William, I trust you are making new friends in Pyongyang?'

'It's truly unbelievable Professor, the excitement here is electric. Can I ask if you have any news of my family?'

'Well, as you Humans say, so far so good. We know that our messages have been received and paper tickets downloaded through the medium of XL100, sorry, your namesake William, so we have located them. However, this is only a one way signal link, and we have no way of knowing what conditions are like where they are. The transfer tickets are only useable for the designated date of travel, which translates to less than twenty four Earth hours and counting, it is now a matter of wait and see.

Time is also limited here in Padstow as the Think Tank is due to be closed down and removed in the next two weeks. Let us hope we can bring them here in the next few hours.'

'I cannot thank you enough, Professor.'

'After all you have done for the process this is the least we can do. As soon as we have any news I will personally contact you. In the meantime please continue your important work at the World Council.'

William took a moment to reflect on what his family might be going through but soon realised it was a futile exercise. He had to concentrate his efforts in Pyongyang 2514 and trust he would be reunited with them soon.

MARY FOCUSES MINDS

Young John Stevenson's recovery was remarkable. It would seem the gamble to let the Cow Pox virus fight the alien infection was paying off. He was no longer contagious and his parents were readying themselves for a return home to Padstow.

'If only we had treated Molly Brady the same way we might not be beating such a hasty retreat from Earth and she may have been alive to witness the new dawn,' Nash was in pensive mood.

'It is highly regrettable, I must admit,' agreed Professor Huntley. 'However, it has focused our minds on a swift withdrawal which I feel will now be the best option for both our species.'

The transport shuttle carried John and his parents back home to the harbour in Padstow. The family were welcomed with relief and sadness that Mary wasn't with them.

They couldn't help noticing how the town had moved on so quickly since they accompanied John to the alien hospital. There were strangers from other surrounding villages sharing stories and planning for the future. The main focus seemed to be on reaching out further. The harbour was a hive of activity. Several new vessels, if primitive in design, were being launched into the water. There was a task force employed on repairing the harbour walls and clearing three hundred years of neglect from its shores. Fields, once on the edge of oblivion, were being prepared for cultivation although, it now being winter, the unfamiliar concept of seasonal variations had to be factored in. Farmers were sharing their equipment with neighbours they never knew existed. Any negative thoughts, and there were a few, were reserved for their *minders* whose extensive footprint on Earth was shrinking rapidly. Locals couldn't help keeping one eye on what was happening across the estuary.

'Looks like they be in some hurry to leave, things is vanishing afore me eyes. Them there flyin ships is buzzin around like bees, you got any news Andy?'

'We've been told they'll be gone from Padstow in no more than two weeks. They plan to retreat to only a few centres worldwide along with their big ships up there in the skies. Then, this time next year, they'll be gone forever.'

'Can't come soon enough for me,tis enough havin new neighbours without they slimy critters still interfering.'

'We have a lot to thank them for, Jake, remember that.'

'That's as maybe but tell that to young Mary's folks. No tis time they was out of us hair. Oh no! Here comes that flamin' rain again, will it never stop. I takes it all back, they was good with weather!'

Andy ran off for shelter, passing Dina on the way.

'Have you heard any news of Karen and Ken? I can't believe they're so far away, with no way to even talk to them. What if they never come back?'

'Don't talk like that we have to trust them *slimy critters*, as Jake puts it. The plan is to send Karen and Ken back with lots of practical advice and knowledge from other people out there who we may never meet in the flesh. When the aliens go, we'll be left to fend for ourselves, again.'

'Is it true they plan to be gone from these parts in less than two weeks?'

‘Seems that way, but Major Main promised to visit us tomorrow, so we can quiz him then.’

‘Ok, I’m off to swat up on some of that medical stuff they planted in the library. I reckon we might have to train up some new nurses to cope with newcomers who plan to live here.’

GERTRUDE AND STAN FROM THE U.I.D.

William's onboard alarm woke them up with a start at 6.30am. Not that they had managed much sleep. Any dreams they may have had could not have been worse than the nightmare scenario they found themselves in. It was worst for Steven and Jane, they had just spent Christmas living a total lie, although some of it began to make sense now, like the way the hotel manager had been reluctant for them to stray out of doors, the constant fog that shrouded the town, taxis to take them everywhere and roast turkey with the giblets still in place.

They dearly wanted to see their son again, to say *sorry you were right.* They had almost forgotten the first *holiday* in Padstow, which as it turned out was another non reality, played out five hundred years in the future. They had travelled through time twice and been unaware both times. Today, with a lot of luck and help from an android, the third trip would reveal the truth they had both missed.

They were planning on telling the truth, as Anita and William knew it, to their interrogators at the Unexplained Incident Department. They figured that, to prove what they had to say was true, a representative of the U.I.D. should accompany them on their train to Bodmin and witness their jump to the 26th Century. That would be the ultimate test of their story. If they didn't go along with it then William would have to blow himself up alongside their captors while the Hawkins made their escape. They agreed that the favoured option would afford the android a few more weeks grace before his batteries expired. He fancied a spot of surfing in Australia, dodging the bullets.

The hotel specialised in gourmet breakfasts. The guests had the enviable choice of Grilled Gerbil with Beaver Black Pudding and the option of a side order of Crispy Chinchilla Tails, or, if that wasn't tempting enough, Rat and Coypu Compote on a bed of Gopher Giblets. The Hawkins opted for the vegetarian option, beans on toast.

'Are you sure we cannot tempt you to one of our specialities. We use only fresh ingredients, reared and shot by local farmers on free range plots. The farmers suffered no stress or anxiety during the kill.'

'No thank you, we're really not that hungry,' answered Jane.

Actually they were starving and would have killed for a full English.

'So, we've got this straight, Anita will do most of the talking, should have no trouble with that dear!' joked Steven, trying to lighten the mood.

'Glad to hear our current situation hasn't dampened your razor sharp wit Dad. The real problem may be if they decide to poke around with Will now they know his little secret. We still need the option of plan B if needed,' noted Anita.

'Don't worry about me' whispered William, 'If they come anywhere near me again they'll get a nasty shock, 20,000 volts right where it hurts!'

'Mum, have you got the tickets safe, we're stuck here for life if we lose them.'

'Don't worry Anita, they're safe in my bag, your Dad will tell you, it's impossible to get into.'

They had just managed to devour a second portion of beans on toast when the heavies arrived. Three goons dressed from head to toe in black. The family couldn't help noticing they were heavily armed and clearly meant business. The hushed whispers and nods in the hotel lobby suggested the uniform was a familiar one and the sympathetic smiles the family received told them the other guests were relieved it wasn't their turn to be whisked away.

'Come quickly with us, there is a car waiting outside, we do not want to attract attention.'

Fat chance of that thought Anita, they were getting used to being driven around in blacked out cars.

As the time passed they realised this journey was going to be much longer than they had anticipated. Any possible escape to Paddington Station might prove difficult to say the least. After a good hour and a half a bang on the roof was their cue to get out. It would appear they had arrived, the location in dense woodland somewhere south of London. An imposing Victorian mansion in extensive manicured grounds seemed an unusual location for U.I.D. headquarters, clearly they had a large budget.

'Please follow me.'

The black clad gorilla led them to a concealed door at the rear of the building, his retina recognition gaining instant access. Swiftly they were ushered down a long and dimly lit corridor, doors leading off either side at regular intervals. William was stocking up his memory banks in case they had to retrace their steps in a hasty retreat. Anita tried looking in the rooms as they passed but was roughly pushed on her way towards a huge oak door in a dark alcove.

A loud rap on the door was answered with a swift 'Enter!'

An enormous oval table filled most of the room. At one end sat a stern faced battle ship of a woman in her sixties. Arranged around her, six other ladies, darkly dressed in various shades of sombre, a popular choice in these parts, they were clearly not in party mood.

'Sit, all of you, yes you too android. As you were made aware yesterday, your case has been referred to us by the regular ineffective police force. Here at the U.I.D. we pride ourselves on getting to the bottom of all cases.'

'ALL cases!' chorused the coven around the table.

'I will admit this is a strange one, quite an elaborate tale, time travel and aliens. Normally in cases like this we could put it all to bed in minutes. You would all be declared insane and at best locked up for the rest of your mortal lives. However, we have you!' She banged her fist on the table and pointed an accusing finger at William. 'We need to know where you got him from, and quickly. He's clearly very advanced. We pride ourselves at the U.I.D. we get to know everything.'

EVERYTHING repeated her six sisters in unison.

'That's right, so who's going to tell us where you stole him from?'

Anita glanced at her watch, it was already 10.45am, and time was not on their side.

'At the risk for being locked up for life, he is actually from the 26th Century and came back with us on a train from Bodmin and, if you want to know EVERYTHING we can help you. In fact, you could save yourself valuable prison space and at the same time solve another case, just by going along with my little plan.'

'Inspector, this female is clearly unhinged, we have our reputation to uphold, swift solutions to unsolved cases, I say we reject the soft option and just shoot them, sell the tin man for scrap!'

'I admire your honesty Gertrude, however, I will remind you that our department has come under increasing scrutiny since this liberal soft bellied government was elected, shooting suspects is no longer a preferred option.'

The Hawkins family were visibly shaken, stretching to hold hands under the table. Paddington Station seemed a long way away.

'I will check the so called android for serial numbers or maker's logo, someone must be missing him. He's quite something, precision engineering, and so lifelike, we could make a tidy profit on the black market.'

A prod to the chest released an electric shock of 20,000 volts sending Gertrude flying across the room in a cloud of smoke and fumes. She lay, a crumpled smouldering heap in the corner of the room.

A team of what looked like garbage collectors entered and shovelled her up into a giant refuse sack, another problem swiftly dealt with.

Anita glanced at her watch 11.15am, she had an idea.

'You look like a reasonable woman,' she said, biting her tongue. 'There is a way for you to clear up this little problem you have with us and at the same time, enlist the services of our William. He could prove a valuable addition to your department, as you can see, he can be very persuasive. Are you ready to listen to my plan?'

Inwardly she was shaking like a leaf and her parents were watching, pondering, *Is this really our daughter?*

Her proposal prompted their captors to initiate private whispering. Gertrude had already been replaced by the repulsive Prudence. They emerged from the huddle with combined sickly smiles.

'We would be interested to hear your plan as long as it can be concluded swiftly, we pride ourselves on resolving problems quickly.'

'QUICKLY' the response was deafening.

Here goes everything thought Anita. 'We need to catch the next available train to Bodmin from Paddington Station. You need to accompany us to witness the outcome. We will literally vanish from your world as the train approaches Bodmin. William will remain behind as a valuable tool in your department. If our plan does not work you will be free to resolve the problem in your own unique and rapid way.'

'Interesting' mused Helga. 'And how do we know this android will go along with your plan?'

'Oh, William is quite subservient, aren't you Will?'

'Absolutely,' replied the android. 'I am happy to serve a new master when you have gone.'

If he could physically cross his fingers he would have done it.

Anita omitted to point out that William's batteries would expire in a few weeks time and could not be replaced. 26th Century technology was not available and AA batteries would not fit the bill.

After a furtive exchange of looks Helga delivered her decision.

'The U.I.D. agrees to your proposal. No one on the adjudication panel can spare time to accompany you, we are far too busy solving ALL cases SWIFTLY however, we will be sending agent Stan to witness the event, please join us Stan.'

The conference room door flew open and in strode Stan, the floor vibrating with every giant step. He stood some six feet seven in his imposing shiny black uniform. His shaven head adorned with an impressive tattoo in the form of the U.I.D. logo. In his arms he gently cradled the most enormous rat the Hawkins family had ever seen.

'Stan is a man of few words but swift actions. If you fail to, as you say, disappear from the train near Bodmin, Stan is instructed to make you all vanish through the nearest window, remember, we solve problems quickly.'

'QUICKLY' came the chorus, Stan joining in.

'William, as you call him, will return with Stan to begin his work at the U.I.D, I believe we can utilise him in a variety of interesting ways.'

Steven, who had been sitting wide eyed and open mouthed, could not resist the question. 'What about the rat?'

'The magnificent rodent, Wallace, is Stan's best and only friend, he is the result of a special breeding programme, hence his imposing stature. I suggest you do not try to cross Wallace, he carries a very nasty nip, not to mention, Stan would be very upset, wouldn't you?'

'YES!' The room shook as the reply left Stan's lips.

'Now, time is everything to us, so be on your way. Stan will accompany you to the railroad station and beyond, we will not be meeting again.'

A flourish of Helga's three fingered right hand dismissed the Hawkins and they followed Stan to a waiting black limo. Anita checked her watch 12.00 noon, they were on their way!

THE CRACKS ARE SHOWING

A message had gone out to Saviorian High Command that the mission on Earth was coming to a close. This put them at the top of the list for next assignments. There would be little time for recuperation and a visit to Vacation Station 4 was simply out of the question. Looking on the bright side, events on Earth were advancing well. The World Council was taking shape and the enthusiasm shown by the delegates was inspiring.

A *Sharing of Experience* session was planned for 3.00pm in the main chamber where delegates now numbered over 3,000. William took his place alongside Karen and Ken, but his mind was not totally focused on the meeting. He couldn't help wondering how his family were progressing in their attempt to jump again into the 26th Century. There had been no word from Dr. Honey and time was running short.

The Session was organised for delegates to share their journey during three hundred years of isolation. It was all quite mundane until a delegate from Siberia reluctantly got up to speak. Boris was a soft spoken man in his late 40's and was clearly concerned about something. With all the talk about the aliens saving the planet and cleansing it of nuclear weapons, he had a worried expression on his face.

'Can I just say something please if I may? Our little village is in the mountains with lots of caves nearby. In one deep cave our people found this big smooth metal object. It has been there all my life and my family before. Some villager's say it has been laying there since the war, well you know what I mean. Nobody takes much notice of it, cannot use it for anything.

'Well, when the darkness was lifted the other day and the strangers came to call, the weather changed, as you have all been saying, no more regular sun and rain that we'd been used to. Anyway, my brother Vladimir, he's just been into the cave and he says the object has started making a noise like a clock, you know, tick tock. Just wondered if it meant anything? Probably not important.'

Many delegates looked puzzled, not sure what to make of it, when suddenly all hell broke loose. Androids appeared from nowhere and escorted poor Boris from the chamber. Everyone else was told to remain in their seats and not leave the room.

Ken turned to Karen 'You remember in your father's library, those photographs of nuclear weapons?'

'How could I forget, you know he tried to make me believe the lies.'

'Yes but don't you think that could be what Boris was describing?'

'Well yes, I suppose it could be.'

'Or some other kind of bomb,' William had now joined in.

'The ticking sound Will, what does that mean?'

'Well unless it is a clock it's not a good sign Ken, that's for sure. Usually it means the weapon is live and a timing mechanism is in operation. If that is the case, it could explode at any time with potentially devastating consequences.'

'I thought the aliens had removed all the weapons while the world slept?' noted Karen.

'That was what we were told,' joined in Juan Carlos from Cali in Colombia. 'They took all the weapons up into space and destroyed them.'

'It looks like they might have missed one and it's become active after all these years,' cried Ken.

Heated discussions spread throughout the conference chamber, a delegate from Texas took the microphone.

'Fellow Human delegates, I think we have a right to know what is happening. This is our planet and if there is any kind of danger we should be informed. I propose we demand answers now. Please raise your hands if you agree.'

A wave of arms shot up around the room, just as the public address system burst into life.

'Human delegates, we ask you to be patient and calm. The Saviorian Security Service is at the scene in Siberia to assist with the situation. You and your fellow citizens are in no danger and this unfortunate incident will soon be under control. In a few moments one of our High Command officials will address you.'

Everyone slowly took their seats and resumed conversations with their immediate neighbours. The scene outside the conference room was far from calm. Surely this must be a mistake, there is no way the android forces would have missed a weapon. Scans were taken over the entire planet to detect weapons and every single one was removed, or so they thought.

Commander Aragon was given the task of talking to the assembled delegates. He had dashed straight from an emergency video link meeting with High Command and had forgotten to turn his Simu-Suit on. Many of the delegates had not witnessed a Saviorian at first hand, having only dealt with androids.

The diminutive figure padded up to the podium leaving a trail of suppurating phlegm and puss in his wake. His bright scarlet head appeared to throb under this new pressure and his yellow green eyes darted from side to side, surveying the scene. As he opened his mouth to speak the stench of partly digested food caused two young delegates to faint on the spot. His first words were delivered with force.

'Shhleem boshumph arrochee, impoo,' then, he realised his mistake, too late for many close to the podium.

Several, wearing their best clothes for their first Council meeting, were instantly drenched by the contents of Commander Aragon's cavernous mouth like orifice. Bile, mucus and curdled, regurgitated entrails swamped them from head to foot. A lone voice in the middle of the room cried out,

'It's nothing to worry about, please stay calm. This is a Saviorian, I'm afraid it's what they look like,' it was Ken trying to reassure the room.

The drenched delegates were led from the room to be hosed down.

'Well that sure proves it, those little creatures are certainly not Human,' observed a lady from Latvia.

Aragon composed himself and quickly switched on his Simusuit.

'Human delegates, I do apologise for my oversight but not my appearance. You clearly feel more comfortable when I wear this hideous disguise, no offence intended. Can you all understand me now?'

Y...yes, was the meek reply from the hall.

'Good, I bring news from Siberia, the situation there is under control, no-one was harmed and the device was safely removed from your planet.'

'Can you tell us exactly what the device was?' enquired Ken.

'Er yes it was actually a er....three hundred and twenty year old thermo nuclear device, which as I say, has now been removed.'

'Excuse me Commander Aragon, it's Ken from Padstow, we have met.'

'Ah yes Ken, good to see you again.'

'Yes Commander, tell me, how is it possible for this device to have gone undetected? You have been telling us, with great pride, how you cleansed the Earth of all weapons. Oh, and another question, was this device armed when you found it?'

A murmur of concerned approval at Ken's question spread around the room.

'These are very interesting questions Ken. Firstly, I must pass on the most sincere apologies from Saviorian High Command for this inexcusable oversight. We are carrying out a complete scan with more sophisticated detection instruments developed over the past three hundred Earth years. In the unlikely event that we find other weapons, they will be eliminated before we leave Earth. In answer to your second point....err... yes, the weapon was armed.'

A general buzz of disbelief filled the chamber.

'So if our new friend Boris had not spoken up, what would have been the likely outcome?' continued Ken.

'An unlikely outcome after three hundred years would have been death on a massive scale, however, the most likely scenario after this passage of time would be a malfunction and an ineffective detonation.'

Shrieks of disbelief were followed by much arm waving.

The delegate from Texas took up the questioning. 'In your desire to save the planet you have set us back hundreds of years as far as Human development is concerned. You plan to leave us soon in such a primitive state that, were we to find any residual bombs we could never make them safe, you are taking the technology with you. We will be left wondering if the next day will be our last just like our forefathers three hundred years ago. Is this the message you want me to take back to my community?'

'Yes, well said' shouted the crowd.

'As I have just stated, we are sweeping the entire planet using all the latest scanning equipment, there will be no residual weaponry anywhere on this planet by the time we leave.'

'That's the point though isn't it,' noted Simone from Normandy. 'You are leaving, no danger to you, we are left with the risk. Having spent three hundred years supposedly protecting us, you are leaving us all with the threat.'

'As it stands, we are not leaving for several months, believe me, any problems will be solved long before then.'

The delegates were clearly not happy with Commander Aragon's answer but felt helpless to influence proceedings.

The Commander continued, 'We would ask you to trust us and remember we haven't spent three centuries of our own lives here to end up watching your planet blow up as we leave. Now it's time to get on with valuable work, preparing you to return to your communities.'

Aragon quickly left the room, on the way out he was passed by another fifty new delegates from recently enlightened areas of the world. Once outside the Commander was ushered away for yet another meeting with High Command.

THE 2.05PM FROM PADDINGTON

On the 2.05pm from Paddington to Penzance all was relatively calm, except for the Hawkins family who were trying to keep everything together. The tickets printed via William's mouth were not for First Class and the carriage was packed with only a few spare seats. Stan took up two spaces at the rear of the carriage trying to look inconspicuous. This was difficult enough but made harder because of Wallace who was attracting a lot of attention. Pet rats were not uncommon but his imposing dimensions were impressive. He was chained to Stan's wrist because pets had to be on a lead at all times.

'Did you have him specially bred, he's tremendous?' asked an elderly lady.

'Yes' replied Stan, a man of few words.

'What do you feed him on?' she was not going to be put off.

'Mostly little old ladies!' was Stan's stern reply.

'Really how interesting, and how....'

'Go away or you're next! 'barked Stan.

Her husband pulled her away. The U.I.D. officer was on duty and duty was very important to the U.I.D. It was bad enough the train being busy but on top of that, he couldn't hear the Hawkins conversation.

'....and you say it doesn't hurt this Time Jump thing?' asked Jane.

'Mum, you've been through it twice before remember.'

'That's the problem, I don't remember, it's all a blur now.'

'No it doesn't hurt, stop asking pointless questions.' Inwardly Anita was a mess, she was putting her parents through hell, and for what. If this didn't work where might they end up? There was still the problem of another return journey home even if it did work.

The buffet car will close in fifteen minutes. We are now selling off a selection of snacks at half price. House Mouse Burgers, Spicy Shrew Soup, Filled Rolls and Panini's, Squirrel Sandwiches and Crusty Coypu Baguettes. Next stop is Plymouth in twenty minutes.

'One piece of luck', noted Steven, 'They haven't checked the tickets this time.'

'Oh I forgot to tell you,' William had rebooted from a battery charge. 'I saw the inspector leave the train in a hurry an hour ago, he flew past the window in a horizontal pose as we left Dawlish, looked surprised, hope he's alright.'

Stan wore a knowing expression as if he might have been responsible for the inspector's early departure.

'We'll be sorry to leave you behind William, what are your plans?'

'Mum, he's a f...ing android he'll probably zap a few members of the U.I.D with 20,000 volts then be sold as scrap when his batteries expire,'whispered Anita.

'I may not have Human feelings Anita but I imagine that hurt, after all we've been through together.'

'Sorry Will, Mum, just a bit on edge that's all.'

'To answer your kind question Mrs Hawkins,' he checked to

make sure Stan couldn't hear, 'I thought I might wait until I'm back in U.I.D headquarters then blow myself, up taking Helga and her coven with me, how does that sound?'

'Well if you're sure dear.' Jane couldn't help herself, tin man reminded her so much of the real William.

The train pulled out of Plymouth with far fewer passengers, Stan moved up the carriage to keep a closer eye on proceedings. Excitement replaced fear as they neared the jump point. It somehow seemed even more important for the family to reunite no matter where or when it was.

'I estimate five minutes to go,' Indicated Stan to William. He wanted to guard the U.I.D.'s new weapon which could ultimately be employed to speed up resolutions to all cases even more quickly.

'Thanks for everything William. I'm sure you will have a blast.'

'Two minutes to go, yes I'll certainly do that. Please say hi to everyone at the Think Tank and especially the Human me, tell him he's got a really nice family.'

'Remember,' called out Stan, 'If you fail to disappear don't worry, I'll vanish you all myself soon enough!' A fleeting evil smile passed his lips.

'Shall we hold hands or something?' asked Jane

'Good idea' cried Steven and Anita …and they were gone.

'Bloody hell!' shouted Stan,' It really was true, what do you make of that Wallace?'

The rat promptly threw up over Stan's nice black shirt.

ZLODICH DEMANDS ACTION

It was Supreme Commander Zlodich on video link from Central Co-ordinations Base. Because of the vast distances between the Base and Earth, there was a time delay, even accounting for Saviorian technology.

'Greetings Commander Aragon, I understand you have been having more technical difficulties on Earth.'

'All in hand Supreme Commander Zlodich.'

'Good, for we have need of your services on a planet in the Piraeus Quadrant, Bellicose Minor heard of it?'

'No, I can't say I have, go on.'

'Anyway, it's a small but quite beautiful, watery planet about a quarter of the size of Earth. It seems that the tyrant ruler of the only inhabited landmass has started behaving in a potentially catastrophic manner. She has begun to eat her way through the entire male population. Queen Eritima, as she is known locally, has been granted God like status and the males are lining up to be her next meal. Bellicose Minor has strong trading links with neighbouring planets that rely on fresh produce from their smaller partner. If the queen continues to feast at her present rate there will be no-one to seed a future population.'

'So when exactly do you need us to leave Earth?'

'Well taking the Queens present rate of consumption into

consideration, no more than two Earth weeks...Hello Aragon, are you alright, you seem to have gone a little pale, are you unwell....Aragon!'

'Sorry Supreme Commander, I must have misheard you, I thought you said two Earth weeks!'

'That is correct, maximum two Earth weeks, and unless you wish to spend a stretch at a nearby Penal Colony, I suggest you cut this link and get prepared...Good bye Aragon.'

The Commander sat in silence staring vacantly at the wall.

Jackie Green burst into the room and he jumped up with a start.

'I'm pleased I caught you Commander, I need a decision on the remaining Human communities still protected. In light of the bomb discovery in Siberia, do we halt the process until the new scan is completed or carry on?'

'Two weeks Jackie, that's all they've given us, two weeks. Queen Eritima is eating all the men and we've got two weeks!'

'Commander, you're really not making any sense, it is not at all like you.'

Commander Aragon requested Miss Green to sit down and explained the Bellicose Minor situation to the Senior Earth Co-ordinating Officer, she was clearly taken aback.

'Did you explain the situation here, did he know about the bomb?'

'Of course he knew, he is aware of everything. It's the Penal Colony for us if we try to delay.'

'Then I need to fast track the rest of the release programme. Can we commission more androids to speed the cleanup operation?'

'Not really, our facilities are being dismantled before our eyes, catch twenty two I think the Humans call it.'

'How long before the scan is complete, we need to reassure the delegates that their planet is safe?'

'Another two Earth hours, its 4.00pm now so by 6.00pm we should have the results. We have to get this right Jackie, nothing short of 100% accuracy will do.'

'Ok. Then, we also need to cram the delegates with life skills information and guides on growing technological abilities at a sustainable rate. We were going to spread this over a few months, now it needs to be done in days, let's hope they can absorb it all in the time remaining.'

'Very well, I suggest we complete the enlightenment immediately, transport as many delegates as we physically can to the World Council headquarters. It might be necessary to send the early arrivals, starting with Padstow, back home now in order to make room for a new influx.'

'Just get that weapons scan result as soon as possible. If it has detected more bombs, it's back to the drawing board.'

William had received word that his family would be jumping at 5.50pm into the Think Tank, District Six, Padstow or what was left of it. The installation had been reduced to a basic core. The surrounding landscape had already been returned to rural fields, ready for fresh cultivation. The complex transport networks which had surrounded most towns and cities had gone. Old primitive road and path systems had been restored, to the amazement of the local Human population.

William was on a shuttle from Pyongyang to the Think Tank, ready to meet his family again, or so he hoped. A decision would have to be made, immediately, on whether to risk an instant return to the 21st Century or stay together in this fledgling world for the rest of their lives. If the entire family jumped back, as they had on their first two visits to the future, the chances of success were better, but what would William decide to do?

ALL TOO MUCH TO TAKE IN

5.50pm, the year 2514, Steven, Jane and Anita stood in the stark surroundings of an unfamiliar laboratory. For a brief moment they stared blankly at the gleaming metallic walls, the bright artificial lights temporarily blinding them. Anita came round first, having some recognition of the installation. Steven and Jane continued to stare, trying to comprehend what just happened.

'Mum, Dad, are you both alright?'

'Wh...where are we?' blurted out Jane trembling with shock.

'You are in what remains of the Fox Institute Think Tank madam,' interrupted a rather officious android.

'Please all of you take a seat while we assess your physical well being. Dr. Honey will be along to brief you shortly.'

'I'm really confused Anita. Is this where we're meant to be, did the time thingy work, is this really the future, how can you tell?'

'Oh yes Mum, that smell is very distinctive, you can never properly disguise the pong of a genuine Savorian, no matter how much disinfectant you use.'

'So you say we've been here before?'

'Twice Dad but you won't recognise it. You see on our previous visits we were fooled by the use of cleverly created scenarios. They wanted us to believe it was still 21st Century Padstow while they observed and used us in their experiments. We were never meant to be aware of the real picture. But here we are and this is the reality.'

Anita turned, 'Well, hello yet again.'

Dr. Honey had entered the room without them realising. 'That was a clever switch of yours you clearly didn't want to stay with us last time.'

'Yes sorry Doc, but the lure of the dance floor was just too strong!'

Dr.Honey looked a little confused at that statement but carried on. 'William will be here in two minutes, his shuttle is just arriving from Pyongyang.'

'Did you say Pyongyang, that's the capital of North Korea isn't it?" Steven had finally come round.

'Perhaps in your time yes.'

'Mum, dad, Anita, thank God you made it safely back!' William had rushed straight from the Hyper Speed Transport.

The family were reunited with hugs and kisses all round. Anita even embraced her younger brother like she meant it.

'Dr Honey, I cannot thank you and your team enough for pulling this off, it is truly amazing.'

'William it's the least we could have done after all the help you have given to our cause.'

There was no time for prolonged family reunions or to go into explanations of recent experiences, events were moving fast.

'Is there any news on the Security Scan of Earth,' asked William, 'The last I heard was there would be an answer by 6.00pm, its 6.15pm now.'

'Nothing yet William, we are expecting an announcement any time.'

'William what's happened to you son? You're all grown up and sounding quite responsible, I can't believe it!'

'Thanks for that vote of confidence Mother, my life has moved on a pace in a really short time, I feel I have purpose here, I can make a difference.'

'William has been very useful to our progress recently and hopefully will continue the good work after we depart.'

'What's happened to this place there's next to nothing left? I couldn't help noticing when I landed, your footprint on the landscape, it's nearly gone.'

'Have you not heard Will, we have to be gone in two weeks, a new assignment or the Penal Colony awaits us!'

This conversation continued while Steven and Jane stared through an outside window looking over the Camel Estuary to Padstow. *Could this really be the 26th Century, nothing seemed too different.* Suddenly a giant transport ship zoomed into view and another shot upwards at a phenomenal rate into space. They looked at one another and realised, it must be true.

Just at that moment Professor Huntley rushed into the room.

'We have news from Central Operations, oh sorry, hello Mr & Mrs Hawkins, and hello again Anita, the real one I take it?'

'Yes, it's me alright,' cried Anita.

'Sorry I've no time for small talk. Dr. Honey, the results have come in from the Earth Weapons Scan, it is not good news. They have detected three more devices from the aborted nuclear war period. They too had become live after enlightenment. All the munitions were located in mountainous areas, hidden in deep cave systems in the Andes, Pyrenees and Atlas ranges. They have all been made safe and removed to our space garbage ship.'

'Surely this must mean a further delay to our departure schedule? We cannot leave until we know all Humans are safe, it would be going against our sacred code.' queried Dr Honey.

'Apparently not, High Command is now entirely satisfied that there are no more undetected devices. The new high tech scanning equipment is 100% accurate and we leave Earth in fourteen days. Which leads me to my next point...' Professor Huntley turned to the Hawkins family.

'I am glad we managed to reunite you all again and apologise for your last leap backwards, which brought you such dangers in an unfamiliar parallel world. However, the fact is we cannot send you back home again.'

'What do you mean?' cried Anita.

'Just what I say, you will have to remain here in 26th Century Padstow for the rest of your lives.'

'But Dr. Honey, you informed me that my family would be sent back again straight away!'

'Yes, and I am deeply sorry William, the truth is our functioning abilities here on Earth are diminishing by the minute, this includes any Time Jump facilities we had set up to bring you here in the first place.'

William wanted to talk to his family but was aware how involved he was in present events.

'Sounds like you planned on staying here anyway, Sherlock. Tell me, how are things going with my android double, she giving you lots of grief I hope?'

'No, she blew her own cover, gone for scrap or spares, something like that. She had me going for a while but I knew it wasn't you. The piss taking was obviously just an act, you know no one can do it quite like you, can they?'

'Thanks Einstein, that means a lot.'

Steven and Jane were finding it difficult to follow the conversation. They were still in a state akin to jet lag with a serious twist.

'Anita, can you explain to me what this all means, I'm seriously confused.'

'Well, it seems that our friends here from outer space are leaving Earth rather sharpish, even though there are old nuclear bombs springing up everywhere. This means the clever little trick of dragging us backwards and forwards in time won't work anymore because someone's pulled the plug. So, we seem to be stuck in primitive 26th Century England for the rest of our natural. No more Eastenders or Match of the Day until they reinvent the tv! All a bit shitty if you ask me Mum.'

'Our friends and family, they won't know what's happened to us, all our animals, oh God! We will never be able to say goodbye!'

'Yes, and I'm afraid William, it's all really your fault,' added Steven. 'You insisted we came back to Padstow the second time.'

'Well, if you recall Dad, you were only too happy to have a free holiday, booze included!'

'Come on you lot,' shouted Anita 'Look on the bright side, oh no there isn't one!'

'Is there nothing you can do Professor Huntley, you were the ones who lured us here in the first place? Don't you use Time Travel to jump huge distances in space?'

'Sorry, I thought I made myself clear, the equipment here on Earth has been dismantled.'

'Yes, here on Earth, but what about on your space ships, you can do it from there, can't you?'

'Well yes, but only in extreme circumstances when our Hyper Drives are not quick enough to get us to a designated problem in time.'

'So it can be done.'

'Hang on Captain Kirk, are you thinking what I think you're thinking?'

'Probably Sis.'

'I told you not to call me that.'

'I do not mean to be rude,' interrupted Dr. Honey. 'But our time is precious.'

'Alright, could you take us with you when you leave Earth then jump us back to the 21st Century once we're onboard, using your ship's facilities?'

'No. I'm sorry, the risks involved would be too great, besides our code of conduct does not allow us to remove species from their home planet, I wish I could help but it is beyond our jurisdiction.'

But not impossible whispered William to himself.

'William, we need you back at World Council with the other delegates to finalise details for our departure,' insisted Professor Huntley.

'Just give me a few moments alone with my family, please.'

'Very well but the transport to Pyongyang is ready to leave.'

William ushered his family to a quiet corner

'I know this has all been way too much to take in.'

'You can say that again son.'

'Right, but we need to be clear headed and decisive about this. We have very little time and the options will not be available to us much longer.'

'Is it right that we can't get back home anymore Will?' asked Jane in a rather feeble voice.

'Just listen to me a minute Mum. We can either stay here in a very primitive world, probably never going far beyond Padstow until the Internal Combustion Engine is rediscovered. Or, try the very risky strategy of sneaking aboard one of the

Saviorian ships and somehow persuading them to jump us back to the 21st Century and home. We may get lucky and by some miracle find ourselves back in our real world or we may be stranded aboard an alien craft in the depths of space for the rest of our lives.'

'What about you Einstein, you're clearly well in with our slimy friends, what would your choice be. You want to stay here don't you to help the new world develop, maybe reinvent the laptop in your own name!'

'Honestly, as long as we stay together as a family that's good enough for me. To stand the best chance of getting home we need to be a four as we were on our first jump. I will go along with your decision but we need to stick together whatever we decide.'

'Thank you son, I know how much all this has meant to you.'

'Oh God! That really is below the belt Sherlock, you'd do anything to stay No1 offspring wouldn't you, sorry just kidding!'

'William, the shuttle is leaving, we need you onboard,' cried an anxious Dr. Honey.

'Just two minutes, this is very important. You have to decide now, do we stay or try to get home?'

'Well son this may be our world but it's not our time, I say let's try and get home.'

'All our friends and family will be looking for us and lord knows what's happened on the farm, so let's go home, Anita?'

'No question, let's get the hell out of here, it would drive me mad, no facebook, no night life, no friends to get drunk with on Saturday night, what we waiting for, Sherlock?'

'I'm with you this time, we don't really belong here. I got you into this mess so let me try and get us all home.'

'William it is now or never, the Padstow Think Tank is shutting down.'

‘Is it right that Pyongyang will be your last contact point on Earth Dr. Honey?’

‘Yes, we leave from there as soon as practical.’

‘Then please take us all with you to Pyongyang, we somehow need to get back to our own time. Once there I will have a chance to plead our case to your High Command. Hopefully I can persuade them to take us onboard and get us home.’

‘By all means take the shuttle to World Council Headquarters but from there you are on your own. I think you will find the answer is no and it will be too late to return with Karen and Ken to Padstow.’

‘Thank you Dr. Honey, as long as there is the slightest chance of getting my family home I’ll take it.’

The shuttle craft hovered over Padstow for seconds then sped upwards and out of sight. It would return just once more to bring back Karen and Ken, armed with practical information to aid the advancement of their society, hopefully in a peaceful and sustainable way.

CARNAGE AT THE U.I.D.

One last full charge of my batteries, well, that damn rat deserved it, kept trying to gnaw at my synthetic ankles. I just splattered him all over the windows of the 17.30 back to Paddington. The public rush to feast on his remains would have shocked even Anita. Not a scrap was left as we approached Reading. Stan was not a happy bunny but he was helpless, promised him the same fate if he laid a finger on me. The rest of the passengers seemed happier with me, well it's not every day there's a free prize rodent on the menu. I promised my black clad minder that I would still serve the U.I.D.

My internal computer indicates a successful jump for my Human friends, now to complete my part of the bargain......

Now approaching headquarters, have asked for a meeting with Helga and the rest of the coven to discuss my new roll in the organisation...

Now in the building approaching the inner sanctum. My sensors have managed to locate twelve Humans being held awaiting a quick resolution to their cases. I must make sure none of them are harmed while at the same time taking out as many of the coven and Stan's henchmen as I can.

Helga awaits me.

'So android, I am told your friends performed their vanishing trick as promised. We do not pretend to understand how it was done, only that it is another case solved quickly.'

QUICKLY was the response.

'It is unfortunate that you felt the need to spread Wallace's contents across the railroad carriage, but this is mere detail. Stan will be supplied with a new friend from our select breeding programme.

'So android, I understand you requested an audience with my Inner Council, make it brief, we have a backlog of cases for you to clear up.'

I move to the centre of the room, in range of all the council members.

'I have only one thing left to say to you, go to Hell Helga!'

William, the most advanced android in the Saviorian fleet detonated himself, taking out every one in the room in a hail of body parts, plastering all four walls with a mosaic of blood and guts.

The U.I.D. would have been proud of his direct methods.

THE STARK REALITIES OF LIFE

The Hyperlink Shuttle arrived in Pyongyang to find the place in a state of high anxiety and confusion. Delegates had been informed of the newly discovered bombs and were clearly angry.

The programme of enlightenment had been accelerated but it had not proved possible to have every community represented on the World Council, there just wasn't time. Even so, rapidly constructed conference centres housed almost 10,000 representatives of the Human race. Although their collective knowledge of technology was limited, they had demanded answers as to why these dormant explosives had suddenly sprung to life. The conclusion was that it coincided with the removal of artificial weather controls and the dark buffer zones. The Saviorians were trying their best to impart as much knowledge in the short time left. The delegates just wanted to be sure their planet wasn't likely to blow up once the aliens left.

Ken and Karen had received word that William was returning from Padstow with some surprise companions. They were anxious to hear how the town was faring so they met them at the shuttle dock.

'William, good to see you, how was your trip?'

'Good thanks, still can't get used to travelling at that speed, oh sorry, this is my family.'

William introduced three rather green looking individuals from the past.

'Wow, some more time travellers, I still can't get my head round it,' cried Karen.

'Tell me about it,' replied Jane, 'My head's about to burst, this still feels like a weird dream!'

'Hi, I'm Ken, Will has told us all about your amazing experiences, good to meet you.'

'Yes likewise, we're hoping he'll fill in all the blanks if we ever get home,' pointed out Steven just before he deposited the contents of his stomach over the reception area.

'Will, we have news that we are to return to Padstow tomorrow for the last time, knowledge in hand, are you coming with us?'

'Eh no Ken, I won't be staying, I'm going to try and get back home with my family.'

'I'm really sorry to hear that Will, I was kind of hoping you would stick around and help us rebuild,' pointed out Karen in a sombre voice. 'There are much worse places than Padstow to settle down. We, I mean you, could have a good life there.'

'Well Sherlock you're a dark horse, still charming the ladies, do you know, she's actually young enough to be your..'

'Yes thank you Anita!'

All delegates please report to your conference room for an important meeting with Saviorian High Command.

'Come on Will, you're still a delegate,' cried Karen, reaching for his hand.

'No sorry, I've got to try and get an audience with Commander Aragon or Jackie Green, you go ahead, I'll catch up with you later, before you leave.'

'How sweet!'

'Shut up Anita.'

In the main conference room Commander Aragon, resplendent in his Simu-Suit, addressed the Earth's Human representatives.

'My dear Human friends,' he was clearly in a rare grovelling mood. 'We are well aware of the anxiety and stress recent unfortunate incidents have caused you. No one was more shocked than I on hearing of more rogue nuclear devices. The fact that these ancient instruments of terror had suddenly become active again added to our deep concerns. Our scientists have been giving their undivided attention to this problem and we are sure this time that there is no cause for further alarm. The Earth is safe for you to return to your communities and start building for the future.'

'What caused them to become active again Commander?' The deep booming voice came from the back of the vast Council Chamber.

'Yes, you haven't told us that, we deserve to know.'

The demanding voices spread across the room. The Commander raised an arm in a plea for quiet.

'Let him speak, we need to know.'

Aragon was growing impatient. 'If I told you the reason you probably wouldn't understand, the explanation goes way beyond your primitive knowledge base.'

'And who were the ones who limited our knowledge to this, so called, primitive level?'

'And who were the ones who saved you from total self destruction, you seem to have forgotten that?' retorted Commander Aragon.

The room fell silent again, they could not counter that. The signs were all there however, Human nature was alive and kicking hard.

'We can no longer be held responsible for the irresponsible actions of our forefathers. We only want to know how to deal with another device if one appears after you have left. After all, you tell us your sacred code requires you to protect intelligent life in all it's forms.'

'Which is why we have concentrated our all our energy into getting to the bottom of this. All Human communities have been released from protective quarantine. The problem was related to this process. There are no more weapons and no means to activate them even if they did exist.

'We implore you to return to the far reaches of your planet and never to mention these unfortunate discoveries again, for the good of your future development. We must leave no footprint no matter how small, of our time here on Earth, this too is part of our sacred code.

'The first delegates must return home today and the last no later than one week from now. Our departure date has been set for 14th January 2515 at 8.00am, we have much work to do, and we wish you well.'

With that Commander Aragon slithered out of the room and androids took over the meeting. When the practical session broke up delegates gathered together in small groups. They agreed that part of the message to take back home must include the nuclear scare. It would be written into their future texts, always to be vigilant and aware that remnants of ancient weapons may still be out there. Quite what they would do if found was another matter. However, the development of technology to safely disarm them would be a priority. It was hoped, for the future of the Human race, that this would never be needed.

Ken and Karen had to rush and prepare for their return to Padstow. Although their time in Pyongyang had been shorter than planned they couldn't wait to be reunited with their family and friends, becoming part of a brave new world. Karen was armed with enough new material to restock her father's library and Ken could go on being the inventor he always claimed to be. He hoped to find like minded friends in the newly discovered towns and villages in his small part of the world. Karen secretly wished William would be returning with them but understood he belonged in his own time in the dim and distant past.

William had failed in his attempt to have a meeting with Commander Aragon or Jackie Green and was getting desperate. He knew that the members of the Padstow Think Tank would be relocating to Pyongyang later that day. He hoped to persuade Professor Huntley, Major Main, Doctor Honey or Colonel Hafey to arrange a meeting on his behalf, even put a case forward between them for a Time Jump attempt while on board one of the ships of the Saviorian fleet.

Their options were diminishing by the minute and were not helped by the sight of Karen and Ken on their way to catch the final shuttle to Padstow. Anita had been wondering which was worse, risking another botched leap through time or being stuck in some medieval future world in a Cornwall even more primitive than the 21st Century version. God forbid, they might even reinvent Jethro. She decided to follow William's path and keep the family together no matter what. As for Jane and Steven, they had only just become aware of time travelling antics and wanted someone to wake them from this nightmare.

'So pleased we caught you before leave. I need you to take a message to one of the Think Tank people, Professor Huntley if possible,' noted William

'It's not too late for you to come back with us, it's much safer than your alternative,' pleaded Karen.

'No we can't, just look at Mum and Dad, they're in complete shock, we need to get them home.'

'Yes I know but you can't blame me for trying, what do you

want me to say to Professor Huntley?'

'Just get him or one of the others to meet us here tonight, we have to be on that ship when they leave.'

'Alright, I'll do my best,' replied Karen in a resigned tone.

'We must be going, said Ken, looking towards the shuttle dock. 'Good luck Mr. and Mrs. Hawkins, Anita. Will it's been a great pleasure meeting and working with you. Karen, we must go.'

A long and tearful embrace between William and Karen said it all and then they were gone, swept up in the crowds heading home. Even Anita resisted the temptation to give her brother a hard time. She realised they had used up their last option, the future lay in the hands of aliens she had mocked for so long.

A BRAVE NEW WORLD

The shuttle dock in Federal District Six was all that remained of the alien footprint in the Padstow area. The lonely figures of Professor Huntley and his team stood waiting for their transport to take them away from the place they had called home for the past three hundred Earth years. When their craft eventually took off for the last time the residents would be left to their own destiny once more.

Karen and Ken stepped from the shuttle and shared warm handshakes with the Think Tank members. Professor Huntley promised to speak to William and his family in Pyongyang, but held out little hope for their plan. Karen wished she had tried harder to persuade William to stay. Once the aliens had left, Padstow might as well be on a different planet to Pyongyang where the Hawkins would be stranded.

The shuttle pad was dismantled by the departing androids as the Saviorians waved fondly to their Human friends for a final time. With a silence that masked the power of their craft they lifted off from their long time base in the Camel Estuary, leaving no trace of their existence, a process being repeated all over the world. Hovering for one last time most of the locals in the fields raised their heads and watched with silent disinterest, and then they were gone in the blink of an eye.

Karen and Ken rushed across the rich green pasture to be greeted by their tearful family. Dina, Andy and Mario had brought with them several townsfolk, some they didn't recognise. For this was the future, a world reaching out again, reintroducing itself, another chance to get it right.

'Kettle's on,' announced Andy as they strode across the fields arm in arm down the lane and home.

HOME VIA BELICOSE MINOR

William was rightly concerned about his parents. They were non responsive to questions and continued to stare into empty space for long periods. They were being checked over by a couple of android doctors as the last shuttle back from Padstow arrived in Pyongyang.

The number of Humans at the vast complex had peaked and now the balance was changing. Saviorians from every corner of the world were gathering together again preparing to leave. They all had their own tales of three hundred years on Earth. Most were looking forward to the new challenge on Bellicose Minor and some wished it could be their turn to go home for once.

Anita had gone to collect her parents from the Medical Centre while William tracked down Professor Huntley and Dr Honey. He hoped the news that his parents were struggling with 26th Century life would persuade someone in authority to allow passage back home from the Mother Ship.

Because there were still many Humans in the facility the order had been given for all Saviorians to wear Simu-Suits in public places thus avoiding anxiety and mess. William caught up with his alien friends on their way to the main abattoir where they were about to consume their first live meal of the day.

'Ah William, your friends Karen and Ken asked us to contact you.'

'Before you say anything, my parents are having treatment in the Medical Centre, could you spare a few minutes to have a look at them?'

'We are in need of sustenance Will, but we will take a quick look.'

'Thank you professor Huntley.'

They all rushed off to the Medical Centre and arrived just as Anita was emerging.

'Oh Will it's good to see you. The doctors say Mum and Dad are both suffering severe shock and nervous exhaustion and will need to stay under observation for twenty four hours. They have been given medication to reduce the anxiety and boost their energy levels. I gave permission to use the drugs in your absence, I hope you don't mind?'

'No, of course not sis. Can we see them?'

'The medication requires complete rest and isolation for at least twelve hours but they did say we would see a vast improvement after that time, oh sorry I didn't see you there Dr Honey, Professor Huntley. The doctors also said many of the problems could have been triggered by displacement disorder and recommended a return to more familiar surroundings once they have recovered properly.'

'Does that mean returning home?'

'I think that is what the doctors were hinting at.'

'Did you hear that Dr Honey? Might that help with our request to join your ship and use it as a way of getting back to our own time?'

'We leave in six days, who's to say your parents will be fit to travel by then. Add to that the fact that there are no Simu-Suits used on our ships, your parents may not like what they see, although I still do not know what all the fuss is about, we are a beautiful species.'

'You must be....'

'Anita please, not now!'

'Our priority is to stabilise the situation on Bellicose Minor, even if it were possible, your return home would not be a priority. Realistically you might be stranded on an alien ship for countless years, do you want your parents to die in space?'

'Dr. Honey is right, you had your chance of a normal human life in 26th Century Padstow, that might have been the most logical option.'

'Listen Mr Spock, the logical option would have been to avoid holidays in Cornwall in the first place, but you lot had different ideas. I think you still owe us big time for using us to find a solution to your little Human problem. You need to get us on that ship and send us home, simple as. What do you say Will?'

'Well yes, I might not have put it quite like that. However, you do like to be thorough when dealing with problems, which is why you've spent three hundred years on Earth. We are still part of your problem, please give us this chance.'

'I can see you are both very determined,' noted Professor Huntley. 'I will put your case to the High Command but ultimately it comes down to the mental and physical state of your parents and the practicalities of having you on board. If we do not think they are well enough, you will all have to stay.'

Anita went to kiss the professor and then thought better of it. Even with his Simu-Suit in place the odour of semi digested raw meat engulfed her senses.

'Can I accompany you to High Command?' enquired William.

'I have all the relevant evidence and arguments clear in my head, your presence would only cloud matters, trust me I will put a strong logical case forward for you to be allowed to join us on our onward journey,' stated Professor Huntley.

'I believe you will professor.'

'Good, now we must get on, our Live Lunch awaits and then it's back to the task in hand. While you wait for news of your parents can I suggest you and Anita help with the remaining delegates preparations for returning home?' asked Dr. Honey.

'Yes, of course, we'll report to Jackie Green straight away.'

It would have been easy for delegates to get on the wrong shuttle craft, such was the intensity of movement in and out of Pyongyang. The roll call of destinations would have confused the most avid world traveller. However, the army of androids had the situation under control, just as they had done throughout the centuries on Earth. Without the androids it is hard to imagine this operation succeeding, after all, it had been android scientists who put forward the possibility of using retro Humans in Saviorian experiments.

William and Anita could not believe the sheer scale and diversity of Human kind represented here, it brought home the immense task undertaken by the aliens, who did it for no other reason than to preserve this so called intelligent life, it was truly a humbling experience. After several hours aiding the evacuation process they were keen to check on their parent's progress. At the medical centre there was some encouraging news. They were allowed to visit, but only for a short time.

Steven and Jane were dressed and resting in a comfortable if stark recovery room. They looked a great deal more relaxed and aware of their situation.

'Ah at last, you two, we wondered when you would grace us with your presence,' smiled Steven.

'Feeling better then are we Dad?' laughed Anita.

'We were just saying, we couldn't seem to take it all in, or make any sense of what was going on, just one mind blowing experience after another,' added Jane. 'These doctors they've been really good, couldn't help us enough, we could do with a few of them at home, they could transform the N.H.S.'

'Androids on the N.H.S. now there's an interesting idea, might save a few quid,' remarked William.

'So then tell us, when do we get to go home, don't get me wrong it's quite nice in here but we need to get back, the animals will have escaped and my Mother will be tearing her hair out. We clearly do not belong here, you know what we mean, don't you?'

'Yes Mum, we agree, first we have to get you both fit and well. Just try and relax and leave the details to us.'

William was still worried they wouldn't get the go ahead to join the fleet, never mind his parent's reaction to the sight of Saviorians in the raw. They would have to be strong and determined and carry a huge supply of sick bags.

'Sorry, we need you to leave now and let your parents rest, they are making good progress and should be ready to leave our facility within twenty four hours,' Android nurse XP204 led them to the door.

'Right we'll be off now, do as the doctors say, oh and Dad, no chatting up the nurses, it's a waste of time they're not programmed to respond to Knock Knock jokes!'

'Alright Anita, you just go and work on getting us home, see you in the morning.'

Outside the doctor spoke to William and Anita. 'Your parents are responding well to treatment and we are pleased with the way their bodies have reacted to, what are for them, alien drugs. They do however need a stable environment in order to properly recover. Any sustained disruption could see a return to anxiety symptoms or worse. You clearly have lots to consider, so I'll leave you to think it over.'

'Yes thank you doctor,' answered William, they walked off deep in thought.

'What do we do now Will, they so desperately want to go home but you heard what the doctor said?'

'If you're talking about keeping them in a stable environment how do you think they'd feel if we stayed here, all this is going soon,' William pointed to the alien's modern comfortable environment. 'They could be faced with working in Asian rice fields, enduring subsistence living for many years to come. You know it will all change when the aliens go. The Humans of today are used to basic life with no modern luxuries, we're not, so the wrinklies would certainly suffer.'

'Good point Sherlock, we just need to lay the facts before them once they are fit enough for rational decision making.'

Suddenly a voice came over the P.A. system.

Can Anita and William Hawkins report to Conference Room C in Annex Six immediately.

'That's us, quick let's go,' exclaimed William.

They caught a Hop-it-Pod to the meeting point as it was some kilometres from the Medical Centre. Dr. Honey and Professor Huntley were waiting for them in an anti-room.

'Please come in and sit down,' Huntley sounded sombre. 'Things are very hectic here but we managed to get a meeting with Commander Aragon and two other High Command officers. They are well aware of your situation of course. We put the case of your parent's well being and also the eternal debt of gratitude we owe you in helping us. They were not too impressed with Anita after she switched with her android double but understand her desire to return to her own time.'

'Ok, so they said no to us hitching a ride, thanks for trying, I guess we're stuck here in the paddy fields forever!'

'Oh please, no, hear us out. Amidst all our complex plans to leave this planet, we have come up with an idea to help you. After all, that is our purpose in life and we should not abandon you now.'

'Are you saying we can leave with you and you'll get us home? Anita was close to giving the little alien another hug but resisted just in time.

'Well, one thing at a time Anita. If the doctors say your parents wouldn't cope with the strain of space travel, you'll be staying here. However, the High Command have given their blessing if you all pass our physical and mental tests. If you do then they will make provision for you to be part of our fleet heading for Bellicose Minor.'

'What sort of medical tests?' said Anita with a worried look.

'Oh don't worry, you'll be fine.'

'No, I wasn't thinking of me, but poor Will here. I mean, let's face it he's not the brightest sparkler in the box, is he?'

The Saviorians looked confused.

'Sorry, just a family joke, please, please tell us more.'

'On one of our transport ships, we will make an area comfortable for Humans to live in. We will try to keep your contact with Saviorians to a minimum, as for some reason it upsets you and there will be no Simu-Suits used on board. Only after we have completed our mission on Bellicose Minor will we be available to spend time on getting you all home, so I am afraid you will have to be patient.'

'Yes, but your mission to Earth has taken three hundred years, if that is repeated we'll be dead before we get a chance to jump,' worried Will.

'We have no intention of taking that long I assure you, our average mission, before Earth, is less than two of your years, so you can see how this job frustrated us all!'

'We can't thank you enough,' exclaimed William.

'How many days do we have before leaving?' asked Anita.

'It should take Five Earth days from tomorrow, if your parents are well enough. We will carry the necessary tests out tomorrow and prepare your quarters aboard one of our transport craft. Be aware however, if any one of you fails any of the tests, then you will all have to stay here on Earth. A successful Time Jump can only have a chance of working with all four of you taking part.'

After a great deal more grovelling and thanks the two species shook limbs.

Anita and William had tasks to perform, helping the accelerated normalisation process to complete on time. They had a renewed spring in their step and realised now, especially in William's case, the 21st Century was where they belonged.

By the end of the day there were far fewer delegates in the vast centre. No sooner had the cavernous meeting halls been erected they were dismantled, packed up and shipped into orbiting storage craft. Once Earth had been evacuated many of the androids would be mothballed, then adapted for the mission on Bellicose Minor. Saviorians would take over the running of the fleet until arrival on the tiny planet. This really felt like the beginning of the end, there would be no turning back now.

FACING THE FUTURE

A great deal of walking and talking had taken place in North Cornwall in the past few days. Life had, in some ways, returned to as it was before the aliens revealed themselves. However, in so many other ways it had clearly altered. The ever changing weather took some getting used to but the biggest change was the opportunity for freedom and discovery. Already elections for representative bodies were being organised between the newly reunited towns and villages. The guidelines passed on by the aliens were very useful but just that, Human nature being what it is, was in favour of more democracy in decision making.

New roads were being laid for carts and horses that continued far beyond the old dark zones, linking their new found friends in neighbouring communities, making it easier to interact and share. Not everyone trusted this new found freedom, preferring to stay put in their own town alongside lifelong friends.

Karen and Ken had much knowledge to impart but in a measured way. It would be a slow process but they felt a huge responsibility to get it right. Mario had recruited two trainee police officers. Andy was asked to take charge of the elections and Dina was busy trying to bring in some medical improvements with the limited resources at her disposal. It would be very difficult to begin with as the aliens had protected Humans from many harmful diseases and viruses through the artificially controlled water supply. Colds and flu would soon make a comeback, not helped by the fact that winter had been reintroduced. The thriving local cottage industries had found new outlets for their winter clothing supplies. Sheep had suddenly become far more important to the local economy providing a boost for wool producers.

For all these people, the aliens had already left Earth. Every day was different now, exciting and frightening in equal measure, but they knew they were in charge of their own destiny. Rivalries had not yet developed, they were still pulling together, so for now at least, the alien wish for a better world was a real possibility, at least in this small corner of the globe.

The whole planet would soon be in this same position as the clock continued its countdown to the Saviorian departure.

GOING BACK ON THEIR WORD

The combination of alien drugs and complete rest was working wonders on Steven and Jane. They were alert and inquisitive, like children let lose in a toy shop. They had joined William and Anita in a Hop it Pod on their way to their important tests. Android doctors had given them a tentative all clear and all four were in good spirits as they approached the test facility.

'Let's go through it again Will, two plus two is what?' asked Anita.

'Very funny, this is serious, mess this up and we're all stuck here for good.'

'Don't worry, we'll be fine, the doctors told us that they are pretty basic tests, at least for Saviorians. In fact, we've already had our physical checks done during our treatment,' said Steven proudly.

They had to walk the last one hundred metres as the Hop-it-Pod tracks were already being dismantled.

'Seems strange, all this lot being packed up and shipped into space,' noted Jane. 'Surely the people round here could make good use of it when these aliens have gone?'

William explained the importance of the world's population starting from a similar level of development and the removal of any external technology was part of that.

'That's enough Einstein, there'll be plenty of time to explain all that on our journey to Belching Moaner, or whatever it's called.'

The tests on the Hawkins family lasted longer than anticipated, over three hours later the family were gathered anxiously awaiting the results. Clearly space travel aboard a Saviorian interplanetary cruiser was rather more sophisticated than five hours on a train to Cornwall. However, Anita, who, for all her bravado was apprehensive of mental testing, thought it had been relatively simple. After all, as one of the androids carrying out the tests explained, they were only hitching a ride. They would not be asked to solve the problem of Queen Eritima's ravenous appetite for the male of the species, which by all accounts, was unrelenting.

The long wait for the results was unnerving the family. For the first time they were seriously contemplating endless days in the rice fields, hoping for someone to reinvent the jet engine to get them out.

'Please come this way, Commander Aragon wishes to have a few serious words with you all.' The android led the way to an outside office and left them. They had been asked to knock before entering. The family were preparing themselves for the worst. William knocked.

“Splooch inumph hoshee' was the reply.

'What was that noise?' enquired Jane. 'Knock again William.'

'Splooch inumph hoshee!' was the rather impatient reply.

'Oh I get it' replied Anita, 'He's gone native. Prepare yourselves, I think you're in for a bit of a shock. I hope you're not wearing any of your favourite clothes, oh no how could you be, anyway, try to keep out of the firing line.'

'Anita, what are you talking about, this is no time for riddles,' cried Steven.

William very briefly explained the need for Saviorians to

wear Simu-Suits in Human company as he opened the door, shielding his parents from the expected deluge.

Commander Aragon was standing in the corner of the room. He was tall for a Saviorian at some four feet six. Turning to face them, his wide open cavernous mouth emitted a stench that physically pinned Steven to the opposite wall of the office. Both he and Jane struggled not to throw up on the spot. William, somewhat used to the hideous sight, tried to stop Aragon from speaking. Anita stood at the door gasping for air. The alien took a small shuffle towards them on his stumpy webbed feet, held up a floppy right arm and spoke.

'Aeoosh flumpiee sook di shoshik poo William.'

A yellow oily puss oozed from his flaying nostrils and trumpet ears as he dribbled half digested fish guts from the enormous green suckers in his gaping mouth. His yellow and red piercing eyes seemed to smile in their direction. The commander was clearly trying to control the volume of slime and gunk emanating from every orifice on his scaly body.

Steven, recovering somewhat, uttered the immortal words 'What the f… is that?'

William responded, 'May I introduce Commander Aragon of the Saviorian High Command.'

The red headed alien lost control of his bodily functions and drenched our intrepid time travellers in a torrent of putrid orange and green bile. The sticky mucus was flecked with the remnants of half digested intestines, the results of a recent meal in the abattoir. Anita, who had managed to dodge a direct hit, spluttered,

'Aragon, for God sake turn your bloody Simu-Suit on before I lose my parents in a sea of slime.'

A pained expression spread across the little alien's bulbous face before he reached for the on switch.

Androids were summoned to vacuum the contents of the

room and guide the family to nearby showers to clean up. Replacement clothing was found and the family placed in a nearby waiting room. William and Anita were very worried that Commander Aragon might have terrified their parents enough to put them off the forthcoming journey. *What was he doing?* Perhaps it was a last minute attempt to persuade the family to stay on Earth? But the High Command had already agreed to their request pending their test results.

'Are you two alright, that was quite a shock wasn't it?'

'That's the worst thing I think I've seen since your uncle George threw up all over your aunty Jean at their Golden Wedding party, lord knows what he'd had to eat that night.'

'One thing's for certain,' added Jane 'I've no doubt now that they're not from our world, ugly little chap isn't he, he would certainly fit well in our rare breeds farm. How do they live amongst all that slime and stink?'

'For some reason they seem to think they're a creation of beauty and cannot understand our view that they resemble foul smelling little garbage tanks on legs,' added Anita.

'And they are the ones responsible for saving the planet? Well you know what they say, looks can be deceptive,' noted Steven.

'So, he didn't put you off sharing a space craft with several thousand vomit spewing creatures?'

'As your dad says, you can't help your appearance. Did you see the look on his poor little face? He was clearly upset by our reaction. No, it's not as if we'll be spending much time with them if they've prepared accommodation for us on our own, I pity the poor little critters, that's all. I mean, paddling around in all that crap, it's just not practical. No, we're determined to go if they are kind enough to give us the chance to get home.'

In the nice clean, stench free office, Commander Aragon met them again wearing his Simu-Suit.

'I apologise if I upset you in any way. I thought it important that your parents see us as our true beautiful selves.'

The family exchanged knowing glances.

'Your reaction still astounds me, but if travelling the cosmos has taught me anything it is this, always expect the unexpected, never judge others by your own high standards.

'Now, as I was trying to tell you earlier, we have the results of your tests. Physically you are all in good enough shape to be passengers on our fleet. However, we are not convinced that Mr. and Mrs. Hawkins would be able to stand the mental stress of space travel. We have a very important mission to Bellicose Minor which requires our full attention.

'Bearing in mind the immense amount of help you, William, have given us on this Earth mission, we can offer to take you with us, but it would be without your sister and parents. As you know, there is a much smaller chance of a successful Time Link Jump with only one member from the original four, but this is the best we can offer you.'

'Just wait a minute' cried out an unusually emotive Steven. 'The doctors and nurses in your excellent hospital assured us we should have no problems being ready to travel, so what has changed?'

'With all due respect, the androids treating you do not have our knowledge and experience. They are highly trained in medical matters but are not programmed to make judgements on hypothetical scenarios. I am surprised they could even articulate such a statement, you may have misheard or misunderstood their verbalisation.'

'With all due respect,' retorted Anita in a familiar sarcastic tone. 'Having spent far too much time in the far reaches of some parallel universe with my brave parents and William's android substitute, I beg to differ.'

'Did she say brave parents, are you alright Anita?'

'Quiet Steven, this is sounding good.'

'I think my parents will agree when I say, William the android made plenty of important judgements on our behalf and was brave to the end. Tin man he may have been but he was all heart. So I suggest you listen to your own androids and take us all with you, if you value your so called honourable code that is.'

'William the android, as you quaintly refer to him, was, along with Anita's replacement, a special edition with experimental features. These allowed for a certain degree of logical independent thought not present in our android medical staff. I am sorry if you misunderstood their comments.'

'So that's it, you're condemning us to a life of work in the rice fields of Korea?' exclaimed William. 'I will not leave my family alone here, either we all go or we all stay here.'

'We have to look at the best way to avoid loss of life, this is our code. We have to maximise your family's survival chances and the best way to do that is for you to remain here. I am sorry you couldn't stay in Padstow with your new friends but that avenue is now closed to us.'

'Please listen we would rather risk the perils of...'

'Commander Aragon!' a security android had just burst into their meeting and began a hushed conversation with the Saviorian.

Even through his Simu Suit the Commander looked visibly shocked.

'Please excuse me I have just received some seriously worrying news which requires my full attention.'

Without further explanation Commander Aragon rushed from the room leaving the family startled and confused.

'It's all going wrong isn't it Steven? We'll never get home now.'

REVELATIONS IN THE CAVE

Commander Aragon was swiftly ushered to a waiting transport shuttle where he met up with Supreme Commander Bolivar who had made her way back from the gathering fleet, where she had been organising departure procedures.

In silence they boarded the craft, instantly lifting off for their destination in the Atlas Mountains of Northern Morocco. Only when airborne did Bolivar speak.

'Reliable android sources say an ancient explosive device has been found in the Owazanate Caves. The device was not on the list of those identified on our latest scan. Our androids are attempting to disarm the live munitions as we speak.'

The transport craft landed at the entrance to the cave and was immediately surrounded by android workers.

'Please come quickly, this way, you need to see this.'

Aragon and Bolivar broke into a lumbering trot, stumbling their way into the dark cave. Additional light was soon provided by android head beams.

'This way please, we are not sure whether to approach him or not, he's standing over the device.'

'What are you talking about, who is standing over the bomb, one of your androids?'

'Please your eminences, this way, into the cave corner, we may not have much time.'

The two high powered Saviorians clambered into the far corner of the clammy dank cave as the lights were trained on a figure crouched over the bomb. As he turned in surprise Commander Aragon was sure he recognised the man's features. 'This is impossible, it can't be you.'

A slight smile broke out on the face of the stranger as he appeared to complete his work.

'William Hawkins, it can't be, you, you are in Pyongyang, I left you there with your family,' Aragon drew nearer to confirm his suspicions.

The figure stood back from the bomb, held up four fingers and promptly vanished into thin air. Androids surrounded the bomb, confirming the fact that it had been rendered completely safe. The methods used to achieve this were a mystery to all present in the cave. It was as if the deadly weapon had turned to stone, matching the geology of its surroundings.

'Androids, did you manage to complete a face check confirmation, who was that man?'

'The Human standing by the ancient explosive device was indeed William Hawkins from the 21st Century.'

Bolivar contacted Pyongyang, 'Please confirm that William Hawkins is present at the base with his family.'

The reply came back in the affirmative, William and his family were in a deep and serious conversation with Professor Huntley and Doctor Honey, none of them had left the base during the mission to Morocco.

Checks were made confirming that no further copies of William the Android had been produced and the face check recognition backed up the fact that this had indeed been the warm blooded Human, William Hawkins.

On the short trip back to Pyongyang every possible explanation for William's materialisation in the cave was explored, as well as his sudden disappearance from the scene. The man in the cave had appeared to recognise Commander Aragon as he held up four fingers, what did this mean? Androids, tasked to search for any residual clues at the bomb site may have stumbled upon something. Aragon and Bolivar continued their discussions on the matter as they approached Pyongyang.

'I need to meet with William Hawkins and his family immediately, it is of the utmost importance.'

VALUABLE CARGO

The Hawkins family were escorted to Aragon's office again, this time under android guard.

'I wonder what this is about?' questioned Anita. 'Dr. Honey and Professor Huntley have not had a chance to put our appeal to Commander Aragon unless they spoke during the journey back.'

'Please don't get your hopes up dear, I still fear we are heading for the rice fields,' Jane was in resigned mood. 'That nice little Mr Honey creature held out little hope of a change of heart from Aragon even though he fully sympathised with their predicament.'

'Please wait in here, Commander Aragon will be along in a moment,' indicated one of the guards.

Aragon was concluding his discussion with Supreme Commander Bolivar. 'So we are agreed Supreme Commander, the entire Hawkins family must accompany us on our journey to Bellicose Minor even with the potential risks involved?'

'We have no choice Commander. William Hawkins must be on that ship and with his family, to provide the best chance they all have to return to the 21st Century. We have both seen the evidence in that cave, he is clearly the key to the continuation of the Human Race once we have left this planet.'

Aragon strode into his office, Simu-Suit in place. The family instinctively stood up, awaiting what was clearly an important statement. The Saviorian stared at William, the memory of the incident in the cave fresh in his mind. He knew it would be impossible to explain the real reason for their change of mind at this moment in time, that would have to wait until the journey to Bellicose Minor had commenced. However, Honey and Huntley had provided him with a way out.

'Please sit, I have been talking with my colleagues about your predicament. As you know we have serious misgivings about you joining us in space. However it is now the feeling of the Supreme Commander and the High Council that we have no choice but to take you all with us to Bellicose Minor and eventually return you to your own time on Earth.'

Anita just couldn't contain her emotions and launched herself headlong at the little alien. She kissed him hard on his Simu Suited face and immediately threw up all over the diminutive creature.

'Oh God sorry, I'd forgotten about your unique aroma, it certainly takes your breath away. Please forgive me I'm just delighted you are now taking us with you.' Aragon left the room for a quick hose down.

'Why do you think they've changed their minds?' questioned Steven.

'I don't know but I didn't much like the strange looks he was giving me, it was like he'd seen a ghost,' noted William.

'The ins and outs don't matter, we are going home and that's what counts.'

'Yes don't complicate things now Einstein, let's just get on that ship. We can ask all the questions we want once we've left Earth,' noted Anita.

Commander Aragon returned complete with fresh Simu- Suit.

'I think it best if we all keep our distance, don't you agree Miss Hawkins?'

'Absolutely!' replied Anita as she shrank into the corner.

'As I was saying, you will now accompany the Saviorian Fleet on its journey to Bellicose Minor. It is not anticipated to be a long assignment and it is now imperative to return you to your own time on Earth as speedily as possible. If there is the chance to let you Time Jump before our mission is complete we will endeavour to do so.'

All the time Aragon was addressing William directly as if the rest of the family did not exist. William wanted to know why it was now *imperative* but decided to wait.

'We will make final preparations for your living quarters which will now be set up on the Mother Ship and not on one of our smaller transport craft as we had originally planned. That way we can monitor your adaptation to space travel more closely and provide you with the maximum of comfort.'

Anita wondered why they had suddenly become the most valuable cargo in the fleet but decided to bite her tongue. She was all for a five star ride whatever the reason.

THE HAWKINS GO CRUISING - SAVIORIAN STYLE

On the day of departure five shuttle craft stood on a low lying plain on the edge of Pyongyang. This was all that remained of the vast Saviorian presence. At last it was time to leave, their work complete, at least that was the belief of the majority in their ranks. The Supreme Council believed they had stumbled upon a possible solution to the rogue bombs still appearing in a few places but the details had yet to be worked out on the way Bellicose Minor.

The Hawkins family now realised the enormity of the situation and were filled with a mixture of excitement and total fear. They had placed themselves in the hands of the Saviorians and had, as yet, no real reason not to trust them.

The shuttle craft lifted off in convoy, watched by the workers in the fields below, many giving a friendly wave. The confusion and disruption of the last few months now behind them, they could live their lives at their own pace again. As they ascended into the clear blue sky, Human heads aboard turned to watch the 26th Century version of their planet receding rapidly. Smoke rose from wood fires in all directions, people crossed the landscape on foot, on horseback and in boats, re-connecting, sharing and learning from neighbours they never knew they had.

On reaching the Mother Ship the Hawkins family were ushered to their special quarters by android guards. There had been no contact with the Saviorians since the confirmation of their inclusion onboard. All communication had been via the very efficient androids. This was all set to change as most of the android crew would be mothballed and then adapted for their mission on Bellicose Minor. Once they were on their way the Saviorians would take over the running of the fleet. The Humans would have little direct contact with their hosts, who would no longer be wearing SimuSuits, this was after all, their domain. However the aliens were well aware of the precious nature of their Human cargo as a result of the revelations in the Moroccan caves.

On entering their quarters the Hawkins family looked at one another in amazement, Anita summing up their thoughts, 'Oh my God!' They were on their way!

TIMES TICKING FOR THE TRELAWNEY BROTHERS

The waves pounded on the rocks around Trevose Head, washing into the sea caves with a ferocity more associated with winter storms. The seagulls wheeled overhead with their distinctive cries filling the air. From the deck of their newly launched fishing vessel brothers John and Simon Trelawney both thought they detected strange sounds on the wind. They appeared to be coming from inside a cavernous sea cave only accessible at low tide. To them it resembled the rhythmic ticking of a clock, sure and steady. They decided to investigate at low tide with a few mates from Padstow.

Tomorrow they would return.

THE CHRONICLES OF BELICOSE

On the face of it the natives of Bellicose Minor had everything going for them. An endless supply of home grown produce sustained by an idyllic climate meant a comfortable life for all. A constant surplus from their fields supplied three neighbouring planets with all their dietary needs. Mineral wealth on Icco, Slunk and Poz paid for their food supply and gave the inhabitants of Bellicose a comfortable standard of living, a perfect trading partnership.

Their largely vegetarian diet was occasionally supplemented with meat from the Vitabump. This illusive hog like creature produced a tender yellow meat which was much sought after. However, the Vitabump could reach speeds of sixty miles per hour on its six powerful limbs. Catching these three metre high snorting beasts was a feat beyond most Bellicosians. Vitabump herds numbered several hundred at a time but when approached they scattered in all directions making capture all the more difficult.

Towns and villages nominated suitable young fit and fast moving individuals to track down and outwit the illusive Vitabump. A peace loving race, the Bellies, as they were referred to locally, had developed few weapons. They did, however, possess a high pitched blood curdling scream which could paralyse the unsuspecting Vitabump in seconds. The problem was getting within the required twenty metre range for the scream to be effective.

Many a calm balmy Bellicose evening had been disturbed by the distant sound of pounding hooves and wild screams as the local groups of fifty heroes pursued their illusive prey. On average a ten day hunt produced a catch of just three startled Vitabump. The succulent yellow meat from one creature could feed up to one hundred Bellies with a rare treat from time to time. However, the effort that went into tracking down the beast meant the feast was reserved for very special occasions.

The only inhabited landmass on Bellicose Minor, Fecundland, had many other species of wildlife which, on the face of it, appeared more docile and eminently more edible than the Vitabump. There was just one small problem, they were all toxic to the Bellicose population. Many a native had lost their life after munching on a selection of these creatures. So it boiled down to plant matter and meagre portions of Vitabump for the peace loving Bellies.

The technological advances made by all of Bellicose Minors neighbours far outstripped those of the docile and a little dumb Bellies. The highly intelligent pigmy like inhabitants of Icco had been the first to develop interplanetary travel. Born out of a distinct lack of essential vitamins and a jealousy of Bellicose and their abundance of edible plant life, the Icco bridged the gap to their neighbours using their high tech Sling Shot Craft.

On the face of it the ingenious propulsion system appeared haphazard in the extreme. A good deal of seat of your pants technology had been refined to produce an occasionally efficient system. An elastic energy beam propelled their craft to Bellicose, loaded up with a valuable cargo of building materials and practical farming tools for example. Accompanying the goods were two brave Icco delivery men. On Bellicose Minor the natives loaded up a huge cargo bay with fresh produce. Timing had to be perfect as there was little room for delay, the energy beam recoiled within minutes of reaching Bellicose. The Icco visitors had just enough time to stamp the delivery notice and wave a fond goodbye before they were wrenched back towards their home planet with a fruit and vegetable consignment.

Contact between the planets was therefore very limited yet essen-

tial for their shared survival. Icco used a similar system to supply the fresh goods to Slunk and Poz. During the initial set up of the delivery system mistakes were made. Calculations on how much energy would be needed to reach Bellicose took time to perfect. Recently merchants sent out to negotiate exchange deals were left in mid sentence when the recoil mechanism whisked them back to Icco before they could close the deal on blue potatoes. There was certainly no time for small talk when you knew any second the invisible elastic band would leave you half way back home in the blink of an eye.

ASLEEP THROUGH IT ALL

'How much of this garbage have you read Einstein, if this was a Science Fiction novel you'd have thrown it in the bin by now?'

'You've hardly scratched the surface yet Anita. Remember what Commander Aragon said, it is essential to gain as much background knowledge and understanding of Bellicose Minor and its neighbours as possible before we arrive.'

'As if we're going to have any say in their plans. So come on how much do I have to read before I get to the juicy bit?'

'We need to understand all the background leading up to the Queen's dramatic change of diet. Commander Aragon wants a Human perspective on the situation.'

'You wouldn't think we were just hitching a ride on our way back home would you.'

'You are just as aware as I am that we are entirely in the hands of the Saviorians, we're hardly in a position to walk to the end of the street and catch a Number Thirty Five into town are we?'

'I suppose you're right, but help me out here, how many pages can I skip to get past the riveting explanation of Icco propulsion systems?'

'Alright, here let me show you, but don't leave out any more than that.' William pointed his sister to the appropriate place to restart her insight into Queen Eritima and compulsive cannibalism.

'Alright I'll give it another try, I mean it's not like we've got anything else to do here. There are only so many asteroids you can count streaking by your window at the speed of light. I should have insisted on being kept in deep freeze like the oldies for most of this journey. They should wake up with a new lease of life if a bit confused. Do you know how much longer they've got in cold storage?'

'I'm not sure, let me take a look.'

William walked to the far corner of their sparsely furnished quarters where the four Suspension Slumber Pods were lined up in horizontal formation. Two remained closed, keeping Jane and Steven Hawkins in a constant state of induced sleep. Their body temperature was reduced as were their heart rates. Implanted dreams were designed to renew and revive the brain. Quite what dreams they were experiencing, William could only guess at. The loud snoring noises penetrating Steven's Pod, led him to conclude they must be satisfying ones. He noted the readings on the display panel, they would both be awake in two Earth days, just in time to prepare for arrival into orbit around Bellicose Minor.

'Two days, that should give you enough time to finish your homework Anita.'

'Blow that, I'll give it a couple more hours to get interesting before I crib the rest from you.'

'You should get a few hours peace and quiet anyway, remember I've got an appointment with Professor Huntley.'

'Oh yes your tour of the fleets Drive Systems, yawn, yawn. Well I hope you think it's worth putting yourself through all that mess and stink, and you'd better have a couple of deep sanitising showers when you get back.'

'I'll be wearing a head to toe coverall, and the smell's not that bad once you get used to it. They're extremely proud if their unique green power plant, it's really quite exciting.'

'Whatever, just stay upwind of Huntley whenever you can and come back disinfected, ok?'

Anita thought she could get away with skipping all the detail concerning dodgy elastic bands and started where William had suggested.

THE YESARWILL REVOLUTION

Queen Eritima descended from a long line of female rulers on Bellicose Minor. The males of the planet are physically strong and very hard working but lack any sense of drive and ambition. While Bellicose females respect the position of the Royal Family, they have minds of their own, and are wary of the power the Queen wields over men.

Although resembling Humans in many ways, the green haired, red skinned Bellies have one unusual characteristic. Rather like some reptiles on other planets, they can shed parts of their anatomies and re-grow them overnight. If damaged, their limbs can drop off and be replaced by an exact copy, causing very little discomfort to the owner. However, the strange thing about this process is it only occurs in males.

During one particularly fierce hunt for Vitabump in the palace grounds a couple of careless fighters lost the use of their legs in the chase. The disguarded limbs were gathered up and prepared for disposal. The unsuccessful hunt had deprived the Queen of her Vitabump treat. She commanded the palace butcher to strip the flesh from the redundant limbs and instructed the cook to prepare a stew with the meat and a selection of tasty vegetables. There had been no history of cannibalism in the Royal Family let alone the population as a whole. She ate every scrap of meat and craved more. It soon became the custom to donate suitable limbs to supplement the Queens diet. As a result her majesty grew considerably stronger and even more demanding. Her appetite for Bellicose male appendages was insatiable and demand outstripped supply. Eritima already had a hypnotic hold over the men of Fecundland and encouraged all females to develop a similar control.

In a desperate state, the Queen summoned her chief advisors to come up with a solution to her voracious appetite. On the island there were many plants which possessed a sap with properties that encouraged obsessive behaviour. One such plant was the colourful Yesarwill, native to the north of the island. The Queens advisory panel suggested introducing an extract of sap into the staple diet of all males in the community. As almost ninety five percent of Bellicose women were in charge of preparing and cooking food for their men folk it would be relatively simple to bring this into their diet. It was promoted as an additional way to care for your menfolk, through a healthy food drink. The persuasive effect of the drug produced stimulants in the brain making the males open to auto suggestion. Note – it is similar to the 'Lap Dog' drug used on Mammiforous One in the Rigel Quadrant.

Batches of Yesarwill drinks were quickly produced and dispatched throughout the female population. The effects were instantaneous and permanent, with no known antidote. The true purpose of this new male dietary requirement soon became evident. Females who had clearly outgrown their male partners could make them an appointment at the palace to meet the Queen. They were more than willing to attend and obey their sovereign's wishes.

Male Bellies went to their deaths with a smile on their faces, having chosen for themselves how they wished to be consumed by Queen Eritima.

DIGESTIVE WASTE DRIVE

'You back already, there's some really cool stuff here Will, I'm well impressed, quite a girl our Eritima, if a bit gross.'

'I thought you might say that. Wait til you read the rest, she's caused some serious problems with her dietary fixations, brought the other planets to their knees. That's why the Saviorians have been called in. A bit more interested now are we sis?'

'I thought you'd stopped calling me that. I do like the idea of keeping the men down, might try and get my hands on some of that, what you call it, Yesarwill Juice if we get down there.'

'I don't think you realise how serious things have become, you really need to read to the end of the report.'

Well, I would have done if you hadn't barged in smelling of vomit, bile and farmyard entrails.'

'I had three showers on the way back here and that's all the thanks I get. Don't you want to hear what I've learnt today?'

'Not really but I'm sure you're going to tell me anyway.'

'Right good here we go then...'

'Oh God I need a drink, is there any of that red wine substitute left, it's not too bad after the third glass?'

'If it means you'll listen, go for it.'

The Hawkins family had been supplied with a selection of replica Earth like comfort items. Some hit the mark but others were worse than the worst Pot Noodle.

'Right, I'm all yours, you have five minutes then I really need to get back to the girl power story.'

'Have you ever wondered where all the excess digestive waste you keep going on about ends up?'

'I try not to.'

'Three hundred years on Earth, plus this little trip, where do you think it has all gone?'

'Give it a rest Geek Boy, you're making me feel sick thinking about it.'

'They've been storing it up in massive silos and now it's propelling us at warp speed across endless space, amazing don't you think?'

'Riveting. Don't even try to explain how it's done although I'm sure dad will hang on your every word once he wakes up. I don't suppose you had the chance to ask how and when the Saviorians plan to get us home did you?'

'Their priority is still the mission to Bellicose Minor but Professor Huntley did say something interesting. They want to talk to us once the parents have woken up, some sort of formal meeting with Nash and his superiors at High Fleet Command.'

'Sounds interesting, but I hope they'll allow us to wear translation belts, I've still not got a handle on the language. I quite like the sound of it but that's as far as it goes.'

'Yes, I know what you mean. It doesn't help when you know some of the words have multiple meanings depending on what day it is or what they've just eaten.'

'Yes clever clogs, just make sure they give us the belts.'

'It's fine Anita, Huntley gave me a belt to use when he showed me the ship's engines.'

‘Good, I’ve only just got used to being in the same room without their Simu-Suits on.’

‘Apparently they’ve been working on adaptations for Bellicose Minor that should be interesting.’

‘Really interesting I’m sure, now go and swat up on your Saviorian small talk, I need to finish my studies on The Cannibal Queen.’

‘

ZLODICH COMPLETES HIS REPORT

With an abundance of male meat on tap the Queen became more selective in her choice of cuts, only selecting the most attractive parts of her victims to devour. Her female courtiers were allowed to eat rejected parts, keeping them firmly in favour of Eritima's eating habits. A new palace extension had to be built to house her majesties spreading waistline but still the men came lining up to give her their all. Over time it became apparent that certain tasks, small and large, usually assigned to the males, were being neglected. Some womenfolk, who quite liked having their men around to perform these duties began restraining them or giving them reduced rations of Yesarwill to stop them sneaking off to the palace in the dead of night. The Queen, an astute if now rather rotund ruler got wind of these underhand tactics. She began to spare a few of the more muscle bound males to work as enforcers. They would root out and free the poor individuals who just wanted to serve their Queen, and get their name on the menu.

Although womenfolk willingly worked the fields, they did not possess the physical strength or speed of their male counterparts. Shipments of produce heading for Icco were becoming slow to assemble and their neighbours noticed. The Queen, formerly a very diligent ruler, showed no concern over this growing problem. Icco, on the other hand, had the populations of three planets to feed and supplies were dwindling. The rulers of Icco decided to take the dangerous risk of sending an Ambassador to stay on Bellicose and confront the Queen. This had never been attempted before. All pre-

vious conversations had lasted as long as the elastic rebound system allowed, minutes not hours at the most.

The tiny envoy was taken to the Queen's grand palace for questioning. The diminutive Ambassador only escaped with his life when Eritima failed to find any worthwhile meat on his tiny frame. He returned to Icco empty handed, extremely worried about the future. If the Bellicose men continued to feature on the Queens daily menu this could become a long term problem.

An emergency meeting was convened between the leaders of Icco, Slunk and Poz. They agreed it would be virtually impossible to force Queen Eritima out of power without the help of a section of the Bellicose population. The logistics of such an exercise was beyond their combined organisational skills. One possible solution would be to send out an emergency message to a neutral organisation. A delegate from Poz, who had travelled extensively in the cosmos prior to being stranded on the desert planet, had heard tale of a race who dedicated their lives to solving other people's problems. He thought they were referred to as Saviorians and would detect any distress signal and respond to it.

This is roughly where we stand now. Once our protracted mission on Earth was deemed a success, we received the orders to proceed post haste to Bellicose Minor and come up with a solution to their pending problem. It is clear from our orders that another Earth Scenario would not be tolerated, we are not about to argue with that. The added complication caused by our Human guests is unfortunate but can only be addressed after the Bellicose situation has been resolved.

This general information bulletin is for all crew members and will be updated as we approach the Bellicose System.

Commander Zlochich.

FEED STATION FRENZY

'Have you read this to the end Will? They won't even think about getting us home until they've changed the Queens diet.'

'To be fair they've always said that. We had the opportunity to stay on Earth 2515 but chose to Time Jump back home when the opportunity arose. At least we have it here in a bulletin so they don't appear to be going back on their word.

Anyway, I don't know about you but I'm starving. Do you want to stretch your legs and have something to eat on the observation deck or stay cooped up here with the snoring oldies?'

'Ok we'll risk it but I'm not walking all the way and have to wade ankle deep in bile and phlegm, we'll catch the Hop-it-Tram, that way I won't need two showers when I get back.'

The Saviorian Fleet housing the Hawkins family numbered over one hundred ships. They had left Earth 2515, some four terrestrial months ago, although the distance covered in Hyper Drive made rationalising their situation difficult. Earth, although still fresh in their minds, was in reality now a microscopic speck in the depths of space. The crew of over 50,000 were themselves unused to Hyper Space travel, having spent almost half their lives on the extended three hundred year mission to save the blue planet.

The caravan of high tech vessels was a floating city, self

sufficient in almost all aspects of life. The only potential weakness in the system was brought about by the Saviorian need for at least one live meal a day. Four complete cargo ships were taken up housing a virtual zoo of assembled animals, fish, birds and reptiles. The stock had been replenished before leaving Earth, which was just as well. Because of their extended stay, supplies from previous missions had been running low. For such a peace loving species their insistence on eating live meat was, to say the least, slightly odd, and their definition of intelligent life forms open to debate. Certainly the animals used to feed this fleet did not fall into that category, as far as the Saviorians were concerned.

The Hawkins family had been given quarters on the Mother Ship and a great deal of care had been taken over their welfare. This was entirely as a result of William's *situation*. One example of this was the Hop-it-Tram transport link, built especially for the four Humans. They could opt for walking alongside their hosts but this would almost always prove messy.

'The tram's here Anita, let's go, what on Earth are you wearing?'

'I'm taking no chances, I think I've covered all bases'. The only part of Anita's body left visible was a narrow horizontal slit for her eyes.

They boarded the Hop-it-Tram and punched the destination button marked *ush klosh* which they had learnt translated to Feed Station. The Hop-it-Tram ran parallel to a service walkway linking most of the major sections of the Mother Ship. The Tram afforded views of the crew as they went about their preparation tasks for arrival in orbit around Bellicose Minor. The diminutive reptilian like creatures, were not unfamiliar to William and Anita after their experiences on Earth. However they had not encountered them in such large numbers. It was still difficult to think beyond their physical appearance to an intelligent selfless being. Short flapping upper limbs waved in recognition as the Human Transport Pod rushed on. There was certainly no resentment regarding the Hawkins presence on their ship.

The tram slowed down slightly and William noticed something interesting off to their left.

'Look Anita, they told us the android stock would be adapted for the Bellicose mission.'

A vast assembly plant with androids at various stages of reconstruction stretched into the distance. They had played such an important part in saving Earth from nuclear destruction and finding a solution allowing their creators to finally leave the blue planet, now they would serve again. Anita was straining to get a better look when the glass screen of the Hop-it-Tram was sprayed with the half digested contents of a crew member's cavernous mouth. The automatic hose and wash programme sprang into action and swilled the mixture of fish guts and bile into the sewage system. A conversation between two crew members had begun, with the inevitable consequences.

'You never get used to that do you? Why don't they try to swallow before they speak?'

Fortunately the accompanying stench could not penetrate the tram's protective outer shell. It was difficult to see the new physical appearance given to the androids but it was certainly different from the convincing Human version deployed on Earth. Presumably they would mirror the physical features of the inhabitants of Bellicose Minor.

It was not clear whether any of the crew would set foot on the planet. If it was in their plans suitable Simu-Suits would also be in production to avoid startling the native population. William couldn't help feeling a little excited at what lay ahead on this new planet. He knew it was really none of his concern but his inbuilt need for adventure, coupled with an inquisitive mind, fed this ambition. He was totally unaware that much more adventure than he could handle was heading his way before long.

William and Anita and to a lesser extent Jane and Steven had made some Saviorian acquaintances back on Earth. Recognising them here on the Mother Ship was somewhat difficult without the aid of Simu-Suits. On nearing their destination at the Feed Station they spotted a tiny figure waving frantically at them from a nearby conference room.

'Someone looks pleased to see us, come on Einstein you're better at recognising these strange little waste disposal units, who is that?'

'I'm pretty sure it's Dr Honey. I'd recognise those eyes anywhere if you know what I mean.'

Dr.Honey held up his three digit hand to stop the tram.

'Please don't let him in, we'll get drowned if he opens his mouth.'

The diminutive alien was jumping up and down in a very excited manner. It was clear he wanted to convey his joy in words but realised after his time on Earth the effect it would have on his friends. Suddenly one of the doctor's colleagues ran up and placed a small device in his sucker covered hand. Instantly Honey's appearance changed to that of a diminutive Human male. Somehow he had acquired a Simu-Suit that had not been adapted for use on Bellicose Minor.

'I'm in dead trouble if they find I've still got this. We're under strict instructions not to wear Simu-Suits around the ship. It just makes it so much easier to communicate with you and the Translation Belt alone doesn't get around the problem you have with bodily functions. Can I come in then?'

'How can we refuse, I'm really touched that you did all this for us, open the door Will.'

Dr. Honey shuffled his way into the Hop-it-Tram and closed

the door, trying to keep out if sight.

'Come on then, what's the big secret you clearly want to share with us?' asked William.

'This conversation never took place alright? I'm for the Penal Colony if Aragon finds out I've spoken to you.'

'Just spit it out Doctor, that should be easy for you.'

'I'm due at a meeting with my bosses which I hear may have an extra significance for you Humans. Word has it they need to get you back to your own time as soon as possible, it's no longer just a favour to you.'

'That's great news but what's the sudden rush?'

'I really don't know the details but when I saw you passing by I just had to let you know, I realise what it means to you all to get home.'

'What do they mean it is no longer just a favour to us, sounds like they need us for something themselves. Come on Honey, you must know more, why do they need to get us home so quickly?'

'I've already said too much, you'll have to wait for the meeting, yes and your parents may be woken up sooner than planned if it's safe to do so.'

A couple of Dr. Honey's colleagues were trying to get his attention.

'Osh umphoshee, ishar oomph', they cried as one.

'They think Colonel Hafey of security might have spotted me with this Simu-Suit on, got to go, good luck!'

Honey slithered out of the tram simultaneously switching off his Simu-Sui,t leaving only the faintest trace of green bile behind.

'I hope he doesn't get into trouble, Dr. Honey is very Human in a lot of ways, I do like him.'

'Maybe, but he still dribbles like the rest of them.'

They were soon at the Feed Station. This was another purpose built room assembled for the Humans to eat in private. It took up a small corner of the main canteen for Saviorian workers. The tiny Perspex fronted room overlooked the huge dining area. William and Anita selected their meals from push button choices on the wall, their menu conveniently translated into English for the Earthlings. Their hosts had tried hard to replicate some of the Hawkins favourite dishes but there were always surprises. William was always reminded of his last Christmas dinner on Earth provided by the android staff where the giblets were conveniently left in the roast turkey, as a *treat.* They both selected a chicken pasta dish. At least they knew the chickens were fresh, they could see them running around the dining room behind them.

Anita sat with her back to the dining room window as she had no intention of witnessing the carnage playing out on the dining room floor. This was the live feeding room where diners selected their species then spent their entire work break catching and devouring their midday meal. There was a smaller dining area where meals had been killed in advance, but this was used mainly by crew members in a hurry. William had a strong stomach but even he couldn't watch for long. Why their hosts would incorporate a viewing window to their eating area was beyond Anita.

'Incredible, and these creatures devote all their lives, over six hundred years, to saving other planets and their civilizations from themselves, amazing. I don't know about you but I'm not hungry anymore, I'll be eating in our quarters from now on.'

DESPERATION

In order to avoid overshooting the Bellicose System the fleet would soon be disengaging from Hyper Drive. More conventional propulsion systems would kick in, giving time to prepare for the mission ahead.

Distress signals from Icco indicated that supplies of fresh produce from Bellicose Minor had almost dried up. The knock on effect was being felt on Slunk and Poz.

Queen Eritima was expanding every day and a special reinforced truck had been built to carry her bulk around. Her ladies in waiting along with other favoured courtiers were spreading liberally while more men folk vanished by the day.

The Queen still commanded the support of the female population.

The Saviorians would have to act swiftly.

DEVELOPMENTS ON EARTH

On their way back from the feed station William and Anita couldn't help noticing a build up of crew members heading along the adjacent walkway. Eventually the crowd connected with the back of a queue funnelling into the main auditorium.

'Something important going on in there,' noted Anita. 'Could be some kind of final orders briefing before we reach this Bellicose place, anyway we're not invited, our own meeting with the powers that be is up soon.'

The Hop-it Tram sped past the auditorium entrance. The Humans would find out soon enough what lay in store.

The tram deposited them at their Life Pod and sped off to the depot. They were welcomed inside by the sounds of a chorus of wrinkly snoring. Jane and Steven could have made a fortune back on Earth with their snorting harmonies.

A flashing light on their Info Screen told them they had a message. It came from Dr. Honey, which suggested he had not been arrested yet. He had conveniently translated it into English for them, saving a few hours guess work.

Your meeting with High Fleet Command has officially been brought forward to First Period 105 New Phase or 10.05 am if you insist on using your Earth time pieces. Your parents will wake up in two Earth hours time. Please be aware they will probably experience a degree of disorientation for a while.

A Hop-it-Tram will pick you up at 09.55am Earth time, please do not be late. Supreme Commander Bolivar and Commander Aragon will conduct the meeting. I will be there to translate where needed. There will be no Simu-Suits or Translation Belts available, so please brush up on your Saviorian language in the little time you have. If you are worried about fallout from our oral secretions please wear the wetsuits provided in your accommodation. Questions may be asked during this meeting however, the authorities stress it is an information based gathering with no alternative scenarios available if you don't like what is planned for you.

Our mission to Bellicose Minor is our prime objective however, developments concerning your home planet demand us to give your situation our immediate attention. Please have a restful night and prepare Jane and Steven for this important meeting - Pish aloosh Honey.

William and Anita stared silently at the screen trying to absorb its content, it's almost threatening tone was not what they had come to expect from their alien friends. It also had a note of panic attached as if their hosts were not in complete control of the situation.

'If this is such an important meeting why can't we use a Translation Belt? Maybe it suits them to keep us in the dark a bit? I still don't trust those little vomit making machines.'

'What I don't understand is what's happening at home. Are they talking about developments in our own time or what happened to us in the 26th Century?'

'We've got a lot to tell the oldies when they wake up that's for sure.'

The siblings were so consumed with the message from Dr. Honey that they hadn't looked through the view portal. They knew the ship had come out of Hyper Drive but hadn't realised there might be something worth looking at outside.

'Wow Will have you seen this, come here, have a look.'

Surprised by his sister's obvious enthusiasm he rushed to the portal. In clear view were the four planets in the Bellicose System. The most distant but largest was Poz, barren and rocky with lakes of yellowish orange, rich in mineral deposits. Spiky mountain ranges shot upwards like cathedral spires, impressive, with a sense of foreboding.

As the fleet circled the planets in a long and slow inspection the planet of Slunk came into view. Just one landmass had emerged from its vast seas of bubbling mud and toxic gases.

The next planet on this fascinating tour was Icco. Next to Bellicose this was the most highly developed in the system. From space it appeared nothing more than a vast yellow white desert with little vegetation. Its wealth lay beneath the surface where most of the population lived.

As they watched in awe Anita and William were left speechless by the beauty of Bellicose Minor. One quarter the size of Earth, it was by far the smallest planet in the system. The one inhabited landmass lay in a turquoise ocean. The verdant green forests and jungles could easily be identified from space, it looked idyllic. It was not hard to see why its neighbours relied on it for most of their food supplies.

'Maybe this space travel has its upside, I'm well impressed.'

'Coming from you, Anita that's quite a revelation.'

'Don't get me wrong I'm still desperate to get home for a legless girls night out but wow, that's quite something. Einstein the wrinklies are going to be gobsmacked when they wake up.'

'No wonder they want to get rid of the Cannibal Queen, millions could starve if she's not stopped.'

'You're not kidding, I mean it's a well known fact that most men are wimps but they need to get a grip and wire her jaws together or something.'

'I must say it would be interesting to hang around and see how the Saviorians sort this one out but it sounds like we might be heading home sooner than planned.'

'Yes, and don't you forget it was you who got us into this mess in the first place, concentrate on getting us home. I've got a bottle of Prosecco with my name on it waiting for me. We're all going home together, that's our best chance of success ok William?'

William knew she was deadly serious when she used his full name and deep inside he didn't want to let her down again.

'You've got my word on that Sis, now let's catch up on elementary Saviorian before the wrinklies wake up.

COME, MEET THE NEIGHBOURS

The Scientists on Icco had confirmed visual contact with the approaching fleet. They'd been in radio contact for some time but the situation was getting desperate. Not only were their own people beginning to panic, the natives of Poz and Slunk had watched their stocks of Bellicose produce dwindle to alarming levels.

This was particularly distressing to the people of Slunk who, over many millions years had grown incredibly tall. It was believed to be an evolutionary attempt to rise above the toxic gasses that spewed from the sprawling mud fields covering much of the planet. One unfortunate side effect of this growth spurt was a distinct loss of short term memory, so every day it came as a complete surprise to them that they were running short of food.

Authorities on Poz were demanding a solution to this desperate problem, at the same time insisting someone else sort it out. The experts in their delegation were a nightmare to work with, always passing the buck.

The Saviorians were quickly realising this mission may not be as straightforward as originally thought. Icco rulers had strongly recommended an urgent meeting between the four interested parties, to be overseen by Saviorian High Fleet Command. The chance of a delegate from Bellicose Minor being present was estimated as slim to nothing as their women were still one hundred percent behind the Queen and the men were still falling over one another to be her next meal.

The fleet would be in position in another twenty four hours and able to travel to any of the four planets in the system in a reasonable time frame. Once a plan had been agreed they would then move into orbit around Bellicose Minor to affect a final solution. Rested from their protracted mission on Earth, Logistical Officer Jackie Green and Chief Organiser Nash would head the initial meeting with delegates from the concerned planets. They would be aided by newly adapted androids who had been briefed on all technicalities relating to the Bellicose system. An initial meeting would be held on Icco to formulate a plan.

However an unfortunate situation on Earth demanded immediate attention which was why Commanders Aragon and Bolivar, witnesses to the final scenes on the blue planet, were taking charge of that particular problem. The fleet were under microscopic scrutiny after their protracted bungling engagement with the Humans.

THEY WERE SUPPOSED TO BE RESTING

Not unlike the ping on your microwave oven telling you the milk had just boiled over, so the warning bell on Jane and Steven's Suspension Slumber Pods sounded, which meant they were about to wake up. It had been recommended that, soon after leaving Earth, the two older Humans should be given additional time to recover from events on their home planet. Implanted dream sequences would help their brains reconcile the events in their recent past, at least that was the theory. This method had only been used on Saviorians in the past so there were no guarantees. However, the contented snoring had to be a good sign.

William helped them from their pods to the nearby seating area.

'Hello son, what are you doing here? God I'm starving, I could eat a horse.'

'You'd better join the queue at the Feed Station, there might be a couple of old nags left!'

'Anita, you're here too what a lovely surprise.'

'You seem a bit confused Dad, do you remember where you are?'

'Well actually now you mention it. I know we redecorated

not long ago but it isn't our sitting room is it?'

'Oh shit, here we go again, so much for sorting your mind out and leaving you refreshed.'

'There's no need to be rude Anita. Perhaps you can fill me in, are we still on holiday in Padstow?'

'Oh you remember that bit, not much more to catch up with! Over to you Einstein, good luck.'

'This really shouldn't be happening. We all thought it would be a good idea to let you and Mum use the Slumber Pods. Mum, you're very quiet, how do you feel, remember where you are?'

'Poosh inshoom sucumpeer ashushoo ump esompee William.'

'Oh great, it gets worse, she's picked up the old dribbling lingo.'

'Don't knock it Anita, this could be really useful for the meeting tomorrow, mum might be able to translate for us.'

'Is that right Mum, while you were snoring your head off you've learnt Saviorian speak?' Jane struggled indicating she was having trouble understanding English.

'Sloosh ush ish pooh,' she exclaimed, clearly frustrated with what was coming out of her mouth.

'I don't think she knows what she's saying, is that right Mum?'

Jane nodded frantically, pointing accusingly at the Slumber Pod. 'Ish pee ugleom.'

'It's no good Mum, none of us have anything more than basic Saviorian, can you not speak any English?'

'Soosh.'

'I know that one, soosh means no.'

'This is doing my head in, we'll have to get Dr.Honey over here, that Slumber Pod's a reject and Dad's one isn't much better.'

Steven had strolled over to the Observation Window, staring

wide mouthed at the fleet as it circled the planets of the Bellicose System.

'These new flat screen TV's are something else, is this another Star Trek film, I thought I'd seen them all?'

'You really don't remember anything properly do you Dad? And mum's not much help, even if she does understand us, she can't communicate in English.'

Just as Anita was about to contact Dr. Honey the ship board Communication Port flashed, meaning they had a message. It was from the Central Surveillance Officer and he had switched the translation mode on so the Humans could understand.

'Our remote cameras installed in your living space have picked up a problem when your parents woke up. I have been instructed to put your minds at rest. Our SSP units are calibrated for use with fellow Saviorians. In addition to this your parents were woken up earlier than planned because of your important meeting tomorrow. Please do not concern yourselves, the unfortunate side effects will wear off gradually over the next hour by which time Jane and Steven should be alert and totally aware.'

'Well that's a relief, they've been through enough over the last few months. This space and time travel certainly messes with your head.'

'I'm just relieved Mum isn't going to turn into a full blown alien spew making machine.'

'Anita, sleemph oolash very rude. I leeroot wooch what you're saying, choorooch clumph, it can be vert soophie you know.'

'Oh great, I think she's reverting back to English. Does this mean you'll be bilingual when your brain unscrambles Mum?'

'I slosh umph a single thing I'm eeripie in Saviorian, eech ukwee my answer must be yuk.'

'Are we in a real space ship, wow, is that a window, those planets, are they real?'

'God, it's like travelling the universe with a couple of infants. Hurry up and snap out of it will you, it's driving me bonkers.'

'Come on Anita, have a bit of patience, they are coming round.'

'I tell you what, you won't catch me sleeping in one of those brain frying pods.'

'With a bit of luck you won't have to. We could be heading home pretty soon.'

During the next half hour Jane and Steven slowly recovered from the effects of their SSP's but unfortunately were still full of questions.

'So what have we missed, I mean how long have we been asleep?'

'Yes, and who decided to umplee slappi in thee ceeloo pods?'

'We decided along with Dr Honey that you could do with complete rest and there isn't much to do during endless days of space. It would have been different if you had brought your knitting Mum.'

'You cheeky umpuloo!'

'You've been woken up at the exciting part. An important meeting with Fleet High Command tomorrow could result in us heading home very soon.'

It was obvious from the resulting conversation that Jane and Steven could now clearly remember leaving Earth 2515 and why.

'So those planets passing by our window are real aren't they?'

'Yes, that's the Bellicose System. God knows how far we've travelled to get here but we are completely in the hands of our alien hosts, so we must do whatever they ask and make their task as uncomplicated as possible, isn't that right Anita?'

'Well yes can't argue with that oh wise one.'

The sound of a Hop-it-Tram stopping outside disturbed their

conversation. The door slid open revealing a powerful looking green haired and red skinned male, clearly not a Saviorian, they knew that much.

'The surveillance department noted that the two older Humans had not eaten since being revived. Your nearest Feed Station has sent along a selection of tasty treats to revive you.'

The odd looking creature placed the tray of goodies on a nearby table and was about to leave when William asked, 'I didn't know crew members came from planets other than Savioria and you speak English.'

'I am android XP140, you clearly don't recognise me from our time on Earth. You should recall that all androids were taken out of service as soon as we left Earth. We have now been adapted to resemble the people of Bellicose Minor in order to blend in with the native population when our mission begins on the planet's surface. I apologise if my appearance confused or startled you. In my time on Earth I was one of the android nurses in attendance when you were undergoing tests in our Padstow Think Tank.'

'That's amazing, please excuse me if I don't remember you but I'm surprised you are allowed to keep memories from previous missions.'

'A very good point sir, only those of us who have proved capable of retaining information without swamping our memory banks have this ability. It can be of use to our masters when a point of historical reference needs to be confirmed.'

'That's fantastic, and this is what the people of Bellicose Minor look like? Slightly strange but a vast improvement on your masters.'

'Anita don't be so rude, thank you so much for the food I think we're ready for it.'

'No problem, if you'll excuse me I have to go and have my Bellicose speech module implanted.'

‘Oh there is just one more question I have been meaning to ask but thought it rude.’

‘If I am able I will help, ask away.’

‘Many of the Saviorian crew use very familiar Earthly names like Nash and Jackie Green while others like Commander Aragon are less familiar, is there a reason for this?’

‘I’m sure they wouldn’t mind you asking. Many of our masters grow tired over their long lifespan and feel somewhat reborn when they adopt a name from another planet. Having spent so long on Earth it is not surprising that they have taken on names familiar to you, I would take it as some sort of compliment, if that answers your question?’

‘What a touching idea, thank you for explaining.’

‘It shouldn’t seem so strange to you Brother, I’ve got lots of names for you.’

With that the android returned to the tram on route to the lab for final adjustments.

The kindest thing that could be said about the hot snacks so thoughtfully provided was that they didn’t move on their own and the taste was better than appearance.

‘So how are you two feeling now?’ William was anxious to assess his parents readiness for the forthcoming appointment.

‘Yes, I think all the bricks have fallen into the right spaces now Son but I can’t speak for your mother.’

‘Feeling much better now William, although I could understand everything going on around me, when it came to talking I couldn’t control what came out of my mouth. I’ll be no use at eoomh meeting, see there I go again, but it’s getting better.’

‘That’s a great relief to both of us isn’t it Anita?’

‘Absolutely, Mum struggles with the English language at the best of times so we don’t want to complicate things. What’s next Einstein?’

'The way I see it we could be out of here by tomorrow. They clearly feel the need to get us back to Earth in a hurry. What I don't understand are Dr. Honey's comments about developments on out home planet. Sounds serious, and it if is how can we help the situation?'

'I bet it's to do with our rare Mongolian goat herd Jane, no one's been looking after them, they may have escaped and run a mock in the village.'

'You're still not right in the head are you Dad? Do you not think it might be more serious than that? Aliens from the 26th Century are not going to delay the rescue of a planetary system because your precious goats are munching through grocer Tom's turnips!'

'Yes Anita, you're probably right.'

'One thought geek boy, when they say developments on our home plant, do they mean now or five hundred years ago in our time?'

'Good point, wow I am impressed. They must mean our own time, why would the conversation be about getting us back otherwise?'

'Oh, please let that be true, I just want to get back to my own house and have a decent soooshawee, sorry cup of tea.'

'I still don't see what makes us so important now.'

'Remember Dad, we've just helped the Human race get its independence back after three hundred years, that's not to be sniffed at.'

'Yes Einstein, but if you hadn't insisted on having a holiday in prehistoric Padstow none of this would have happened.'

'Actually it was me winning that competition that soomsh us to Cornwall in the first place. If we'd decided not to go we wouldn't beoos here now, how did we get in such a mess?'

'If I understand it right, and believe me several times I've woken up expecting it all to have been some weird dream, the Saviorians manipulated events to help them out of a sticky situation.'

'You're right dear, none of us are to blame. Let's just hope things are not that bad back home and we can pick our normal lives up again.'

The window portals slid shut blocking out the view of the Bellicose System, ever nearer now. It was time for some much needed sleep for Jane and Steven, free from the influences of their SSP pods. A monumental day lay ahead for the Hawkins family.

'Switch that bloody light out Anita!'

KAREN CAN'T BELIEVE HER EYES

The Trelawney brothers returned directly to the safety of Padstow harbour with the strange ticking sounds from the sea cave still echoing in their ears. They had abandoned any attempt at fishing and made a quick dash back to port. The continued harbour reconstruction meant a hive of activity welcomed the cries from the deck of the New Dawn fishing vessel and soon a crowd had gathered on the quay.

'Calm down young Simon, youm makin no sense yellin like that,' Old Jim Dakin helped secure the New Dawn and Simon Trelawney clambered ashore. 'Now tell us again what's this all about?'

'Well, we was just getting our gear out when we hears this funny noise comin out of nearby cave.'

John had now joined his brother on the quayside. 'Yes, but the swell out there's something fierce so we couldn't get that close.'

'Yes John, but close enough to hear it. Like the tickin of Granny Lockwood's grandfather clock only great deal louder.'

'Yes and wem sure there was some sort of red light flashin, casting reflections on yon cave walls.

'Twasnt firelight nor nothin more regular like?'

'No, so we thought we might go back at low tide, try and clamber in there for a proper look.' '

‘Might be an idea to let young Ken or Andy’s maid Karen hear your yarn. Could be somethin them there aliens left behind,’ suggested Mr Dakin.

‘Good idea Jim, come on Simon we’ll go track them down.’

Ken and Karen were to be found in the library putting together some practical tips on building a crude mechanical seed drill. When they heard the story from the Trelawney brothers they headed to the New Ship pub where some interested locals had gathered for the latest gossip.

‘You got any idea what this might be Ken?’ asked Jim Dakin.

‘Karen and I have been thinking about it on the way down here but we don’t want to alarm folks for no reason.’

‘Don’t talk in riddles Ken we know it’s not no Grandfather clock, so what be it?’

‘Well, continued Karen, ‘before the Saviorians left they unfortunately discovered a number of stray bombs left behind from that nuclear war the aliens put a stop to. They had another sweep of the planet and assured us they had all been found. Sounds like John and Simon might have stumbled on another.’

‘Holy cow, bomb you say, sounds dangerous to me, might she blow up on us or somethin?’ yelled Connor Luckham, an excitable young farmer from Little Petherick.

‘Let’s not get too worried, if it is an old bomb it’s been there for over three hundred years. The chances of it exploding must be extremely slim.’

‘Them there aliens should come back and fix it for us.’

‘Oh yea and how do ye propose tellin them, yellin up into the sky ,or sendin some smoke signals? They be miles away now, won’t hear you up there you daft cabbage.’

‘Alright boys this won’t help, we’re on our own with this one,’ pointed out Ken.

‘If you Trelawney boys are up for it I’d like to take a look tomorrow. We could go out with the tide and step in the cave at low water if the weather's set fair.'

'I'll be coming too Ken, together we might see a way forward.'

'No point trying to dissuade you Karen, and your input would be valuable.'

'Andrew Dawe reckons, judging by sea and wind conditions, we're set fair for tomorrow.'

'I think we should keep this bomb idea as quiet as possible, no need to worry the town folk at this point. Let the Trelawney boys, Ken and the young maid have a nose in the morning and take it from there.'

'Good idea Jim, right who's for a game o euchre then?'

'What do you think Ken?' asked Karen as they strolled back towards the library.

'Sounds suspiciously like an old bomb to me, we've certainly been left in the lurch by our alien friends. So much for promising us they'd found all the explosives.'

The next day with the tide on the turn the four brave souls readied themselves to sail out of Padstow harbour aboard the New Dawn. In true Padstow tradition word had spread to every corner of this tight knit community who now crammed the quayside to wave them off, armed with homemade pasties and supplies of ale. John and Simon were pretty sure they could remember the location of the sea cave. It was not that any of these new seafaring folk were familiar with the North Cornish coastline having only recently been released to the world outside their own little town.

Within an hour they were lying off Trevose Head and Simon spotted the cave entrance. Today's sea was relatively calm as predicted and a narrow slither of sand indicated the cave entrance was exposed and partially dry.

They manoeuvred the small fishing vessel into place and

rowed the last few yards, avoiding the rocks, to the cave entrance, where they grounded the New Dawn. The wind had changed direction overnight and they strained hard to hear any unusual sounds.

'Are you sure this is the right cave boys because I can't hear anything except the gulls.' noted Ken

'I must admit that ticking sound seems to have stopped.'

'Let's have a look anyway, it's quite a deep cave by the look of it.'

'Ok Karen, but you step careful like, it's hell of a slippery in ere.'

As they advanced they stopped every few steps listening for any strange sounds, and for a second John thought he heard and maybe saw something, but if he had it must have been his imagination, there was nothing there.

'Did anyone bring a lamp?'

'Yes, here in my bag I think,' said Ken.

He lit the wick with a taper and shone the flickering light around the walls. They were about to give up when Karen thought she saw movement in the far corner.

'There, shine it over there, look!'

The flame picked out an unusual metallic object the size of small beer barrel resting on the cave floor.

'Where the hell did you come from?' shouted John.

Crouched alongside the rusting cylinder was the figure of a young man, he looked up from his work and smiled, at the same time somehow transforming the bomb to stone. Karen, close to fainting fell into Ken's arms. The young stranger appeared to raise two fingers as if in the act of counting.

'Dear God, it can't be you, you left with the others off into space. William is that really you? Please talk to me.'

With that the stranger was gone, vanished into thin air.

They searched every inch of the cave but he was nowhere to be found, gone in the blink of an eye. They approached what they had thought to be the bomb but all that remained was a smooth barrel shaped rock.

'Who did you think you saw Karen, you're as white as a ghost?'

The girl stared at the space where the figure had last been, her eyes wide with disbelief.

'Come on tell us maid, I never caught sight of his face.'

'Ken, didn't you see him, his face was as clear as day. I've missed him from the moment he left Pyongyang.'

'William Hawkins? You know that's impossible.'

'Yes, yes it was Will, I'm sure of it.'

'But there was no way for him to get back here from the other side of the world, all the transport left with the aliens.'

'I don't care, I know what I saw, Will it was Will. Please come out Will, you can't have just vanished, I really miss you Will.'

They all searched again, Karen even calling his name again through a veil of tears, there was no one.

'Must have been a trick of the light maid, no other explanation for it, nothing out of the ordinary here unless we've got the wrong cave,' noted Simon.

'I did see something move Karen but as Simon says, flickering light can play tricks with your mind. Any road we'd better head back to the boat, tide's turning we can head home soon.'

As they left the cave they checked for any strange sounds on the wind or lights from other caves, there was nothing. Karen was left hoping William had somehow returned but couldn't explain his sudden disappearance from the cave.

She might spend the rest of her life wondering, she cut a forlorn figure as they turned for home.

PROBLEMS PILE UP

Overnight the news from Bellicose Minor indicated the situation had worsened. The delegates from the neighbouring planets were demanding their meeting with the Saviorian Fleet be brought forward.

The Mother Ship had moved hastily into position orbiting Icco. Demands had been made for more senior officers than Jackie Green and Nash to travel to the planet so now Commander Bolivar was to join them. This meant a delay in the scheduled meeting with the Humans. Once again the Saviorians were faced with a delicate situation, balancing the two emergencies, and the eyes of their masters were trained on them.

The Hawkins family were rested and ready for their 10.05am appointment. They were just about to jump on the Hop-it-Tram when a message flashed on their Communications Port.

Sorry to inform you of a last minute change of plan. Your meeting with Fleet Command has been delayed. Please wait in your accommodation for further information.

'It's worse than bloody Southern Rail what do you thinks going on Einstein?'

'It could be something to do with Bellicose Minor, the Queen might be asking for seconds!'

INSULTS ON ICCO

A shuttle craft with a delegation of three Saviorians and a crew of Androids headed for the surface of Icco. Newly designed Simu-Suits and android adaptations would be used for the first time. These gave the Saviorians the appearance of Bellicose natives. It was hoped this wouldn't confuse or upset their hosts but they needed to be tested at some point.

As the shuttle craft hovered over the planet's surface nothing could be seen but a yellow and white windswept desert. Its topography exhibited little in the way of hills or mountains, a barren and inhospitable place. They landed at the co-ordinates provided by their Icco hosts with no sign of life or welcoming party.

Commander Bolivar was attempting to communicate with the Icco delegation when the ground began to shake. Their shuttle was descending beneath the deserts surface on a hydraulic platform cut into the surface. It came to rest a good hundred metres below ground level.

The Communications Screen burst into life with the image of what appeared to be several of their hosts crushing to get into the picture. The image of six or seven pigmy like creatures with wild black hair and oversized heads would have seemed comical to a human observer. Saviorians however, had seen it all before on their travels and smiled politely in return.

The close connection between the Icco people was clearly not just a physical one, becoming evident when they spoke, each taking turns in contributing.

'Welcome,'

'to'

'Icco.'

'please'

'join'

'us'

'in'

'our'

'Central'

'Square'

'just'

'outside'

'your'

'ship.'

Jackie Green and Nash exchanged glances as if to say this could become annoying.

They stepped outside the protection of their craft but were pleasantly surprised by the sub-terrainian atmosphere. The air was fresh with a comfortable temperature of twenty one degrees. The Icco people clearly possessed a highly efficient filtration system that circulated air throughout their cavernous underground world. Their welcome party had nominated one senior dignitary to speak for them all, which was clearly a relief to the Saviorians, although there was a good chance someone would jump in.

'The entire population of Icco welcome you to our beautiful planet. We all appreciate you answering our distress message and are sure you will come up with a swift solution to the Eritima problem. Your remarkable resemblance to the Bellicose people is a surprise to us all, but might give us an advantage in removing the Queen from power.'

Commander Bolivar explained the use of Simu-Suits and androids to disguise their natural beauty.

'That's'

'brilliant.'

'Remarkable!'

'Well'

'done,' exclaimed the assembled Iccos.

'Our friends from Poz and Slunk await us in our Conference Room. Unfortunately no one from Bellicose Minor was willing or indeed able to join us.'

The Saviorian delegation boarded a transport shuttle and sped off down a nearby connection tube bound for the conference centre. Their diminutive stature made them well suited to the dimensions within the Icco world, the same could not be said for the representatives from Poz and Slunk. The shuttle took a good ten minutes to reach its destination even though it travelled at breakneck speed on its smooth rubber wheels. The noise on approaching its destination was deafening. Crowds of Iccos were lining the trackside shouting and screaming approval of their intended saviours.

They were ushered into the Conference Room where the delegates from Slunk and Poz stood to welcome them. One unfortunate representative from Slunk promptly struck his head on the ceiling, sat down in agony only to stand up again and repeat his unfortunate actions. Their propensity for short term memory loss could prove awkward in forthcoming negotiations.

'You people really should think of others when we get together like this. Your minute chairs are totally inadequate to accommodate our larger frames.' The senior delicate Poz did not stand on ceremony. 'I must say I am surprised to see representatives from Bellicose Minor here, does this mean the Cannibal Queen has eaten her fill of your men folk and we can get our supplies of food back again?'

'Unfortunately not, these are our esteemed guests from the Saviorian Fleet, come to help us in our hour of need. They are in disguise as Bellies, ready to blend into the background of that troubled planet.'

The delegate from Slunk stood up again to speak, banged his head, looked confused and collapsed into his undersize chair.

The president of Icco, Fuzz, brought the assembled delegates up to speed with the increasingly dire food situation.

'Our last six visits to Bellicose Minor have seen no deliveries of food deposited at the pickup points. Equally worrying, our visiting merchants saw no sign of life at the formerly bustling depots. Reports say Queen Eritima has almost all males enslaved in her palace compound, sharing them out with her ever expanding coven of cannibalistic females.

'Our stock of fresh fruit and vegetables is diminishing fast and we can no longer pass on supplies to our neighbours on Slunk and Poz. This is causing friction between our peoples, something we have never experienced before. General Rotundia, have you anything to add from a Poz perspective?'

'You're damn right I have, it's a disgrace. The people of Poz feel betrayed and left to starve. We have two weeks supplies left and we will not ration our population, so get your finger out and sort it Fuzz!'

'Thank you for your usual constructive observations. I take it we will not be counting on any practical support from you?'

'Damn right, you sort the problems, we complain, that's the way it is.'

'Professor Whatmee how are you coping on Slunk? Please don't feel you have to stand up to respond.'

'Thank you err..'

'Fuzz.'

'Yes, thank you President Fuzz, what was the question? Oh yes, I think we have just ten days worth of food to distribute to our people, is that right Doctor Ivorgot?'

'Sorry, what was the question again?'

'Yes err.. Fuzz what did you ask me?'

'Supplies, how much food have you left?'

'Yes food, well Ivorgot how is it looking?'

'Didn't I tell you Professor, ten days? Our food seems to be running out, can anyone enlighten us?'

'I'd enlighten you with a slap in the face if I could reach that far up', noted the irate Poz, General Rotunda. 'When we've had meetings before you have recorded discussions to remind you what has been said, why are you not doing so this time?'

'Did we, what a good idea, right recording device now active.'

Commander Bolivar had heard about enough. She got to her feet and the room fell silent.

'If this is an example of how you go about solving major problems it's no wonder you called for us. Can we get down to business? There is no time to spare as we have another serious problem to address on board our Mother Ship.'

'Well said Commander, we are not helping matters with needless squabbling, please continue Commander Bolivar.'

'Firstly, in order to prevent food shortages in the short term I am willing to authorise a shipment of live meat from our Farm Ships to each of your three planets. This should keep you going while we deal with Queen Eritima.'

An audible gasp of horror circulated the room. The watching Iccos were not sure they'd heard the Commander right.

'Did she say live meat?'

'No we must have heard that wrong.'

'She did you know, I think I'm going to be sick.'

'Quiet!' President Fuzz was growing increasingly frustrated. 'I'm sorry Commander but could you repeat your offer, I don't think I heard you correctly?'

'Yes, the Saviorian Fleet do not have limitless supplies of fresh meat but we can provide you with enough animals to feed your populations in your hour of need. Our reputation for being kind and selfless creatures is founded on countless examples similar to this one.'

'Well err, that is indeed very generous, but you see the truth is err,'

'Oh come on Fuzz just tell it like it is, Commander we are all vegetarians, couldn't stomach eating meat let alone the live version. You're just one step away from the Cannibal Queen, you'll have to do better than that Bolivar, am I not right Professor Whatmee?' With his usual tact General Rotunda had put his substantial foot in it.

'Sorry we don't eat meat do we Ivorgot, at least I don't think we do?'

'I can't remember ever eating meat Professor, I think I'd know if I had.'

'I'm afraid we are all strict vegetarians which makes the situation with Queen Eritima all the more repugnant,' squirmed Fuzz.

Commander Bolivar was on her feet ready to leave the meeting but was restrained by Jackie Green and Nash.

'Please Commander, we cannot leave now, these creatures are desperate and hopelessly inept at the same time. We cannot walk away, you know that, especially after our prolonged mission on Earth. The penal colony awaits us if we fail this task.'

'Yes I know you are right Jackie, forgive me. My mind keeps

straying to the Human problem, very unprofessional. Why did we ever agree to take the Humans with us after leaving Earth?'

'Now is not the time Commander, do you wish me to continue on your behalf?' enquired Nash.

'Not at all, let's get on with it. I apologise for the oversight regarding your dietary preferences. We can offer you a supply of fresh fruit and vegetables from our stores and I will ask our scientists about the possibilities of developing a temporary system to grow your own produce, counteracting the harsh climatic conditions on your planets.'

'That's more like it,' commented General Rotunda.

A degree of order returned to the room. Whatmee and Ivorgot reviewed proceedings so far without the need for further disruption. Practical help would clearly not be forthcoming from the planets in need of rescue, so, as with many of their past missions, the Saviorians found it was down to them to solve the problem alone.

Commander Bolivar continued, 'As you are probably aware, we are a peace loving race and will not resort to force to remove Queen Eritima from power. We need to set up a viable opposition to the Queen and persuade enough natives that her eating habits are not conducive to the long term health of the population. Our team of highly developed androids will infiltrate the Bellicose society and foster the idea amongst the female population that their men folk are worth keeping away from the Queens dinner table. We have developed some harmless drugs to help in their task. It is also important that we create a sustainable alternative to Eritima once she is deposed.'

'This is all well and good but how long do you think this plan will take to work? Only we demand that life is orderly, regimented and predictable at all times,' General Rotunda once more demonstrated his diplomatic skills.

'General I implore you it must be obvious, even to your good self, that the Saviorians are here to help with no advantage to themselves. We do not want to alienate them before their work has even begun' Fuzz was clearly exasperated by the General's intervention.

Professor Whatmee was losing patience himself and stood up to make his point more forcefully, but banged his head on the ceiling and collapsed in his chair.

'Well if there are no further questions of any importance we need to make progress with this mission,' Bolivar was clearly frustrated with the apparent lack of appreciation of their efforts and indicated she was ready to leave the conference room. 'President Fuzz, if you could show us back to our craft I will contact you when we are ready to implement our plan.'

'Certainly Commander and on behalf of all delegates assembled here you have our heartfelt thanks for what we hope will be a swift solution to our shared problem.'

'Well thank you President, I can clearly see the amount of work the Icco people put into making your alliance work. We will send emergency supplies down to all three planets straight away.'

'That's right, get to work, the people of Poz are starving you know, put your words into actions Bolivar,' General Rotunda stood and indicated where the door was with a dismissive gesture.

'Safe journey back to err where are they going? Oh bother!' Whatmee and Ivorgot were left sprawling on the floor in a predictable state of confusion.

'Well done Commander that took a great deal of self control.'

'I do not wish to discuss it Jackie, let's just get the job done and leave them to it, incredible!'

The whole party were relieved when their shuttle delivered them back to the Mother Ship. All they needed on top of this was the Human problem, an altogether more complex issue than Queen Eritima.

I'LL EAT IN, THANK YOU

The Hawkins family had waited an entire Earth morning with no further news and they were now in need of food and an explanation.

'I wouldn't mind but they brought you wrinklies out of cold storage early for no good reason.'

'It's nice to see you too Anita,' noted Steven.

'So shall we go and eat at one of the Food Stations? I could do with some fresh air,' noted Jane.

'You go ahead but leave me out, I've had enough of watching poor innocent creatures being chased around a room to the point of exhaustion only to have a leg bitten off by a slobbering little alien.'

'Surely you're exaggerating Anita, you know it wouldn't be the first time.'

'For once she is right Mum, they certainly are messy eaters. However, we must remember, as I've said before, this is their world, their normal behaviour and we are the guests.'

'You three go but I'm going to pass on throwing up again if you don't mind. I'll send out for something vaguely edible from our extensive Eat In menu.'

'I would still like to see the Food Station at first hand. If there is any animal cruelty taking place I may make a formal complaint to the authorities.'

'Good luck with that Dad.'

A Hop it Tram was summoned and Anita was left to stare at the beauty of the Bellicose system of planets. Her eyes wandered to the vast blackness of space beyond. Earth was out there, somewhere, but it might as well not exist, such were their chances of reaching it again. She was overwhelmed with a feeling of helplessness as she tucked into her freshly delivered parrot pie.

NOTHING BETTER THAN SAVAGES

Commander Bolivar's party reported back to High Fleet Command, careful to omit the frustrating aspects of their Inter Planetary Conference. Androids were to be sent to Bellicose Minor and supplies of vegetarian items to the other three planets. Thoughts could now turn to the Human problem with a rearranged meeting time of 7.00pm Earth time. Commander Aragon, Dr. Honey and Major Main were to brief the Humans on their return to Earth and the secret mission attached to the process.

'I'm lodging a formal complaint to the relevant authorities. I have never witnessed such barbaric behaviour towards innocent animals in all my life. I had to stop your mother before she caught sight of what was going on, truly shocking.'

'I did warn you Dad.'

'Is that all you can say Anita? You work with animals just like we do, your friend Honey, he needs to know what's going on.'

'Dr. Honey has live lunches just like the rest of his kind, it is part of their everyday lives.'

'I'm surprised at you William, you have some influence with these creatures, can't you make them see this is totally wrong?'

'Unfortunately it's the way they choose to live and we have no power to change that.'

'Well I'm having nothing more to do with them, call themselves intelligent advanced beings, they're nothing better than savages!'

'We all agree with you Steve but if you want to get back home to your so called civilized world we need their help, we are in their hands.'

'It's all very well for you to say, Jane, you didn't see the carnage.'

'You enjoy a good steak on a Saturday night Dad.'

'That's different, I don't chase the poor cow round the restaurant first.'

'I don't think the Saviorians would see it that way, it still ended up in your stomach.'

'I'm talking animal cruelty here, it's disgusting.'

'This conversation is a complete waste of time, we need to put our morals aside for one moment. The universe has many different ideas of what is normal, just look at what is happening down there,' William pointed to the window and Bellicose Minor beyond.

'There's someone in authority clearing her way through her own male subjects, let's try not to be judgemental.'

'William Hawkins for Prime Minister, that's what I say. Now can we find what's happening with our ride home?'

No sooner had Anita asked the question when a message flashed up on the Com. Screen.

Your meeting with High Fleet Command will now take place at Phase Three 05. Your transport will pick you up at 6.55 Earth Time.

'At last, now please Steven, try to put the thought of live lunches out of your mind and co-operate with our hosts, they are our ticket back home to some sort of normality.'

'Alright Jane but I'm still not happy.'

Another message flashed up on the screen.

Professor Huntley would like to meet William in the Main Engine Room at 3.00pm Earth time to complete his tour of the ships' propulsion systems. A Hop-it-Tram will pick him up in good time, please attend we feel he will find this additional part of the tour enlightening. Due to the restricted space in this part of the ship we ask that he come alone. We ask him to confirm that he will attend by pressing the green button on the com screen now.

Without hesitation William complied and pressed green.

'That's funny, I was sure the tour was complete. You three don't mind if I go? If it's anything like the first tour it should be fascinating.'

'No you trot along and get enlightened Einstein, us mere mortals will satisfy ourselves with a game of Corner the Cow or was it Devour the Donkey. These board games are all the rage in high Saviorian Society.'

'Anita please, your father is still trying to keep his anger in check. I must say Will, you're very much flavour of the month with our hosts. Still I suppose you've spent a lot of time with them, especially back on Earth, helping them sort out whatever they had to sort out.'

'You mean the continued existence of Human life on Earth?'

'Yes, that's it dear.'

WILLIAM'S MISSION REVEALED

The Hop-it-Tram arrived and William was waiting to board. After a journey of no more than a couple of minutes it arrived at the destination. William thought it strange, this wasn't where he remembered the Main Engine Room to be. The doors opened and he stepped onto the walkway. There to meet him were Dr Honey and Major Main, in full Human Simu-Suits.

'Sorry about the confusion William but we need to talk with you alone, please this way.'

They entered a small briefing room to be met by Commander Bolivar, also in her old Earth Simu Suit. She looked visibly shocked when their eyes met.

'It really was you in that cave. I know we had all the confirmation possible but I didn't quite believe it until now.'

'I'm sorry, you've completely lost me, have we met before?'

'Please excuse my somewhat confusing welcome. I am Commander Bolivar, we met in a remote cave in Morocco but I fear you will not be aware of that. Please sit down Mr Hawkins and we will try to explain, can you continue Major Main.'

'Thank you Commander. If you recall during your time in Pyongyang, not long before our departure from Earth, we had some problems with rogue munitions left over from your planets intended nuclear war. As part of our cleansing operation we assumed all WMD's had been removed and disposed of in our orbiting refuse vessels. The detection systems used when we arrived on Earth three hundred years ago were clearly lacking in some way, we had inadvertently overlooked a few munitions. Our updated scans identified these missing weapons which we cleared out straight away.

We were just about to depart for Bellicose Minor when the call came to visit the remote cave system of Owazanate in Northern Morocco. To our frustration our androids had located another long lost explosive device. Departure from Earth was in a few hours and as you are aware William, once we leave a planet we never return. We had to make the bomb safe before we left. Our androids led us deep into the cave. Android head beams lit up the far corner of the cave and stooped over the explosive device was the figure of a young Human male working at defusing the bomb. Commander Aragon recognised the Human who turned with a smile, raised four fingers and promptly vanished. Our androids confirmed the figure as being William Hawkins.'

'How ridiculous! I've never been to Morocco, never mind to a remote cave with a bomb in it. You've got the wrong man, it wasn't me.'

'You are correct in one respect. The William Hawkins we see before us at this moment in time has not been to that cave, but it was you.'

'How incredible, as my sister Anita would say, someone needs to take more water with it. It's simply not possible.'

'Yes it is possible, we have the ability to time travel, though we rarely use it. Remember, we brought you from the 21st century. We used time travel to bring you to the 26th Century, did we not?'

'Yes you are right, I still can't quite get my head round everything that has happened, so forgive my inability to grasp it all.'

'Yes off course, we must move on. While on our journey to

Bellicose Minor our scientists have been working on the technology we think you used in the Moroccan cave to defuse the bomb and turn it to stone, and we believe we have succeeded. I have to admit to you now, if it were not for what we witnessed in that cave, none of your family would be on this ship now. We want you to fulfil your destiny and enter that cave, history demands it. We also believe there was more than one explosive which you personally made safe. You held up four fingers, which gave us the clue that it was part of a sequence.

All this would not be necessary if we had done our job properly and removed every residual bomb on the planet but as we are not permitted to return we again need your help. This is particularly true following the distressing news we received yesterday. High Fleet Command reported a very large explosion they are sure originated on planet Earth. As yet we have been unable to ascertain the extent of damage or loss of life, but it does not look good.'

William was left in a state of shock with many more questions than answers. He didn't know whether to be angry or excited by the prospect of potentially saving the newly developing world again. He had so many questions in his head he couldn't speak.

Commander Bolivar continued, 'Our amazing scientists believe they have developed a device capable of placing the wearer anywhere in space and time almost instantaneously. Working on a highly sophisticated version of your ancient Satellite Navigation System, locations anywhere in the known universe can be pinpointed and the wearer transported there at any point in time. We have tested the system quite extensively between our sister fleets and it appears to work well. We do not intend using it other than for this mission as we are opposed to the general use of time travel, as you know. We are proud to call it the Jump Suit and will go into the technicalities if you agree to go ahead.'

William afforded himself a little smile at the chosen name for this amazing development and he knew Anita would certainly find it amusing.

'So before we go any further we would appreciate hearing your reaction William, would you be willing to help us one more time?'

William finally managed to unscramble his brain to speak. 'I can't pretend to understand how I could possibly be in a Moroccan cave and at the same time your headquarters in Pyongyang. I suppose it is no more remarkable than being transported by train to the 26th Century, I may have to trust you in that department.

'Although, how can I trust you when you appear to have put the lives of millions of my fellow Humans in danger by failing to remove all the WMD's in your time on Earth? Does this recent explosion on Earth mean I failed in my part of the operation to defuse the remaining bombs, am I already dead?

'You are asking a lot of me, clearing up your mess for you. I know you saved my planet from nuclear destruction three hundred years ago but you spent the next three hundred years trying to find a safe way to leave. In lots of ways you are to be admired, selflessly combing the far reaches of space for problems to solve at no little risk to yourselves, but you are far from perfect.

'Why does your sacred code prevent you going back to a planet to check all is well?'

Major Main tried to explain. 'The moment a mission has been brought to a successful conclusion we must leave, taking with us all traces of our time there, minimum interference for maximum effect. Earth proved to be a great deal more complicated and we admit we spent far too long there. It was only when we brought your family to that time that we found the means to leave. We cannot break our code for that itself would be a failure.'

'So you would rather put my life and those on this *new* Earth at risk than break your precious code?'

'Our hasty departure from Earth was a regret but we were under pressure to leave for Bellicose Minor. All our installations and personnel had been placed back on our ships. Your appearance in that cave gave us the opportunity to remove any lingering threat to the newly liberated Earthlings. In a way we are returning to Earth, just through you.'

'I can see I'm not getting anywhere with this argument. However, you have been very clever in placing me in a position where my family can't get home unless I help you first. You know I couldn't refuse when there are lives at stake and I can help.'

William knew he was in a no win situation but this didn't stop his inward anger at their approach to this enormous problem.

'You are still free to go home with your family when the time is right, why would we deny that, after all we did promise you. But please William, help us clear up the problem on Earth, you will be helping millions of your kind at the same time.'

'Assuming I do agree, what is your plan, because I still can't get my head around the idea? I'm not saying a definite yes, I have to visualise it for myself first.'

'With our newly developed Jump Suit we can place you back on Earth at a moment in time before we left for Bellicose Minor. We can place you at each location where we believe there were residual bombs. You will be able to jump instantly from one location to the next until all the munitions have been neutralised, and then we jump you safely back here.

'Because of the utilisation of time travel your family will not know you're missing, you will arrive back moments after you left. We are not in a position to say whether the explosion we detected on Earth will be erased from history by your visit, but we hope that will be the case. It is only after arriving on

Earth that the bomb locations will be detected using sophisticated tracking devises built into your Jump Suit. You will have no control over where your Jump Suit takes you, so don't think you can visit old friends while you're there.

'It goes without saying that if you happened to meet your other self back on Earth it could prove fatal for you and probably many others, avoid this at all costs. Do not be tempted to interact with anyone during your mission, you should behave and appear as if a ghost to anyone who sees you. There will be no direct communications with us during your mission but we will trace you as best we can and bring you back if there is any real danger.

'Once you have removed these residual munitions we will honour our promise and send you and your family back home to the 21st Century. It is up to you whether you tell the others after you return, but please do not complicate matters by telling them before you jump. When we meet your family later today it will be all about getting you home safely, they are not to know about your extra little task.'

'So, when are you planning to send us back to Earth?'

'It is scheduled for 9.00am tomorrow Earth time.'

'And if I happen to get blown up or the Jump Suit fails and I get stuck on 26th Century Earth, what happens to my family then?'

'We will still attempt to send them home after explaining about your secret mission. However, you know very well it is more difficult to get any Time Jump right when the original party is missing a member, they could end up in another parallel universe, but we don't plan on that happening William. As you say on Earth, we have your back, we'll take care of you.'

'If I hadn't experienced all I have in the past few months I would say you are all completely, thoughtlessly mad. Yet strange as it may seem, I sort of trust you, backed into this corner as I am!'

'So you will do it then?'

'I must be crazy but yes, after all, if you saw me in that cave then I have already done it.'

Commander Bolivar approached William and they shook limbs, the Human with a cold feeling in his heart.

'You are a credit to your species, we will not let you down. Dr. Honey, can you give Mr Hawkins the information tablet?'

'Certainly Commander.' Dr. Honey reached up to embrace his friend, 'You must take this device and study it carefully between now and tomorrow morning. It contains details on how to make the devices safe and how to operate the Jump Suit. It goes without saying that you must not let the rest of your family see it, they would probably try to persuade you not to do it.'

'You're certainly right there although Anita would probably be helping me into that Jump Suit!'

'If you have any problems understanding our English translation or any practical aspects of the mission, try to communicate this to us before tomorrow morning. Now I feel you must go, you have been separated long enough from your family and they will start to worry.'

Bolivar explained she would not be at the evening meeting but in order that it run smoothly Earth type Simu-Suits would be allowed complete with Translation Devices. William was relieved to hear this as none of the family relished being sprayed in mucus and freshly munched entrails, perhaps a partial admission of guilt on their part.

On the Hop-it-Tram ride back William started looking at the instruction tablet and uttered the immortal words,

Oh Shit!

It slowly dawned on him the enormity of the task ahead.

THE QUEEN SMELLS A RAT

The first delivery of emergency food supplies was on its way to the planets of Poz, Slunk and Icco. However this could not be allowed to develop into a long term operation, the Saviorians still had a huge fleet to feed. Fresh fruit and vegetables were continuously grown on their agro ships and their diet, as we know, was primarily made up of fresh meat, but they could not afford to be generous for long. There was talk of capturing some of the native livestock on Bellicose Minor, toxic to the natives, but the tests needed to prove suitability were not a priority.

Androids were about to land undetected on the planet, mainly disguised as native women, to ultimately infiltrate the palace complex in an attempt to get close to the Queen. The Saviorian scientists had been hard at work developing an auto suggestive drug that could change the mindset of the Queens' followers. However, without being able to test this on Bellicose females they could only estimate how effective the drugs might be.

In more worrying developments, the Queen was taking steps to completely close down the docking ports for incoming Icco craft, thus permanently cutting off the supply lines to neighbouring planets. In addition, male labourers had been hard at work expanding the Royal Palace complex to house more willing food supplies. The Saviorians knew time was not on their side and all available resources had to be thrown at the problem.

Normally after a full cooked breakfast the Queen was at her most contented. She was even known to have a laugh with her female advisers about which fit young male they might share for dinner. Today however she was not at all happy. Her neighbouring planets, who had leached valuable resources from her beloved Bellicose for centuries, had turned on her. They had invited in roving do-gooders, threatening to spoil her party by cutting off her supply of fresh meat.

'Sister Zoe, bring me up to date with news from outside the palace complex. Are there any reports of intruders landing on my beautiful island? Do we even know what they look like? I need information.'

'Your Majesty we have eyes to the skies and patrols on the shores. Any males not in line for consumption are willingly aiding our sisters searching in the towns and villages and as yet there have been no reports of outsiders on Fecundland. We have no idea what they look like but there must be some physical differences, coming from deep space as they do.'

'Our spies on Icco, have they not updated us?'

'You will recall Your Majesty, that you ordered the closure of all space port links with Icco, there is now no way for them to get back and report.'

'Damn it, yes you are right! We are on our own Sister Zoe, time to secure what we have. The latest phase of palace expansion is complete, yes?'

'It is Your Majesty, room for two hundred more males with many more camping outside awaiting their chance to *serve.*'

'Then we need to change our strategy, we need to expand again, increase our freezer capacity, bring them all into this great palace, leave the women out in the countryside, they are better off without their men and they know it. Our larder will be full and we shall survive any invasion.'

'If I may point out just a couple of practical problems with your plan Your Hugeness?'

'Well, what is it Zoe? You know above all my Ladies in Waiting, I value your opinion, a bit.'

'Having dried up our supply of white goods such as freezers from Icco, not to mention high tech security fencing and surveillance equipment, it might be difficult to expand further, Your Immenseness.'

'Then we use what we have Zoe, the men shall build wooden fortifications to reinforce our defences and dig salt pits to preserve their fellow's fine meat until there is room in our freezers. Now go and make this happen, time is against us but we shall prevail Sister Zoe. Oh and while you're at it, fetch my lifting device and Monster Truck I am in need of some exercise.'

'Yes at once your Excessiveness.'

The ever reliant android army of the Saviorian Fleet had already landed on one of the small uninhabited islands of Bellicose Minor. They brought with them the very latest Invisibility Cloaked Landing Craft, to use when making landfall on Fecundland. They would use the island of Notineere as a base for missions to the Bellicose capital. It was hoped that the mission could be completed successfully, using androids alone. That was the theory anyway.

The plan was a simple one. The Saviorians were confident that the latest android assimilation as native Bellies would be convincing enough to fool the population. They came armed with a powerful drug, which, if administered properly, would alter the mindset of the population, encouraging them to rebel against the Queen. Low key operations would start in outlying towns and villages. The plan hinged on the androids being able to gain the confidence of local females and get them to try their new Elixir of Life. The scientists had not been given sufficient time to test the longevity of the potion so androids would have to work swiftly. If tests on villagers proved the persuasive nature of their potion then the androids could advance with local support to the palace.

Three quarters of the androids landing party were posing as female Bellies to reflect the worrying position on the ground, the first group of six entered the village of Idlick.

The sheer beauty of the place was lost on the synthetic brain of the androids. No works of art would spring from the inspirational backdrop of green valleys, sparkling cascading waterfalls and verdant bright flowers which the place had in abundance.

'When you've finished digging them potatoes the washing's nearly dry and ready to press, so put your back into it. There should be time to chop a load of firewood before you get my breakfast on.' A young red faced woman was barking orders to a much older man.

Most of the prime male stock was already in the palace production line, this must have been her grandfather, not on the Queens shopping list. He had a resigned and rather forced smile on his exhausted face, no doubt a result of the Yesarwill drug administered to the entire male population by their benevolent ruler.

The female androids were posing as messengers from the palace, accompanied by their male servants. They carried forged documents from Queen Eritima to the entire female population, inviting them to try out a new health drink, developed as a protein substitute for the missing Vitabump. The much prized creature was not being hunted anymore because of the lack of male hunters. The Saviorian scientists had aptly named in Vitalift, one of their creative moments. There was not a Bellie on the planet that didn't crave a portion of Vitabump so it should be an easy sell. It claimed to give an instant energy boost and enhanced physical strength, more than enough to keep any remaining men in their place.

The women folk of Idlick certainly liked the idea and flocked to the Village Hall to get their free sample. The androids had set up a fake demonstration of the drinks' powers, showing before and after effects of its potential. With all the women of the village dying to try this magic potion it was time to move on. One android would stay behind to observe the true effects of the potion. This process was being replicated in towns and villages large and small where females demonstrated similar levels of enthusiasm for this gift from their Queen. The men folk continued in their obedient stupor under the influence of the Yesarwill drug, but things were about to change.

ANITA DISCOVERS PLANS FOR WILLIAM

'We were about to send out a search party William, started to think you'd been abducted by aliens, but, oh yes, you already have been!'

'If that was an attempt at humour Dad I'd start working on your material before we get home,' noted Anita.

'We barely have three hours before this meeting and I still can't string a sentence in Saviorian together.'

'Oh that reminds me Mum, they've agreed to wear Earth Simu-Suits and Translation Belts when we meet, so relax.'

'So come on number one creep, you haven't told us the latest revelations from the engine rooms.'

'What, oh err yes, nothing you'd be interested in Anita. They did give me this fascinating information tablet on their vision for propulsion systems in the future. Actually I might have a look at it now if the rest of you don't mind?'

'Words fail me Geek Boy, promise me you'll get a life once we get home.'

'You carry on Son, we need to finish our game of Corner the Cow, your Dad just needs to devour Daisy and he's won.'

'Leave it out Jane, I despise this game, imagine how it would go down with the PC crowd at home, you'd be locked up for just looking at the box.'

'Right then, I'll only be an hour or so with this stuff, I want to read it while it's fresh in my mind.' He needn't have bothered explaining, the others were nearing the conclusion of Corner the Cow and the stakes were high.

This highly classified information, translated for you into English, must not be shared with any Human. The tablet will not accompany you on your Time Jumps so technical instructions must be memorised before the mission commences.

William began to read the operations manual with intense concentration but shuddered at the section entitled Possible Side Effects on Human Subjects.

We must point out that due to the fact that this system has only been tested on androids, there may be unforeseen implications for the Human who jumps. We are confident that the technical side of the operation will proceed as predicted and, as this particular subject is young and healthy, there is no reason for him not to return intact. There is however, a five per cent chance he may deposit a small part of his anatomy at each location, which would be impossible to retrieve at a later date.

It would only have been normal for William to have had second thoughts and he fully intended asking more questions later in the day, however, his overriding feeling was one of excitement. As he read on he was unaware of his sisters' presence over his shoulder.

'Is this something you'd like to share with all of us?'

William gasped when he realised Anita was reading the text with him. 'Oh God! How much have you seen?'

'Enough to know you're not reading a manual on puke powered propulsion systems.'

'Quiet, don't let the wrinklies hear us, they don't need to know about this, you don't need to know.'

'Too late for that Einstein, this gives a whole new meaning to the phrase Jump Suit doesn't it?'

'Honestly Anita this would be one revelation too much for the parents, please!'

'Right but I want to know it all, you can't keep any of this from me after all we've been through.'

William quietly ordered a Hop-it Tram to the Observation Deck. He knew Anita would not be satisfied until she'd heard all the facts.

'Where are you two off to?' Jane and Steven had been preoccupied on the floor trying to locate a missing udder from Corner the Cow.

'Just want to show Anita something from the Observation Deck, we'll take the tram, shouldn't be long.'

'Want us to come with you?'

'No it's alright Dad, we'll be back in plenty of time for our meeting, see you later.'

William and Anita boarded the tram. The doors had only just closed when Anita started.

'I only caught a glimpse over your shoulder but this looks seriously weird, even by your standards.'

'Look Anita we haven't got long so you'd better stay quiet and just listen for once.' William began a somewhat abridged version of the plan to defuse the rogue bombs. As he explained the details to his sister he was having trouble himself believing what lay in store. However, it did help him get his head around the situation and his complex roll in all of it.

Anita had uncharacteristically remained silent throughout his explanation. When William finished she reached out and grasped his hand.

'You really are a brave son of a bitch, one hundred percent bonkers, but brave.'

'Now you really are getting me worried. It's fine, I'll be back before you know it, actually, I might be back before I know it.'

'And you believe their version of the facts, because some of it is pretty farfetched? They are totally taking advantage of you, you know. The more I learn about our hosts the more I detest them.'

'I know this much, they had no intention of bringing us all this way to Bellicose Minor, we would be working in the Pyongyang rice fields now if they didn't believe I could do this. We are here as much to get them out of trouble as to get us home, so yes I do believe them, whatever their motives.'

'I can't understand why, after all we've been through, you had no intention of letting me in on the plans.'

'I didn't want to risk the wrinklies finding out, they've been through enough as it is.'

'So now what? You want me to pretend I know nothing when we have this sham of a meeting tonight?'

'That's exactly what I want you to do. If everything goes well I should return more or less the exact second I have left and we all get to go home together.'

'Yes. But if you don't come back what do I say, Will, *oh yes he's just popped to the shops for some milk, don't think he'll be long.*'

'Don't worry, you'll still get to go home in time for a few rounds with your girlie mates on Friday night.'

'Don't even joke Will.' Anita quickly brushed away a tear before making a quick recovery. 'I tell you something Geek Boy, you'd better bring me back one of those Jump Suits, they look well cool.'

'I'll see what I can do.'

The spontaneous hug said more than words ever could, interrupted only by the doors hissing open as they were returned to their accommodation pod.

I DIDN'T PRESCRIBE VITALIFT

'I tell you there are some Bellies out there just not doing their jobs. Still no news of an alien invasion on our shores?'

The Inner Council of Queen Eritima's Court was in emergency session. The Cannibal Queen was surrounded by her most senior advisors, Sisters Zoe, Sarah and Tiffany, all powerful females in their own right but all in possession of a common Bellicose trait, they were just a bit dim.

'May I say, your Highness, we were all a little surprised by your latest proclamation.'

'What are you talking about Sister Sarah? I have not made a proclamation of late.'

'Yes you have and quite brilliant if I may add, but how did you collect the extracts needed for such quantities of drink?'

'Can we have a supply for the ladies of the palace?' added Sister Tiffany.

'Stop at once. I have no idea what you are talking about but someone had better explain.'

Sister Zoe joined in 'I have an Aunt still living in Obahere just north of the palace. The entire female population have been given a new drink prescribed by you in a written proclamation. It claims to contain extracts of Vitabump which enhances physical strength and power over males. Apparently you have called it Vitalift, a very catchy name if I may add.

Your popularity has gone through the roof, so can we have some?'

'I have no idea what you are talking about, wait a minute, do they know who's been handing these drinks out, did they recognise their faces?'

'No, they thought they must have come straight from the palace on your orders.'

'Quick Sarah, Tiffany, organise a party of sisters to go out into all the villages and towns and stop this, let's hope it's not too late, the aliens are here!'

The Saviorians authorities were as pleased as they could be. All supplies of the fake Vitalift drink had been distributed and consumed with enthusiasm. They now awaited reports back from their androids on the effects of the drug.

COSMIC MANURE

'We've only got half an hour before this meeting William, what do you think they'll make us do?'

'What do you mean Dad?'

'Well, do you think it'll involve train tickets or going through strange tunnels like the last time?'

'I shouldn't think so, we're not on Earth any more are we.'

'As long as there's none of that Parallel Universe stuff. I'm not being forced to eat rat sandwiches,' pointed out Jane.

'All four of us will be going home together this time, everything will be fine.'

'I hope we're all going home,' mumbled Anita under her breath, before getting a nudge in the ribs from her brother.

'What did you say dear?'

'Oh nothing Mother, just my warped sense of humour again.'

The Hop-it-Tram picked them up promptly and the destination display indicated they were heading for Conference Room Three. It was close to early evening feeding time and the walkways were teeming with hungry crew members on their way to the Feed Station. The conversation was clearly animated, most likely debating the progress on Bellicose Minor. The glass cleaning system on the tram was working overtime removing phlegm and bile from the windows as the Humans sped by.

'You say our hosts will be wearing Simu-Suits at this meeting?'

'Yes Dad, they promised as a special gesture to speed things up.'

'Thank God for that, have you seen the carnage out there? I still say it shouldn't be allowed.'

'Don't start again Steve, with a bit of luck we'll be out of here soon, look, I think we've arrived.'

The tram made a slight detour away from the main walkway to a quiet branch line. As the doors hissed open Dr. Honey and Major Main were again there to meet them, Commander Aragon was already seated in the Conference Room.

The Major spoke first. 'What a pleasure to see you again Mr and Mrs Hawkins, I trust you are having a comfortable journey with our magnificent fleet?'

Jane nudged Steven before he could comment.

'Yes we are thank you, but we are anxious to get back home now.'

'Please come inside and meet Commander Aragon again, I know you spoke at length while still on Earth.'

Major Main guided Anita, Jane and Steven into the Conference Room while Dr. Honey held William back.

'Have you managed to digest the instructions manual?'

'Yes but I only had time to read it through once. Unfortunately Anita was reading over my shoulder so she is aware of what is planned.'

'And your parents?'

'No, that's the last thing I want.'

'Can you trust Anita not to tell them?'

'Oh yes, for once I'm sure I can.'

'Good, we will proceed with the meeting and assume we are planning for all four of you to return to 21st Century Earth together. You may keep the instruction tablet until tomorrow morning but you cannot take it with you on your mission. This way please.'

William and the doctor joined the others around the huge circular table.

'More secrets Einstein, planning to save the rest of the universe while you're at it?'

'Quiet Anita, you promised.'

'Now about your Time Jump back to your own place in history.' Commander Aragon was abrupt in his manner and a little ill tempered. 'As you may not be aware, the mission to Bellicose Minor is at a delicate juncture, we can barely afford the time to solve your plight, we have just one chance of getting you all home in one piece.'

William bit his tongue, was Aragon not also aware that he was going to risk his life to save the Saviorians a long spell at the nearest penal colony?

'We have put the infrastructure in place to afford you this opportunity, but let me make it clear, if the jump is not successful you will either spend the rest of your lives as honorary Saviorians or spray your organic matter across the cosmos like a fine manure. However, I am confident in our scientists and all will be well. Now I must go, there are many more important matters requiring my attention, I will hand you over to Major Main and Dr Honey to go through the procedure for your departure tomorrow.'

With that Aragon shuffled out of the room, switching off his Simu Suit on the way and leaving a trail of yellow green bile in his wake.

The family sat open mouthed and speechless. It was left to Major Main to rescue the situation.

'The Commander is under a great deal of pressure to produce a successful outcome from this Bellicose Minor operation, I apologise for his somewhat abrupt manner. If you will allow me I can explain just how we intend to get you home.'

'What's there to tell, sounds like we're destined to become cosmic manure,' noted Anita the only one of the family with a functioning jaw.

'Not at all, the chances of that are very slim and after all, you have already completed the round trip on more than one occasion.'

Yes, and we all know where the second little jaunt took us.'

'As you well know Miss Hawkins, that was because your party was missing one original member, William, and that will not happen this time.'

Here's hoping, thought Anita.

'Please pay attention to the following instructions.

At 08.00 hours Earth time you will proceed to Sky Lab One, dressed in your original clothes from 2014, we have managed to duplicate copies of these for you. No other clothing or items used on your stay aboard the Mother Ship can accompany you as they may compromise your jump.

'We do not have the transfer space available aboard this ship to send you back via the First Great Western Continuity Link. This time we have mocked up a black London taxi cab. All being well you will depart from Sky Lab aboard the mock up taxi and arrive at Paddington Station aboard the genuine article in the year 2014 with half an hour to spare before your train departs for Cornwall.

'It will be just as if nothing unusual had happened. Whether you retain residual memories of your time here in your future is unclear. It will be up to you how you take it from there. One thing is certain, none of this will have taken place back in your own time.

'If you share any of this with fellow Earthlings at best they will believe you've been drinking, at worst, you'll be locked up with no sign of a key.

'The jump in the taxi should be similar to your previous train transfers, with no physical discomfort and all reasonably seamless, do you have any questions?'

'So it will be like rewinding an iplayer to the first episode and pressing play to continue our lives?' asked Jane.

'Your words mean little to me Mrs Hawkins.'

'What Mum means is our lives will start again from a point just before we left on our original journey to Cornwall and anything after that point will not have happened?' asked William.

'Exactly, you get to continue your lives from that point, but this time we will not be controlling your journey. It will be up to you and the state of your memory whether you actually get on that train this time. The future course of history could depend on that one simple decision. This is one of the main reasons we do not like to use time travel in such a random way.'

'Yes, but if we are left with no residual memory of our future adventures we will have no reason not to board the 12.05 for Bodmin Parkway station,' noted Steven.

'Thanks for that Pops, I'll tie a knot in something to jog my memory.' Anita's reply was determined but lacked any real belief.

'This sounds like the perfect outcome for us, but what if everything doesn't run smoothly, what is the scenario then?' asked Steven.

'To be perfectly honest with you Mr Hawkins there is little point in dwelling on alternative outcomes, they are all out of your hands. My best advice is to think positively and trust in our fine scientists,' stated Dr Honey. 'Now I suggest you spend your last few hours aboard our fine vessel relaxing. Major Main and I will see you in the morning, William, a quick word if you would.'

Karen guided Jane and Steven in the direction of the tram, as she had a fair idea where that conversation may be leading.

Once out of earshot Dr. Honey spoke, 'Just before your planned jump back to Earth make your excuses for a moment. A trip to the toilet always seems of suitable use to Humans. This will give enough time to fit you unto your Jump Suit and send you off on your rescue mission. If all goes well you will emerge from the toilet successfully relieved and ready to head home for the last time.'

'It's exhausting just thinking about what might be involved, can my body stand the strain?'

'Will, you are young and fit, there is no good reason for you to have problems. Just avoid any direct contact with anyone and stick to the plan dictated by your Jump Suit. We have huge confidence in you, based on our brief time together.'

'Come on Will, the wrinklies want to go,' shouted Anita from the Hop-it-Tram door.

'You seem so attached to these slimy little creatures Son are you sure you want to come home with us?' asked Steven.

'Yes, quite sure Dad, I'll be as relieved as you to see the back of them and get in that taxi tomorrow believe me.'

'Good, now let's take this tram for one last tour of the nicer parts ship before we leave.'

THE SISTERS SEE THE LIGHT

Events had moved on rapidly on Fecundland. The effects of the fake Vitalift drink were already being felt. Women in all the towns and villages were seeing the men folk, those left that is, in a completely new light, praising and encouraging their every move and generally finding them incredibly attractive. They had stopped administering the Yesarwill drug and there were signs the men were regaining self belief and independent thought.

When conversation turned to the Queen the natives were appalled at how dire the situation had become. There was even talk of storming the palace to save fellow males from becoming part of Sunday Lunch. The androids now integrated and immersed themselves in local life, encouraging the revolt and helping to plan a march on the palace. It would not be an easy task to dislodge the colossal cannibal from the throne of Bellicose Minor however, as they now knew the Queen was aware of their presence on the island and she would defend her right to six square meals a day to the end.

The Queens High Council of Sisters in the shape of Sarah and Tiffany had reached the outlying village of Ovahere where they attempted to track down Sister Zoe's Aunt. They wanted to know if any strangers had been seen handing out free Vitalift drinks. Zoe's Aunt could not be found but the ladies from the palace had a rude awakening on reaching the village hall. They were apprehended and tied up by the local women folk.

'We know who you are, two of the Queens special friends,' shouted an elderly villager. 'You been munching on the meat of our men folk haven't you? Well we've seen the light and things are about to change. Just to show there are no hard feelings we would like you to share a drink with us, it's delicious.'

Sarah and Tiffany were forced to swallow the Vitalift before being released. They had only reached the edge of Ovahere when the potion began to take effect.

'I'm not quite sure the Queen's got the right to munch and nibble on our men folks succulent bits do you Sarah?'

'Now you come to mention it Tiffany, it does seem a tad extreme.'

'Yes, I know my old man Richie was happy to be part of breakfast a couple of weeks back and I did enjoy his kidneys fried in a little garlic and butter, but is it right?'

'Same with my old man, a month's gone now since the Queen had him done five ways, and now I actually miss him.'

'What gives her the right to grow fat on the flesh of our fellas, just cause they're too weak to resist her rotund regalness?'

'It's got to stop Sister, we must rescue what's left of our men folk.'

They were not aware that during their conversation they were being followed. The two androids posing as village folk caught up with them on the path to the palace.

'Afternoon ladies, can we join you?'

'Suppose so, but we have urgent business with Queen Eritima, so need to move quickly.'

On the way the androids explained who they were, which was no easy task. They had a fresh supply of Vitalift and with the help of Sarah and Tiffany they could smuggle it into the palace.

'The Queen sent us out to track you down but instead you found us. I must say your appearance is somewhat of a surprise,' noted Sarah.

'Yes we thought aliens would be, you know, little slimy four eyed creatures, but you actually look quite normal, you know like us.'

'That's a long story which I fear we don't have time to go into right now. We notice you've sampled our Vitalift drink, very revealing isn't it?'

'You can say that again, what a cow that Eritima turns out to be, she needs taking down, like yesterday,' shouted Tiffany.

'Yes quite. Do you think you could sneak us into the palace and help us administer the rest of our Vitalift supplies to your fellow courtesans?'

'You try and stop us sister, it'll be down their necks quicker than a round of shots on a girls night out, then our ten tonne tyrant'll be toast.'

'Good, at least I think that's good, it's rather hard to follow some of your local dialect. We do however have two potential problems. Firstly, we are not certain how long the effects of our drug will last, so we must act quickly. Secondly, your men folk in the palace need persuading that their prime function in life is not to be part of the Queens staple diet. Our scientists are working on a reversal drug for the Yesarwill potion but until that materialises we could still have problems.'

'Tiffany and I, we've never had a problem with men.'

'No, and once we get the Sisters of the palace juiced up with your Vitalift we'll be ready to bring down her Majesty, now come on let's get to it,' added Tiffany.

On their final approach to the palace gates they picked up several more native women and other parts of the android force.

In order to gain access to the palace Sarah and Tiffany needed to give the impression that this little band of warriors were in fact prisoners being brought back to answer to the Queen. Sister Zoe met them at the Western Palace Gate with a degree of suspicion.

'Welcome back Sisters, may I ask who this band of women folk are?'

'High quality new recruits for the Palace Household Sister Zoe.'

'Really Sister Sarah, they look far from high quality to me.'

'I beg to differ,' argued Tiffany. 'They should scrub up well and they're very keen, aren't you girls?'

'Oh yes, fair desperate we are to serve her Glorious Majesty.'

'Keep them good for nothing men folk in their places that's what I say.'

'Been waitin for this chance for ages, can't believe our luck.'

Unconvinced Zoe changed the subject.

'This is all very well but you were sent out to track down the aliens who've been distributing this so called Vitalift drink.'

'If you'd give me a chance I was just getting to that very subject,' exclaimed Sarah, at which point she pushed two of the Saviorian androids forwards feigning their capture.

'We caught these two carrying supplies of the fake potion with the intention of passing them on to our unsuspecting women folk,' added Tiffany.

Androids XB102 andXB307 were now face to face with Sister Zoe, close enough to deploy their recently developed Mind Manipulation tool. This could only be used once by each android before having to be reset by the Saviorian scientists, thus limiting its use to serious situations such as this. As XB307 spoke Sister Zoe's mind was altered to accept everything suggested by the android.

'What the Queen is doing is cruel and evil, she needs to be stopped and your men folk released from this nightmare. Unite with this group of brave villagers to bring down Queen Eritima before another Bellie goes on her supper menu. Drink some of this wonderful potion, your mind will be then be clear and focused.'

Tiffany passed Zoe a cup of Vitalift which she gladly accepted, gulping it down like a pint on a Saturday night.

'How did you do that, I'm well impressed? Mind you she was never one to refuse a drink,' exclaimed Tiffany.

'It's a new development from our scientists, it's never been used in the field before but it seems to work.'

'Right come on Sisters, no time to lose, let's drink the drink and spread the word, Queen Eritima is toast!'

Zoe swung open the huge wooden palace gates and the growing band of freedom fighters and androids spread the message throughout the palace. More and more villagers poured through the open gates heading for the Queens Munching House. Extra android forces landed with supplies of the new antidote for the Yesarwill potion and at last a successful Saviorian mission was in sight after the failures of three hundred years on Earth, nothing could go wrong now, could it?

I JUST NEED TO USE THE TOILET

No one in the Hawkins family got much sleep that night, especially William. In the solitude of his Sleep Cradle he read the Saviorians instruction manual over and over again, so much was out of his hands. The Jump Suit controlled his actions and ultimately his destiny. He just needed to follow guidelines and avoid direct contact with any Humans he encountered on the way.

Anita too was finding sleep difficult. She had the added burden of knowing what William had to achieve before their attempted jump home. She was well aware that if they had to leave without him the rodents or worse could be waiting for them in some other parallel universe.

Steven and Jane did manage some sleep, dreaming of less complicated lives on their farm back home. None of this really made sense to them, so if it could be erased from their memories for good, all the better. If they were honest all this scared them witless but it was out of their hands, as it had been from the moment they travelled to Padstow on those free tickets.

William was finally enjoying some fitful slumber when he was woken by the high pitched beep of an alarm call and the smell of a full English breakfast. The whole family were soon awake, stirred by the 6.00am siren. Breakfast had been laid out with place names attached for clarity, the feast arrived via a ceiling drop down table.

Anita was not a happy bunny 'How come you three get eggs, bacon, sausages and all the trimmings and I'm served up shitty muesli and plain f...ing yoghurt? I'm not having this, give us one of your sausages William, I'm famished.'

'I think you should read what it says on the back of your place card first.'

'What's that got to do with the price of a pint Einstein?'

'Alright I'll read it for you.'

Dear Earthlings in order to replicate the morning of your departure from Earth in 2014 in as much detail as possible we have provided you with the breakfast you consumed on that very morning. In this way the feeling you have in your stomach when you arrive back home will match that of when you left for Cornwall, continuity is the key. Enjoy- Dr.Honey.

'If I recall Anita you were following a strict diet in order to impress your then boyfriend John, a relationship which came to an end before our second journey into the future.'

'Yes alright Dad, thanks for that not too subtle reminder, but I'm still bloody starving, you don't want that bacon do you Sherlock you must be stuffed by now?'

'Best do what Dr Honey suggests, we don't want to spoil our chances of getting home for the sake of a rasher do we?'

'Hand it over Geek Boy, unless you want your little secret passed on to the parents here.'

William hastily pushed his plate in Anita's direction, his mission was far more important than a portion of pig.

'There that wasn't so hard was it?'

'What secret's this Anita?'

'Oh nothing really, only that young Will here has the hots for Miss Nottingham Photo and Media 2014, who he won't have met yet when we return to Earth, isn't that right Will?'

William just forced a half smile, pleased to see his sister was keeping her side of the bargain.

At 07.30am Earth time the Hawkins family stepped aboard the Hop-it-Tram for the last time. They were wearing duplicate clothes to those worn on that April morning 2014 provided by the Saviorian History Department, complete with the now infamous train tickets Jane believed she had won. They had nearly come full circle, which would be completed by their imminent Time Jump. They were consumed with their personal thoughts but William's heart was racing just a pace quicker than the others, his monumental task yet to be completed.

Their tram rolled gently up to Sky Lab One. Through the sliding glass door they caught a glimpse of the mock up black taxi cab waiting to jump them back to the 21st Century.

'Wow, it looks so real, it could almost be the exact one we arrived in at Paddington Station, how do they do it?' exclaimed Jane.

'Yes they certainly are a clever bunch of vomit spewing midgets,' added Anita

'Welcome to Sky Lab One and the final phase of your journey home.' It was the voice of Commander Aragon from the Bridge of the Mother Ship

'He sounds a bit brighter than yesterday,' noted Steven

'Can I say it has been a pleasure knowing you, especially young William with his enthusiastic contribution to the cause.'

'Oh here we go, don't get that fat head of yours stuck in the taxi door will you, creep.' Anita couldn't resist but she knew exactly how much he was contributing to their cause.

'You will be interested to know our mission on Bellicose Minor is going well and as we speak our android forces are spearheading a march on Queen Eritima's Dining Room.'

'That's why he's sounding so cheerful, and here's me thinking it might be because of the live pig he devoured for breakfast,' noted Steven.

'Good luck with your Time Jump especially you William,' and he was gone.

Jane and Steven just glanced at each other but William and Anita knew what Aragon meant.

'Good news all round I think!' exclaimed Dr. Honey as he and Major Main shuffled up to meet the family in Sky Lab One.

They had activated their Simu Suits for the farewell meeting, in order to keep the Hawkins dry and free from a shower of fish guts and entrails

'Good, you are wearing the clothes we have provided, it is most important that we replicate your appearances from your first journey.'

'How did you manage to produce these duplicates in such detail?' asked Jane

'Believe me Mrs Hawkins this is child's play compared to some of the tasks we have to undertake. Now please, time is running out, we need you to take your places in the taxi sitting in the exact positions you occupied on your original taxi ride.'

'No Mum, you were on the left hand side, me in the middle with William on the right. Dad, you were in the front with the driver. That's a point we have no driver.'

'Do not worry Miss Hawkins if all goes to plan he will appear once your jump is complete.'

'How's the time?' William asked when they were all seated.

'Five minutes to eight, why?' enquired Steven.

'I just need to go to the toilet, I'll only be a couple of minutes.'

'You can't go now. We jump in five minutes, you'll have to cross your legs dear, there'll be one on the platform in London!' exclaimed Jane

'Oh let him go Mum he's just like a Cornish seagull, everything goes straight through him in no time.'

Anita had known this was coming but still couldn't fathom how it could possibly work, time certainly was a strange concept.

'You've got four minutes now William, hurry up!'

He was already out of sight and being kitted out in his Jump Suit while receiving last minute instructions, then in a flash he was gone.

THE QUEEN HEADS FOR SWAMPITSLUDGE

'Zoe where are you? I'm starving, bring me fresh meat, I command you.' Queen Eritima had not eaten for over an hour. She could not physically move from her specially enlarged chair and the usual line up of willing male offerings was clearly missing.

'Sarah, Tiffany, have you returned from the outside, what news of the alien invasion?'

There was no reply from any of her Inner Circle. The Queen attempted to extract her bulk from the massive chair only to roll flat onto her severely distended belly like some gigantic beached blubberous whale.

The doors to the Queens inner sanctum burst open under the weight of several hundred Bellicose men and women, plus a substantial band of alien androids. They swarmed through the doors and surrounded the sprawling mass of their once powerful Queen.

'I demand an explanation,' blurted out the strangely high pitched voice from the sad sight that confronted them.

The astonished expression on the faces of the men in the room spoke volumes. With the effects of the Yesarwill potion totally cleared from their systems many felt physically sick at the sight of their queen and the thought of what had become *normal behaviour* in the headquarters of their beautiful island. Amidst an atmosphere of mixed elation and pent up anger, Sister Zoe spoke,

'It is time to put an end to your evil reign of cannibalistic cruelty. On behalf of the Sisters of the Palace and all inhabitants of Bellicose Minor you are hereby banished to the uninhabited island of Swampitsludge, just as soon as we have constructed transportation sturdy enough to support your massive bulk.'

Android XP146 spoke up, 'We may be able to help you with the logistics of that operation if you wish to speed up the process.'

'That is very kind and may I take this opportunity on behalf of all Bellies to thank you and your masters for rescuing us from this awful curse.'

The crowd cheered as one, even though many were unclear just what had happened and who they were thanking.

Queen Eritima was heading for a slow death at the hands of the Blood Suckers of Swampitsludge unless she could outrun this eight legged beast from the bogs, unlikely in her present state, but at least she had a chance unlike her male victims.

The question was, who would now step into the deposed Queen's shoes? A difficult choice but one made possible by the intervention of the remarkable Saviorians and their fearless band of androids. Links would have to be re-established with the neighbouring planets and trade lines put in place again by the time the aliens departed on their next mission, the aliens could not continue with their emergency food supplies for much longer.

FIRST JUMP

Melt water from the roof of the ice cave dripped onto the dull metal surface of the ancient rusting metallic object, hissing on contact. A red warning light glowed ominously in the cold dark cavern near Norilsk in Western Siberia. In the days before the *nuclear destruction*, over three hundred years ago, this was a remote coal mining region of old Russia and a storage depot for nuclear weapons of war. During the time of Saviorian quarantine the area had been void of Human life and had clearly been overlooked during their worldwide sweep for weapons. Yet now it had been discovered, one on the shortlist of live rogue bombs which threatened the fledgling new world of post Saviorian protection.

Smack! His shoulder made contact with ice encrusted rock. Clearly this Jump Suit would take some mastering. His jumbled senses were trying to come to terms with his situation. One second he was zipping up this high tech time travel jacket in the relative safety of the Sky Lab One toilet, the next he was freezing his bits off in a dank cold inhospitable cave.

His instructions were to let the sophisticated Jump Suit guide his every movement. Was William simply the physical means needed to carry out the disarming process. His hands were drawn to a glass panel through which a number sequence was visible. The display read 1004 the last digit jumping back and forth between three and four. An activated countdown had clearly jammed at this point which reassured William somewhat. However, before he could rationalise the situation his hands were guided to a switch beside the numerical display which he moved upwards without apparent control. The red light was immediately extinguished and the outer shell of the ancient armament started to cool. His left hand was drawn to an internal pocket of his Jump Suit. This pocket supported five plastic bottles of grey liquid. He removed the container labelled No1 and carefully unscrewed the stopper. Without any conscious effort he poured the contents of the bottle over the top of the now lifeless device. The strange unidentified liquid had the immediate effect of turning the bomb to stone, matching that of the limestone cave. While William was trying to figure out how he had carried out this tricky operation without any input on his part, he suddenly held up one index finger as if to indicate the completion of the first task. Then a thought struck him, a deeply troubling thought. If he was to have no control over the tasks he was performing why hadn't the Saviorians simply sent one of their excellent androids to carry out this highly dangerous mission? If all they required was a body at the point of delivery why did it have to be him? He blamed himself for not realising this sooner, asking more questions.

Was William simply here for the ride? The Saviorians would have a lot to answer for when this was over, if he survived it.

WHAT'S HE DOING IN THERE?

'Should we go and hurry him up? What's he doing in there, we're nearly out of time.' Jane was getting anxious and the clock read 07.57, three minutes to jump time. 'Why couldn't he just hold on, it's not like he's old and can't wait?'

VISIONS FROM THE PAST

With the blink of an eye his location had changed. His nostrils filled with the salty brine of the open ocean. A faint breeze wafted in from an unseen portal. Again he found himself crouched next to a rusting barrel shaped object, slightly different from the previous one. This one was emitting a rhythmic ticking sound along with an eerie red glow. He could make out a similar digital display but this time the countdown was active.

He waited for the Jump Suit to take control of his actions as before but nothing happened. Unlike his time in the inhospitable ice cave, William felt that he was not alone. He thought he could hear distant voices some of which had a rather familiar tone. He wanted to find out where the sounds were coming from but he needed to concentrate on the task at hand. If the Jump Suit had somewhat malfunctioned he would have to complete the job on his own.

He searched near the digital display for a switch but he could see nothing. He could now distinguish several voices one of which was female. William felt he recognised the rise and fall of a faint Cornish accent,

no, it couldn't be.

The Jump Suit was still not responding and he was close to panic. He reached for the red light which flipped forward in his hand revealing a switch beneath, this must be what he was looking for. In desperation he moved it upwards as with the previous device, the light went out and the ticking ceased. Peering at the digital display the countdown had frozen at three hundred and fifty. Taking heart he reached inside the Jump Suit and removed the bottle marked two. Without delay he proceeded to pour the grey liquid over the device. The chemical reaction caused the metal to change to a stone like state as before.

It was then that he realised he could identify two of the voices, incredibly he believed they belonged to Karen and Ken from Padstow. He instinctively smiled and wanted more than anything to reach out and embrace Karen, the urge was almost overpowering. Her voice echoed off the dank cave walls. He wanted to speak but no sound came from his lips. He was about to give in to temptation and reach for her when the Jump Suit sprang into life, compelling him to hold up two fingers.

'Dear God, it can't be you, you left with the others, off into space. William is that really you? Please talk to me.'

Then he was gone.

The horse drawn cart was travelling at such speed he was nearly thrown sideways and into the dust. Coming to his senses William realised he was alone on the back of a flat bed cart. The driver was unaware he suddenly had company.

His mind was still in that sea cave with Karen but his body certainly was not. While clinging tight to the side of the bouncing wagon William's eyes were soon drawn to a large object covered by an old dusty blanket keeping him company, and within touching distance. The Jump Suit was clearly functioning again as his hands automatically reached out to remove the blanket.

So that was it,

thought William, *the reason why they hadn't used androids to destroy these rogue devices, this all powerful Jump Suit had not been tested properly at all. They had been rushed into finding a way around the problem on Earth and he was the available solution, someone who could think on his feet and improvise if necessary.*

Come to mention it, the Saviorians were very good at getting others to do their dirty work. If not their brilliant androids then some unwitting native from another planet. Maybe, William mused, *he couldn't fault their good intentions, but were they really the selfless creatures they would like everyone to believe? Wasn't he the one taking all the risks?*

There was no time to dwell on that idea as the dusty red blanket flew backwards from William's hands, landing on the sun baked dirt track behind. He turned to see the now familiar shape of an ancient armament tied by ropes to the floor of the cart. The driver of the primitive wagon must have caught a flash of red out of the corner of his eye. Turning to see what had spooked him he was shocked to discover he had company on his dangerous journey.

He had only taken his eye from the track for a split second, but long enough for his nearside front wheel to collide with a stray boulder, causing the cart to shoot into the air, landing on its side. William was thrown clear or the ramshackle cart while the bomb casement tumbled down the scrub covered slope to his left. The driver had not been so fortunate, his left leg appeared to be trapped under the substantial bulk of his cart. His faithful horse had galloped off to a safe distance, turning now to see where his master was.

Williams' first instinct was to attempt to free the young man's leg but the Jump Suit had other ideas. He was dragged down the slope against his will to where the rusty bomb lay. No matter how hard he tried his legs would not carry him back to free the helpless man. William remembered again the warning,

do not interact with the native population.

Without thinking he found himself working on the ticking mechanism of the bomb.

This was a larger and more sinister looking device than he had seen before, but the Jump Suit seemed to be making light work of the detonation mechanism. Quickly the count downs stopped and warning lights extinguished and William found himself reaching for container number three inside his Jump Suit. As he poured the grey liquid over the large rusty devise he could see that the man was still trapped but conscious. He could hear him shouting,

'Por favor Senor, por favor!'

He knew as he felt his arm rise in a three fingered salute that there was little time. He knew he couldn't leave the poor man who was clearly in pain. The only way he could free himself to rush and rescue the stranger was to remove the Jump Suit and risk being left behind in the Mexican Desert.

Instinct took over as he unzipped the suit and released himself from its grasp, hoping that it would only function with him inside. He clambered up the sandy slope to the overturned cart. Trying not to make direct contact with the driver he put his back to the side of the cart, dug his heels into the dirt and pushed with all the strength he had. To William's astonishment the cart creaked and slowly raised a few inches from the track surface, long enough for the diminutive Mexican to drag his left leg clear. William immediately lowered the cart and dashed for the spot where the Jump Suit lay. Not thinking of the possible consequences he thrust one leg into the powerful piece of Saviorian technology and promptly vanished.

After staggering onto his one good foot the driver looked everywhere in an attempt to thank his good Samaritan but he was gone, vanished into thin air. He searched the immediate area for the prize he had dragged from the disused mine but all he came across were boulders and brush.

Still struggling to dress properly, William fell headlong into another location, fraught with danger.

A drip of cold water directly entering his right eye confirmed his suspicions, another cave. On his arrival, four fast moving figures ran in the same direction, away from yet another now familiar metal object. He could hear their voices as they scrambled for the light.

'Slushee umph cooshugpoo' cried one voice.

'Ashoolumph umph yugoshi' cried another.

William recognised the language but sadly not the content, it was Saviorian and they were probably androids. That could only mean one thing, he must have arrived here at a time when the Saviorians were still on Earth.

Could this be the cave in Morocco where he was spotted by Bolivar and Aragon?

He tried to concentrate on the task in hand and was relieved that his Jump Suit appeared to be working properly after being discarded in the Mexican dust. He managed to stop the countdown at 4751 and was just pouring the contents of bottle number four over the bomb when something made him turn and look up. There in front of him was the diminutive slimy creature better known as Commander Aragon. To his surprise the high ranking Saviorian spoke to him in English.

'This is impossible, it can't be you.'

William smiled as he completed his work, he had learned that direct verbal contact was out of the question.

Aragon continued, 'William Hawkins, it can't be you, you are in Pyongyang, I left you there with your family.'

William was seriously tempted to complain about the substandard, under tested equipment which was endangering his very existence, when he realised how futile that would be. Especially since, to the best of his knowledge, the Jump Suit had not yet been developed.

Commander Aragon was getting too close so William stood back from the rock, which moments before had been live and dangerous, held up four fingers and vanished from sight, on to his fifth and final mission.

WHERE'S THE TOILET?

Steven was now getting extremely agitated, 'Two minutes to eight, excuse me I'm going to find that son of yours, this is ridiculous! Where is the toilet?'

'Please remain seated Mr Hawkins, he will be back in time, in fact that might be him coming now.'

Dr. Honey only just managed to persuade Steven to retake his seat in the front of the taxi. Even he had little idea how the mission was progressing, but while there was time there was still hope.

ONE FINAL MISSION

He found himself face down on a cold concrete floor in almost complete darkness. As he struggled to his feet and peered into the gloom he could hear his own tentative footsteps echo back from distant walls. The air was stale and dank with a residual air of foreboding.

This is no cave, thought William, the cavernous space was clearly manmade.

With his eyes slowly adjusting to the blackness he thought he could make out a faint red glow in the distance. He was getting no assistance from his Jump Suit which worried him greatly. He decided to walk in the direction of the glow. If there was a stray bomb that would be the most likely source. He made slow progress as he counted his steps towards his goal, every footstep had its own dull echo. He couldn't be sure but William felt that the enormous building was completely empty except for the glowing object looming in the distance. Certainly there were no obstructions to stumble over to impede his progress.

He was counting his steps in his head as he advanced on the increasingly imposing form in front of him, five hundred steps already. He got the impression this was a much larger object than any of the others he had encountered and still his Jump Suit was not responding, he had no idea how to make it work.

After over seven hundred steps he estimated the cylindrical object to be five times larger than the ones he had already made safe. It suddenly occurred to him there was no ticking sound attached to this monster, there hadn't been since he arrived. However, the red flashing light was almost blinding.

Another fifty odd steps and he was there.

When the light flashed on he could see the whole space around him, this was the only object in an enormous hanger. On the floor next to the bomb was painted the number 5,025. He could now make out other numbers in sequential order, rows and rows of them.

Could this enormous hanger possibly have held over 5,000 bombs?

He felt sick to the pit of his stomach.

What had led the world to this desperate state three hundred years before? Just how many weapons had the Saviorians made safe and swept up in their attempt to rescue this savage planet? Was it any wonder that a few strays had been missed?

With no help from his malfunctioning Jump Suit he began examining the monster weapon. He could see no instrument panel, just the smooth outer case of the bomb. It appeared to be in much better condition than the others he had worked on, probably because of its protected location. Luckily he noticed an old step ladder propped up on the adjacent wall which he grabbed and placed next to the silver weapon. After testing the first few rungs he felt safe to start climbing.

He could now see over and along the top of the imposing object. There appeared to be three sets of figures housed beneath a clear Perspex cover. Beside this display he could make out a green button marked Open. After some deliberation he pressed the button and the instrument panel, somewhat jerkily, slid open. While leaning over to examine the display he was distracted by something scribbled in red under the thick layer of dust. Brushing the dust away with the back of his hand he could see the words

FAULTY – REJECTED.

He had no time to decide whether this was good news or not.

His attention reverted back to the numerical display. Three sets of numbers but two of them had already reached 000 and the third was actively counting downwards from 98.

William could do with his Jump Suit coming to his rescue right now.

The red light was no longer flashing but deepened to a constant blood red, 75 and counting. Were there any instructions on the body of the bomb to stop the countdown? He frantically searched, what was this? A metal plaque bolted to the body of the weapon. Again he rubbed away three centuries of dust and grime. In raised gold letters he read the inscription.

WE THE PEOPLE OF THE SIXTY FIVE STATES ON OUR GREAT NATION DEDICATE THIS SUPERIOR WMD TO OUR GLORIOUS DICTATOR DANIELLA THUMP SENIOR. MAY IT HASTEN OUR RIGHTFUL POSITION AS RULERS OF A NEW CIVILISED WORLD

As the countdown reached 25 this was not what William expected or wanted to read. He barely had time to contemplate the significance of the message. His Jump Suit was as much use as a paper overcoat in a hail storm as he searched for bottle number five.

The display read 15 as he placed the last and largest bottle in his hand, he thought of his family waiting for his return from the toilet. He hoped they would be able to return safely home without him. He hoped that the imminent explosion would be contained enough to avoid any loss of life in this brave new world.

Three......

Two.......

One......

he threw the grey liquid from bottle number five over the bomb at the moment of detonation.

The force of the explosion blew the roof from the enormous

storage facility, sending debris in all directions.

THE 12.05PM FROM PADDINGTON

'That's it, one minute to eight, get out of my way, I'm going into that toilet!' Steven was a man on a mission. 'I can't believe he'd leave it so late, what's he doing in there?'

Dr. Honey blocked his path, 'Mr Hawkins please. I think I can hear William coming now, please get ready to leave.'

And there he was, looking like he'd been pulled through a hedge backwards. William was back from his mission to save the Earth. The Jump Suit had sprung into life on the count of one and he was dragged back aboard the Saviorian Mother Ship. There had been just enough time to change back into his Earth clothes but he still looked dishevelled.

'William you look dreadful, where on Earth have you been for the last four minutes?'

Where indeed, thought William.

'Sorry Mum, I think that Saviorian sausage disagreed with me, I've just thrown up in the toilet. The Saviorians can clear up my mess for a change, they're happy wallowing in that stuff.'

'Wow Einstein, are you going off your alien friends?'Anita asked.

'Let's say I've had more than enough, I'm ready to go home.'

William had been plucked at the very last second from the explosion. His action of throwing some of the contents of bottle No. Five in desperation had limited the size and effect of the explosion and no lives were lost, according to the Jump Suit. His mission had been a complete success but there was no time for celebration or recriminations, just a knowing if slightly embarrassed nod from the Saviorians present acknowledged their awareness of how things had gone.

Back aboard their mocked up taxi the Hawkins family were given their final instructions,

'Those of you who were wearing an Earth style time piece when you arrived at the transport station to depart for Cornwall in April 2014, please make sure it is set to the time 11.35am. This is the time you exited the taxi and therefore the time you will arrive back from the 26th Century.'

Steven and Anita had watches on so they set the time as instructed.

'Good luck Earthlings, it has been an honour to meet you, especially you William, we will always be in your debt.'

William bit his tongue and said nothing, all he wanted now was to get safely home, he was still in a state of complete shock and couldn't quite believe he was still alive.

An impressive collection of Saviorians had assembled by now to witness the Time Jump. In a blinding flash the Hawkins were gone, leaving the empty taxi cab on the Sky Lab floor.

With the Bellicose Minor mission nearing a successful conclusion Commander Aragon had just announced exciting instructions for the fleet to head to the nearest Vacation Station for a well earned if belated rest. The androids would be placed in cold storage, after they had cleared the mess produced by the thrilled Saviorians.

The taxi deposited them in the proximity of Paddington Station with half an hour to spare. They were all looking forward to their trip to Padstow, including Anita who was happy to get as far away from John as possible after he had dumped her for the blonde Latvian shot putter.

The platform number came up and they rushed to the gate. Jane's four free tickets showed they were all seated together. William searched his pockets for his phone to take a photo of this happy family occasion.

'Hang on a minute what's this?'

William emptied the contents of his pockets onto the table in front of him. Fifty three pence in change ,a piece of jigsaw puzzle showing a cows udder, the remains of a cheese and pickle sandwich, his smart phone and a strange bottle with the number Five printed on it. The dregs of a grey liquid remained in the bottom of the container.

'What the hell's that Einstein, some new geek energy drink?'

'I've absolutely no idea where that came from.'

'I didn't know you were into doing jigsaw puzzles son?' asked Jane.

'No, I...'

As he spoke strange images formed in his mind, none of which made any sense. He returned the bottle to his pocket.

'Are you going to take that bloody photo or what?'

'What? Oh yes. Smile please, hold up your tickets, say cheese.'

'Happy holidays everyone.'

The End or Just the Beginning?

ABOUT THE AUTHOR

Alistair Dalziel Wright

Born in Stranraer, Scotland, Alistair moved to Nottingham, age eleven and later met his wife Karen at Clifton Teacher Training College.

A successful teaching career took him to Colombia, Mexico and London before moving to Padstow in 1990 to buy a quayside restaurant and later holiday accomodation.

A challenge to write a short story in 2014 sowed the seeds of "The Hawkins Scenario" which was revisited after retirement and became the book you see before you today.

His sense of fun, love of Padstow and travel shine through this far-fetched, fast moving tale.

Printed in Great Britain
by Amazon

60476602R00271